THE DATURA
SOLUTION

THE DATURA SOLUTION

Book 1 in the Max Foreman Series

PATRICK FAURE

Copyright © 2016 by Patrick Faure.

Library of Congress Control Number:		2016908368
ISBN:	Hardcover	978-1-5144-9391-5
	Softcover	978-1-5144-9390-8
	eBook	978-1-5144-9389-2

All rights reserved. No part of this book may be reproduced or transmitted in any form or by any means, electronic or mechanical, including photocopying, recording, or by any information storage and retrieval system, without permission in writing from the copyright owner.

This is a work of fiction. Names, characters, places and incidents either are the product of the author's imagination or are used fictitiously, and any resemblance to any actual persons, living or dead, events, or locales is entirely coincidental.

Any people depicted in stock imagery provided by Thinkstock are models, and such images are being used for illustrative purposes only.
Certain stock imagery © Thinkstock.

Print information available on the last page.

Rev. date: 05/26/2016

To order additional copies of this book, contact:
Xlibris
800-056-3182
www.Xlibrispublishing.co.uk
Orders@Xlibrispublishing.co.uk
739844

PROLOGUE

1993, Mambatu Province, Africa

The rain had started to fall two days hence and it had not stopped or relented once since then. It was a typical African rain, dense and thick, as if the raindrops were made of a different type of water than in Europe, a heavier water. It created a deluge against which neither of the two men could protect themselves. The drops exploded on their backs and splattered with a vengeance, as if to punish them for what they were about to do. Their raingear had long become completely ineffective, and they had discarded it. Water saturated every piece of clothing they wore and every part of their body was wet. Their special purpose combat fatigues integrating a pattern of dark green and black were now a perfect match for the equatorial forest environment. They both had given up using their ponchos, except to protect their combat rations from the rain while they ate. Now, they lay prone on the slimy forest ground which was slowly turning into a swamp. The variety of insects crawling about them left them indifferent, as long as they were not the dreaded army ants. They concentrated instead on hiding their presence from the Cuban soldiers who patrolled the area, an occurrence that was rarer and rarer due to the weather. They spoke loudly, announcing themselves from a distance, even in the rain, oblivious to the potential presence of any enemy. In contrast, the two men had not exchanged a word in over a day. Not that they experienced any type of disagreement, but rather out of respect for each other and in abeyance to the US Army strong noise discipline. They were veterans of many such missions and knew that their survival depended on fully focusing on their mission. They slept in turn, according to the rhythm of a well-tried routine that they had practiced many times. Their physical discomfort was of no concern to either one. As they said at Fort Bragg, 'Physical discomfort is a state of mind'. They practiced meditation techniques to ensure their minds were always in control of their bodies. They had in fact welcomed the rain which was their greatest ally. Rain would hide any sound they could make while moving to their objective and it would allow them to fully benefit from the effect of surprise. Any ambush was far more likely to succeed when taking place in inclement weather. Each man carried a pistol with silencer, a combat knife, and the developmental TM-16 a combination crossbow-M16 that allowed the shooter to switch between a conventional M-16 and a composite crossbow. This weapon had been conceived to allow a sniper to be totally silent, a quality that no rifle-equipped silencer could ever achieve. Hopefully, they would not need to use it. The two men waited for night to fall and prepared for their mission. They switched on their night-vision goggles, and although the devices were basically useless in the heavy rain, they would still allow them to distinguish the temperature generated silhouette of any enemy soldier. At close range, they would serve to identify any booby trap or claymore mine that might have been set up. Luigi said a quick prayer, kissed his medal of the Virgin Mary, put it back inside his fatigues, and they set off.

They reached the Tactical Operations Center (TOC) of the Brigada Che Guevara a few minutes after midnight, so that they would be ready to strike at zero-one-hundred hours. With the exception of the vicious rain hammering the vegetation and distant military equipment, they could hear no other sounds. That was perfect because the Cubans could not hear anything but the rain either. Perimeter guards were more occupied protecting themselves from the deluge and from any venomous snakes than watching out for potential intruders. They knew that the closest enemy unit, a regiment of French Foreign Legion paratroopers, was over 500 miles away, and the US units had not even landed yet—if they ever came. Their commander, El Diablo, had reminded them a few days before that 'these fucking Legionnaires were nothing but a bunch of pussies that even had been defeated by the Mexicans'. Knowing the weather would prevent any airborne assault, the Cubans had settled in the overconfident comfort that they were safe from any military attack. Their appallingly lax security illustrated this belief. The two men estimated that the Cuban encampment was barely operational, and the only visible defence outside of the standard foxholes manned by forward observers was a string of barbed wire that had been hastily strung around a few tents. These tents included the readily identifiable tent of the brigade commander, which stuck out by its hexagonal shape and greater size. Neither man could see any type of anti-personnel mines. There were no lights in the camp, and it seemed that everyone was sleeping. Luigi tapped Max on the shoulder and pointed to the Observation Post or OP immediately to their right. With the heavy rain falling unabated, there was no way any of the soldiers could see anything or could even hear the stealthy assassins. Luigi and Max, having received a fully permissive Rule of Engagement, had already decided to take no chances. *Leave no witness behind.* Crawling in unison with the supple efficiency of snakes, they moved without a sound and quickly reached a position around and behind the OP. They slithered into the foxhole as each took one target and swiftly ran his combat knife across the throat of the two Cuban soldiers manning the OP. The gurgling noise of the blood rushing through the severed carotid artery was the last sound either Cuban soldier ever made. With their vocal cords severed, they could not raise any alarm. Even with the rain, Max felt the warm blood of his victim run down his combat knife and onto his right hand. As he sliced the neck in a smooth motion, pulling the guard's head back, a fountain of blood spurted from the men's throat, and the tiny droplets mixed with the rain fell back into a spray on Max's fatigues and face. *I hope the fucker did not have AIDS or some other shit.* Death came quickly to both sentinels. Luigi and Max proceeded unimpaired and faced not a single challenge as they reached the commander's tent, except for the desultory obstacle of the tentative barbed wire perimeter. Feeling secure that no attack would take place, the barbed wire had not even been alarmed. In the darkness and the rain, they saw one man who was supposed to be on guard by the commander's tent entrance, but was instead sitting, his back leaning against one of the tent poles. He was bundled up under his poncho, trying to remain dry. Although he was probably sleeping, no risk could be taken, and Luigi quickly dispatched him before he even knew he had been killed. The tent was zipped up. Unzipping it was out of the question, as it made a very distinctive noise that even the rain would not hide. Both men knew that the zipper screech would immediately wake up the occupant. Max took out a box cutter from his pouch and sliced through one of the heavy canvas panels, using the tent post to support his cutting. In this manner, the operation was practically noiseless. Luigi went in and the inside of the tent became fully visible through his night-vision goggles now that they were no longer impaired by the rain. He did not bother to look at the items decorating the large tent and instead identified the man lying on the field bed. The white parade uniform of a general was hanging on a clothes hanger attached to the centre pole of the tent. It was wrapped in a protective transparent garment bag, a testimony to the man's carefully managed vanity. Luigi tightened his grip around the combat knife's handle, and for the third time in less than twenty minutes, he cut the throat of an enemy combatant. He saw the general open his eyes in terror, unable to see who was killing him in the total darkness. The man thrashed about needlessly in his field bed, as life was already draining out of his body. The blood pulsed out in a torrent from his carotid artery, turning bright green in the sights of the night-vision goggles. It flowed so fast, it could not even be absorbed by the bedding and started dripping on the floor. Death had come very quickly to El Diablo. Luigi wiped his knife's blade and his hands on the general's field bed. He then pulled a small waterproof container out of his fatigue shirt pocket. From its contents, he selected a playing card bearing the four of diamonds, ensuring he left no trace of blood or a fingerprint on it. He then placed it carefully on the lifeless body of the general. The calling card would be a reminder that the operation had been the work of the Four of Diamonds, a US Army secret unit that had never been acknowledged or identified, and whose motto was 'Leave No Witness Behind', as was printed on the back of the playing card.

Luigi exited the tent and asked Max to go in and verify that General Luis 'El Diablo' Perez-Castro was indeed dead. Max came out, made a thumbs-up sign, and using a military adhesive, he closed the tent and camouflaged the trespass so that it would not be discovered until morning. Both men made their way back out of the TOC the same way they had come in. Forty-eight hours later, Luigi and Max, clean-shaven and wearing business suits, entered the Henry Todd Building in Rosslyn, Virginia. They took the elevator to the eleventh floor and dialled the code that allowed them access into the offices of the Zantex Corporation. Colonel Kelly was waiting for their report. In Cuba, on the same day, Juventud Rebelde published a lengthy homage to El Diablo who had tragically died of a heart attack while defending the cause of communism in Africa.

CHAPTER 1

1994, Washington DC

George had waited until the massive station clock had indicated 6:32 p.m., holding on to the absurd hope that she would have turned around and come back. But the chair next to him had remained stubbornly empty. A few moments before, he had watched Lena's slender figure reluctantly walk towards the departure gate, her red fox coat negligently wrapped around her, and her green scarf peeking out from under her blond hair. He had wished her to turn around, to look at him one more time, so that he could engrave in his mind her beauty. She had not turned around, even as he followed her silhouette disappearing down the long hallway among the other passengers. He had followed her with his eyes as she rode the escalator down to the departing trains. He knew that she could not have left him if she had looked back. He knew the intensity of the sadness she was experiencing, a sadness whose strength could only match the intensity of her passion for him. He had watched her finally vanish into the nothingness of absence. He was still sitting at the table, her empty glass of white wine, the only reminder of her presence in his life. He thought about how he had caressed her slender hand, how he had barely touched her, and how she had shuddered at the reminiscence of the touching that had revealed her passion to him three days before. She had taken his hand and had pushed it between her legs, where he had felt her dampness. He had not wanted her to go. He did not know her well enough yet to be ready to let go. He had wanted time to stop, the hands of the clock to be frozen by some catastrophe that would shut down the station and prevent the trains from leaving. He had wanted her for himself in these precious moments that their unavoidable separation had made even sweeter. He had been overwhelmed by an uncontrollable desire to let her know how vulnerable she was making him, him the diplomat who was known for his ruthless negotiating skills and for his absolute stoicism. Yet he knew that his attachment to her was at most a fad. He had experienced this with every woman he had ever met. He would never be able to be faithful to her, however much he liked or loved her. When she had stood up and packed up her bag, he had made every effort possible to hide the sorrow, the sorrow that can only come when you have the knowledge of certainty. He had hoped that in a sudden reversal, she would abandon all pretence, fall back into the chair, in tears, telling him that she was staying, that the rest of the world did not matter, that the only person worth living for was him. He would have controlled her entirely then, and would have had her at his mercy. But she had to go. They both knew it, and he had accompanied him to the station to make sure she would leave. She had taken the decision on her own, and he had come along to support it, regardless of his feelings.

He slowly finished his beer. He savoured the taste of the Abbaye de Saint Martin beer that he had started when she was still there, next to him. It was a taste that he would always associate with her. Just like he would always associate the slightly acrid flavour of her intimacy and the perfume of her body to Guerlain's Jardin de Bagatelle. He longed to hold her again in his arms, to walk into a restaurant with her, and be the instant focus of attention. She made him an extraordinary man, while he knew that despite all of his efforts, he was simply common. He did not want to go home. He needed the stimulus of the crowd around him. How he wished he had given her a last kiss in public. He knew that if he had done that he would never have let her go. He wished he had told her in a gentler way that he loved her, even if deep inside him he knew it was, if not a lie, at least a half truth. He had not been good with those words. They had rushed to his lips, he had pronounced them hurriedly, as if he had been hiding from them, as if the words had been a way to actually hide the depth of his doubt. He was sure that at that moment he undoubtedly had thought he loved her. How many women had he said that to in the last year? In the last three years? She had not responded, as if she had guessed his true inner thoughts. She had simply squeezed his hand, and let it go at that, as you forgive a child's misplaced word. He knew his words should have been better articulated, that he should have taken better advantage of the situation, that he should have allowed her to enjoy the full expanse of their meaning. He was not pleased with how he had pronounced them. He wanted to take them back, to do it again, to slowly, deliberately tell her, so that the words would be more like a caress than an obvious statement. He had jeopardised his entire life to be with her. If the Department of State learned that he was having an affair with Elena Alexandrovna Krasnaieva, the wife of the Russian oligarch who was suspected to be the head of one of the most powerful crime syndicates in Russia, his career would be over in a blink. Despite the risk, he had not been able to resist the physical attraction and the desire to possess her that he had felt for Lena. But this was not the first time that he took such risks in this city. He got up. His leg hurt like he could not remember it hurting before, as if the dishonesty of his behaviour had concentrated into the old motorcycle injury. He limped to his Suburban with federal plates in the station parking lot, so that he could drive home. As soon as he got in the car, he called her. There was no answer. He closed his eyes, and rested for a while. He thought about who Lena really was. A pretty model from then Leningrad, without much education, but with a beauty that had made her the poster girl for the Krassiva line of women's clothes, and who had had the luck or the misfortune of being noticed by Oleksandr Krasnaief. They had been married at a sumptuous wedding attended by the billionaire jetsetters—that also included the Russian Prime Minister—at the highly exclusive Guana Island. George had become well aware of these facts, as he was in a habit of googling all the guests of dinner parties he attended. He had been well aware of Lena's husband's fortune hours before he had met her at the Russian Embassy. He had googled her husband first, and he had found out that the man owned billions of dollars' worth of industrial assets, that he had mansions in every fashionable resort or city: London, Porto Cervo, Miami Beach, Cayman Island, Sydney Harbor, and that he had recently given his wife a multimillion dollars yacht, The Princess of Russia, as a birthday gift. The man's picture was that an oafish brute and reminded George of the bust of Sulla. His eyes seemed to protrude out of their sockets like those of an ox, and the picture suggested that he was covered with body hair. He saw a photo of the man in swim trunks, and it confirmed that he looked like a gorilla. George wondered how any woman could possibly have sex with such a repulsive man. Then, he realised that money, especially the amount of money Krasnaief had accumulated, could make even the ugliest man look attractive. He had fantasised how his life would change if he could become Lena's lover, or even, he thought without a trace of humour, her second husband. He had inquired with the US Embassy in Russia, and they had confirmed that Oleksandr Krasnaief's fortune exceeded $22 billion. He almost fell asleep dreaming about the future. He came back to reality with a jolt. It was already almost seven, and he was expected at the Embassy of South Korea at eight. He still had to drive home and change. He could not wait any longer. He put the car in gear and took off, the blue strobe lights of his government vehicle parting the traffic in front of him. He called Lena. He wanted to make sure that she had not changed her mind; that she was actually catching the train;

that she was not coming back. Thankfully, it did not happen. She was in the train, and it had long ago left the station. There would be no happy ending for her that day. He drove in a daze, only thinking about how he could ensure she would become hers. He drove passed places on M Street where they had been, where they had shared their joy at being together, from where they had staged excursions in the park, and where he had kissed her under what had become their tree. There was no stoicism left in him. It had given way to an irreversible decision to make her his wife, at whatever cost. He arrived at home, the place where they had spent so many nights and yet so few as well. The familiar surroundings had become foreign without her. Yet he felt her presence there. He saw her fumble with her pocketbook trying to find the lipstick she always lost at the bottom of it. He saw her smile as he waited for her to find it. He saw her as if she was standing right there. He reached for her, but it was only a phantasm, she was not there. He thought how such a beautiful and rich woman would make a political career possible, how the Georgetown house he had bought a couple of years before would become the centre of the Washington high society, and how senators would beg to be invited to dinner parties hosted by Mrs Elena McMillan. At the same time, he realised he had been smitten. He climbed the flight of stairs slowly, trying to push back the point in time when he would have to go in the bedroom and find her gone for good. He opened the door. He could still smell her perfume in the air. It was too weak to indicate her presence, but strong enough to remind him of it. He remembered the night before, a happy night. He remembered the passion of the embrace as they kissed and how he had squeezed her against him, knowing it would be their last night together. They had conspired to not talk about the separation that was unavoidable. And he had never once hinted at the fact that he knew how wealthy she was. They had responded only to one urge: satisfy their need for each other.

The cell phone rang. It was her. She was calling from the train. She had locked herself in the bathroom to have some privacy. She was in tears, incoherent from her pain of having left him behind and from fear at what she would tell her husband when she saw him again. He got very concerned, as she spoke on without making much sense of all the situations that she was trying to deal with: him, her work at Krassiva, her husband waiting for her in Sankt Petersburg. She did not lie well. He became filled with anxiety and worry about her well-being, and despite it, at the same time, he experienced the intense pleasure of knowing that she was desperately in love with him. He hoped that this would last, as she was the opportunity of a lifetime. She was his ticket to bigger and better things. He needed to ensure that from this point on she felt he experienced the same passion for her as she did for him. And finally, she came out with the fatidic three words 'I love you'. She had never told him this affirmatively. Of course, she had told him she had fallen for him, that she was crazy about him, that she was in love, but never before had she told him 'I love you' with such conviction and yet pain, for she was now a hundred miles away. He would have squeezed against him if he had been able to, and he admitted he missed the warmth of her supple and perfect body more than his words could describe. He had to give her the strength to face her husband. Yet, for the first time, he spoke to her as if she were a business asset. She was a business opportunity, and he could not let it slip away. They had only spent a week together. He needed to build on this, make sure she did not consider their time together as simply an adventure. He reminded her of the song they sang together when they had gone running in the park a few weeks earlier 'Up in the morning with the bloodshot eyes, it is another Tequila sunrise!' Since she had locked herself in the railroad car's bathroom, she was able to sing it again with her delightful Russian accent over the phone, and the change was immediate. She went from crying to the good memory in a millisecond and soon the clarity and the purity of her laughter filled his ears. She was back to normal. It was high time! Now, he had to rush to shower, shave, put on his tuxedo, and drive like the devil to the Korean Ambassador's residence where dinner would be served promptly. On the way there, he received a text from her. She promised to call in the morning. He was delighted—it would not be a simple fling. Now, as he drove into the park surrounding the residence, he was himself again, ready to charm anything out of anybody.

After the party, to the surprise of his host, he had left alone. This was such an unusual event that the ambassador joked and asked him if he was feeling alright, as George was well known for having a passion for pretty women—and for not being able to resist any. But tonight, he had only one person on his mind: Lena. He drove home, served himself a whisky, and sipped it slowly in the lightless living room. He undressed and climbed in the bed, trying to find the trace of her perfume, of her body's smell. Faintly between the pillows, on the bed he could find her. This is where her head had rocked from side to side as he brought her to orgasm time after time. This is where the tsunamis of amorous passion had overwhelmed her in a way she did not even know they could, where she had lain exhausted, on the brink of passing out night after night, as he catered only to her pleasure. This is where both he and she had discovered the passionate woman she was, the orgasmic Venus that was hiding behind her reasoned and shy daily appearance. She had given herself to him, and he had allowed her to discover herself a new woman. He was as pleased by her own satisfaction as by his. Yet, he had to admit that she made love without the sophistication he expected from a woman as wealthy as she. She had been surprised by too many things, and by how long and powerful his lovemaking was. She had told him that one of the things that had attracted her to him was his virility, and night after night, he made sure she understood what the full meaning of virility was. She discovered ways that the hands of a man could touch her that she had never suspected. She loved his hands. And he showed her that his hands loved her entire body. He caressed her head, feathered over her face, tickled her spine in a way that made her shudder from pleasure, he rubbed her arms, pinched her nipples, teased her clitoris, massaged her feet, touched her thighs for long moments before finally allowing her to explode as he went back to her intimacy. He glorified her in as many ways he possibly could and she pushed her athletic and strong body towards him, indicating how much she loved it, how much she enjoyed it. It was an unending series of pleasure waves, of orgasms that burst out of her in exhausting vibrations and with a violence that almost looked painful. She was receptive to all of his lovemaking. She was on a voyage of discovery, and he was leading her there with all of his energy. From the very first day, because of his vast experience with women, he had known how to read her body, how to measure the pressure he had to put on certain parts, how to moderate the rhythm, how to increase the speed or the intensity of his touch, when to stop, and when to start again. He had not had enough much time to fully get her addicted to his lovemaking. At the beginning, she had been apprehensive, fearing that under the polished and virile varnish, the lovemaking would be as disappointing as with her husband. But as soon as they had exchanged their first kiss, hesitantly to start with, and then with a passion that she had never experienced, when he had softly massaged her head through her hair with his elegant and powerful hands, she had realised that his persona was indeed extraordinary. That very instant had been the point of no return. He had undressed her, ever so slowly in the deliberate manner that showed that he put her satisfaction ahead of everything else. She was too naive to realise that the reason he had known not to rush things was that he had the experience of countless amorous liaison. The mere manner in which he touched her had already caused her to shake uncontrollably in expectation of the lovemaking. He had taken his time, spending so many moments caressing and rubbing her back that she was aching for him to turn to her shapely breasts. He was an accomplished lover, and he knew what she wanted—just as he knew exactly what all women wanted—but he had made every effort not to hint that he knew. This was part of the skill as well. When he had finally consented to barely effleurage her nipples, she had almost collapsed. She was longing to his touch all over her, but he had refused to be carried away by the immediate desire she had for him. He was an accomplished artist. He had undressed her, one piece of clothing at the time, dropping each on the floor, and ensuring he caressed her, kissed her, and coached her into following his rhythm. Only once she had been totally naked, had he taken her by the hand and led her into the bedroom. He had asked for nothing in return. He had not been preoccupied with his own pleasure. He was there for her, and for her only and alone. Her first orgasm had been so violent, she had kicked him in the head with her knees. She was a passionate woman, but a woman who had been deprived of sexual satisfaction for so long, that he did not have to use the full measure of his skills. The lovemaking went on for hours until she could not stand it any longer, until her body was so satisfied there was no longer any way she could receive pleasure. She realised after that first evening that no other man could ever satisfy her again. 'How can I survive after our paths part,' she had asked. He had responded that the only way was to make sure they never parted. He knew from other women that when he would be gone from her life, she would be left with her hunger for him, for the passion he had created in her. At a point in time in the uncertainty of the future, she would be left with the memory, and she would enjoy the memory of these precious moments. She would never again be satisfied. It was a great moment of revelation. He joked that he was like Socrates, that he had allowed her to discover the inner truth about herself, and it was impossible to hide that truth any longer. She did not know about Socrates. Every night became more intense. Every wave of pleasure created more pleasure. Every action created more desire. Every satiation created more hunger. Every act became more sophisticated. Every penetration became more intense. Every abandon required more abandon. Acts that she thought were unachievable were achieved. Penetration she had imagined to be too painful procured her pleasure so intense that she passed out. He had won her over. A more sophisticated woman would not have been that impressed, she would have pushed him far harder, she would have asked for more exotic positions, for more pornographic sex, and for more intensity. Not Lena. She was too simple for him, and he was too experienced for her.

Yet, now, he had gone over these nights in his head, despite the whisky, he was not able to find any sleep. He needed more sexual activity. The desire to touch her skin, which had a special quality of softness, excited his virility beyond limits, to the point where he could stand it no longer. The pain in his loin was physical. He regretted not taking the beautiful Korean woman home, the one who was a top fashion model, and whom the ambassador had so kindly seated to his right at the dinner. The woman had made verbal, physical, and highly suggestive advances. He imagined that he had taken her home. Lena would never know about it. He tossed and turned and dozed off for a while only to be awakened by a nightmare. He was at the office, at the State Department, overlooking the street. He was absorbed in a secret document, and he did not hear her arrive. He felt a tap on his right shoulder. She had returned in the glory of her nudity, with her radiating blond hair reflecting light like a halo around her head. Surprised, he got up, turned around, took her in his arms, and kissed her with the pent up passion of the separation. In front of the entire office who would have no doubt about their liaison any longer. He felt the sensation of her tongue touching his as if it was real, and horrified by the consequences of the event on his career, he woke up in a sweat. The sensation of the kiss had simply made the matters worse. He got up to go to the bathroom, fully erect. He thought of her even more and he imagined seeing the reflection of her face into the mirror. He decided that no matter what, he could live with his decision. He sat on his bed, and knowing the futility of his attempts to find sleep, he dialled the number of Sun, the Korean woman. She was not even asleep yet, and he convinced her that he would make her night memorable. Within an instant, he had dressed, jumped in his personal car, an AMG-Mercedes, and was on his way to K-Street where she was staying. At six in the morning, he woke up to the noise of the jets overflying the hotel, and that were starting to land at the Ronald Reagan Airport. He was exhausted by the lovemaking that had been savage—Sun was an expert lover who had demanded far more than Lena could ever—and by the lack of sleep. It would be a rough day in the office! This is when he remembered he had to brief the Undersecretary of State on the Rwandan situation… He tried to enjoy the warmth of Sun's body for a while longer. Time passed. He did not want to get up. He was dozing off again when the telephone rang. He did not answer, although he knew who it was. He got up, agreed to a time to come pick up Sun that evening for dinner, and rushed to his car. While driving home, he dialled Lena's number, explaining that he had been in the shower when she had called, and that he was now on his way to the office. In his line of work, he was used to lying. Contrarily to the night before when she had cried on the phone, she was upbeat. He felt that she had weathered the first night away from him well. He rejoiced at the sound of her happy crystalline voice. It meant his investment was safe. When she hung up, he was happy but knew it was a long way uphill before he could capitalise on their liaison. He had no qualms about using her. Of course, he had strong feelings for her, but he could have had strong feelings for tens of women. He admitted to himself that she was special only because she was rich. 'Shit,' he thought, 'If I wanted a wife, Sun would actually do better than Lena.' And in fact Sun had three advantages. She was free, she was a much better lover, and she was far less dangerous. He thought that there would always be women like Sun around, once he was rich. Lena called him again while he was getting dressed. He did not want to have her call him every five minutes. But he knew what she wanted, and he would talk to her all day long if that's what she wanted. He promised to call her again, later. He preferred to be in charge of the times when he called to ensure it did not interfere with his meetings with Sun. He cursed silently thinking Lena would probably want him to talk to her as she went to sleep. He would have to invent a meeting at some embassy or another. He stepped outside to get the *Washington Post* and had his coffee in the sun room while reading the paper. He washed his coffee mug and went on to the office. On the way out, he called Lena again to tell her how much he loved her.

CHAPTER 2

The Covent Garden fortune teller is a London institution. Her location can be easily spotted because at all times of day, a queue of supplicants stretches out into the square from her booth. Men and women of all ages and races come there to consult her because she is one of the only ones left in London who still practises her art in a public place. But on that cold day of January, there were few people perambulating the old market, and there was no line now that flurries had started to whirl around the capital. The fortune teller had failed to see any signs on the way to work, her vision obscured by the snowflakes. She had no indication that this day would be different from any other in her life. When Max approached her booth, he saw her looking into the distance. She was not a remarkable woman. Tanned, wearing a grey print kerchief—Max thought she probably was not aware that she was wearing the colour of death in Roman tradition—she was bundled in a heavy dark blue winter coat. Behind her, a Merlin blanket covered the entire back wall of the booth, its stars and planet a faded shade of white in an almost black sky. In front of her, the table covered with an old blanket—that was not exactly engaging—was ready: the stones, the runes, and the tarot cards were awaiting her next customer. Max decided to have his palm read. As he got closer, he saw her gypsy features: a fine nose, a sensual mouth, despite her age, which he estimated at about fifty, and when he sat down opposite her at the table, he was drawn to her piercing light blue eyes that were totally unexpected. At the same time, Max was looking into her eyes, she was suddenly taken over by an ill-feeling, a bad omen, she said. She wondered what had caused her such discomfort for a fleeting moment, but then her business sense took over. Here was a man who was young, elegant, who apparently was well off, so there was no sense in providing anything but her regular service. She told him her rates: palm reading, five pounds, but this allowed you no questions. For ten pounds, Max could ask her three questions (like the genie jokes, Max thought). He chose the ten-pound reading. At the moment she grabbed his hand to read his palm, she could not help but cringe back from him.

'What's the matter?' asked Max anxiously.

She hesitated. 'It is, it is. . . I have never seen this in my life.'

'What?' asked Max with unrestrained curiosity.

'It's probably. . . No it is there with you!'

'What?' asked Max again, truly annoyed this time.

'I am not sure what it means, but death is right next to you! I have never seen her that close to anyone before! I can see her, like I can see you. And she knows I can see you! She is standing by your right side, which is actually a good omen for you. Death on the right side means she is not after you.' Max thought the woman was half mad, but he had decided to be open minded, so he let her continue.

She could not relate the appearance of death on Max's right side with the Tarot death card. In Tarot, Death is symbolic of the ending of a major phase or aspect of someone's life that may bring about the beginning of something far more valuable and important. 'A door closes while another one opens,' she explained. 'It helps put the past behind and gets a person ready for new opportunities and possibilities.' But, the face of death she was seeing next to Max was not that of the Tarot Death knight on a white steed. This was the face of death herself. It was a hidden form in a black hooded cloak, her eyes shining like fluorescent white lights inside the hood. The gypsy wondered how she knew death was a woman. She realised she had no information to state so, and that it was simply her shape and demeanour that made her decide she was a woman. Regaining her composure, the fortune teller looked at Max's palm with increased interest. She manipulated it for a moment, looking at Death and at Max in turn, careful to choose words that would not anger Death, or upset her client. The gypsy knew that Death was not for Max, but she had to wonder if that was an omen meant for her. Slowly, with some hesitation in her voice, and yet the conviction that she was right, she declared: 'I have never seen a longer lifeline than yours in all my years.' She was in awe. Turning his hand towards him, she showed him, 'Look, it starts on the top of your hand, right behind your index finger, and it goes around all the way to the articulation of your wrist. Death is not for you.' She laid his hand softly on the table and decided to read the runes to understand why Death was there. She was motivated by her own fear of the vision. She took the stones, rubbed them in her palms, her icy blue eyes squarely reading into Max's soul, and she rolled them on the table. She said nothing, simply looking at them as they stopped moving. She then looked to Max's right, obviously searching for a sign from death herself. Max felt strange, as if the gypsy woman was actually communicating with Death. He looked over his shoulder, but could see nothing. After what seemed an eternity, the gypsy said 'Death is your permanent companion. She will not let you have any other. She is the only one who will be on your side constantly until the day she takes you. Wherever you go, Death will be with you.' For the first time in her life, she actually had a client who was a puzzle for her, and one who showed up with such a powerful figure riding with him. It was an ominous and unique event in her life. She knew it would never happen again, and she wanted to understand. Who was Max? Why had Death chosen him as a companion? What would his life be like? She put the runes back in her bag and pulled one at random. She turned it over. It was Dagaz. Death would not interfere with him. He would accomplish his goals. But the price would be personal. She pulled another stone. It was Fehu, one of the three Mother Stones, the rune of prosperity, good luck, and unbridled creative energies. She interpreted for him: 'Death is your companion, she will be travelling with you, hitting at your enemies and friends alike, but she will be your ally, however cruel she may be. She will make you suffer, but she will allow you prosperity and success. You should not fear her for yourself. You are protected by Fehu. But be careful, the wolf lives in the forest. You will have to face it, and you will then be free.' She saw Death almost vanish. 'Once you defeat the wolf, you will be free. Death will leave your side. Somewhere, you were cursed and you must fight the wolf to break the spell.'

'Who is the wolf?' inquired Max.

'I cannot see who the wolf is. My powers are not that great, but I know he is there, lurking for you in the darkness. I can hear him.' She reached in the bag again and pulled Ansuz reversed. She warned Max. 'Ansuz reversed will haunt you, with failed communications, and missed opportunities. You will fall out of harmony with the universe. Your path will become unclear, and those who portray themselves as your friends will give you false advice and spread malicious rumours. This is when you will meet the wolf. You will know him. He will be all-powerful, and he will have many followers. He will bring you to your knees. He will inflict pain and he will seem *invictus*. Only a valiant man, a true warrior, can ever defeat the wolf.' She stopped, out of breath, almost fainting, but she regained her composure. She reached again for a rune. She grimaced as she saw its face. Hagalaz. The hail rune. She saw Max's concerned look. 'I see chaos, destruction, and disruption on a primal level. There will be setbacks, but Fenu will still protect you.' For the fifth rune, she pulled Elhaz. 'Elhaz is the elk. Elhaz is also Algiz, the Protector, in the old Anglo-Saxon language that only two of my people can still speak. The elk will give you the power to protect yourself and those around you. It will bring you the thrills and joy of the successful hunt. You are in a very enviable position right now, because you will be able to maintain what you have built and reach your current goals. Your most terrifying ordeal will be meeting the wolf. But the elk and Algiz will watch over you. The elk will be your greatest ally. You cannot fight the wolf without him. You must meet the elk first, then, and only then, you can take on the wolf. You will overcome and be stronger. But this will not shelter you from the malefic influence of Ansuz and Hagalaz.' The gypsy was now drained. She pulled away from Max. 'Come back another time. . .' Without another word, she pulled a cord and was instantly hidden from sight as a heavy curtain decorated with a star motif came down in front of Max. Confused by the revelations, he got up and tried to remember everything the gypsy woman had stated. He crossed the street, sat at one of the many cafes bordering the square, and ordered a large beer. Before he could forget everything, he started to write down the prophecies. He had no idea how close to reality they would eventually prove.

CHAPTER 3

1998, Rota Air Force Base, Spain *(13 October 1998)*

The C-130 Hercules was sitting in a remote spot away from the lights of the airfield. Its ominous black silhouette devoid of any visible markings and battered by the rain of an early autumn storm was completely invisible in the darkness. The cockpit was unlit, and the two men approaching it, although they had walked less than a half mile, were drenched. Despite the load of military hardware and the weight of the parachutes they were carrying, their stride was dynamic, and they walked standing tall against the storm, fully focused on their mission. They had chosen to walk to the airplane rather than to be driven to avoid yet another person being aware of their activities and of their whereabouts. Both of them were matched in size. A casual observer would have said they were six feet tall and would have been about right. Max Foreman was just over six feet and had joined Steve Uvenchko at the airfield a few moments earlier. He had arrived from a special training session with French Commando School Number 4. He had travelled by train to avoid having to disclose his name and identity to the airlines, and thus the authorities. Not that it would have mattered much since he was travelling under a fake identity provided to him by his unit, the Four of Diamonds, or FOD as they called it.

Max had insisted in a last training session to ensure he would arrive in top form, even though it had meant being separated from Rebecca, or Reb as she was known to her friends, for an additional week. Steve had joined him from Gibraltar after a brief bus trip and a long walk from the bus depot. Both of them had carefully avoided any contact with anyone and had spoken to none of their travel companions. They had stayed at the BOQ (Bachelor Officers Quarters) and had made sure they had no contact before meeting at Hangar 56, a rarely used hangar at the far end of the maintenance line. There, according to the instructions they had received, they had found webbing, two sets of Generation-4 Night Vision Goggles, known as G4 NVG, GPS Universal devices, specifically designed desert camouflage uniforms with Ghillie suits, four unfolded parachutes, commando knifes, field glasses, entrenching tools, C4 with detonators and remotes, four nine-millimetre Berettas with four clips of sixteen rounds of ammunition and silencers, two hybrid assault/sniper rifles with scopes and silencers, and eight thirty-round clips, eight assault hand grenades, NBC masks, two anti-tank MILAN missiles with one firing computer and tripod, one Harris Falcon HF Radio with crypto, Meals Ready to Eat, and older version C-rations, soft skin canteens of two sizes that were filled with about fifty litres of water, first-aid kits, compasses, arctic sleeping bags, two mess kits, six thermal grenades, several Sterno cans, and two rucksacks. Two envelopes filled with currencies from Algeria, and Morocco, as well as dollars and euros had been placed on top of the parachutes. Without exchanging a word, they had started to work. There was no need to talk. They were professionals and exchanged data only when it was critical to the mission and to their survival. Both of them considered that any other communication was a waste of time, effort, and precious silence. They had both discarded the spare parachutes—at the attitude they were jumping, either the main opened and it was OK, or it didn't and there was no time to open the spare. They folded their own parachutes, using the buddy system to verify the quality of the folding. They then packed the rucksacks starting with the rations, and layering the packing from least urgently needed to most likely to be used upon landing. They tested the weapons mechanisms, holstered the Berettas, packed the assault rifles on top of the rucksacks, and with the rucksack loaded in front of them and roped, they had loaded the canteens of water and started on the walk to the aircraft. There were no instructions, mission orders, or ROE (rules of engagement), since all of the instructions would be received after the plane had taken off. They had only received a one-line message up to then: *Report to Hangar 56, Rota Air Force Base at 2200 hours, 13 October.*

In the weeks coming up to the mission, they had trained in the Mojave Desert of California to get accustomed to the harsh weather conditions they were going to find in their area of operation, even in October, and more importantly to rehearse the mission. They knew the mission entailed the ambush and destruction of an armoured privately owned Mercedes, but they did not know either the exact location of the operation (although they knew it was to be North Africa) or the identity of their occupants. They had rehearsed it a total of fourteen times over a ten-day period, the last time with live ammunition and a remote-controlled car—they had not used an armoured Mercedes, but an older Chevrolet Impala to simulate the size and mass of the car. Satisfied that they had mastered the mission, Steve had gone home for a week, while Max had stopped to see Reb for a couple of days and had flown straight to France for a last preparation with Commandant Bosquet who was an expert in North African operations. By the time they reached the dark shape of the airplane, the rain had penetrated every layer of clothing despite the rain gear. The two men entered the aircraft which was in complete blackout. In the cockpit, the crew was working with NVGs to prepare the machine for take-off. It had been agreed that there would be no unnecessary meeting between the crew and the special team. Greetings, exchanges, and other cordialities were unnecessary and there was no need for the crew to get acquainted with their passengers for security reasons.

Steve simply banged on the door of the crew compartment according to a prearranged pattern to indicate they were ready while Max was activating the mechanism to close the door. Not that it made any difference since the plane was not pressurised and would be flying nap of the earth to defeat the radars of the countries they had to fly through. Painted in black radar-absorbing paint, with its transceivers turned off, and the advantage of the foul weather, the plane would be undetectable as a war plane to any radar except to AWACS aircraft thanks to one special digital signature on the top of the airplane exactly at the geometric centre of the wings. The pilot had simply received a flight plan and the drop-zone GSM coordinates. When he reached the location, he would simply turn the green light on, and both men knew what they had to do. It clearly was not their first mission.

Neither Max nor Steve had any previous background that had made them predisposed to the type of mission they were embarking upon. Max was a highly educated philosophy scholar who had a passion for Greek philosophers and was as apt at quoting Plato as Heraclites. Fluent in five languages, he had been born in Monaco and after completing the course of study at the highly competitive and elitist Ecole Normale Superieure, he had been invited to finish his Doctorate in Philosophy at Columbia University in New York City. Within a week of successfully defending his doctorate thesis, he had received notice from the French army that he had to fulfil his one-year conscription in that organisation. Since he had neglected any type of relationship with the French conscription offices, he would be incorporated as a private. Unfortunately for France, Max had fallen in love with Rebecca, a young woman from Georgia, and being aware that one could fulfil French conscription by serving in the US Army (this went back to the days of Lafayette, he had been told), he had enlisted in the US Army. Within less than a year of joining, he had become both a US citizen and an officer in the Signal Corps. His career had been a normal one, except that the army quickly became aware of his language skills, and wanted to add more. Two years after he had become an officer, the army sent him to the famous University of Southern California to get a technical degree. From this point forward, his career had been anything but normal. While serving on the NATO staff, he had been contacted by a mysterious officer who had invited him to participate in a Top Secret program code name LICHI KLESH. The name of the program was never explained, and the classified orders to report for an interview in Suite 1703 in the Rosslyn Building in Rosslyn, Virginia, where the warning of disciplinary action if he were to disclose the very name of the program to 'uncleared individuals', had been ominous. When he arrived for the interview, Max was made to wait for over one hour in an empty room, without magazines, facilities, or even a window. He received no indication that anyone was expecting him or even cared that he was there. Max figured that this was a test, and he simply meditated according to the Zen meditation he had learned with an Arizona Zen master who had spent two months teaching him how to make abstraction of his surroundings, even when the surroundings were on top of Huachuca Mountain and included hundreds of rattle snakes. When a colonel finally asked him into his office, Max was fully rested and his mind was as sharp and prepared as it had ever been. The interview lasted several hours, first with the colonel, then with a panel of three officers including an infantry general who did their best to destabilise him, to anger him, and to cause him to lose control of his temper and composure. That day, nothing could distract Max from the interview. The stress that they had wanted to build simply fell flat—they had not expected the power of Zen, Max told them as the end of the interview. In any case, his language skills were essential, especially French and Italian. The army had great concern that the dying conflict between the Soviets and the Afghanis so-called Freedom Fighters, backed by the United States, was creating a population of Islamic extremists that were returning to their home countries with nothing better to do that wreak havoc. The United

States had engendered the next wave of conflict, and the cost of victory against the Soviets in Afghanistan had a price that would turn out to be staggering. Already, the US Army was creating programs to address the issue, and this is what Lichi Klesh was all about. This is how a top Greek philosophy scholar had become a trainee at the Center for Specialized Warfare at Fort Bragg, North Carolina, and how his name had disappeared from the official records of the US Army. He should have been given a new name to be used on his uniforms, but his personality was so well known within the US Army, that a new name would simply have added unnecessary scrutiny to the program, and it was decided that he should keep his own name.

His teammate, Steve, had been an even more unlikely candidate for LICHI KLESH. Born from a low-income family in Salina, Kansas, where his father was a manual labourer on the grain elevators, he had joined ROTC in order to get a scholarship at the University of Kansas where he had graduated with an Industrial Arts degree. He had had no time to use it, as immediately upon graduation he had been transferred to the US Army Infantry School at Fort Benning, Georgia, to attend the Basic Officer Infantry Course, and for the first time in his life, he had actually travelled outside Kansas. From that point on, he had simply moved along the infantry world, reluctant to get the airborne wings, or the Ranger tab. He was approached to join the program because he had finally agreed to join the Special Forces community and had demonstrated a rare quality to endure physical discomfort. Steve had then accepted a three-year exchange assignment with the South African army and had quickly been a contributor to the South African Special Forces Brigade, popularly known as Recces. While his initial service in 1 Recce lacked the international flavour that he was longing for, Steve had excelled in bush warfare and had participated in operations in Namibia and as far north as Angola. He had then been transferred to 451 Para, the old 5 Recce, which specialised in long-range infiltration, where he had acquired the skills that would prove critical to his selection to LICHI KLESH. He had experienced the long and arduous approaches to target areas, moving at night, digging in during the day, avoiding enemy forces and the locals, while carrying the heavy weight of a combat load and navigating in all types of terrain without the help of the GPS which could have given his position away. He had crossed rivers that looked so black on a moonless night as to look as a bottomless precipice—rivers that harboured man-eating animals as well as the threat of microbiological and incurable sickness—and whose water loaded with minerals, all types of detritus and hippopotamus dung, stunk up the fatigues, and made you uncomfortable for hours after reaching the other side. He had survived on bugs and lizard meat, while trying to conserve rations, drinking the strict minimum amount of water while he travelled in conditions from freezing rain to deserts, all the time not uttering a word, not making a sound, always on the alert for the noise that could bring death. But now he knew that whatever happened out there, he could survive on his own, capable to rely on his skills, stamina, and willpower to return to base. Upon reaching the target area, he had experienced hiding right in the middle of enemy territory, while taking notes, counting soldiers, making maps, and identifying military hardware, under the very nose of soldiers who had no discipline and wallowed in an orgy of blood, murder, and rape. At times, he had been tempted to pull the trigger as he witnessed the multiple rape of a young girl before she was made to kneel and her throat was simply slashed, her blood pulsating out of the open wound. He was revolted at the meaningless sadistic torture and senseless beating to death of a helpless prisoner. Then, its torturers had beheaded him and had used his head as the ball for a game of soccer. But he would have compromised his mission as well as himself, and in the end, they both would have been killed. This is why the Recce had trained him. At times he had penetrated right into the heart of an enemy position to conduct a detailed reconnaissance. Once he had been seen and he had had to kill the man with a swift thrust of his commando knife into the enemy's mouth. The knife had come out on the other side of the skull, and when he had pulled it out, the brain matter had squeezed out of the man's mouth. And after he obtained the information, he had to exfiltrate, to go back through all of the same challenges that he had faced on the way in. Except he was weakened by days of poor dieting and lack of water and the rucksack was heavier with every step—there was no way to dump its contents as he went, as this would have resulted in leaving a trail behind him. He was in even greater danger on the way out, and he had to make a conscious effort to slow down, force himself to think rationally despite the lack of sleep and food, and focus on the processes he had practiced so many times in training. Whatever atrocities he witnessed on the way out, he had to suppress the urge to intervene, and he had to make it through borders where he was always in danger of encountering a random patrol. He had to face wild animals, especially lions that he feared most. If his infiltration was discovered, the enemy could deploy hundreds of soldiers in an attempt to find him, catch him, and make him talk under torture. He would have to outwit them and outlast them. They would set up interdiction lines he would have to cross, and they would sit in ambush for days waiting for him to come through. They had all the time in the world—he did not. He carried perishable information; he had no food, no place to hide, and he was exhausted. They would hunt him down by helicopter, by truck, and they would seek their own Special Forces upon him. He would have to survive, go back to the fundamentals of escape and evasion, and not panic—he would commando march, hide, lay low, backtrack, go in the opposite direction that he should have, and kill only when he had to, even if he did so with absolutely no hesitation. But all of this took its toll on him. After over fifteen hundred miles on foot, he would finally reach safety, barely able to articulate a few words, reduced to 160 pounds, and ready for a stay in the hospital. He would turn in his report and be driven by ambulance to the seven floor building where nurses and doctors knew he had come back from hell. They would patch him up, repair him, rehydrate him, and he would be ready for the next mission. During his years with the Recces, Steve had appreciated people who could keep their mouth shut and did not flinch under fire. He had thus built formidable teams that operated with pre-scripted scenarios, did not need to communicate and were always predictable in the way they would react to unforeseen situations. They were truly silent teams. After three years, he too had been approached by a mysterious US Army officer who had introduced him to a classified program code-named LICHI KLESH. The existence of the program was itself classified as well as the names of all of its members. The major had not identified himself, nor had he given Steve any way to contact him. He had appeared one evening, as Steve was coming out of the Phalaborwa Officers' Club, and he had disappeared with the same stealth as he had arrived with. The conversation had been brief: a simple statement of mission, professional conditions, and the request for a yes or no answer within twelve hours. Steve was not married, had no girlfriend, and could easily agree to the one condition that he had to basically disappear. He would be paid as normal, would benefit from a liberal expense budget, no questions asked, and would immediately be promoted to the rank of colonel. He would participate in Lichi Klesh for ten years and—if he survived—retire with a full pension equal to 100 per cent of his salary. The arrangement reminded him of the Roman legionaries and he was sure that whoever had drawn up the terms had done so with the purpose of linking the program to the Tenth Legion of Julius Caesar. At precisely five o'clock in the morning the following day, Steve's telephone had rung. He was already up and about and preparing for his daily ten-kilometre run. The question was brief: 'Yes or no?' Steve simply answered, 'Yes'. Normally, he would have packed his military gear a simple task since his equipment was always ready to go by the front door. But he lived in an apartment and had some personal things, and a car. He figured that he was meant to leave them behind. His clothes could be replaced, his car was nothing special and worth a few thousand Rands, and the few personal items he had could probably be packed in a duffle bag. He went out in the still cool early morning air, knowing that this would be his last run in South Africa. But Steve was not one to reflect unnecessarily on the unavoidable changes that life brings. By eleven he was packed: civilian clothes, a few personal items, his laptop, the military gear, and most importantly, two hand guns with four clips of ammo. At the stroke of twelve, the officer showed up to pick him up. He was amazed by how little Steve had packed. They proceeded down the stairs to a waiting unmarked car. Once they had loaded the gear and they were sitting down, the officer continued: 'I am taking you to the airport; you are flying to Fort Bragg.' These were the only words they had exchanged that afternoon.

This was how Steve got to meet Max. From that point on, they were paired: the sophisticated scholar, fluent in five languages and capable of operating incognito in multiple countries (something Steve would need a long time to learn), and the experienced Recce soldier, who would be able to teach Max the secrets of survival in hostile environments (something Max could muster relatively quickly). Following that day when they met at Fort Bragg, neither Max's nor Steve's lives had ever been the same again. For Steve, who had spent three years operating in the bush, the training had been like a vacation, but for Max, who had not had that experience, every day brought him to the edge of exhaustion. Yet he managed to make it through the course. There was no graduation ceremony and no diploma. They were called in turn to an anonymous office where a colonel simply shook their hand and told them they had successfully met the course requisites and were being assigned to a caretaker, from whom they would get their orders. During the first year, they had trained even more, going to the extreme SF Escape and Evasion School then to Fort Benning, Georgia, for the never-ending nine-week Ranger School. At the same time, they qualified on all the weapons in the arsenal of the US Army and the Russian Army. They were then sent on an infiltration training mission in France: it had consisted of a drop in Northern France and the mission had been to reach and penetrate the military port of Toulon, observe activities there during three days, and return to Northern France without being caught by the Gendarmes, the population, or the French DST. This event had been remarkable in that thanks to being born in France, Max had been the only operative to have fully accomplished the mission out of the thirty soldiers who had started it. Steve had shown his shortcomings being caught after only six hours into the two-week-long mission. They had participated in real missions in the Saudi Peninsula, in the Philippines, East Timor, and Pakistan. During this entire period, Max had been surprised that his relationship with Rebecca had become even stronger and that Steve had managed to find a girlfriend, marry her, and even have children. Steve had also been shot twice, and despite his French experience, Max had been caught once on the island of New Caledonia where he had been beaten, starved, questioned, and beaten again. In the end, he had exploited one moment of inattention by his rebel captors to jump off a cliff into a river, as Geronimo had done at Fort Sill, and swim five miles with the flow of the Guekaipir River before commandeering a small rowboat and making it back to civilisation. His daring escape and the information he had collected had allowed the French forces to liberate four hostages that had been held captive for several months. However, he was too valuable to the US Army to continue such nonsense and he had been transferred to urban operations. He had said goodbye to Steve and had started undercover work in Europe. That Steve and Max should be reunited in the same mission was highly unusual at this point in time.

One hour into the flight, the co-pilot came into the cargo bay and handed Max, who was the ranking officer, a sealed envelope marked Top Secret. Max opened it and found a two-line message: *W2°52'33"78 – N30°54'42"39 – Mercedes 600 SE Black – 01956 106 27 – 14-15 OCT – engage and terminate all.* However cryptic the message had been, neither Max nor Steve needed any further instructions. The message included a clear set of latitude and longitude that both men had known for a long time was on the road to Tamanrasset. The description of a car and a license plate that was clearly Algerian and described a Mercedes licensed in the city of Mostaganem. The dates indicated when the action should take place. With these data, they had received Google Earth pictures together with classified satellite photos of the area which they consulted with the focus of men whose life depended in remembering every detail of the terrain. And now they knew that the mission would take them to Algeria, roughly 45 miles east of the Moroccan border and 300 miles south of the Mediterranean and the city of Melilla. The exfiltration would be difficult as the terrain was flat and offered little place to hide. A photograph of the occupants of the car had been included, a superfluous piece of information since neither man would ever have a chance of seeing them at that close a range.

CHAPTER 4

A new day had dawned, a new day once again without any news and without any sign from her. There could be no email, no voicemail, no text message, since she was spending Christmas and New Year with her husband in their Sydney Harbour estate. He feared for his future, and his days were filled with anxiety. It was not an anxiety that resulted from the need to have her emotional presence, her intellectual complicity, and to experience again the great intimacy they had shared. It was the same anxiety that a lottery winner experiences when he realises his ticket bears the winning numbers, and he is suddenly overwhelmed by the fear of losing it. He would have lied if he had stated that he needed her sexually. Since they had managed to sneak a visit in Paris a month before, he had had several partners, and all of them had been better at lovemaking. Sun had gone back to Korea, but she had introduced him to her best friend, a Taiwanese woman named Xin, who was the best lover he had ever had. Since the two women were bisexual, Sun shared Xin with George as a way to 'get them together'. Now, rather than thinking about Lena, George was obsessed with Xin's body and techniques. Although he hated to have an exclusive partnership, in the past three weeks, they had been together almost constantly. He figured that once they had exhausted the thrill of novelty, they would simply part ways and never see each other again. But the inventiveness they both displayed showed that the time for their parting ways was not in the near future. Lena had now become a secondary thought—more than anything he needed her reassuring, he needed to know that he could still attract her and that she would come to him with the fortune that her husband had already shared with her. Yet, he also knew that the longer she stayed with him, the less likely it was that she would eventually leave him. This was a constant apprehension, not a fear, but it was a permanent thought that disturbed the anticipation he experienced of seeing Xin again. Xin expected luxuries and wanted to be impressed. At the rate he was spending money with her, the small amount of inheritance that remained after he had bought the house in Georgetown, together with his State Department salary, would not last more than four to six months. But, by then, his liaison with Xin would probably be over in any case, so he did not care. On the other hand, Lena complained every time she could talk to him that it had been a long time, a very long time, since they had seen each other and it was clear to her that these absences simply were not sustainable. He could feel that she was sincere, and that she experienced genuine pain, sadness, and loneliness. When he talked to her, he had to sound true as well. He had to switch from his nights of debauchery with Xin, to the sad lover who longed only for Lena. He had become very good at it. Of course, Xin would pout during his calls with Lena, and one time, she had purposely sent an entire pile of plates crashing on the floor while he was talking with Lena. He had had to pretend he was in a restaurant and that the waiter had dropped the plates. But the explanation had left Lena unsatisfied as she had not been able to hear any background noises. To avoid such situations, from that point when he talked to Lena, he kept to himself, limiting his conversations to the confines of his office. He could only think of the end-goal, the day when he would have Lena to his side, her fortune, her elegance. He imagined how he would then be able to progress his diplomatic and political careers. Then, the horrible days of counting every hundred dollars, the nightmare of running out of money, and his inability to purchase a Ferrari would be over. He would be able to breathe again, to let his ego run wild in a city where egos had to be backed by money.

He wondered what would happen if her husband ever found out about them. Surely, George would be disposed of. He would divorce her, and simply get another pretty girl. In fact, Krasnaief did not need her. This is when George started to think it would be advantageous if her husband could have some sort of accident. He got caught in the fantasy and actually thought it through. It would be impossible to organise in Russia. George knew no one there, and in any case, it would impractical. However, when Krasnaief travelled to Europe or to North America, it would be possible to organise something. Although George had never killed or participated in the killing of anyone, the fortune at stake certainly made it a consideration. Through his work at State, he knew that such operations were conducted every day. Of course, Executive Order 12333 prohibited the assassination of foreign leaders, but it did not extend to the assassination of enemies of the United States. What if Krasnaief could be disposed of in that manner? There would be a time of mourning, and after a few months, he could propose to Lena, she would become his wife, and he would have it made! He recollected the ways he had seen to terminate people: gunfire, knifing, poison, plane crash, car accident, induced heart attack, and suicide. Of the six, he eliminated the most unreliable ones: knifing, car accident, and suicide (certainly Krasnaief had no reason to jump off a building since he was making more money than ever). In the office, he rummaged through some of the files to find other ways people had been killed. Then, he recalled that the chemical used to stop the heart from beating in cardiac surgery was potassium chloride. He also remembered that the lethal effects of potassium chloride had led to its use in lethal injections used to carry out death sentences. This is the chemical that Doctor Kovorkian used in his thanatron machine. This was the obvious solution. He would have to resolve three problems: first, find potassium chloride in injectable form—this was the least challenging issue, since it was available from Internet drug resellers; second, he would have to find a way for the potassium chloride and Krasnaief to be at the same place at the same time; and third, he would have to find someone to do the injection. The fantasy killing became a project in the blink of an eye. And how would Lena react to this death? A heart attack was not an unlikely scenario, as every picture he had seen of Krasnaief showed an almost obese man, with eyes protruding out of their sockets like those of an ox, and every article denounced his excessive drinking and smoking. There was even the report of an incident when he had been part of a diplomatic mission to the United States. He had arrived so drunk at a state dinner, that he had tripped on the carpet and in an effort to prop himself up and keep from falling, he had reached for the first thing he could grab. Unfortunately, it was the punch bowl which had been filled with several gallons of red artillery punch. It has failed to stop the fall, and as Krasnaief had fallen on to the ground, the entire content of the punch bowl had emptied on top of him and had splattered guests who had had the bad luck of being too close to him. Krasnaief had been taken back to his hotel so that he could be washed and so that he could sleep his drunkenness off. Immediately, George seized upon the idea. This was the opportunity. He had to manage to reproduce the same incident and be sure he was in the vicinity. He would not even need another person to inject the potassium chloride then. He could do it himself!

When the news reached Lena, she was indifferent at best. In the past months, torn apart by her love for George, she had been seeing mystics in Russia, and two of them had predicted life-shattering events. She knew that the only life-shattering event she could experience was the death of her husband. The quantity of vodka he consumed on a daily basis and the absolutely constant smoking of cigarettes allowed any prediction of his death to be highly credible. He had gotten fatter, more obnoxious, and more repulsive. She gagged every time he came in her bedroom and demanded sex. Fortunately, it was rather quick, because it only took a few minutes for him to fall asleep in a drunken stupor after he lay down on her bed. In the past three months, she could not recall seeing him not drunk. She wondered how he managed to conduct business deals, but guessed he had other people do it for him. She had even started to think of how to get rid of him, when the news made the effort of thinking about it entirely redundant. Her first thought was of George, and how happy he would be to learn of the death of her husband. She was in Yalta, and her husband had been part of an official delegation to England. George had told her he would be out of reach for a couple of days as he had been invited to go trekking in Idaho. She tried to call him in any case, but he did not answer. George at that time was on United Flight 933 from London to Washington under a false identity. He had killed his first man, and it had been a cinch. He had had himself added to the list of invitees at the Annual Aluminium Industry Congress, and had just waited for the appropriate moment to intervene. He had shadowed Krasnaief all night, and as predicted, the man had drunk incalculable amounts of vodka. He had even brought his own stock of Beluga vodka from Russia, since it was not available in England. Dinner at the Ritz was followed by more drinking at the Mayfair, where Krasnaief was staying. George had accompanied him there, pretending to be interested in aluminium production and a joint venture with an Italian producer. In the meantime, he was ensuring that Krasnaief drank even more. Finally, at about three o'clock in the morning, Krasnaief had tried to get up to go to his room. He had not been able to stand up, and since George was still around and was the only person he knew, he had sought his assistance to stumble to his room. George had manhandled him to one of the elevators, and on the way up, he had fallen asleep and collapsed. George had immediately pulled out the syringe filled with six grams of potassium chloride, and without hesitation, he had injected the entire amount into Krasnaief's interosseous vein, just below the fold of his right elbow. After he had reached the seventh floor and had pulled Krasnaief out of the elevator, he had called the reception and requested help. Krasnaief was very much still alive at that point. Rather than waiting for assistance to arrive, he had then gone back down using the stairs and had disappeared into the night so that he could go back to his own hotel, change, and grab a taxi to catch his plane at seven fifty-five. While walking along the embankment, he had thrown the syringe into the Thames and had wished it a good trip to the North Sea. Now, an anonymous traveller in Economy Class, he came off the adrenaline high and surrendered to the exhaustion of the past day, dozing off in the middle of a sentence of the book he was reading.

In accordance with Krasnaief's wishes, no autopsy was conducted, despite the Metropolitan Police's refusal to release the body unless one was performed. Finally, the Russian Embassy had to intervene, stating that Krasnaief had the status of diplomat and that any investigation would be completed upon the return of the body to Russia. The embarrassment of the situation had delighted Fleet Street, as it showed once more that oligarchs were nothing but the most common people. Photos of the beautiful Lena made the front page of the Daily Express which declared her to be the most desirable heiress on the planet as it was assumed she would inherit Krasnaief's colossal fortune. In Russia, rumours were going around that Krasnaief had been murdered, that his death was suspicious, and that he had fallen victim to one of the other oligarchs who wanted to claim his empire. Lena had addressed this in an interview on the main Russian TV channel, ORT. She had given a precise description of Krasnaief's last days, spent between drinking orgies and vomiting, passing out anywhere in the house, not even bothering to shower or change clothes, while at the same time smoking $50 cigars as if they were mere cigarettes. At one point, she had not been able to stand the smells, the obesity, the filth, and the sexual assaults, and she had packed up and gone to Yalta. She added that there was no way this death was anything but the natural conclusion of years of excesses, and not taking care of himself. Per the deceased's wishes, the funeral took place at Isaakievskiy Sobor in

Sankt Petersburg in the most Russian tradition. The prime minister, who had been present at the wedding, was also there. The coffin was draped in a Russian flag with the double-headed eagle and carried by a delegation of Russian sailors from the Baltic Fleet. A large photograph of Krasnaief was placed on the coffin, adorned with a black ribbon, and had been carried in the cathedral by his two brothers. Lena was the most elegant widow. Dressed in a Nina Ricci black dress, she wore her long blond hair in a chignon and had switched from her red fox coat to a black sable one. Her faced hidden behind the black gauze of her hat, she maintained herself with a dignity that had been admired by all. And when the body had been entered, she had dropped a red rose on top of the coffin and had walked to her waiting Rolls Royce with the measured steps of an empress. As soon as she had been in the car, she had poured herself a glass of Mumms Champagne and had called George to tell him she would meet him in Munich two weeks forth, after the reading of the will—the content of which she knew already—and the settling of a few affairs. In the few minutes that the conversation had lasted, George had noticed a significant change in her. She was no longer the naive blonde who was deeply in love with him. He had sensed that she had become the leader of a multibillion empire. He would have to be very careful in the future. Nevertheless, there was no need to cancel any of his evenings with Xin.

CHAPTER 5 (14 OCTOBER)

« Il y avait un homme en moi qui voulait a tout prix avoir raison ». Stefan Zweig

'Every Friday, Mustafah Guermoulian, an Algerian of Armenian descent, a former Freedom Fighter currently living in Algeria and operating Network 16 of the Armée Révolutionnaire Islamique (ARI), drives from his compound in the region of Bechar to visit his ailing brother in El Bayah, via National Road 6, known as N6. He travels in an armoured Mercedes with two of his key associates. It is also believed that Mustafah is planning to take over leadership of not only Network 16, but also of the ARI by force. Because the current leader of Network 16 of the ARI is a CIA operative, who is positioned to take over the ARI following the assassination of his leader, Mohammed Ben Bellaouid, it is imperative that he prevented Mustafah from taking over the Network. Your mission is to prevent him from doing so and to terminate him. A tracking device has been installed on the car and will alert your GPS receiver when it is within ten miles of your position.'

Now, while they were waiting for the Mercedes to appear around the bend in the valley below, Max and Steve started readying their temporary home in order for their departure. The attack in broad daylight did not make it very easy to exfiltrate from. But because it was being conducted in a remote area, and without a police station or an army barracks within twenty-five miles, the two men had agreed that they had plenty of time to reach an alternate position, dubbed Position Beta, and situated eight miles east from their location. Position Beta did not appear to be an obvious refuge for someone looking to hide, as it was mainly composed of medium-sized boulders that had been left undisturbed for hundreds of thousands of years and presented no touristic value. Their main attraction was that they were unremarkable. The two men were in top physical shape, and even with their equipment, while they were training in the Mojave Desert, they had consistently averaged a running cadence of seven and a half minute per mile. On three different days, they had even been able to run eight miles in just under an hour. Thus, it was anticipated they would need just about an hour to reach Position Beta, which was the rendezvous point with a Navy Seahawk helicopter from the aircraft carrier USS Nimitz. The exfiltration would take place under the cover of darkness, with the Seahawk flying NOE (Nap of the Earth) both ways. By flying NOE, with a very low-altitude flight course, the Seahawk would be able to avoid enemy detection and potential attacks in what was sure to have become a very high-threat environment by 0100 hours Zulu Time when the pickup was scheduled. They had rehearsed that phase of the operation a number of times, and both men had been able to escape detection in a similar environment, thanks to the highly sophisticated Ghillie suits they were carrying with them. The suits were fitted with electronic gizmos that jammed and fooled any heat detection devices and they had been put together with an exact colour match of the terrain at the spot chosen for exfiltration. Despite the fact that it would take them an hour to reach that spot, Max and Steve felt confident that they had plenty of time to get there before 'all hell broke loose' as they path went East–South East, and the road—which any vehicle rushing to the scene would have to use—went North from their foxhole. In addition, it was calculated that any police or army vehicle dispatched to the site would need at least forty minutes to arrive, and by that time, they would clearly be out of visual range. Furthermore, although their presence would have become obvious by that time, the terrain around the area was mainly stone and it was unlikely that their escape path could be traced from footprints. The plan consisted of rappelling down the South slope of the craggy outcrop, so as to leave no indication of a flight to the East. The ropes were also equipped with a remotely controlled explosive device that would detach them from their anchor point so that they could be collected and hidden at the bottom and suppress any indication of their existence. They had set up the ropes during the last part of the night, making sure to camouflage them with rocks and dirt. But in any case, they were ready, and the only thing needed was to throw them over the side. The issue of the photographer came up again. As the two men sat in the foxhole, waiting, Max brought it up again. If the photographer was indeed an agent of the Algerian government or of the Islamic Revolutionary Army, the mission was compromised. This was obvious. But this also meant that there was a mole within Lichi Klesh. Steve dismissed anew the very notion of the photographer's presence being anything but fortuitous, but Max pressed him. 'Steve, you cannot be that fucking stubborn, Goddammit!' he almost yelled. 'We are in a mission that has a high fucking probability of being goddam compromised and you refuse to look at all the possibilities. Do you want to fucking die here, or what? The only reason you and I have survived thus far is because we always looked at all the fucking aspects of the motherfucking problem! I would suggest we spend the next couple of hours thinking how we are going to get our asses out of here once the fucking Algerians show up!' Steve still was not convinced. Max thought that accepting the mission had been a huge error: there were too many agencies involved. Lichi

Klesh—whoever they were—was the first one, and outside from belonging to it, it was so compartmented that neither Max nor Steve knew anything about it. They were given missions and either accepted them or not, but there was never anyone who was identified as belonging to Lichi Klesh. That Max knew his handler had been due simply to chance and the fact that he had recognised his voice over the phone. So, who were the people actually manoeuvring them on the chessboard? Were they even the US Army? Then, there was the CIA, since the mission had been organised to cover a CIA operative and allow him to control the activities of the IRA. And there was one thing Max knew for sure: one could not and should not ever trust the CIA. Then, of course, there was the Air Force, who had flown them there, and finally, the Navy. Both of these services were jealous of the army's ability to conduct such operations especially when they had to risk their lives and equipment to bail them out without ever getting credit for success. And finally, there was the Army Intelligence Agency. All of these organisations had compartmented layers of bureaucracy that prevented the free flow of information and certainly hid the person responsible for any failure behind so many classified programs that the president himself could never access them. Max wondered why he was doing this shit. And now, his partner, one of his closest friends refused to see the reality of the whole situation, wanted to stick to the plan, and count on their stealth to escape. Steve could not even comprehend that the organisation might in any way be compromised, and that there was a distinct possibility that they would not catch a helicopter home at two in the morning. Max was despairing of having Steve understand that, and blamed Steve's softness on the comforts of being married and father of children. A family man simply was not cut out for this sort of missions and risk. Max thought that like when you play chess, you should consider all of the possible movements of on the chess board. Steve was losing his patience: 'Max, we have a shitload of stuff to do here before we engage the target, we should focus on it rather than fucking around with some fucking shit you are inventing!'

Max was absolutely incredulous at the attitude of his friend—or was their friendship actually unravelling at this very moment? 'Steve, there is no need to be pissed off! If you think everything is honky dory, at least fucking think of Emily and of your kids. Are you willing to gamble that we are absolutely fine here, and that you will see them again? Are so sure of it as to refuse to even look at other alternatives? What if other people have already sentenced us to death? What if other people have already decided we are not going to make it out of here? It happens all the fucking time. Remember the operation in Nicaragua? They thought they were coming home as well. Have you seen them at Bragg lately? No! And you know why, because they didn't fucking make it! And you know why? Because that fucking Marine colonel changed his fucking mind about what is the 'national interest of the United States' while they were on the ground on a mission! That's why, in case you fucking forgot! Nobody even knows we are here! Our handlers don't even know, remember? The fucking air crew that dropped us off does not even know *we* are here!' But rather than appeasing Steve, these words just made him doubt his former friend—for in his mind, there was no longer any friendship: "Max, I think you got cold feet! I think that since you met Rebecca, you simply are no longer cut for this type of work, and you are fucking scared!' Max could only find one answer to this: 'Fuck you, Steve! Fuck you to hell!' He pitied his former friend, and he knew that their ten-year friendship had just disintegrated in a couple of minutes. Steve was not even his partner now; he had become a liability, a liability whose obstinacy could cost him his life. As they were preparing the escape from the foxhole, Max focused on playing in his head all of the contingencies. The sleeping bags would be destroyed, the excess food also—but Max disagreed and decided to keep his. The two men were no longer operating as a team. They no longer even spoke, like spouses in a marriage gone bad. Steve went about making his rucksack as light as possible to ensure he could run the eight miles in under an hour, while Max was packing for another contingency: surviving in the desert. He knew he was right, and he knew something had gone array in this mission. He was preparing a route of escape to the South and then due west into Morocco. He had thought about all possibilities. If they had been compromised, Algerian forces would be looking for them. At first, right around their position, and then always further, using circles of increasing diameters: five kilometres, ten kilometres, fifteen kilometres, and so forth. The area would be buzzing with helicopters and other aircraft, an activity which the US AWACS were sure to identify. And there was no way that the captain of the Nimitz was going to risk his crew and a $30 million aircraft to see them either shot down or captured to rescue an assassination team. The logic was cold and it was one that they all accepted: the Special Warfare team knew what mess they had put themselves in, and they had agreed to it when they had signed up that at times their exfiltration would be impossible. No officer in the chain of command would ever question the carrier captain's decision. If his own crew was to be captured, that would force him to commit more resources, even supporting a rescue operation with the F-18 Hornets, and this would risk triggering a dogfight with the Algerian Air Force. Surely, none of the F-18s would be lost, but how many others would have to die to get these two guys out? Again, in previous situations, no captain had ever been criticised for avoiding an armed conflict with another nation. Max knew this very well from his days working in the Office of the Joint Chiefs of Staff. While the US Department of Defense valued human life above all and certainly valued it more than the cost of a helicopter, putting other lives at risk was an equation that was easy to solve. If four lives were lost to save two, the net result was two more deaths than had been necessary. While every attempt would be made to save these two lives, the captain was responsible to ensure that the risk was not excessive from the start. Max calculated that the helicopter would never come and that his only chance of survival was to go in a direction that was absurdly illogical: South into the expanse of the Sahara Desert rather than North or West to the safety of the populated areas of Algeria or to Morocco. By two in the afternoon, all packing was done, but Max's rucksack was at least twice the size of Steve's as he had also taken as much water as he could carry. The weapons were at the ready on top of their packs, the 9mm in their body holsters, and the MILAN ready to fire. Steve had polished the field glasses so that he could confirm the identity of the target—his task on this mission was twofold: first serve as the spotter and second provide close-range security as Max fired the MILAN missile, in case intruders appeared. The thermal grenades had been placed on top of the equipment to be destroyed, and the two of them sat down to wait. At the last moment, they would remove part of the roof to have more freedom of movement and have 360-degree vision. At 16:17:23, the digital device emitted a small beep. The Mercedes was arriving within range. Max removed the missile tube cover, took up the firing position, and activated the firing computer of the MILAN device. He was calm, but the adrenaline was already pumping in his veins and he could feel his heart beat accelerating despite the fact that he had not moved. He confirmed with relief that all lights were green as the system booted itself. He took as comfortable a position as he could, put his eye on the reticle, and placed his finger on the trigger. Behind him, Steve had peeled back the roof of the shelter and was observing the area, while focusing his attention to the road, which they could see appear around a bend about three miles away. Traffic was light but was consistent with their observations the day before, so neither of them paid much attention to it. Especially Max who was now absolutely focused on finding, identifying, and servicing the target. During these short moments, everything else was Steve's responsibility: confirming the target by identifying it was the correct license plate, ensuring perimeter security and eventually, providing perimeter. Max was certain he could not miss the Mercedes. Although the MILAN was not a new generation anti-tank missile like the US-made JAVELIN which was a fire-and-forget, the French missile was without doubt the best of the older generation. When fired, it was first propelled by a charge of compressed air which avoided the backfire of other missiles and prevented the missile form emitting a cloud of smoke, thus not giving away the shooter's position. As the missile reached a distance of 100 metres after launch, the rocket engine ignited and started to propel the missile that flew to its target at a speed of just under 520 kilometres per hour. This resulted in the missile being slightly slower over the first thousand metres than over its last thousand metres, and it required 14 seconds to travel the entire distance of 2,000 metres which was its effective range. The only thing Max had to do was keep the crosshairs on the car, and the computer would relay the flight data to the warhead through the wire linking it to the computer. After a wait of a few minutes, the car finally appeared around the bend. It was too early to shoot. Max would wait until Steve could confirm the license plate number and tap Max once on the left shoulder. Once the car reached the point which both of them had agreed would be the optimal engagement area, Steve would tap his right shoulder twice, indicating it was time to shoot. During the whole time, Max would be tracking the car with the active missile computer. When Steve tapped him for the second time, Max fired. The missile was liberated with a slight whoosh, and it dipped a little bit before starting to glide forward. It was like playing a videogame, it was like being in training. As expected, a puff of smoke indicated the missile had fired properly. The seconds ticked away, and Max was fully absorbed by flying the missile. He did not really see where it was, as it rarely kept a trajectory that was visible from the reticule until the moment of impact. Max knew the missile would hit the target as long as the crosshairs were on it at the moment of impact. Mentally, he counted the seconds '. . .thousand five, thousand six, thousand seven. . .' At thousand eleven, the missile appeared in the reticule. The car was moving faster than anticipated. Thousand twelve. Thousand. . . he did not have the time to say thirteen. The impact was square on the passenger door. At first nothing happened. The car did not slow down and did not explode. Then, Max saw it stagger sideways to the left, cross the median, as if pushed by an invisible hand, and as it did the anticipated ball of fire engulfed the entire vehicle. The temperature was high enough to melt steel, and the oxygen ignited from that heat. Everyone in the car was already dead, as the armouring steel of the door was turned into a superheated mist. One breath burnt the lungs irremediably; the blood boiled instantly, death was welcome and almost instant. The car continued travelling across the road, off the pavement, flipped over and finally came resting back on its wheels as it left a trail of burning debris behind it and above it. As pieces fell back on the road, it ignited the hardtop. The car was now a blazing inferno belching ugly black smoke from its burning tires. Max confirmed that no one had escaped the hit. He keyed the pre-programmed signal on the radio, indicating the mission had been accomplished, and disconnected it. As Max turned around to throw the radio on top of the pile to be destroyed and start evacuate the foxhole, his predictions were proven right. At that precise moment—he involuntarily glanced at his digital watch that indicated 16:14:46—his nightmare started. It was still the afternoon of October 14.

CHAPTER 6

Max's focus was completely broken when he felt Steve fall heavily on him, his full weight almost pinning him down into the foxhole. At the same time, he felt a warm liquid spill onto his right arm, and he knew instantly it was blood. The quantity of it told him Steve was either dead or close to it. One look at him, and Max realised the horror of the answer. Where the back of his head should have been, there was simply a massive hole that had taken out the entirety of the cranial bone and its content. Max did not have the time to feel anything about it, he did not have the time to process any information except that if Steve has suffered this wound, it had to be because people had been shooting at him, and if they were shooting at Steve, they certainly were shooting at Max as well. He wondered where Steve's brain was, not because of some gruesome curiosity, but rather because he did not want to step on it. As he thought that, he also thought that he had been right, that he had to send the duress signal, but foremost, that he had to shoot back. He lunged for his rifle, noticing that Steve had been using his pea-shooter (the 9mm pistol), and Max could not figure out why. Throughout the few seconds, Max did not even have a sense that bullets were flying about him. The events had been too quick. He first found Steve's rifle, and simply shot a quick burst of bullets. Immediately he heard and felt the impact of enemy bullets all around him. He finally reached his own rifle. Using Steve's with his left hand, he again shot a controlled volley of three rounds. Then, he popped up and shot one bullet with his own rifle, hitting one assailant squarely in the chest and sending him reeling backwards in a mass of exploding ribcage and dying flesh. He peered to the left and saw another one coming. One round. He recognised the familiar muffled report of the silencer releasing a second deadly vector, and the man fell backward, his head exploding in a spray of blood, bone, and brain. When he again released a burst of three bullets from Steve's rifle, the response was far more hesitant. He ventured to look out and saw yet another assailant that was attempting to find some cover. Max took his time, carefully lined up the scope crosshairs on the man's body. The bullet hit him in the small of the back and pushed him off his field of vision. Max knew he had broken the man's back and the bullet had probably disembowelled him. Suddenly, there were no noises. If more enemy combatants were coming, they were now seeking cover, which meant that Max's position was even more precarious. He could not let them recover. He could not let the momentum slip away from him. He grabbed four hand grenades, and rifle in hand, he stormed out of the foxhole, firing randomly. He saw the three men he had just shot and realised there could only have been four of them. The fourth one was running as fast as he could down the hill to the safety of an official looking car painted with the colours of the Gendarmerie Nationale. Max aimed at the car first, ensuring that he rendered it inoperative—something he would regret later. He meticulously shot the two wheels facing him and put a third round into the engine compartment. The runner turned around and tentatively took aim at Max from an unstable position. The bullet hit and chipped a rock about six feet to the left of Max. Max took aim and shot the man in the back, but at the last moment, the man lunged to the side and the bullet ripped through his right leg. He tumbled forward, picked himself up, and continued running. Max could see that he only had a flesh wound. During that time, the assailant that had been shot in the lower back made a desperate attempt to grab his rifle. Max shot him a second time, and this time he hit him on the side, puncturing a lung, and most likely taking his heart out at once. He did not move again. The fugitive was about to reach the radio in the car. Max assumed the prone position, took careful aim at the zigzagging man, and this time he hit his left shoulder blade. From the way he fell, Max knew he had shattered his entire shoulder, and he bounced awkwardly while letting out an agonising scream. It was only a matter of time before he bled to death. Yet, Max could not take the chance that he would reach the bloody car radio and he decided to go after him. The man's pain was intense, and he had dropped his rifle. He was far from wanting to fight—there was only a desire to survive. Max saw it in his eyes as he quickly caught up with him. The man was now non-ambulatory, but he approached him with the greatest caution. Max did not have any time to waste: his life depended on his expediency. He had to run back up the hill, get his rucksack, rappel down, and run for at least an hour before reaching some safety. The man started begging for his life in French: 'Ne tirez pas, ne tirez pas, je dirai rien! J'ai une femme, j'ai deux enfants, je vous en prie ne me tuez pas!' He started wailing in Arabic, then back in French. He was crying, and Max guessed he was shouting his prayers. Max pulled out the 9mm from the holster, chambered a bullet, and shot him in the head. He turned around and ran back up the hill as fast as he could.

 He rushed to the Falcon radio, reconnected it and packed as fast as he could while it was rebooting. He took his rucksack and threw it over the side of the hill, while he was releasing the rappelling rope. He returned to the foxhole, keyed in the distress signal, thus scrapping the extraction mission, and threw the radio on the pile with everything that had to be destroyed. He took four additional canteens of water, ripped Steve's dog tags from his neck, put them in one of his chest pockets, and armed the thermal grenades. He ran to the edge of the cliff, hooked up the D-ring to the rappelling rope, slung his rifle across his back, put on the leather gloves, and he slid down into the abyss. Less than fifteen seconds later, he was on the ground. He activated the remote control and within another a few more seconds, he was able to pull the rope down. He gathered it and hid it as best he could. Then he started running south in the infernal heat of the late afternoon. Max had just killed seven people and had been the witness to his former friend's death, yet he felt nothing. He felt no remorse, no sadness, no regret, and no compassion for any of them. It was as if his conscience had been removed from his being. He only had one thought and that was to put as much real estate as possible between him and the men he was certain were coming after him. Worst of all, there was no place to easily hide in the plain ahead of him. The boulders that were his Position Beta, now seemed completely inadequate. Fortunately, Max still had his Ghillie suit and that was going to be his salvation. He ran at the same steady pace he always did in training and in operation, the pace that would allow him to run a mile in seven and a half minutes. Except the weight of the extra load slowed him down. It was the first time he ran with so much weight. He tried to tighten up everything he was carrying, and yet he felt every piece of gear jingle and pull to one side or the other, he felt the weight of the water slowing him down and he realised he was nowhere close to running seven and a half minute miles. He wanted to go faster to escape the prying eyes of the helicopters that were sure to be coming after him. As he ran, he tried to calculate his progress, he tried to divide time into miles, and miles into minutes and hours. His mind travelled back to another time, a time when the world was benevolent, a time before he knew about the cruelty and the savagery that he was now participating in. It was a world that had been cocooned, a world that felt good like a warm blanket on a cold winter evening. It was time when he was in junior high school and had to participate in mental calculation exercises in Monsieur Aubert's class. He hated the mental gymnastics required and he hated even more getting it wrong. For a year, every Tuesday at nine in the morning, the entire class, student after student was submitted to the humiliation of getting it wrong. At first it had been easy simple problems such as 85 times 26, with simple tricks: multiply 85 by 100, divide it by 4 and add 85, for a total of 2210. Max remembered getting this one right. But then, calculations had become more and more complex and only a handful of students had been able to keep up. Max had been one of them, and now as he recalled the class and thought of some his friends of back then, he was delighted to have been good at mental calculation. He had a very hard time concentrating as his feet tried to avoid the traps of the uneven ground, his balance constantly on edge because of the excessive weight of the rucksack.

The heat beating down on him quickly became unbearable. He never looked behind him, but he could feel the activity of the Algerian army in his pursuit. He sensed the presence of the soldiers, and he focused only on one thing: reaching the safety of Position Beta. He could not get his mind to give him an answer on how fast he would get to the boulders, and he was no longer sure they were not a mirage. He had been running about thirty minutes when he heard the first helicopter. He threw himself on the ground without a millisecond of hesitation. He opened the rucksack, pulled the Ghillie suit out, and covered himself with the garment. At the same time, he had oriented his body towards the direction where the noise had come from; he had pulled his rifle, uncovered the reticule of the scope, and had chambered a round. He knew that if he had to, he could shoot the pilot in the head and take the helicopter down. In the prone position, he slowly adjusted his posture to take full advantage of the terrain, like the turbo fish that slowly digs himself into the bottom of the ocean. Max remained alert to every sound, to every indication a helicopter was approaching. He soon realised that the search was clearly taking place around Hill 752. Logically, there seemed to be a lot of activity focused on that piece of terrain and on the area to the west of it. Max assumed from the movement of the aircraft that they thought he was still on Hill 752. It was now approaching dusk, and Max knew that it was to his advantage. The Algerian army did not have a night flight

THE DATURA SOLUTION

program, and the darkness would ground their choppers. He played the scenarios in his head. If he had been in their place, he would have alerted a company of infantry, and by now they would be on the road to look for him. It would take only four vehicles, each going in a cardinal direction from Hill 752 and using long-range Xenon searchlights to find him. If they had done that, he would have had very little chance to escape, and he thought that just maybe, they did not want to find him. But he also knew the Algerian army, and their mode of operation was not the most ambitious, and they may have simply been unmotivated. As time passed and there was no indication of the search coming his way, he relaxed and even took time to drink some water. Soon it would be dark, and he would be able to keep moving, but he would also feel the grip of cold and he would have to manage the difference of temperature between the day and the night.

As the sky turned purple, Max got up and started running again, and as soon as it got dark, he put the NVG on and continued unencumbered. He thought of nothing except survival. He thought of all the miles he had run with his friend John Davies, he thought of all the soldiers in the world who were running like him, and he thought how lucky he was to be in a position to have a chance to escape and to see Reb again. In the back of his mind ran a constant movie, a movie with Reb as the star. Now, as his mind started to numb because of the mental exhaustion and stress of the day, he could only think of her. In the greenish landscape of the night vision he saw her face, he saw her dimples as she smiled at him. He was already hallucinating as the bitter cold bit at him, and he saw her naked body, athletic and thin. He grasped for her as if she were right next to him, and the brutal cold vanished under the warmth of her embrace. Then, he realised the impossibility of the task ahead of him. He also realised that he had paid no attention whatsoever to how fast he had been travelling. He had not counted his steps, he had not taken azimuths with his compass. He had been moving forward, away from Hill 752 without any discipline. He cursed himself for being so careless. He recognised in a panic that he had no idea where he was, whether he had run in a straight line or had run east, which would be the end of him. He was exhausted and confused and could only think of Rebecca. He needed to get hold of himself. He stopped and caught his bearings. He had long passed the row of boulders that would have been his salvation, and he had passed the next range of hills. He looked at his watch: it was three twenty-six in the morning. He had been moving for six and a half hours, more or less. He slowed down to a walk. He suddenly became aware that he had been shuffling rather than running, and that his speed could not have been over four and a half miles per hour. It meant that he had run about thirty miles—the distance Roman legionaries normally walked in one day. He decided to take a rest. But he also thought that it was time to go west. He laid an azimuth at 270 degrees and started heading in that direction. He was no longer running. He couldn't. He was now barely walking not even briskly. He gained the consciousness of the excessive weight he was carrying. He stopped again meaning to sort the stuff and repack it, but then he decided against it. Better to transport excess luggage a little further until the sun came up and he could rest for the day, he thought. Then he would have plenty of time to sort the stuff out then. There was no need to waste precious time in the middle of the night. The night was to travel, the day to rest. He looked again at his watch; it was four in the morning. He tried again to mentally figure out how long he had gone. Then, he remembered he had just done that and that he was moving west. His legs were aching, his back was killing him, and he knew he had to jettison some of the stuff. He stopped. He could go no further. In any case, it was now time to dig a hole that would allow him to spend the day in hiding. The sun was already over the horizon by the time he collapsed in the hole, absolutely spent by the efforts of the previous twelve hours. He drank some of the water, finally took his combat boots off, lay down, covered himself with the Ghillie suit, and assembled some of the gravel, rock, and sand on top of him. He emplaced the breathing tube and fell asleep within a couple of seconds.

He woke up to soon. The sun was high in the sky. He listened for every small sound, intent at not being surprised by an enemy, which he was expecting to pounce on him at any moment. He lay there in the warm ground, more a tomb than a bed, and he did not even need to urinate. His mouth was dry. He wiggled him arms towards the canteen, and drank a few sips. He conducted a systems check of his body: he had a headache, his feet were sore, his legs had muscular pain, his back was sore. By altogether, it was not so bad. He still had at least six hours before he would start moving again, he would have more time to heal. To pass the time, Max tried to recite De Bello Gallica: 'Gallia est omnis divisa in partes tres, quarum unam incolunt Belgae, aliam Aquitani, tertiam qui ipsorum lingua Celtae, nostra Galli appellantur. Hi omnes lingua, institutis, legibus inter se differunt.' He gave up, knowing that he would never remember the rest, but it was good to recite Julius Caesar in the middle of the desert in a situation that was as desperate as he had once experienced as a captive of pirates. He drifted again into sleep, his mind too empty to stay awake after this single effort. He woke up again a couple of hours later, starving. He carefully got up, ensuring he made no noise, and also hearing his articulations creaking like a wood floor. He ate one of the C-rations, drank more water, and started to sort his gear. The sleeping bag was useless, so were the ammo and half of the weapons. He could not carry them, and he would not need them in any case. One rifle and one pistol would be amply sufficient. He abandoned the rest in the foxhole, with one of the empty canteens, and the NVGs since ambient light provided enough vision during the night, especially because the first quarter of the moon had appeared in the night sky.

CHAPTER 7

Their wedding was the wedding of the year. In the National Cathedral adorned with American and Russian flags, the guests kept arriving as if the bride and groom were royalty. The press photographers and the paparazzi had taken the best positions as early as midnight to snap the best pictures of the celebrities, political figures, and jetsetters that were expected. George had been right, everyone absolutely loved Lena. She had impressed by her beauty, her elegance, her natural aristocratic demeanour, her lively personality, and by her sophistication. George had a hard time believing that this was the same woman he had met two years before. The first thing she had done was to provide the funds to entirely renovate George's Georgetown house. After over $5 million, the house was the epitome of elegance and good taste. Thanks to this work, when she was in town, George and Lena had been able to hold the most desirable dinner parties. The first parties had regrouped industry people, people Lena did business with or wanted to do business with. Then it had been senators and representatives, and finally, it had been cabinet members. One evening about three months before, the Secretary of State, George's boss, had been a dinner guest and she had suggested that a leadership position in one of the embassies might be a possibility. Lena had indicated that she had so many connections in Spain that this country may be a great choice.

Now, on this auspicious wedding day, the high society of Washington, Sankt Petersburg, and Moscow was present in the building. Because he had been a personal friend of Oleksandr Krasnaief, the prime minister of Russia had accepted the invitation and it had been decided that he was the one who would 'give' the bride away. But since the Russian PM was there, the United States had decided that the vice president should attend. So, this personal celebration between Lena and George had created an opportunity for Russia and the United States to conduct high-level meetings and consultations, and George had been recognised as the catalyst for the event. At the same time, the highest ranking members of the Orthodox Church had travelled to Washington to participate in the ceremony and conduct a series of meetings with their counterparts in the Methodist Church. George was increasingly being recognised as a man of vision. And as a wedding present, the Secretary of State had given George a letter assigning him as the US Ambassador to Spain, according to Lena's wishes. The Queen of Spain, a personal friend of Lena's, had been the first person to present George with her congratulations. Of course, for Lena, there had been instant US citizenship, and the Secretary of State had personally presented her with her new passport.

For all the attention, pageantry, and eminent guests, the fact remained that Lena was truly in love with George, or at least had been truly in love with him at one point, but the union with the up and coming ambassador was something that she had started to use to her advantage. Her acquaintance with the most important political figures in the US as well as Russia had recently benefited her business more than any other event. George, on the other hand, was awed and upset by her changes. He was awed because he had never thought that the naïve woman he had met could metamorphose in the sophisticated businesswoman she had become. But he was upset because he realised that although he would benefit from her wealth—the Georgetown house renovation proved it—he would never be able to control her or the wealth that he aspired to owning. And Lena still made love like a peasant. This is why an inconspicuous guest had been invited. Xin continued to be George's lover, and he had even been able to have one of the wildest sessions he could remember the night before, as Xin had invited over her cousin, also from Taiwan. The lesbian love scene they had orchestrated had rendered George insane with desire, and they had partied until the early morning hours. Now that he was going to ship off to Spain, he wondered how he could move Xin and her cousin to Spain as well. There was no way he could not take them along. Despite the unusual duration of the relationship he never tired of Xin, and she got better all the time. There was absolutely no sexual act she would not perform, however unusual, perverse, or gross. He could ask her for anything, and she would do it. If he did not ask her, she would propose it. They had developed so many innovations, that she had even consigned them to a little black book. And, of course, she had managed to film their most pornographic adventures so that they could enjoy them again. Together, they had also experimented with cocaine, and the drug had increased their pleasure as expected. He thought about it and internally chuckled as he drove with his new wife to the wedding reception at the Mandarin Oriental.

Life took a turn for the better for the Honourable George McMillan, a man of relatively modest origin who had struck it rich, and who, thanks to his Russian wife's political astuteness, had become a Washington and a global celebrity. Her wedding present to him had been a Ferrari Enzo, while his wedding present to her had been a forgettable pearl necklace. With his limited means, there was no way he could compete against a million-dollar car. He had done his best in a half-hearted way, and it showed. It was frustrating and humiliating. He could have done better before, but now, he was also paying for all of Xin's expenses, showering her, and now her cousin, with gifts. In truth, his financial situation was dire. He had taken a line of credit on his house, which only six months before had been debt-free, and this line of credit was almost already exhausted. There was no way he could continue that way. He had to get access to her money and finally get some relief. Especially that Xin was expecting more—he was now a billionaire, and she was expecting billionaire's gifts. Her latest request—she never demanded anything, but rather suggested—was a house in Georgetown; 'just like yours' she had added. With the amount of sex tapes they had done together, she had an enormous amount of materials to blackmail him, if she ever wished to. Xin was quickly becoming a massive problem. Yet, he was oblivious to it because she delivered in the bedroom, and at the end of the day, it was the only thing that counted for George. Xin had totally bewitched him. He thought that he could never find a woman like her again, a woman who would share him with multiple women, and find sexual pleasure at watching him have sex with them. The fear of losing this sexual connection and not finding a replacement for her led him to never say no. And now that he was an ambassador, there was no way he could ever say no to her again. Unless, of course, she was made to meet a fate similar to Krasnaief's. . . But Xin was far more intelligent than that big oaf had been, and she probably had made copies to be released to the press in case anything happened to her.

Lena continued to travel extensively between Russia, the United States, and now, Spain. George had managed to find a suitable villa for Xin and her cousin. In order to pay for it, he had started to steal from Lena. But he had not been able to find the millions he needed to buy Xin a house. In the meantime, Xin's perversions continued to drive him insane. She had recruited two Spanish girls and had managed to get them to fornicate with a donkey while she had sex with George. George had happily joined into the activity and was now an addict of zoophilia. Over the following days, Xin had surpassed herself, finding new depravation, where even George could not imagine a scenario. When Lena was absent, Xin was always a guest of all embassy events, and she was shameless in approaching women she saw as potential lesbian partners. At such an event, this is how the wife of the French ambassador found herself in George's bed with Xin, while her husband returned home to his own mistress, appreciative of Xin's ability to get his wife distracted for a few hours. In fact, Madame Fournier-Lenotre had remained at the residence for four straight days and had happily become Xin's sex slave, even agreeing to the vilest zoophilia acts. The woman was even more sexually insane than Xin and had even taught her a few things! George could not cope with the sexual perversions and the delivery of his duties at once. And he was far less interested in his duties than in the sexual activities with Xin, and now Michelle. The two women spent those entire four days naked, caressing each other, having sex with each other, and preventing George from thinking about anything but their insatiable sexual appetites. George hated for Lena to come back. He found sex with her utterly insipid and started having problems not only maintaining an erection but simply having one. One night, when Lena suggested he seek help, he slapped her so hard she fell down on her knees. He got dressed, went to Xin's villa, and found the women naked as usual, and Xin whipping Michelle who was hanging from the ceiling by her arms. Xin offered the whip to George and begged her to whip her as well. The sadistic cycle of their relationship had started, but unbeknownst to George, it went both ways. And the following night, it was him who was whipped and suffered the humiliation of being raped.

After the first slap, it had been easy to continue. Lena had noticed that when he beat her he became aroused, and if the price of sex was a few slaps, then she accepted this type of relationship without a problem. George never thought that Lena could be introduced to Xin, and thus his relationship with Lena became more and more painful to both of them, with sex sessions punctuated with beatings, and less and less access to her money as he went on beating her. He had managed to get Xin a house in Georgetown, nevertheless, and the fact that he had introduced her to Michelle had fully satisfied her. Yet, every day, Xin cost him in the neighbourhood of $5,000. At the end of the year, it amounted to almost $2 million. She called it wealth transfer. He called it prostitution. But he wanted her more every day. From the outside, the McMillan couple was still the perfect couple. He made sure he never bruised her where it could be seen, and things were for the best. Once could never have guessed that the two of them were yelling at each other, abusing each other, and were now at the point of hating each other. She was at the residence less and less frequently, which suited him just fine. Using her name for leverage, he had started to invest heavily in Spanish real estate, an activity that was strictly forbidden by the State Department. But, as George thought, everything he did was strictly forbidden by the State Department. . .

CHAPTER 8

It was the fifth night that he had been running. He had always liked number five because it was the day of his birthday. But on this occasion, he cursed number five. He was exhausted from the previous four nights of running, and his entire body ached. He tried to ignore it, but there was no hiding it, with each step demanding more control of the pain that was running through his feet, his legs, his back and his shoulders. In the same time he was suffering a burning sensation in his stomach caused by the overwhelming hunger pangs. He had focused all of his attention on keeping his feet healthy, as he knew that any blister could be catastrophic, could soon become unmanageable, and would leave him stranded in the desert. As he had always done in training, he was wearing ladies' socks made of fine nylon over which he wore the heavier US Army–issued wool and cotton socks. The principle was that the nylon would soak up the sweat and thus stick to the skin and protect his feet from the rubbing of the socks against his skin. This was a true and tried method to avoid feet injury, and up to now, it had always worked for him. But there was no remedy to the constant rebounding of the combat boots on the rocky terrain, and at times, he could feel the shockwaves travel up his spine all the way to his brain, which was sore to a permanent headache that had started sometime on the third night. His second concern was to spare his legs for he knew that any sprained ankle or pulled muscle would slow him down so much that he would lose any hope of reaching the border with Morocco. It was true that he had never sustained any ankle injury, but now, in the loneliness of the great expanse, with enemy soldiers looking for him—or at least he thought—he was becoming obsessed with the fear of a sprained ankle. His third immediate worry was water. He had carried his eight litres as well as the Steve's eight litres, and he had calculated that he had to ration himself to one litre per day not to run out. This was pure insanity, as he was in a country where the army recommended drinking eight litres a day, or eight times more than was available to him. He tried not to think about these problems. He looked at the positive side of it. He had three combat rations left, he had three litres of water, his feet were not injured, and his legs could still carry him. Everything else he ignored. He continued the routine he had followed the previous four nights. He ran for 100 paces, and he walked for 100. This was the marching method known as 'marche commando' he had learned at the French commando school. This allowed a man to travel much further and much faster than either walking or running alone. Walking was slow, and running, well, it was impossible for a man to run for eight hours straight, night after night. Commando marching allowed extending the distance one could run, while being much faster than walking. When he was on the move, he thought of nothing except survival and detecting any suspicious movement. He assumed that by now the Algerians had either given up looking for him, or they had figured out what he was up to and were simply waiting for him at the border. He did not fear the second eventuality and was mentally prepared for it as he advanced towards his goal. He was far more concerned with the minefields that were said to lie between the two countries. He did not want to run for eight days and then suddenly fall victim to a stupid anti-personnel mine. As he marched, he was ceaselessly repeating army Jody calls, and although he knew them all, they ran out very quickly, and before the end of the night he had mentally sung them hundreds of times. After every song, he used Airborne Ranger as his refrain:

> Two old ladies, lying in bed.
> One rolled over to the other and said.
> I wanna be an Airborne Ranger!
> I wanna live a life of danger.

He used all of the energy he had to put real aggressiveness into *Ranger* and *danger*. Somehow this carried him through the night. But he knew he was getting weaker by the day. He should have been eating the equivalent of 8,000 calories the way he ran, and yet, he barely had a thousand at his disposal. He was losing weight and his fatigue pants were already too big on him. Yet, he maintained his discipline. He took a rest every hour on the hour for five minutes. A rest meant that he walked leisurely. He did not want to sit down, as he feared he would never find the motivation to get up again and run. He commando marched from sun down to sunrise. In fact, as soon as he saw the east become lighter, he started looking for a site to dig-in for the day. Once he had located a suitable site, in a depression, or under the cover of a boulder, he'd stop running, and start digging his lodgings for the day, which were more of a shallow grave than a bed. After he had finished his work, he would eat his main meal of the day, the can of what the army called food was in the C-ration, as he kept the crackers, jam, peanut butter, and whatever else was edible, such as the sugar and the powered milk, for breakfast. Then, he drank half of the remainder of his water ration, lay down in his sleeping position, and covered himself with his poncho, and pulled the dirt, gravel and rocks that were available to achieve invisibility. He did a thorough job of it, taking the time to collect as much dirt as possible. He kept his rifle close to him, wrapped in the cloth that muffled its banging during the night and that kept it free of grit and sand. He placed the breathing tube in his mouth as he gathered the rest of the sand and gravel over him, and he usually collapse into deep sleep. He remained constantly aware of his surroundings. Years of training had resulted in his mind waking up at the slightest unusual noise. The advantage of sleeping during the day in the desert was that all the animals also slept, and human activity in this part of Algeria was non-existent. Of course, he did not sleep the full hours of the day, and when he woke up it was the toughest part of the day. It was the time of day when his brain could not avoid thinking about her, and when he missed her so much, he felt a physical pain deep in his chest. It was the time of day when he knew she was undressing, going to bed, and he could project her image in his brain, so that her presence became almost real. This is when the ordeal became a torture. By now, she would have known that something had gone wrong, that he was lost somewhere in a place that was to remain classified to her. She had expected him to come back within the week, and now if was almost two weeks. He wondered how she was coping with it. He felt a deep sadness come over him, and every evening, when he had to get up and go, the sadness was more and more intense, more and more distracting. He could see her in the house, pretending as she always did that everything was 'just fine' as she would say. And yet, she would be unable to share her anxiety and her sorrow with anyone, as she did not even know where he was. She would be depressed, she would be awaiting the phone call or the text message, and she would feel despondent, not knowing where to turn for information and for support. In fact, there was no place for her to turn. She was not even his wife. As far as the US Army was concerned, she had no legal existence, and she would never know what happened to him if he did not come back. He was filled with sorrow and horror at that thought. One late afternoon, as he lay there unable to move under the heavy blanket of the desert soil, he felt her presence in a physical way. He felt someone taking his left hand, and pressing her finger into his, as only she did. He felt the great pressure between his fingers of her fingers squeezing his hand, and he also felt as if her arm was resting on his forearm. He knew it was her, only she had ever held his hand in this manner. He wanted to hold her longer, he wanted to feel her entire body taught with desire next to him, he wanted to make the moment eternal, but slowly she went away, as if telling him he had to keep going, as if pushing him to come back to her alive. She has visited with him, she had reassured him that she was with him always, and now, it was up to him to go back and find her again. Yet, in his sand and rock bed, he wondered if he was not starting to hallucinate already, if he was not losing it after only five days, while he was still at least 80 miles from safety. Using the commando march method, he estimated he was progressing at a rate of about 4.5 miles per hour. That meant that he had already covered about 150 miles. He remembered the training month he had done with Steve one time at Fort Benning, when they had run fifteen miles per day for thirty days, for a total of 450 miles. Now it was his fight for survival, and he had to cover 230 miles in eight days. He did not doubt he could do it, but as the days passed, he wondered if he had calculated right, and if the water would last that long.

Late afternoon was the time of day when he felt the ache in his shoulders and upper back, when he became conscious of the amount of lactic acid that was building in his legs, and of the pain it created, when he felt the hunger pangs in his stomach, when he realised how thirsty he was, when he wondered whether he would ever get out of it alive, when he felt guilty for abandoning Steve's body to the Algerians, when he thought of home, and when he built the scenarios that would lead to either his survival or his death. Being an atheist he did not pray, and not once during the ordeal did he feel compelled to seek help from an imaginary being. He was driven but an irrepressible urge to live. It was not the thought of his girlfriend, of home, or duty, or any such concept that kept him going, it was a sheer desire to live. He followed the process that he had followed every day to the letter. It was his routine for survival. At times, his mind started wondering and becoming incoherent, and this is when the routine took over. There was no mistake. When the sun was almost over the horizon, he would come out of his hiding place, massage his feet and legs, put his socks and combat boots back on, and he would eat the remnants of the C-ration, which he would leave behind. He would wash it down with four gulps of water—just enough to fool his body in believing he had drunk something. Then, he would pee, and he would recover the liquid which he drank as well. He would allow himself another gulp of water, bury whatever he was leaving behind, and by the time night had fallen, he was ready to march again towards the salvation of the west, and of Morocco. At the start, his muscles were cramped up and cold, and the discomfort was unbearable. But as he started marching, they would loosen up until the cold desert air made them ache again. This is another reason he could not stop, the night was frigidly cold, and many times, he started shivering as he felt the cold bite at his fingers. Yet, he pushed forward, oblivious to the pain, constantly repeating the songs he had learned at airborne school. He would motivate himself by thinking of the unbelievable marching power of the Roman legions, and across the millennia he reached out for strength to the officers of the 10th Legion, men like Gaius Fabius or Antistius Reginus, and he hoped that if he had to die, he could do so with the same dignity they had demonstrated. On the fifth night, he became concerned because he stopped urinating regularly. There were no longer enough liquids, and he became scared that his kidneys would fail. Then he remembered to monitor his heart rate and his respiration, as he knew that their permanent increase would show that he had lost over 5 per cent of his body fluids, and he would have to do something about it. He could not monitor his blood pressure or his temperature, but he was aware of the sleepiness that was slowly creeping over him during the night, even as he walked. He also knew that once he got the headaches, the nausea, and the paresthesia, he would have to drink no matter what and forget his rationing, as his situation would have become more severe and would require immediate correction. He knew he could not last more than one or at best two more days like that, and that if he did not reach Morocco soon, he would surely not survive. He had kept his 9mm so that if he needed to, he could end his suffering in the vast expanse where he had seen no other human since the day of the ambush. Now he did not even focus on his well-being, he solely focused on following the W for West on his compass. It was make or break time, and he stopped concerning himself with his body. If his kidneys failed, he still would be able to survive for at least a few days. And all the way, he built the doomsday scenarios, then he would reject them, but the fact was that he was slowly and imperceptibly losing control of his mind. He somehow felt part of the 10th Legion, he imagined Gaius Julius was there, giving him orders, guiding him. Yet, he did not realise these were hallucinations. He had not urinated in at least eight hours, his skin felt like it was shrivelling and he felt confused and dizzy. He knew the symptoms well for having experienced them during training in Arizona, and he was familiar with the next step. He would probably get swelling of the brain as his dehydrated body would start producing particles that pulled water into the cells. Then he would go into severe dehydration—if he did not suffer from it already—and he would be in hypovolemic shock, when his low blood volume would cause a sudden drop in blood pressure, and death could happen within minutes. He finally grasped the inevitability of his death if he did not remedy the situation some time a little after one o'clock in the morning of the sixth night. He threw all caution to the wind and drank an entire day's ration of water. It had a dramatic effect of well-being, and yet, as he carelessly threw away the empty canteen without burying it first, he felt short-changed. He needed far more water. He resumed his march. An hour or so later, he realised how careless he had been, and started having nightmares about the Algerian army finding the canteen. His mind told him to go back to retrieve it, while his body told him there was no way it could take two extra hours of marching. He became paralyzed by the conundrum and almost stopped moving all together. Unable to make any decision, he hesitated, took a few steps back, then turned around and started going forward again, before stopping and figuring out what to do. His

THE DATURA SOLUTION

brain had entered the no-man's land of incapacitation and had become a useless organ that sucked blood out of his legs. He lost precious moments, trying to fight indecision and hesitation. He was no longer the competent US Army officer he had been six days before. He was simply a man lost in the night in a hostile environment, a man who like Steve would not return home unless he collected his thoughts. He made extra efforts to focus, like a drunk driver who makes huge efforts to stay to the right side of the central yellow line. For the first time since the beginning of the mission, he got thoroughly scared. And at that very moment, a voice deep inside his lame brain started chanting the Airborne Ranger song, and suddenly he was moving forward again. He did not think of checking his compass until he had been marching for about thirty minutes, and he realised the mistake as he had been going South instead of West. He cursed at himself, certain that this short delay would cause his death. Now, he would not be able to calculate where he was in relation to the border any longer. For the first five nights he had kept a mental tally of his progress, counting the steps, adding them, and with the help of the map figuring out how far he had to go, but on this fatidic sixth night, he had lost the count entirely. He was simply surviving, moving forward without concerns about how far he was. With a jolt, he wondered how he could possibly fight if he ran into the enemy. He was in no condition to fight effectively. He understood that he was no longer able to aim a rifle and take down a target. If he ran into the Algerians, he was a dead man. And he started thinking that he was dead anyhow, he had almost no water left, was exhausted, was suffering from the effects of water deprivation, and would never see Reb again. He started to sob, but there were no tears. He wished Steve had been with him; with two people it would have been easier. Then, for the first time in sixth nights, he tripped and fell. The fall took the breath out of him, but brought him back to his senses. He was on all four on the ground, the pain shooting through his left knee, attempting to regain control of his breathing. And the fall re-energized him, as if it had allowed an internal voice to talk to him. 'Get up and walk' the voice told him. He recognised the voice of his airborne instructor, Master Sergeant Kemp, telling him to get off his ass, stop feeling sorry for himself, and fucking get going. Suddenly, he was back at Fort Benning, he was running on the airborne track, and he started moving again, remembering to check he was going west. Yet death was now his constant companion, he could feel its cold breath in the nape of his neck. He could feel the sharp blade of hardened steel already chipping at his vertebrae. He could not think about anything else, except how to avoid it.

Even the silence had become a burden. For days, he had heard no sounds except the thumping of his boots on the ground or the scratching of his entrenching tool as he dug his bed for the day. He longed for the noise of a human voice outside of his own, he longed for the clinging of beer glasses at the local pub, he longed for the roar of a jet plane screaming as it took off, and most of all, he longed for the screaming of a Formula 1 engine. People had told him the Sahara Desert plays trick on your mind, and he experienced it several times a night. He thought he heard noises, he thought he heard people talking to him, and at times, as he was moving forward, he would suddenly turn around convinced that someone was right behind him, trying to catch up with him and talking to him. He hallucinated that Steve had actually not died, that he had simply dropped back a few paces, and that he was now running after him calling for him to wait. A couple of time, Max actually stopped. Then he realised he was losing it, and made up his mind to ignore all voices. Where were they coming from? From over the Atlas Mountains, or from way down south in black Africa? He knew there were no noises, he knew they were no voices, they only existed in his head, and yet, desperate as he was to be rescued and to end the ordeal, he could not bring himself to accept reality and to ignore these sounds that were reaching from an unknown world, as if extraterrestrials had suddenly started talking to him. He could find no respite from them, and at times, he even heard the rotor blades of imaginary helicopters biting the air. Then, he did not know whether to hide or to run towards them as they could be either enemy or US Navy helicopters. The cold did not help his mental capabilities, and he lost track of his running for entire hours, incapable of focusing on anything but solving the enigma of the silence which gave him no rest. He lost time, and the voices rendered him hesitant. He did not trust his hearing any longer, and he just wanted to control it, he wished he could have closed his ears like one closes one's eyes. Peace came with the sun, when he was able again to see correctly, and when the hot air muffled noises, when his eyes were witnesses to the emptiness around him. By that time, solar reverberation was so strong that Max could almost hear the air evaporate. And there were the flies. He could not figure out where the fucking flies could come from. There were none at night, but as soon as the sun warmed up the frozen sand, flies were all over. They found their way to any part of his body that was not completely covered by the Ghillie suit, the poncho, or the sand and rocks, and they would bite with a vengeance. Once he was entirely covered, they would even found their way down his breathing tube and try to get into his, sucking every possible drop of humidity out of him. But soon, he came to regard them as an ally, because he knew the moment he was not being bitten at all, then he was completely covered and protected from any person looking for him. Yet, he was also convinced now that no one was looking for him any longer and that all his precautions were useless and simply resulted in him losing more precious time.

So he kept going throughout the nights, his mind incapable of forming any useful thought or advice. Only the routine he had established saved him. Moving like a broken automaton, he dug his hole, ate his C-ration, drank his water, laid down, covered himself with sand and gravel, used the breathing tube, and fell asleep, hoping this would not be his last day on earth. He woke up in the hottest part of the day—it must have been noon. The quality of his position was poor, and he could feel the sun burn through his fatigues. He did not react. He knew well that he should cover himself up, save any water he had in his body, and prevent it evaporating. He also realised that he'd better reach Morocco that night, as it was impossible that he could continue further. He figured that he must be another thirty miles from the border—he had allowed a 10 per cent risk factor in his calculation. On a normal day, he could easily cover the distance in less than six hours, but now, all bets were off, and he doubted he could reach the border within the night. His mind was still unclear about what to do about it, so he decided to just lay there and do nothing. The man of action had been eroded by the desert, and he was simply an organism not even trying to survive. As his thoughts drifted from what he wanted to eat, to what he wanted to do to his girlfriend when he saw her again, to the type of car he wanted to buy, to the drinks he would have at the bar of the hotel in Morocco, he made a tremendous effort to regain control of his brain. He focused on Technical Manual 27-4 Desert Survival, which he knew by heart—or at least he had known it by heart at one point, not so long ago. Pressed for time, as he did not want to spend another full day in search of the border, he decided to wait until four in the afternoon and take his chances using the last hours of daylight to reach the border before the night was over. He got up hesitantly, finished his C-ration, and finally looking at his watch (he could not read it when lying in his position), he realised it was already five in the afternoon. He gathered his meagre possessions, his rifle, and his water, and started walking. He was incapable of any significant running at the beginning of his progression every day, so he took it easy for about one hour, before the lactic acid could be processed, and started running only after the pain was sufferable. As he moved forward, he saw the glint of what he thought to be a weapon a few hundred metres ahead of him. Fully awakened from its torpor, his brain jumped into action. He unlocked his rifle scope, and using it as a telescope, he tried to identify the threat barring his road, and what he saw made him shudder. It was a single stand of concertina wire stretched across the border between Algeria and Morocco. He had spent the entire day not even two miles from the border. Now, a new energy came over him, and he actually started running towards the salvation of Morocco. He remained careful not to go too fast and inadvertently run into a minefield, but as luck would have it, there was not a single obstacle between him and the concertina. He lay down, and making himself as thin as possible he crawled under the wire. The razor-sharp blades of the wire cut through his fatigues and into the skin of his left arm, but it was only a scratch, and within minutes, he was in Morocco. He was safe at last.

Now he had to get away as quickly as possible. In the euphoria of his success, he drank more water, as he was sure he would be soon rescued by a friendly soul. And now, regardless, he could march north. But he also had to dispose of some of his arsenal. There was no way to keep the rifle or its ammunition, and even the 9mm had become a problem. Despite his advanced state of fatigue, he picked an area not far from the border, but he did not have sufficient strength to dig the hole destined to hide this lethal hardware, so he knelt down and started the job. Long gone was the day a week earlier when he had dug an entire foxhole in a couple of hours. He struggled to scratch the ground. He forced himself to dig deep enough to bury all of the military hardware and all the clues that could link him to a military organisation. He tried to civilianise his appearance. He wondered what he looked like. He had not washed, combed his hair, or shaved in a week. The only hygiene he performed consisted of brushing his teeth, dusting his feet, and ensuring he spread some Vaseline between his buttocks to avoid chaffing. He then placed all of the military items in the hole: the Ghillie suit, the pistols, the ammunition, the hand grenades, the magazines, and finally, the rifle. As he deposited the rifle into the hole, he suddenly was taken over by a deep sadness and he started to sob uncontrollably, as if the rifle was a friend of his. He had not shed a tear for Steve, but now, as he buried his rifle, he started crying and long tears rolled down his cheeks for this piece of cold steel. And he realised he was crying because the rifle had saved his life—he could not and did not have the force to feel anything any longer. If somebody had asked him if he was missing Reb at this very moment, he was not sure he could have answered, and he was not even sure he could have sorted out who Reb was. He forced himself to cover the hole and to pack the dirt on top of it, and with his rucksack basically empty for the first time in seven days he felt lighter even if he could hardly move. It took him several moments to re-orient himself and to figure out which direction he was supposed to follow. It took all of his brainpower to get him going west again. Within half an hour of leaving the burial site, he ran into a dirt road, and he started following it northward. He was now so weak that he walked like a drunkard, a few hundred yards later, his body gave way entirely and he collapsed as a pile of dirty stinking clothes enveloping his emaciated body around which a thousand flies were busy extracting the last drop of sweat from his drying skin.

CHAPTER 9

> Intelligence is the ability to optimally use limited resources to achieve a goal. —Ray Kurzweil

Max regained a certain level of consciousness as he was riding in the back of a Peugeot utility vehicle, bouncing around in the dust of the dirt trail. He was not doing well. The state of exhaustion he was experiencing and the movement of the car made him positively sick. He barely had the time to lean over the side of the vehicle to vomit. But he did not vomit anything except bile. He realised that he was having a bilious attack. He also understood that his liver was no longer operating correctly and that it was not supporting the thousands of necessary functions to keep his body healthy. He also wondered if the driver of the vehicle—he suddenly became aware that someone must be driving, and that the same someone had to have put him in the back of the car—had given him any water. As he recovered and lay back down onto the bags of rice the car was carrying, the driver looked back and through the small separating window told him in heavily Arab-accented French 'Te fais pas de souci, je t'ammene a l'hopital.' The only thing Max could answer was 'De l'eau.' He was dying for a drop of water. But the man said, 'I don't have more, you drank everything. I take you to hospital!' Max's world was spinning, he fell back into oblivion. He could not understand whether it was sleep, loss of consciousness, or a coma. For the entire time he was in the car, he drifted unpleasantly between consciousness and this no man's land of the brain he could not define. He felt the pain of the ordeal in every one of his bones, in his head that was pounding, and in his stomach as he leaned over again to spit the bile that had collected in his stomach. He did not even know what the man looked like, and he did not care. The road started climbing and he knew they were going up the Atlas Mountains. He closed his eyes and continued to laboriously breathe through the dust picked up by the car. He was desperately thirsty and he once again went out. He woke up as the car slowed down to enter a village of earth-baked building. As the car made its way to the main street people would stop and look at the strange package it was carrying, and Max understood they were looking at him, wondering where such a wretched creature could have come from. He could see in their gesturing they did not think much of his chances of survival. For Max, it was like a dream when the dreamer is slipping down into an abyss and cannot do anything about it. As he lay in the car, the Berbers looking at him with the same disdain as people look at the homeless, he had a vision of how elegant he had looked about a month and half before at the dining-out when he had worn his dress blues impeccably pressed, his black tie adjusted to perfection, his hair nicely trimmed, his white shirt starched, and Chantal at his arm in her beautiful black cocktail dress. They had been the focus of remarks about elegance. Now, not one person at that evening would even have recognised him. He was so weak he had lost the ability of moving his arms, but he did not care because he had survived—at least until then. The car stopped in what looked like a shopping centre. The driver jumped out, telling Max to stay there—as if he was going to move. . . A few moments later he came back with two men who looked like nurses, and a wheelchair. Surely, Max thought, they have an emergency somewhere—what about me? Only when they approached the vehicle did he understand that the wheelchair was for him. He wanted to refuse to use it, he wanted to walk in, but his brain was completely shut down, and he could only let the two nurses pull him out of the truck and man-handle him into the wheelchair. He heard voices speaking Arabic, and a question in English about which language he spoke. 'Français' he was able to whisper through his parched lips. But they did not speak any more. They entered the coolness of the dispensary, and they wheeled Max to the emergency area. Although many people were waiting, he was given priority over them. The orderly asked him he could get himself onto the bed. Max made an effort that took out the remainder of his strength and manage to sit there. Another nurse arrived with an IV pole while one of the two who had rolled him in put in an IV needle in his arm. The treatment had started with the first goal to rehydrate him with a mixture of electrolytes and water. They also brought him a solution that tasted somewhat like Gatorade and asked him to start drinking it as if his life depended on it. They also inquired if he had a headache, and when he said yes, they seemed very concerned. The orderly started a second IV. Max would only learn later form the doctor that he had a severe headache most likely because his brain had started to swell due to the dehydrated body producing particles that pull water into the brain cells. The doctor informed him that he had been within less than an hour of developing hypovolemic shock, when the low blood volume causes a sudden drop in blood pressure that brings about death within minutes. The doctor had commented, 'You are a survivor.' Max wanted to answer 'Only if you knew,' but kept his thoughts to himself.

The recovery was slow, but within a couple of hours of arriving to the dispensary in the village of M'Hamid on the edge of the Sahara, Max had been able to take his first shower in eight days and to finally shave. He was given a set of fresh pyjamas and he had been told that his filthy clothes had been sent to cleaning. For the first day, the people at the dispensary were concerned about his not dying— for obvious reasons—and he was able to sleep. Of course, he was concerned about the events of the previous ten days, but he needed to rest first. He was unable to focus on anything yet. He simply was too weak. On the morning of the second day, he was woken up from his dreamlike world by the appearance of two uniformed officials who came to inquire what had happened to him. It was a friendly visit to make sure no foul play had taken place, to make sure Max 'What is your last name, sir?' had not been the victim of assault. But it became clear they wanted to know how he had appeared in the Moroccan desert, and if his vehicle had been abandoned, they would be happy to go and tow it back to town. Max played the confused card and avoided answering, but he knew that these tactics would only last so far and that he would soon be made to explain himself further. A further visit confirmed that his suspicion was correct. At ten in the morning, a captain of the Gendarmerie Royale Marocaine came into his room with a sergeant and asked him very pointed questions. He had arrived especially from Zagora to question Max, who had not yet been declared a prisoner, although he was sure this would soon happen. The interview was cordial, the captain—elegant in his impeccable grey uniform—showing all the restraint and courtesy of a cat who is ready to pounce on a hapless chipmunk. But the message was clear: Max was suspected of foul play and there was no fooling the Gendarmerie.

'You know, Monsieur, that it is a crime to lie during an investigation, so for the last time, what happened to you?'

'Frankly Captain, I cannot remember. The only thing I can remember is waking up in the back of a Peugeot camionette and being taken here. Anything before that I cannot remember.'

'How did you get in Morocco, Monsieur Lefort?'

'I arrived by plane from Paris, I guess. I cannot recall anything.'

'Monsieur Lefort, this is an outright false statement. There is no track of anyone named Pierre Lefort entering Morocco. Either by plane or by boat. And we know you did not arrive through Algeria because they have not records of you. So, let's try another approach: which hotel did you stay at before your adventure?'

Max was grasping for straws. 'The Sheraton in Marrakesh? I have no idea, but since I always stay at the Sheraton, it is possible that I was staying there. I think to remember I was in Marrakesh.'

'Alright, Monsieur Lefort, we'll check that. But how did you come to be in the desert twenty miles south of here? Who took you there?'

'Again, I do not recall. I cannot think of anyone I was with.'

'And the money that you had with, what about the money? Dollars, euros, Algerian dinars, what were you going to do with that money? Were you planning to buy hashish, Monsieur Lefort?'

Max was hoping that a doctor would come in any moment, just like in the movies, and would tell the captain that the patient needed rest, and that he should come back in the morrow to question him. But time passed and no such event took place, and even when the orderly brought in a plate of couscous for lunch, the captain did recant, and Max could only play the amnesia card. It was not a winning hand. He knew that soon he would be charged with entering Morocco illegally, and as he would be in a holding facility, the police and the gendarmerie would have plenty of time to look at all the crimes committed in the area in the previous two weeks and pin one on him. Or worse, they could discover a stash of drugs and accuse him of carrying them into the country. If they went looking for stuff where he was picked up by the camionette, they were sure to find the military gear he had hastily buried, and things would only get worse. He knew he had to make every effort to prolong his stay in the dispensary to regain this strength, but he also knew there was a tipping point where he would not be able to escape any longer. His Level C training in Escape and Evasion at Naval Air Station Brunswick had clearly taught him that the probability of an evasion being successful was much higher the closer it was to the time of capture. Since Max was not a captive yet, it would be advisable to escape before he became one. He simply did not want to jeopardise his health. He had come so near dying that he did not want to chance it. The captain finally left after about three hours, and he was tired.

He did not realise how slowly his conscience had been regaining power over him. At first, he simply dismissed the early signs, a slight discomfort in his abdomen. He put it to the fact that he was sick from the water he had drunk on the way to the hospital, or maybe, it was simply the remnants of the bilious crisis. And he went on with his day, building the strategy that would continue to fool the police officers who were becoming more assertive by the hour. But then, the discomfort turned into a constant low-level pain, the same thing he had experienced the first time he had jumped out of an airplane. It was not fear this time, it was apprehension, he thought. He realised that the presence of the police in and outside his room was bringing this in. He had not given a thought to any activity of his conscience. On the third day he could not stand the underlying discomfort any longer. He wanted the feeling of unease to disappear, he wanted to feel well again, he wanted not to have this pressure in his stomach. And it came suddenly, an irresistible need to vomit. He barely had the time to reach the bucket, and he emptied himself. He lay there, on the bed, drained by the effort, his mouth still registering the acrid taste of the liquid. It was no longer bile, it had come straight from his stomach. He did not ring for help. When he had recovered sufficiently, he rinsed his mouth, and the images appeared to him as he was controlling his breathing: Steve's exploded cranium, the blood and the brain matter staining his own fatigues, how he had simply pushed him aside, not giving a thought to him as he fought for survival, the bullet ripping through the chest of the one man and spraying blood and lung into a geyser as the man was twisted backward, the other bullet ripping through the hip of another man and the bullet that went through his lungs, deflating him like a party balloon, and finally, the last man, begging him with tears in his eyes to let him live, to let him return to his wife and kids. He was overcome by a strong dislike for himself. How could

THE DATURA SOLUTION

he have done such things, how could he have inflicted such pain? How could he reconcile the humanist values that he was so attached to with the agony of fellow humans? He tried to rationalise the situation, remembering that one of the greatest men of Greece, a humanist for sure if the term had existed then, Pericles, had also been a warrior, and that he must have inflicted far more suffering on other men than Max would ever. He rationalised that he had had no other choice. His life had depended on killing. And he thought that preserving his own life was worth all of the sacrifices he had expected from the men he had killed. Was this right? He submitted to himself that he was being taken over by emotions, by a sentimentality that was foreign to him. He knew that if he ever shared these thoughts with his handler, Jim, he would simply disregard them, and he would be dismiss him as a wimp, as a pansy, as he said. Max would be removed from the unit and branded as an officer who let his emotions interfere with the mission. After all, his handler had spent seven years in Vietnam conducting tens of political assassinations, and he had the photos under the glass of his desk to prove it. Gruesome photos that he relished in showing, and which the general had demanded he removed from public view. Jim had pretended to start removing them, but as soon as the general had walked out of the room, he had declared to all to hear 'Fuck him! I don't give a shit what he says! If he does not like it, he can come and try to kick my ass in removing them. I don't need this fucking job! Fuck that motherfucker! He is lucky I don't fucking shoot his fucking ass! Faggot!' Jim always packed two Forty-Fives, so any threat of shooting someone had to be taken seriously. But Max also knew that behind the façade, Jim was subject to nightly nightmares that left him in sweat, panting for breath, and unable to sleep for hours on hand. Max knew because he was one of the two persons who actually were aware of Jim's personal hell. The first one was Ng, his Vietnamese wife, whom he had almost killed one night during one of his crises, and who now slept in a separate bedroom with an armoured door, and bars to reinforce the lock. She never ventured out of the bedroom during the night, because she was terrified that Jim would actually kill her. The other was Max, because Jim had needed to tell someone, one evening as he was getting sauced on Bourbon and Coke at the Officers' Club. He had confided that he had been the youngest Special Forces Colonel in Vietnam and that he had volunteered to spend seven straight tours of duty there, and what he had done during Operation Coyote was killing people who opposed the Saigon regime. He had killed over 140 people, men and women, during his seven years there, which amounted to 1.6 per month. He was looking in his Bourbon, and he had told Max that he had awful nightmares about it. This is when he told Max that one night, he had woken up with Ng sleeping next to him, and still living through his nightmare, he had confused her for one of his targets, and he had started to strangle her. She had fought hard to stay alive, and in a last ditch effort to survive, she had managed to grab the heavy light off the nightstand and hit him on the head, cutting a gash on his skull that had required eight stitches. The sudden pain and the immediate flow of blood had brought him back to his senses, and he had released her to run to safety to a neighbour who had called the cops. He had been booked for domestic violence, and only after he had explained the reason of the attack to Ng, had she recanted and decided not to press charges. 'Why don't you go in therapy,' Max had suggested. But Jim was not about to do so. He considered that a sign of weakness. Jim continued undeterred that this incident had had a far greater impact on his life. The police report publication had allowed the families of his victims who had already filed a class action suit to find him. Subsequently, Jim had been served the court papers indicating he was being sued in US Federal Court by the families of the victims. Although they had tried and failed to bring criminal charges against him, they were now seeking monetary compensation, and every dollar Jim made went to his defence fund. He was a man pursued from within and from the outside. That evening, after realising he had said way too much for his own good, he had told Max that if he told any of this to anyone, he would kill him. Max had every reason to believe that he would indeed. In his dispensary bed in M'Hamid, Max wondered if he was becoming like Jim. Surely not, Jim did not share Max's humanist values, and on top of this, he liked killing people, and Max didn't. Or did he? Max tried to sleep again, now that he was aware that it was his conscience tormenting him rather than a physical ailment. He thought about Chantal, but she was so far away, and so many things had happened since he had left that he wondered if she was still a reality. Was she still there? Was she still waiting for him? The anxiety shook him out of his torpor. For the past three days he had enjoyed the comfort of the dispensary, the comfort of the building that was muffling all outside noises, and he had almost forgotten that he should be getting home, that he should check out as soon as he could. He got up and decided to go for a walk in the corridor. He was prevented from doing so by the police officer who was mounting guard at the door. Seeing this, he faked weakness, as if he was fainting, forcing the policeman to catch him from falling and accompanying him back to his bed. He lay down, thanked him, and closed his eyes. The guard closed the door and Max assumed he resumed his duties outside the door. Max quickly got up again, and verified that his clothes, which had been cleaned, were still in the nightstand. He took them out, and stored them under the mattress to ensure they would not be taken away. The matter of hiding his combat boots was more difficult, and he decided to push them under the bed, out of sight. It was essential that he keep his combat boots since the bulk of his money was hidden in the soles and the heels. As long as he had money, he could get anywhere in Morocco, even if he left a trail behind him, he would be one step ahead of the authorities, and he had all of the choices, like the white side at chess. The black side could only respond to the white's actions. He started making plans for his escape, for he could not possibly stay there. He was in the middle of Plan B, when Police Inspector Taoufik Saftir entered the room. In a few hours, Inspector Saftir would wish he had never heard of Monsieur Lefort.

CHAPTER 10

With Police Inspector Taoufik Saftir in the picture, it was now time for Max to adopt a more sophisticated approach and use the counter-interrogation techniques he had been trained in but had hoped he would never have to use. But there he was, and the consequences of his mismanaging the interrogation could have dire consequences on his future. He mentally prepared himself for all of the techniques he knew: direct, incentive, emotional, increased fear up, decreased fear down, pride and ego, pride and ego down, futility, establish your identity, repetition, file and dossier, Mutt and Jeff, rapid fire, and silence. It was obvious that Inspector Saftir would not have the time to test all of these techniques, but Max was thus prepared to counter any of them. Especially the repetition technique which could show very quickly that Max was lying. This was exactly the technique the inspector selected, and it demonstrated beyond any doubt that he considered Max a hostile element, since the repetition approach is pursued to induce cooperation. The technique consists of asking a question and listening carefully for the answer, and then repeating both the question and answer several times using different words and formats. By doing this with every question, the interrogator causes the person being interrogated to become so bored that he answers the questions fully and almost candidly simply to keep the interrogator from repeating things over and over. It would take Max extreme focus not to fall in the trap. This also has the advantage of putting the interrogator fully in charge. Of course the inspector could not know that Max had been trained in resisting the technique and had greater self-control that the petty criminals the inspector normally interacted with. Max seized the opportunity to regain his composure and delay the interrogation. The inspector had been pushing for an answer on how two dog tags obviously belonging to a US soldier had ended up in Monsieur Lefort's pockets. 'What about these?' he asked, plopping them on the bed? Max used the same repetition technique and repeated the question, 'What about these?' It went on all afternoon, with Max simply repeating the inspector's questions and not answering a single one he was asked. A fully frustrated Inspector Saftir left Max after almost three hours of questioning, warning him ominously that he would be back in the morning. 'We are going to see a lot of each other in the next few days,' the inspector stated as he left the room. Max thought that he would be quite disappointed upon his return.

At dinner time, Max asked for more water and was rewarded for his requests with two bottles of Evian water. At about seven, the doctor came to visit and found him in very good shape compared to the state he had arrived in, and he ordered that the IV be taken out. Normal oral hydration would suffice from this point forward. As soon as he had left, Max went once again to the window, which although on the ground floor was overlooking a small cliff into the oued below. Max had also managed to figure out from an article in the paper that M'Hamid was at the southernmost extremity of Nationale 9, which would eventually lead him to Marrakesh. But there were a good 220 miles before he could get there. The question of how to get there had an easy answer, he had to find some wheels: there was no way he could go on foot. But first, he had to climb down the cliff. He went to sleep early, and using his training, he set his internal clock to wake up at midnight. Max had the capability to wake up at precisely the moment he wished to awake. He was well aware that the guard was outside the door and that any noise he made would attract his attention. He woke up as scheduled, undid his bed, and tied the two sheets end to end. He did not bother to knot them as people see in movies since this only would have consumed time and served no purpose. He then slowly moved the bed towards the window so that he could tie one end of the sheets to it and use the bed as an anchor. He then dressed, took some dollars out of his boots, put them in his pocket, and finally, he grabbed the bottles of water and put them in the side pockets of his desert fatigues. He did not block the door, since this would have made noise. However, he wetted the pillow cover and laid it tight against the bottom of the door in case the guard would notice the draft of cold air after he opened the window. He had noticed that the window made a screeching noise when it was opened, and he had collected the fat from the lamb in the couscous to grease the hinges. This had produced an excellent result, and when Max finally opened the window after climbing on the bed, it moved without a sound. He threw the sheets out of the window and immediately started climbing down. Although they did not reach the bottom of the cliff, the final few metres of descent were far from difficult, and less than two minutes after leaving the room, Max was walking west in the bed of the oued in the direction of Nationale 9. He had decided that his first priority would be to acquire a burnoose—the long cloak of coarse woollen fabric with a hood, usually dark in colour, worn by Berbers and the Arabs throughout North Africa—but he was unlikely to be able to do so after midnight without drawing unnecessary attention to himself. As he climbed back out of the oued into the village, he was conscious of his conspicuousness, and he walked close to the walls. As he was rounding the corner of the Kasbah, he saw a light in a shop, and against all expectations, there was a man half asleep who was still tending his shop. He hesitated to go in and decided to push on remembering this mantra of evasion, which is to put as much distance as fast as possible between you and your pursuers—and especially not to leave a witness behind. As he was making his way out of M'Hamid using the main street, he saw a bicycle that someone had negligently leaned against the wall of a house. Careful to make not a sound, he tiptoed to it, lifted it on his shoulder, and carried it that way for about 200 metres. Once he estimated he was far enough, he put it on the ground, climbed on it and started pedalling towards Marrakesh. Max was an excellent cyclist and participated regularly in criteriums as well as triathlons, and although he had been weakened by his escape from Algeria, he managed to set a respectable pace on a bicycle that was far from a performance machine. Within one hour, he had gone the thirteen miles to Tagounite. By four thirty in the morning, he had cycled through Zagora, even managing to steal a burnoose that had been left to dry overnight on a clothing line. At daybreak he abandoned the bicycle in the valley of the Draa and had reached Ouarzazate, intent on finding a trucker who would be amenable to give him a ride to Marrakesh. Logically, he knew this would be the time when the dispensary staff would realise he had disappeared. They would alert the guard, and he would call the inspector who would come personally to investigate while chewing up the guard for not doing a better job at watching Monsieur Lefort. Inspector Saftir would alert the Sûreté Nationale, and the Moroccan police forces would be looking for him, more or less. Putting these thoughts aside, Max quickly found a rendezvous point for truckers who were on the way to deliver produce and dried goods to Marrakesh and he negotiated a ride on one of them. The driver asked no explanations, as he was interested only in making a few dollars. He looked like someone who did not particularly like the police of the gendarmerie. He offered Max a seat in the cab and even gave him a few dates, and they were on the way. The driver was silent, which suited Max just fine, and they did not exchange one word during the three hours the ride lasted. Max dozed off despite the laborious climbing over the Atlas Mountains. He woke up as the driver pulled onto the parking lot of a small roadside café. As they were reaching Marrakesh, near the Almekis golf course, the police had already set up a roadblock. Max told the driver to slow down to allow him to jump. The driver smiled and wished him good luck. Max opened the door and swiftly jumped out, disappearing from sight towards the Amanjena Hotel. He was far from being home yet.

Inspector Saftir was pissed off. How could he have thought that this half-dead guy was incapable of escaping? And now he was convinced he had something big to hide to take the chance to run away. But in a sense, he really did not have any reason to hunt him down. As far as the situation stood right now, he had not been charged with anything, he had seemingly committed no crime in Morocco, and he should really have been free to leave the dispensary as he wished. Yet the fact that he taken the risk to climb out of the window and down a cliff was the proof that this guy was guilty of something. He got back into his Volkswagen Jetta and went back to his office. He sat down behind his desk and the day took a twist he could never have expected. *Hagalaz*. Within a few minutes of seating down, he had the visit of an officer from the Moroccan Counterespionage Agency (MCA). The conversation had focused on Monsieur Lefort in which the MCA was apparently interested. Taoufik would never comprehend what happened next. His mind could not keep up with the speed of the action. He could only reconstruct part of the chain of events. He was talking to the MCA guy, when this guy had stood up and had shouted something at him in Arabic. The next thing he knew, he had been thrown against the wall as if the guy had hit him with a powerful ray machine like you see in the science fiction movies. Then the guy had walked out, locking the room behind him. In the meantime, Taoufik had fallen to the ground from the impact of the force that had projected him against the wall. He had scrambled back to his feet, rubbing his head that had hit the wall rather hard. He still could not make any sense out of it. He got back to his chair and picked up the phone to call the Sûreté and report this weird incident. Taoufik talked to Chief Inspector Mansour and had explained to him what had just taken place in the office, and the Chief Inspector had told him to go unlock the door. Taoufik had done just that, and as he was coming back to sit on his chair, this is when he suddenly felt the warm liquid run down his stomach, reach his crotch, and slide down both his legs. This is when he understood he had actually been shot. Getting back to the phone, he told the Chief Inspector to call the police emergency number, although he knew there was not much to do about his condition. His lungs had been shredded by the hollow point bullet, and the blood vessels severed. He instinctively knew the arteries had been damaged. *A few more minutes to live.* He had already started to lose control of his body functions, and a stream of urine mixed with the blood flooded his chair, gushing onto the floor and mixing with the red of his life, being pissed away. He also realised that he was deaf from the gun firing in such close quarters, and that he could identify the smell of gunpowder lingering in the office. He cursed at himself for having been caught so stupidly off guard. He started drifting away from reality, while at the same time struggling to keep his body from going into shock. In the middle of the ghastly scene in which he was now an actor, he knew that allowing his body to drift into shock would mean the end of his life. Although he knew there was not much hope to ever come out of this one. It must have been a 45, he thought. In the same time he started wondering why anybody would shoot him for talking about Monsieur Lefort. And it suddenly dawned on him that the guy had not been an agent of the MCA. He grabbed for a pen: in his dying minutes he would write down everything he could remember, he would write about the interview, about the dog tags, about the escape. He could barely put two words together. The pain hit him all at once. In a blink it became unbearable. *This is how it feels to be shot in the chest.* He realised he should have called medical emergency services himself. He went for the phone but could not dial 17. The pain was so intense he barely managed to think. He imagined saying, 'I have been shot, in my office, I am bleeding to death.' Then words rushed to his brain of his wife telling him 'have a good day, dear'. He sure wished he had kissed her tenderly, but how was he to know that he would die that day? Today? And yet, this is exactly what he was doing. He finally looked for something to stop the bleeding with. A box of Kleenex! He mangled it open and stuffed the entire content into the hole in his chest. The bleeding did not even slow down. He needed to get out of the office, nobody would find him. . . He struggled to the door, leaving behind him a stream of blood. He got to the hallway, stumbling like a drunk . . . holding on to the wall with his left hand while desperately trying to stop the blood from flowing out with his right hand. He swivelled right and collapsed with a heavy thud, a dead body falling within sight of the building reception area. His last thought before he hit the ground was for his wife. He called her name, 'Raissa!' and as his last breath left his body, as his brain went black forever, he had a vision of Raissa taking him in his arms, gently lifting him up, and carrying him into the bright light of the afterlife.

Death is your companion. In Marrakech, Max had gone into the Amanjena Hotel, had ordered breakfast, and had proceeded to the clothes shop to finally dress in civilian clothes for the first time in over two weeks. He had then placed a call to the US Embassy in Rabat. He had asked to speak to a Colonel Andrews. He did not introduce himself. He simply stated 'Code 353' to which the colonel was supposed to answer '464—Lima Kilo', indicating that Colonel Andrews was read into the LICHI KLESH program. Upon getting the correct answer, Max simply then stated '446', indicating he needed a safe room activated in accordance to the protocols of the program. Colonel Andrews acknowledged by answering '446, Jones', indicating that the room would be activated under the name of Jones. Max would simply have to ask for the message at the front desk for Mister Jones. As for the hotel, there was no need to specify which one was to be used, as the program had a preset protocol for this as well: first on the list was the Hilton; if there was no Hilton in that city, next was the Hyatt, and failing to have a Hyatt, the third choice was the Sheraton. So there was never any need to state which hotel to go to. Max added one more instruction, 'Triple Seven', which meant he needed some

THE DATURA SOLUTION

firepower, as he did not doubt for one moment that Inspector Saftir would send a bunch of his goons after him. And Max, although ignorant of the fact that the danger came from somewhere else, was still in the survival mode. He knew that in regards to the Moroccan authorities, he was on the same level with an escaped convict. He needed protection. Now, the next challenge was to get from Marrakesh to Rabat. Max eliminated all possibilities that required any type of identification and any that would make him a sitting duck. In the end, he came to the conclusion that there was no good solution and he had to opt for the least compromising one. He hesitated between the train and a chauffeured limo. For a hundred dollars, the concierge got him a Mercedes E Class with chauffeur and by two in the afternoon, the chauffeur pulled up in front of the Goethe Institute in Rabat and Max got out. He walked away from the drop off point, ensuring the limo driver was not keeping track of him, and he started walking down Avenue Ibn Hamz towards the Hilton. He grabbed lunch at a small restaurant, and an hour and a half later, Mr Jones was in Room 708 overlooking the lush landscape which had been engineered around the hotel. He went to the bathroom, lifted the top of the commode, and found the hardware that he had hoped for taped with duct tape to the underside of the cover. It consisted of a 9mm Browning equipped with silencer and provided with four clips of fifteen rounds each. For sure, Colonel Andrews had been generous in his anticipation of ammunition. He thanked him mentally. Also wrapped around the weapons was a small plastic bag containing $2,000 in used notes and a passport in the name of Mike Jones, which only needed the picture added, a standard operating procedure when calling a Code Triple Seven. Once Max had an ID photo, he would simply leave the passport and the picture at the reception, dial Colonel Andrews who would send someone to pick it up and return it later with the photo added, courtesy of the US Consul. All of this was done without any of the parties having contact with each other or even knowing the identity of the person on the phone, for Colonel Andrews was certainly not 'Colonel Andrews'. Both men were operating in the murky waters of false names, offices they did not occupy, functions which were entirely bogus, and people who did not exist. The only authenticating element in all of this was a classified name and three codes they had exchanged. They knew they were on the same team and this alone allowed them to operate in concert. After taking a hot shower, a quick nap, and shopping at the Hilton shop for a change of clothes and toiletries, Max had a proper dinner at the Dar Al Andalous restaurant and rejoined his room where for the first time in three weeks he would sleep in a regular bed. Although he wanted to call Rebecca, he resisted the urge to do so because he would have compromised his position and survival, as he had no doubt that all hotel conversations were monitored by the Moroccan espionage services. In the morning, he would get a throw-away cell phone and call her from it. He barricaded the door with the armchair in the room, sticking its back under the door handle, and pushed the desk against it. He ensured the window was locked and balanced one of the desk lamps on its edge so that he would be woken up by it crashing on the floor in case of an intrusion attempt. He locked and loaded a round in the pistol, and certain that he would be able to hear someone trying to come in his room, he went to sleep, keeping an ear open, just like a cat.

It is only in the morning that the precarious situation he was in hit Max in the face, when he read the paper that had been left by his front door and he read it on the way to breakfast. It was right there, in bold letters on the front page of the national newspaper Le Matin: 'Assassinat d'un inspecteur de police a M'Hamid'. As he read the article, he realised that his alter ego Monsieur Lefort who has escaped from the M'Hamid hospital was the prime suspect. Max knew full well that the assassination was no coincidence and that it was a direct consequence of the inspector being so interested in his case. Max concluded that the Algerians, having failed to get him on his way out of the desert, were now pursuing him in Morocco. Since the murder had taken place less than ten hours after his escape from the dispensary, Max congratulated himself for having had the perspicacity not to wait any longer to flee. If he had, he was convinced that the assassination of Monsieur Lefort would have made the title page of the papers as well.

CHAPTER 11

Le Matin's article changed all of the plans Max had elaborated. It was as if the opponent had had a secret weapon and suddenly used it against him in a game of chess. It was so sudden and so unexpected that all of Max's previous pattern-recognition facilities were unable to compute a solution. He had to abandon all of his plans and apply recursive reasoning to regroup and react. First, he eliminated the steps he should absolutely not take. There would be no calling Rebecca since he had to assume that the enemy had no idea of his identity and of the link between him and her. Despite the incredible desire he had to call her, such an action would most likely result in putting her at risk as well as in giving his adversaries a clue as to who he was. Second, there was no sense in trying to get out of Morocco, because whoever was after him would simply follow him across the next border as they had done here. Third, he could not keep meandering in public and open himself to recognition as Monsieur Lefort, and that meant that the safe room he was occupying was not safe any longer. If Colonel Andrews' superiors linked Max to the assassination of Inspector Saftir, the colonel may well receive orders if not to turn him in, at least to no longer cooperate with him. He could not be sure of his loyalty, even under the LICHI KLESH program. It would not be the first time that the United States sacrificed a peon to satisfy a foreign government and in this case it was even worse. Turning Max in would pacify the Moroccan government by turning in the presumed assassin of Inspector Saftir, it would pacify the Algerian government since Max has dispatched four of its gendarmes, and it would also pacify the extremist ARI group by showing them that the US government did not hesitate to turn in its own citizens when they were conducting assassination missions. Max's only saving graces were that he had used a French-made anti-tank missile and that thanks to his ability to speak French as his mother tongue, everyone involved thought he was French. He thought about what he should do, and the consequence of each action. And as he did so he constructed a hypothetical scenario that reflected what happened if he made a certain move. He had to consider what his opponents would do if he made a certain move, and he had to determine what was the best move for him, and the best move for his opponent. Again, he was playing a game of chess and he reflected that playing chess did not require only intelligence but also being able to plan ahead and plan how the opponent was going to react. Based on the murder of Inspector Saftir, Max had only one advantage: he knew exactly who his opponents were.

The first thing Monsieur Lefort, aka Max, decided to do was to address a letter to Le Matin to absolve himself, thus lifting some of the suspicion off him and allowing the Sûreté to look for the real murderer or murderers. He went to a paper store and purchased a common writing tablet. He sat down at the terrace of the Hilton Café and started writing:

> Monsieur,
>
> I have the honour of being the Monsieur Lefort of recent interest to the press and the police. I read your article and noticed that the police as well as your paper credited me with the assassination of Inspector Saftir, whom I had the opportunity to meet and respected greatly. I must tell you that although it is tempting to impute the murder

to the last person he interrogated, it would have been impossible for me to commit such a crime as at the time it took place I was on the way to Marrakesh where I arrived at around nine thirty in the morning as the concierge at the Amanjena Hotel will be able to verify. It is therefore physically impossible for me to have been in Marrakesh at 9:30 a.m. and in M'Hamid at 10:00 a.m. I have since moved on to Rabat where I normally reside.

Yours Truly,
Maurice Lefort

Once he had written the letter, he tore the page off and went to the Hyatt Hotel where he asked the concierge for a piece of paper and an envelope. Ensuring he did not touch the paper with his fingers (so as to not leave finger prints) he went back to the privacy of his room at the Hilton, where he proceeded with writing the entire letter in upper case letters with his left hand (so as to render writing recognition impossible). Once he was done, he took the Hyatt envelope, and using the same precautions, he folded the message and slid it inside. He was pleased to see that the Hyatt was using self-sealing envelopes so that no saliva was required to glue the flap. He then went to the post office and mailed the letter to Le Matin at 17, Rue Othmane Ben Affane, Casablanca, to the attention of the chief editor. This would give him twenty-four hours during which he could put his plan into action. After accomplishing this first phase of his plan, Max wondered the city in search of the perfect setup, since he had decided to ambush the killers looking for him. He had thought about the consequences of his action during his recursive analysis. He knew the people after him were the ARI. It had to be a two-man team. If he did not kill them, they would keep pursuing him, first in Spain, then in the United States, and he would have to kill them in any case. If he did kill them, it could be possible that another team would follow them, and he wondered how many teams the ARI would send after him. Experience with other avenging activities showed they had little appetite to send more than one team after a person they had condemned to death. The problem he saw with his plan was that Colonel Andrews would know instantly that Lefort was Mike Jones, and his cover would be blown, and all hinged on Colonel Andrews having or not received orders to turn him in or not. The key was to ensure that everyone continue to believe that there was a Monsieur Lefort someplace. It was similar to the movie North by Northwest where Mister Kaplan does not exist, but everyone thinks he is actually Cary Grant. Max was glad to have seen the movie several times. He would apply the same technique. He went to a phone booth and reserved a room at the Hyatt under the name of Maurice Lefort using a pre-paid credit card he had bought from Western Union. He then identified a taxi driver whom he judged would not mind making an extra $50, and asked him to go check in as Monsieur Lefort while Max waited in the cab. The hotel clerk was sure to ask the taxi driver for an ID card, but Max ensured his accomplice had an extra small piece of paper with General Grant's picture on it to take care of that detail. Less than ten minutes later, the taxi driver came back with the room entry cards. Monsieur Lefort existed and he had a witness of his existence. Max encouraged the taxi driver to tell the funny story to all his colleagues, as he was sure that sooner or later his pursuers would go that route to enquire about him. Since he had no intention to ever occupy the room it made no difference if the authorities showed up in his room. Max only had to wait patiently for his pursuers to find him. In the meantime, Monsieur Lefort virtually appeared at several places, making reservations at a restaurant, at the theatre, and at a hammam. He went to none of them, as he prepared to spend another night in the hesitant environment of the Hilton. As he was having dinner, he realised he had to yet change room again. He then would have three rooms in Rabat: one in which Mike Jones was supposed to sleep, one that was Monsieur Lefort's at the Hyatt, and one that was to be his safe room—he would have to see which identity he could muster. He only had two passports left, and he also had to extract himself out of Morocco, a task that would not be easy after the hell that was going to break lose at the Hyatt if things went according to plan. Max figured it would take another twenty-four hours for his pursuers to find him, so he had plenty of time to relax. He went back to his room, decided to use a French passport belonging to Jean Tardieu, and he went to get another room, ensuring that he had never seen the registration desk clerk. He then transferred his toiletries to that room and went to dinner as Mike Jones since the restaurant hostess recognised him from the evening before. He continued to think of the trap he was going to set. It was already sorted out in his head. He knew that the assassin would ask for Monsieur Lefort's key pretending to have lost his wallet during a night on the town. The assassin had to have good social engineering skills, as the clerk was sure to ask him for some sort of identification. It would undoubtedly lead to some type of discussion. Max would wait for such a man in the lobby bar while pretending to be drinking. He would casually get in the same elevator as he. He would then simply shoot him in the elevator. He had already wrapped the Berretta in a plastic bag to avoid the powder fumes spreading in the elevator and the spent cartridge rolling on the floor. One bullet would be sufficient, square in the back of the head in the nape of the neck. He would already have the pistol in hand because he had picked a black plastic bag with the double 'C' of the Channel brand and it would be hidden in it. So there would be no need to pull the pistol out of his pocket or some silly gesture like that which would only cause a draw with his opponent. He figured nevertheless that he had another two days to wait before his assassin would show up.

 The first of these two days Max spent visiting Rabat, a city he had never been to before. He did the tourist things, ensuring that he accompanied his walks with nice meals and plenty of water. At the Hyatt, life was disturbed by persistent calls to Monsieur Lefort's room, and by the no less insistent visit of Le Matin reporters demanding access to Monsieur Lefort. The morning of the second day, Le Matin duly reported on the letter of Monsieur Lefort to the paper. After perusing the article, Max spent the day planning his escape from Rabat and from Morocco. He could not possibly stay in the Hyatt after shooting whoever was coming after Monsieur Lefort. There were videos in the hallways, and he would be seen entering the elevator and coming out of it. The body would be found and it would only be a matter of time before he was discovered. The problem was there were no planes in the middle of the night. He decided that he would return to the Hilton even if his comings and goings could be associated with suspicious activities. While looking at ways to leave Morocco, he decided there would be far too much scrutiny on air travellers. Hence he took advantage of the beautiful fall day to walk to the Rue Abou Faris El Marini and rent a car with chauffeur to take him to Tangiers the next day—he would have rented a car without chauffeur but he had no drivers' license that matched any of his passports. Plus this allowed him to rent the car without giving an identity or a credit card. Max had come to love cash payments in the last few days. He agreed that he would be there at 10:00 a.m. the following day. Once in Tangiers, he would charter a boat and ask to be dropped off on the Spanish coast. If dollars could secure such a service, it would be fine, it not, he had a Beretta and he would not hesitate to use it. After completing this task, and having another nice dinner, this time at the famous Villa Mandarine, rue Ouled Bousbaa, he walked back to the Hilton. He went into the bedroom belonging to Jean Tardieu, unlocked the safe, and took his Beretta out. He checked it for cleanliness then took the plastic laundry bag from the closet and placed the pistol in it. He checked that the trigger was not encumbered by the bag, and he sealed it with Scotch tape he had purchased the day before. Once he was satisfied everything was okay, he put the pistol in the plastic Channel bag, waited until about ten in the evening, and went to the Hyatt and settled at the lobby bar while sipping slowly on an eighteen-year-old Glenfiddich. He waited. He had taken a book in French with him, Le Joueur d'Echecs by Stefan Zweig, but he had finished reading it before anyone showed up. He waited until three o'clock in the morning and was almost ready to give up when he forced himself to consider that three in the morning was the time when people are the most vulnerable, the least in control of their senses and capabilities, and the most apt at making errors. As if on cue, a man came stumbling in through the rotating glass doors. Max knew it was him instantly. He dragged himself to the front desk as if completely drunk, and vociferated that he wanted the card to his room, that he had been robbed and that he had no card, no money, and no ID. He was perfect as a drunk. He almost fell as he pretended to slide off the front desk, barely managing to remain standing, and he asked for his key.

'What is your room number, sir?' asked the clerk.

'My room number? I am Monsieur Lefort! That's my room number!' the man stated, in a pure French accent, slapping his hand on the front desk in a gesture that caused the clerk to jump in surprise.

'Yes, Monsieur, I know you are Monsieur Lefort, but what is your room number?'

The drunk pretended to make an effort to remember, then slowly he stammered, 'Five . . . Six . . . and the last I don't remember' he burst out laughing. The clerk said, 'Okay, it is five-six-three, will you remember?' 'Oh yes,' answered the would-be drunk, 'I am on my way.' While he pretended to stagger to the elevators, Max stood up, and slowly followed him, offering assistance as the drunk tried to push the call button. 'Thank you,' he said, and he grabbed Max to remain standing. Max was amazed at the detail of the setup. The guy had even poured alcohol on himself to stink like a drunk. But Max was not fooled. As they entered the elevator, Max already had his finger on the trigger, and he had long ago removed the safety. The drunk was stuck in his role and has to continue pretending to be inebriated. 'Which floor?' asked Max. The man continued his acting 'Fi-Five.' Max punched number 5. As soon as the doors had closed, he turned slightly to the right to ensure he could fire effectively, and he squeezed the trigger. The man's eyes bulged from both the surprise and the shock. This time he grabbed the railing to maintain himself straight. 'This one was for Inspector Saftir,' Max told him. It was a useless sentence as the man was already dead. He could not stand any more. Slowly he emitted a swooshing sound, as if he was deflating, his head rolled forward, heavily crashed against the mahogany wall of the elevator, and came to rest on the beige tile floor. Max knew he no longer had to fear anything from him, and frisked him. As a good assassin, the man had absolutely nothing in his pockets, but Max found a shoulder holster containing a .40-calibre Glock with laser sights. Max pocketed it, and as the elevator reached the fifth floor, Max grabbed the man under the shoulders and acted as if he was helping him to his room. Anyone who would have seen them walking would indeed have thought they were two drunks coming back to the hotel after painting the town. Upon closer observation, one would have noticed the copious amount of blood already staining the men's clothes, and by that time the assassin had already dead over one minute, and he was now relaxing his bowels. Max took the key card from the man's pocket, opened the door, and manhandled him onto the bed, face down. He almost gagged from the stench of blood, shit, and piss that the man had released as he died. He took his jacket off that had been stained by the dying man's blood, calmly exited the room, closed the door, and walked to the stairs. He waited until the clerk was distracted and went out looking for the second man. There, still with his Chanel bag in his right hand, he pretended to be looking for a taxi. Spotting a Peugeot 405 with a driver he went towards it, seemingly to inquire if this was a taxi. The driver signalled him to shoo away, but Max could not take this as an answer. So he yelled out, 'Are you in service?' The only answer he got was a movement of the driver's right hand towards the left inside flap of his jacket. Max took the Chanel bag and aiming as fast as he did during competition, he led go two bullets. The first one hit and broke the windshield! 'Fuck me!' he thought, as his field of vision was obscured, while throwing himself towards the left of the vehicle, where the driver did not have a field of vision. Max had no idea if he had actually hit the driver, although he thought he had. The only certainty he had was that three bullets had been fired. Two were his, and the third one had grazed his left arm, tearing the sleeve material. Max reflected mentally that when one exposed himself to firing guns, sooner or later one bullet had to make its way to him. He did not have much time to think because whatever wound he had inflicted to the driver was not fatal. He heard the son-of-a-bitch open the door of the car and get out of it. Max kneeled up to the passenger window (another one that is going to break, he thought), and squeezed the trigger again twice in succession. This time he saw the shadow if the driver jolt forward—he had been hit. Max ran to the back of the car, rounding it to the left side, but the driver was waiting for him, and let go of three bullets that hit the bodywork and one tire—the air starting hissing out and Max noticed movement by the front door of the hotel. Max could not wait any longer. He lunged forward and liberated another three bullets in the direction of the driver. Two missed, but the third one hit him in the face as he was attempting a last effort to save himself from certain death. Max was down to five bullets in the magazine. The driver suddenly felt nausea, and a stream of vomit erupted from his disfigured mouth, washing the blood and the teeth away. For a moment, he lay perfectly still and as he realised he was drowning in his vomit, he made an effort to survive. Max could not believe how many bullets he needed to kill the guy—how he regretted his Colt 45 . . . Max half-crawled to the driver and shot him a last time in the back of the head, execution style, to make sure he was dead. The driver no longer existed. Max did not wait to see the result of the last bullet, it was not necessary. He retreated to the shadows of the trees, brushed himself off, and made his way back to the Hilton and its service entrance, where he would go to Jean Tardieu's room on the seventh floor. He hesitated between staying there and leaving before the cops were called to the scene. He had planned to stay in the room until morning to allay suspicion.

THE DATURA SOLUTION

Whoever was missing from their room had to be the murderer. The cops would probably mistake the first killer for the non-existent Maurice Lefort, Mike Jones would be nowhere to be found, and he would be the prime suspect, and as for Jean Tardieu, if he were in his room, nice and tight, sleeping, he would be beyond suspicion, except for the fact that his face was all over the surveillance videos helping the fake drunk to his room, a drunk that was later found dead in his bed. So Jean Tardieu called the reception so that they could prepare his bill, and get him a taxi for the airport. He packed the blood-stained clothes in the second laundry bag, he packed it in the AWOL bag he had purchased the day before, then he reloaded his Beretta, took the Glock out of the safe, packed them each in a Hilton hand towel, put them in the AWOL bag, shaved, put the shaving kit in the bag, zipped, and he walked out. Thirty minutes after his call, he was on the way to airport, and he had been sure to tell the clerk that he was catching a General Aviation flight to Ouagadougou. Up to then, his plan had worked, even if there had been a little more collateral damage than he had wanted. As soon as the taxi had left, Max walked in the direction of Nationale 6, turned right and using this thoroughfare, he took the downtown direction so that he could get to Rue Abou Faris El Marini and the chauffeured car that he had ordered for 10:00 a.m. On the way there, Max stopped at a bistro to get a coffee, and to his horror, his picture was on the eight o'clock news as having a link with two murders the night before at the Rabat Hilton. The TV reported that Maurice Lefort was found dead in his room, and that a second man, yet to be identified, had been found dead next to a sedan that was riddled with bullets. The suspect's name was Mike Jones, an American citizen who had been seen in the company of the victim as he rode the elevator. Since no wallet, identification, or money was found on either victim, it was assumed that the alleged murderer had killed both men simply to rob them. The US Ambassador had been called to ensure the full cooperation of the United States in helping solve the murders. Max drank his coffee, left a few coins for its amount on the counter, and walked smartly out of there. He avoided all main thoroughfares, any place where there could be a cop, and he hoped that no one who had seen the news crossed his path.

He remembered the Evasion and Escape exercise in France, where he had been captured within 200 metres from the goal to reach because he had underestimated the ability of the French Gendarmes to track his movement. Thus, he approached Rue Abou Faris El Marini very gingerly. He took one of the throw-away cell phones and called the limo service at nine fifty-five to tell them that he had had a long engagement at the Central Bank of Morocco (which was about 500 metres away) and that he should be picked up there rather than at the office. A few minutes later, he saw the limo leave the garage, and as he had suspected, it was followed by two unmarked police cars. The limo service guy had watched TV and called the cops to set up an ambush, and now the cops and the limo were rushing to the Central Bank. More disheartening of course was the fact that the authorities knew of his plans to go to Tangiers, thus making it impossible for him to rejoin the city. And he did not have a Plan B. He thought about commandeering one of the other limos by force—he could easily do that—but he also was sure the cars were equipped with a tracking device, so it was out of the question to use any of those. And where would he go that would allow him to get to Spain. Suddenly, Morocco had become a very small country, with no place to hide. He had relatively little room for manoeuvre and he had too many equations to solve to be able to get to a quick decision.

CHAPTER 12

The United States ambassador had called an emergency meeting of his special staff for 10 o'clock. At the set time, everyone was entering the bubble. The bubble is a heavy-duty Plexiglas room that is suspended inside a regular on rubber shock absorbers deep inside the embassy. It has no window, and this is where the most confidential and critical meetings take place. To cover the voices of the participants, in case an electronic sweep would miss a bug, a noise generator is activated as soon as the lights are turned on. It makes meeting in that room rather uncomfortable especially since the table and chairs also made of Plexiglas give very little elbow room. The entire staff consisting of the head of Public Affairs, Economic Section, OSC (Office of Security Cooperation), USDA (US Department of Agriculture), FBI, Peace Corps, US Commercial Service, US Agency for International Development (USAID), plus the military attaché, the Head of Mission, and concealed in the group, the CIA Chief of Mission whose identity remained a mystery, was assembled when the ambassador arrived. The ambassador, a former Wall Street banker whose personal fortune was in the upper hundreds of millions of dollars, was smartly dressed as always. That day he wore a charcoal-grey Hugo Boss suit, a chocolate and fuchsia Ferragamo custom tie with matching pocket kerchief, and an absolutely radiant white shirt from one of the sops on Seville Row. As usual, Mark Schoenberg wore a tan as if he just walked in from a summer sunbathing session in Saint-Tropez, his hair which he managed to die with just enough black to make it a constant and invariable salt-and-pepper colour, heavy on the pepper, was flawlessly arranged, and his fingers were perfectly manicured. A personal friend of the vice president, he had asked for the post in Morocco because he spoke French and Arabic, enjoyed the country, and figured he would spend three of four years there, away from any potential damaging crisis, and would have plenty of time to investigate business opportunities. As a matter of fact, he was now investing heavily in developing tourist infrastructure in Marrakesh and had financed the building of new houses that were destined to be bought by affluent Western personalities and would sell in the neighbourhood of $3 to $4 million. Ambassador Schoenberg therefore saw any type of activity reflecting negatively on the United States as a personal affront, and one that could jeopardise his financial returns. While he was a charming individual, suave and polite, and whose erudition amazed all around them, he was also none for his frank manner of speech when things went wrong:

'I know one of you in this room knows about that son of a bitch! Talk to me,' he started.

'I have nothing to do with it,' immediately intervened the military attaché.

'Great, then find out who does,' the ambassador fired back. 'I don't give a flying fuck if you have nothing to do with it! The prime minister called me this morning while I was having breakfast at the residence and asked me for a report by noon, for Christ's sake! So, if you don't know fuck about it, find out! FBI, what do you have?'

The FBI guy hunkered down—he did not even know what the ambassador was talking about, but he bravely answered, 'Sir, we are working on it. We'll have a report to you by eleven fifty-five.'

'Listen, I don't want your usual fucking reports of shit that summarised what the papers say. I want you to put men on the street, and I want you to find that motherfucker and I want you to take him in. You understand?'

'Yes, sir!'

Then the ambassador went around the room. Nobody knew anything. When it came to Colonel Andrews, who was officially the OSC, he denied any knowledge. The problem was that the ambassador was not read into the LICHI KLESH program and there was no way that Colonel Andrews was going to compromise it. The meeting ended after less than ten minutes. The ambassador was still pissed. He looked at the faces around the table, and he added in a menacing voice:

'Anyone who knows something about this guy and does not tell me, I'll have his ass. I'll crucify you to the fucking wall if you don't tell me the truth! Everybody back here at eleven forty-five. And I want news, not bullshit or what the TV tells me. I want him found, I want him arrested, I want him off the streets!'

Colonel Andrews was unconcerned by the threats. He had one loyalty and one only. It was to the US Army and to the program. He could not care less about Mark Schoenberg. As a matter of fact, he would do anything he could to help the guy, whoever he was, if he asked him. But he also knew that he would never call again, not now when the situation was deteriorating so fast for him. Colonel Andrews thought that if this guy was able to get out of it, he was very, very good! And mentally, he wished him good luck.

The CIA Head of Mission went straight to the encrypted phone in his safe and dialled Langley. He was sure that the so-called murders in Rabat were not random and that if they had been carried out in the middle of the Hilton, there was a good reason. He wanted to know which agency was controlling the operation and what the planning had been to start with. Surely, an operative would only have shot two people in the middle of the capital of Morocco in self-defence. It could not be part of a regular operation. The answer he got was not what he wanted to hear. The CIA had no idea what was going on—it was not one of their operations, and Defence did not know either. When

Langley had talked to the Pentagon, the only thing they had been told is that the Pentagon knew nothing about anything. The CIA Head of Mission immediately knew that someone was lying—such an operation could only have come from the Pentagon or from the CIA. Since he would normally have known about a CIA event ahead of time, or at least post-event with cabled instructions, he was sure that the Pentagon was responsible. Then he tried to figure out who within the Pentagon would have done that: he immediately eliminated the air force and the navy. This was not their type of operations. It left the marines and the army. He had never heard of marines going to this type of urban environment, so it had to be the army. And the army operated so many black programs that were layered like an onion that there would be no way to link whoever was now in country to any program. The thing that mattered in this case was that the guy or guys who were involved were without doubt US Army, that the operation was highly classified, probably Commander-in-Chief Eyes Only, and that the operatives had taken the steps in self-defence. Then, he recalled an article he had seen in the *Marrakesh News* about a man who had appeared in M'Hamid out of nowhere from the desert, and he knew this was the same guy. He looked for the article online and found the report describing a man who had collapsed from exhaustion and thirst and who had barely survived the ordeal, and how the competence of the medical personnel at the M'Hamid had saved his life. This triggered another question. Where had he come from? He decided to call his counterpart in Algiers. What he got from him was the key to understanding the whole enigma.

'What do you mean "what is going on in Algeria?" Haven't you heard? We are in some shit! One US Army major dead, three members of the ARI blown up in their armoured car, four gendarmes killed in the counter-ambush, one of them at close range, a bunch of military gear, both French and American found burnt at the bottom of a foxhole, and you asking me what is going on? Shit, I thought news travelled faster than that! The French of course are denying any knowledge, and we have been denying any knowledge as well, except we have a damned US Army major to send home in a freaking coffin. How do you explain that to the freaking Algerians?'

'Well, I guess we have the answer to what is going on in Rabat, then.'

'What is going there?'

'What is going on is that whoever was with your army major survived that someone has been hunting him down, that the massacre has continued on this side of the border, and that the entire Moroccan police force is after him, and that the ambassador wants him caught and turned in!'

'You cannot do that,' screamed the Head of Mission in Algiers. 'If you do that, it will confirm Algerian suspicions that we have conducted assassinations in their country, and this is NOT what we want as the US is backing the regime of General Ben Ouali in the upcoming democratic elections in December. If you guys do that, all of Algeria is going to support the candidates of the Islamic Revolution and we'll end up with ayatollahs running the fucking place! You'd better debrief your elephant and have him call mine!'

The elephant of course was the ambassador, because the saying around the embassies was that watching ambassadors work was like watching elephants fuck. It made a lot of noise, produced lots of dust, and no one could see any results for twenty-seven months.

At eleven fifteen, the CIA Head of Station (HOS) walked into the ambassador's office.

'I hope you have good news and that the son-of-a-bitch has been caught,' barked Ambassador Schoenberg.

'Actually, Mister Ambassador, it is far worse than this,' confided the CIA HOS as he sat down in one of the Ethan Allen leather armchairs the ambassador had ordered from the US upon arriving at the embassy a year earlier. 'Ambassador Monroe in Algeria and you need to talk, you see, the entire thing started in Algeria, and

Ambassador Monroe wants us to help the guy escape to prevent the ruin of the upcoming elections in Algeria in less than two months.'

The CIA HOS explained what he had discovered and how everything fit together from the operation that had started on 14 or 15 October, one could not be certain, until today. Ambassador Schoenberg listened with scepticism. 'What about the VP wanting the guy off the streets?' he asked.

'Sir, the fact is that the VP does not know about it and talked to you without referring to POTUS (President of the United States). The reality of it is that the VP is not briefed into the program and that the operation was given the green light by POTUS under a highly classified program.'

'And then, they send some fucking imbecile who cannot tie his shoe laces to execute it, and turn the entire country into a slaughter house,' mocked the ambassador.

'Sir, with all due respect, the guy is pretty competent: he serviced three major ARI terrorists, killed the four special gendarmerie unit guys coming after him, survived running two hundred and some miles in the desert and apparently ambushed the guys from the ARI who were coming after him, and he is still on the run!'

'Yeah, you right,' reluctantly admitted the ambassador who had suddenly gained respect for 'the guy' as they called him now.

He thanked the CIA HOS and dialled Ambassador Monroe in Algeria, using his secure line. Ambassador Monroe confirmed the narration of his CIA HOS and reported that POTUS himself had called him to instruct to exfiltrate 'the guy' as cleanly and as smoothly as possible. Of course, when the order had been issued, neither of them knew that 'the guy' had already exfiltrated himself into Morocco. 'The president's instructions were pretty clear, Mark, get the guy out of there and get him back safely,' Ambassador Monroe added. Mark reflected about the number of classified and compartmented programs that were being run, and he wondered how anyone could keep track of them. And then, his mind wondered to his investments, and he asked himself if they would be affected by the bad press about Americans coming to Morocco and killing innocent citizens. Then he thought how he had taken so many precautions to make sure nobody could trace his investments to the United States, and especially to him, since he was in clear violation of US laws and of the code of ethics under which ambassadors were supposed to operate. He looked out of the window into the palm tree garden and half-smiling he murmured, 'One does not get rich by abiding with the law. Okay, Mark, time to go to the meeting.'

The eleven forty-five meeting took an altogether different direction. The ambassador excused all except the military attaché, Colonel Andrews, the FBI Bureau Chief, and CIA HOS.

'Guys, one of you is not telling me the truth. I know it's not Greg (CIA HOS), I know it's not the FBI, so it's one of you two army guys. Before I go get my ass chewed by the prime minister, I would greatly appreciate actually knowing what is going on. So, who will start?'

The military attaché took the floor:

'Sir, I have no idea what is going on. You know that I am not involved in any operations outside of information gathering and that my clearance is only limited to Top Secret. And if anything is going that involves termination of personnel, it is clearly above Top Secret, and I would not be cleared for it.'

'So this leaves only one person. Colonel Andrews?' insisted the ambassador.

Colonel Andrews counterattacked effectively taking the wind out of the ambassador's sails:

'I would love to assist you and the staff, but first, I would have to know what is going on. I have not a clue what you are referring to, please enlighten me!'

The ambassador had Greg explain what he had deducted from his observations, and had been confirmed by the US Ambassador to Algeria.

'Now, can you help us, Colonel Andrews?'

'Sir, I have no knowledge of the operation in Algeria, nor do I know of any operation that was intended to take place in Morocco. However, if the intent is to assist a fellow army officer, then I am available, of course.'

'Okay. I have to leave now, I would like to meet again here at two, so that we can review any new data and agree on a plan of action to get the guy out of our flower bed. Wish me good luck!'

And the ambassador walked out. The four of them looked at each other, trying to figure out what course of action could be envisioned. Under the circumstances, it was unlikely that they could do much. On his side, Colonel Andrews could not really help without divulging his belonging to LICHI KLESH and would not volunteer any of the information that could be of use. The FBI chief decided to dispatch two agents to see what they could get out of the Hilton personnel, the military attaché returned to his office to deal with a pressing matter for the Army Intelligence Agency, and it left Greg and Colonel Andrews walking together to the cafeteria. 'What do you think, Ryan?' asked Greg, who had a good professional and personal relationship with Colonel Andrews.

'I think the guy is excellent, and I wish I could help him, but no one in this embassy has clearance to know who he is and what he is doing,' added Ryan.

'Not even you?'

'Even me,' lied Ryan.

Ryan went back to his office and called his LICHI KLESH handler over secure lines to receive instructions. Of course, there were none, since he had no need to know. He was simply to do his best to help a fellow officer, but nothing more could be offered. There was no way to contact the guy. It was up to him to find his own way out of whatever situation he was in, and that was the end of it. At the afternoon meeting, there was no news of the guy, and no coherent course of action could be agreed to except to continue searching for clues of the guy's presence. The FBI had no gleaned new information,

THE DATURA SOLUTION

the army could only wait to see if either would be contacted, and the CIA was simply putting the pieces of the puzzle together. Greg had found out that the guy could not have shot Inspector Saftir since he had been shot with a Glock and Greg had confirmed with the army that such weapons are not in the US Army inventory. That information was passed to the Moroccans who were still trying to figure out who the two people were who had been shot at the Hilton. One was still suspected of being this Monsieur Lefort, while the other had to be Mike Jones, Greg reported. Upon hearing this, Colonel Andrews had a hard time not bursting out laughing, since Mike Jones was the guy . . . only he knew that, and he was not about to share it with anyone else.

Having spent most of the day in the Medina, where he hid while having lunch and buying yet another set of clothes, Max tried to figure out what to do next. He relied on Colonel Andrews thinking the same way he did. If he had been Colonel Andrews, he would have gone down the list of hotels on the protocol list and would have rented a room for him in that hotel. Max knew there were no other American hotels in Rabat, so the next one on the list was the Sofitel. Max made his way very carefully—he had been described during the noon hour news as armed and extremely dangerous—to the rue Al Maddal Cherkaoui. He had bought a panama hat and a pair of sun glasses to hide his face and thus was able to avoid detection, especially since he had changed clothes as well. Because he was now identified as an American, he spoke in his native French to the hotel clerk who immediately handled him an envelope addressed not to Mr Jones, but to Monsieur Jeaunes, exactly like Max had pronounced it. He went to the toilets, locked himself in a stall, and opened the envelope. In it were another $2,000 in cash, a MasterCard, in the name of Monsieur Dupont, a French passport with the same identity, an airplane ticket for the next day at 09:05 a.m. Royal Air Maroc flight AT972 from

Casablanca to Madrid, the ignition key to a car licensed 93722-1, the key card for room 341, and a note:

'I am trying to do my best to get you out of here. Embassy trying to locate you to do the same. Of course, they are a few steps behind. Good luck. PS—the car is a grey Citroën C5, leave the key inside and park it at the airport parking. We'll recover it later. It is not completely unmarked and untraceable. You owe me a beer.'

He took the airplane ticket, tore it into tiny pieces, and flushed it down the toilet. Monsieur Dupont would not be arrested by the Moroccan police as he tried to fly out of the country. And although he had not slept in thirty-two hours Max was not about to go to bed yet. He made sure that no one was in the bathroom, he opened the window and climbed out into the hotel garden, sure as he was that if he went out the front door he would be immediately followed. There was no Steve around to tell him he was paranoid, and whether he was or not, in his situation, he could not possibly be paranoid enough. Knowing that he could not trust everybody, Max had made the decision to not trust anybody.

CHAPTER 13

Like every morning, the commander, Special Warfare Office, was being briefed prior to the teleconference meeting with the Joint Chiefs. The briefing was routine until the incidents of Morocco were brought up.

'And who is running this program?' asked Lieutenant General Bernard.

'We don't know,' replied with embarrassment Colonel Hightower who had was briefing the incident.

'What do you mean you don't know?' The general surveyed the room. 'Does anybody know who is running this goat rope?' The general was not amused nor was he trying to be amusing. In fact, the general was on the verge of losing his temper, a habit his staff knew all too well.

'Sir, we have asked everybody we can possibly ask, and this one is so deep into the black, that the name itself is classified' added Colonel Hightower. 'We simply cannot find a trace of evidence that a program even exists.'

'So, you are telling me that a fucking C-130 from our air force dropped two officers from my army in the middle of the fucking desert, that they killed ten motherfucking people, that one of them got killed, that we have one still alive shooting fucking people left and right, and that not a soul on my fucking staff knows who is in charge of it?" General Bernard had already given up making efforts to control his temper and to moderate his swearing, and by the end of the tirade, he was practically screaming.

'Yes, Sir, this is what I am telling you,' Colonel Hightower answered without flinching. 'Ever since we got the cable from the embassy, we have been looking in every possible corner, at Bragg, Benning, Meade, and at the Pentagon, and we cannot even find the program, anyone who is associated with it, and even less who could be running it.' Colonel Hightower had personally spent the last forty-eight hours trying to find the program, and despite his years at the Pentagon and at Bragg, he had come back empty handed.

'So, again, let me get this straight: when Admiral Pointdexter asks me about the Morocco situation in about thirty minutes time, I am supposed to tell him that my entire fucking staff has been incapable of finding anything about it, right? Gentlemen, we will all look like jackasses!' The general hit the table with his fist.

'Sir' continued Colonel Hightower totally unperturbed, 'it appears that the orders were classified POTUS Eyes Only and that he personally gave the green light for the operation in North Africa. As far as the nature of the program is concerned, no one that I have talked to even recognises its existence, or will even accept that its name exists. It looks like the program is so compartmented that any member would not know any other member, and it also looks to me that classifying its very name, makes it impossible I can only surmise that the members receive instructions in a pull down process, as is common with other classified programs. If this is the case, members would simply have a telephone number to call which reroutes them to the right person in the program. They probably have a set of codes that identifies them as a member, and they have a very effective set of verbal SOPs and ROEs.'

'Gentlemen,' the general continued, 'I want you to get to the bottom of this. Hightower, you are in charge, you take Reynolds and

Hunter, and you go find out what is going on. I don't care if you sleep or eat, I want this fucking thing sorted out by tomorrow's briefing. You have your orders.'

The general got up to leave, but the colonel went on:

'Sir, if I may,' interjected Colonel Hightower. 'I would rather pursue this on my own, and keep this entirely between you and me. I have no way of knowing who is in the program, and if either Reynolds or Hunter are part of it, then I will never get anywhere.'

The general saw the wisdom of his staff member and agreed. 'When can you have any results?'

'Sir, I have no way to tell, but I will brief you every day on my progress.'

'Okay,' agreed the general. 'In the meantime, Reynolds, you take over for Hightower—I want him dedicated to this 100 per cent of the time until we have an answer.'

He left the room so that he could go to the bathroom before the start of the teleconference.

Colonel Hightower was a veteran of Special Forces (SF) operations, and he was also a very political officer with two tours of duty at the Pentagon, one on the army staff, and one on the Joint Chiefs staff. He had been repeatedly promoted ahead of his peers, and he was by four years the junior of any colonel in the army. It was public knowledge that he would make his star at the next promotion board. He was a calculating officer who had never done anything unless he had planned to his advantage, and despite his smooth style, he had upset many of his peers. But even his detractors had to admit that 'he was going somewhere,' and they were not. So he must be right. Colonel Hightower saw this challenge as an opportunity to kick the anthill while at the same time continuing to ingratiate himself to one of the most powerful three stars in the US Army. Like many officers who had come from SF where operations were undercover but clearly military, he had a hard time dealing with the black programs and was frankly less than a fan. In his experience, they had proven time and again that no one was controlling them, even less managing them. And now, here was a clear case where there were already eleven casualties and nobody could tell who they were (even the operatives' names were undoubtedly fake), what was their purpose, and who had ordered the slaughter. Colonel Hightower doubted very much that POTUS would have given his agreement to such a mission, especially one which included such a large number of civilian casualties. He was determined to get to the bottom of it.

One person who was not enthused at all by Colonel Hightower's zeal was Eric Sandstrom, the CIA Manager for North Africa. When he was given a transcript of the conversations in General Bernard's office and the transcript of the calls Colonel Hightower had made afterward, he had been livid. Eric Sandstrom had been the advocate for the ambush against Mustafah Guermoulian, personally briefing POTUS and convincing him of its benefits. Now, he already had egg all over his face, and his competence and reputation were certainly at stake. His career as well. He feared that the colonel's prying into his affairs would compromise his master plan. He and his team been working for years to infiltrate and take over the Armée Révolutionnaire Islamique. This was going to be the supreme coup of his career: have a CIA agent run an Islamic terrorist organisation. The imperatives of national security could not be derailed by a colonel, however competent or ambitious he was. He had to be stopped before he could get to the front door. He called in one of his most trusted staff members who had just been reassigned from the field thanks to his connections. He had certainly been right in not asking, but demanding that the man be reassigned to him.

'Charlie, here is the file on Colonel Hightower who works at Special Warfare for General Bernard. He is a bit too nosy these days; so, here is what I want you to do. I want you to put him under round-the-clock surveillance. I want all his phones tapped, I want to see the transcripts in soft format myself. I want you to be able to tell me when he farts, at what time he takes a shit every day, and when he bangs his old lady assuming he can get it up. Got it?'

'No problem, boss.'

Charlie was not a man to discuss anything or to have any questions. You gave him a mission, he executed it, and he knew how to be discreet and cover his tracks. With Charlie on the case, there was no way Colonel Hightower would know he was under surveillance, and most importantly, there was no way any information about his movements, whom he talked to, and whom he met, would escape Eric.

Once he was done with the videoconference, General Bernard called his aide for a cup of coffee and told him to ensure he was not disturbed for the next thirty minutes. Using a disposable cell phone, he then called the LICHI KLESH operations number in Canada, area code 418 in Quebec Province. From there, the call was rerouted to various locations around the world that made the operations centre a completely virtual organisation. When the prompts came up, the general entered his personal code of 115, and he was connected to the Ops Centre. The general wanted to know when 1162 (the code for Operation Beartooth) would be concluded. The Ops Center asked for more credentials and confirmed that Operation Beartooth had been concluded with the expected positive result. When the general objected to the answer, the Ops Center simply hung up, per protocol. It made no difference that it was the man in charge of LICHI KLESH who was calling. He should have known that any event taking place either after the expected result had been achieved or after the team had been exfiltrated was classified as being outside of the operation. As usual, there was no contingency plan in place to cover situations such as the one in Morocco. The operative was on his own. The general put the phone down, extracted the SIM card as well as the memory card, and shredded them. Things were out of his hands and he could only hope for the best.

In the meantime, the events in Morocco were being reported by the international press, and he was sure he was going to be called by the president to explain on this little problem. Since General Bernard could not confirm that he had a LICHI KLESH member at the embassy in Morocco, he called the ambassador personally. He got the rundown of the situation there, with the assurance that everything was being done to find the guy and get him out of the country as fast as possible. During that time Colonel Andrews was preparing to go pick up a certain young Moroccan lady for a drink at the fashionable Hassan Hotel. As he pulled out of the embassy garage, he clearly saw the unmarked Moroccan security services car pull out behind him and follow him to the hotel. He wondered if they would be following the Citroën he had left for Monsieur Dupont. He decided against calling from the car because his phone was sure to be tapped, and he figured the Sofitel phones were also tapped—he had no way of warning Monsieur Dupont.

While Colonel Andrews was pursuing his dreams of the Thousand and One Nights in the company of a creamy brown-skinned beauty with dark eyes shaped like those of a gazelle, which reminded Greg of Paul Eluard's poem La Capitale de la Douleur

> La courbe de tes yeux fait le tour de mon cœur,
> Un rond de danse et de douceur,

Colonel Hightower was actively trying to figure out the who, what, where, when, and how of the guy. But by mid-afternoon, he had made no progress whatsoever. He could not go and interview the president whom he knew now to be the only person to have knowledge of the Morocco operation. Running out of options, he decided to call his West Point roommate, Colonel Gary Irvine, who was working at the White House Communications Agency. After chasing him down for an hour, he finally connected with him and he asked for the big favour: who from Special Warfare had visited the White House between let's say 10 and 15 October. At the end of the day, Gary had come through. He had a list of five names: two one-stars, two colonels, and General Bernard. It would be fairly simple to know exactly what the other four officers had been doing at the White House. It would have been normal for General Bernard to be on the list because he only had to ask for an appointment through his aide or his secretary to gain access to POTUS. At the same time, Colonel Hightower was receiving his information, Charlie was listening in on the conversation. Charlie realised the importance of the information and at once got a time slot with Eric Sandstrom. As Charlie briefed him, Eric remained impassive as always. This was one of his traits. Once Charlie had finished, Eric asked him if it was all he had, then joining his hands as if praying, he remained silent for a long while, thinking carefully at the available courses of action, trying to see several moves down the road into the future, like a chess player. After about ten minutes of silence, reluctantly, he started to express his thoughts.

'Charlie, this Colonel Hightower is becoming a real issue. He is coming too close to the. . . No, let me rephrase this. His actions are in the process of compromising the national security of the United States and endangering a long-term antiterrorist operation. At last count, the Algerian operation has cost the life of at least a dozen people, to include a highly trained US Army officer. What really bothers me is that it was clearly a top secret operation. Actually, it was classified POTUS EYES ONLY. The fact that our team seems to have been ambushed immediately after they had disposed of their target indicates without a doubt that we have a mole somewhere in the organisation, and if not a mole, a traitor. I have no facts to support this, but when I know, I know. And I would not be surprised if the man who betrayed the organisation was the man in charge of it.' Eric paused to let the information settle. 'If the colonel is left to his own volition, he is a dead man anyway, but before he ends up at the bottom of the Potomac, he will have ruined our own operation. This cannot be left to happen, as our man in Algeria is in the process of becoming a key leader not only with the Islamic Front, but also with Al Qaida. If the colonel discovers anything and goes reporting to the general, our man in Algeria is as good as dead. It is one individual against the other. The difference is that the individual in Algeria is far more valuable to our national security that Colonel Hightower. I regret it profoundly, but the choice is crystal clear. We have to take care of him. I want to avoid unnecessary suffering, and especially anything that would cause a police investigation. We need something normal, like a car accident. I don't see any other way out. I am already in the shit as it is, but if he keeps on putting his nose where he shouldn't, we are really *in* the shit.'

'Not a problem,' replied Charlie, 'I already had a plan and I have everything on standby. After the call to the White House, I knew it would come down to that. I came to the same conclusion as you: there is no way out of this one. It will be done as elegantly as humanly possible, don't worry.'

Since Eric had had the offices of General Bernard and his entire staff tapped—an effort that was repetitive because of the insistence of the general to have his office swept for electronic listening devices every month—Eric Sandstrom was perfectly aware that the general ran LICHI KLESH. Since General Bernard was one fourth Navajo, Eric was the only one to know the rather careless—Eric thought this was a good word—link between General Bernard and the name of the program, which meant 'red snake' in Navajo. This also showed that the establishment of the program was a Bernard initiative and that he ran it entirely from his office in Roselyn, away from the prying eyes of the Pentagon and other staff wienies who might have proven to be inconveniences.

The course of the next day was rather perplexing for Colonel Hightower. First, he was refused an appointment with General Bernard. He could not understand how a man who was so anxious to have a report every day could refuse to see him. Hightower clearly remembered having proposed a daily meeting and the general agreeing. Then, as he checked on the two one-star generals, he found out that one did not exist—he was nowhere on any army record, and he was not even on any of the official results of the generals promotion boards—and the other one had actually been visiting the NATO military headquarters at Mons, Belgium, on the date when he was supposed to be at the White House. The protocol office at SHAPE was adamant the general had spent the entire day in SACEUR's offices. As for the colonels, they as well did not exist on unclassified army records, and since Colonel Hightower had no 'need to know', he was denied access to their whereabouts. It was a fact that despite his great field and staff experience, Colonel Hightower's disdain for black operations had prevented him from truly learning about them, and particularly gaining access to individuals who would talk to him 'off the record'. He was approaching the current problem with a naïveté that would have caused General Bernard to laugh at him. But the conclusion of his research was obvious: the only person that he could ascertain had actually visited the White House was indeed General Bernard. Colonel Hightower also reflected on the fact that General Bernard had ordered an electronic sweep of his office to take place twice a month. This could only result in two things. First this sent a message to whoever was eavesdropping that the general knew they were listening in on him. Second, the sweep ensured that the bugs were active at all times because they needed to be replaced on a regular basis. Through this process, he had also learned that the alleged cleaning lady was working for Langley and was the one replacing the bugs. The reason he was keen on the bugs is that he could set up bogus meetings, feed disinformation to Langley, and also make sure that if a problem arose it would be shared with Langley without the need of a meeting. It was an old Soviet trick he had learned during his multiple visits to Moscow at the time of the Soviet Union. When you were in your hotel room, you only had to say that you were thirsty for a glass of whisky, and a few moments later, the babushka watching the floor would mysteriously appear with a glass of whisky. In the same manner, the general would mention a problem, and many times it would be solved without him having to call anyone. Colonel Hightower only understood this partially, because again, he had not embraced the way of Special Warfare. He failed to recognise that by assigning the inquiry to Colonel Hightower, and subsequently refusing to see him, General Bernard had clearly identified him as the problem to be solved. The general could only hope that 'the problem' would be solved quickly, because he knew that the colonel would figure out *he* was LICHI KLESH.

Two days after the last meeting between Eric and Charlie, the Metro section of the *Washington Post* ran the summary of a traffic accident in Arlington:

> A 42-year-old army colonel was killed in a four-vehicle crash on Virginia Route 27 in Arlington Thursday afternoon after the car he was riding in was rear-ended. The crash occurred just after 6:30 p.m. when an eastbound car stopped to make a left turn onto Columbia Parkway. It was struck from behind and pushed into westbound traffic where it was hit by a truck, said Captain Peter Hill of the Arlington Police Department. Two other cars, one eastbound and one westbound, ran off the road to avoid the collision, he said. The driver of the car, Colonel John Hightower, a highly decorated Army officer, was taken to the Virginia Hospital Center in Arlington where he was pronounced dead on arrival. Hill said a second occupant riding in the car with Colonel Hightower was injured in the crash. He was taken to Bethesda Naval Hospital for treatment. His medical status and name were not released. Colonel Hightower, a member of the Special Forces, had recently returned from a tour of duty in Afghanistan.

Colonel Hightower received a military funeral attended by General Bernard at Arlington Cemetery. At his funeral, he was decorated posthumously with the Legion of Merit. His wife and two children did their best to remain solemn, but when taps was played, the colonel's window sobbed uncontrollably into her sister's shoulder. At the same time, another colonel, who knew nothing of the events of these few days was doing his best not to meet Colonel Hightower's fate.

CHAPTER 14

Colonel Hightower had been a prudent man until his fatal accident on Virginia Route 27. It was almost unconceivable that he could have fallen victim to such a murder, if not for the disdain and underestimation he had borne for black programs. The truck driver had not even been found, after he had allegedly left the scene of an accident. Of course, the Virginia State Police had issued an APB (All-Points Bulletin), but Captain Hill had no illusion that he would be found. In his eyes, knowing the background of the victim, and the fact that the other passenger had been a Special Forces officer as well, he was of the opinion that it had been a murder rather than an accident. None of the other drivers had seen anything, and the witnesses could only describe the driver of the truck as Hispanic, 'probably Colombian' had stated one woman, although on which grounds she had made this remark could not be ascertained. Captain Hill's suspicions turned to the passenger of the car who had not been gravely injured, and who may have been there to ensure the colonel had actually died, maybe by preventing him from breathing while he was still under the shock of the accident. The autopsy had revealed no reason for death, as there were no grievous injuries, and no sign of a heart attack. The cause of death could only be determined as 'cessation of breathing'. However good the ambush had been, Colonel Hightower had documented the inquiry he had been conducting, and he had written down every single detail of his phone calls, conversations, and suspicions, not only since the beginning of the inquiry but since his assignment to the Special Warfare office, going back eighteen months into the past. The notes included a computer USB, several recordings of conversations, and an extensive set of written documents with places, events, and names of the people involved. Knowing that in the event 'something happened to him' whoever would be the recipient of these notes would be in danger, Colonel Hightower had racked his brain as to who should receive them. The first step had been to find a lawyer's office that could be trusted, and by trusted, he meant one that could not possibly be linked to Special Warfare, Special Operations, the CIA, or even the Pentagon. He had decided that such an office did not exist in the Washington DC area. Therefore, he had spent many hours vetting potential lawyers as far as possible from any military installation. Since he had access to classified files, he had also made sure that none of the lawyers had any military background and that they had never held a security clearance. He had settled on a small single-lawyer office operating out of a modest office on Main Street in Milroy, Pennsylvania. This was sure to avoid suspicions since Milroy was also the colonel's hometown. His instructions to the lawyer were clear, in case of his premature, violent, or suspicious death, these documents were to be handed over to the person on top of the list he had also provided. The list had three names, and if the first person on the list was no longer available, it had to go to the second one, and again, if this person was no longer available, it had to go to the third one. In case none were alive, then the package had to be sent anonymously to the offices of the *Washington Post*. Of course, the lawyer had no idea of what was in the documents which were delivered sealed and time-stamped. All payments for the service were in cash and in person, and no receipt was ever issued linking the colonel to the lawyer.

The colonel has spent months figuring out who should be the recipient of these secrets. Not only because he wanted them to be used wisely, but because their mere existence was proof that the colonel had violating the trust of his security clearance, and that this could lead to an inquiry after his death that would blemish his name and reputation. He had had to search all corners of the Pentagon to decide on three officers he could trust. The packages remained in the lawyer's office for several weeks after the colonel's death. It was only about two months after his passing that his widow, going through his papers, found a closed envelope addressed to her. Within it, was another envelope, preaddressed to the lawyer in Milroy, and a note:

> *'Cathy, if you find this envelope, it is because you have started sorting out my papers after my death. If my death was the result of a violent act, an unexplained event, a suspicious military event, or an assassination, mail the enclosed envelope to the addressee. Please ask no questions as it would endanger you and the children. The addressee knows what to do once he gets the instructions.'*

Cathy, the recently widowed army wife, had known from the start that her husband's death had been suspicious, but she could not pinpoint any fact, and could only harbour resentment at the army. In her curiosity, she decided to open the letter, but was disappointed to read a simple sentence, 'Please proceed as agreed', without even a signature. The signature was replaced by a single sentence, 'Speaking in confidence, for I should not like to have my words repeated.' She assumed it was a code that her husband had agreed to with the lawyer to show the authenticity of the instructions. Had she been a Plato scholar, like her late husband had been, she would have immediately identified this sentence as belonging to the dialogue between Glaucon and Socrates in Book X of the *Republic*. She typed another enveloped, put the letter in it, and mailed in a few moments later from the Arlington Post Office.

When the lawyer got the letter two days later, he was sorry to learn of the death of his client. He broke the seal of the envelope containing the list of three names and started the task of identifying the whereabouts of a certain Major Peter Edwards, who could be known under a different or different names, with a last known address and telephone number in Fayetteville, North Carolina. When the lawyer reached that number, the woman who answered acknowledged that Peter Edwards had lived there, but that they were now separated, that she had no idea where 'the bastard' had gone, and that she did not care! She let him know, however, that he was probably in DC, 'screwing his whore'. While the lawyer did not think that the second part of the sentence was very useful, at least he had a lead to the DC area. Not that it made his task any easier. Mrs Edwards seemed to be less than inclined in cooperating, and such sensitive material required personal delivery in the hands of this Peter Edwards. The lawyer wondered how he could possibly find the individual. And since it was quitting time by then, he decided to forget about his challenge by drinking a glass of 15-year-old Glenfiddich. Finding Peter could wait another day.

Eric had clearly put the events surrounding Colonel Hightower's death behind him. There was no way the Virginia State Police, however suspicious, could ever link the event to the CIA and to Charlie who had been perfect in disguising himself as a Hispanic truck driver. As for the passenger in the colonel's car, he had met the colonel for a meeting an hour earlier and had simply asked the officer for a ride down to Arlington, which the colonel had agreed to give him. It was the first time they had met, and since he, too, was an officer, albeit in the Marines, there again, the trail went nowhere. It was perfectly normal for officers to meet, discuss certain things out of the office, and move on. The marine officer had provided his meeting agenda, together with the notes of the meeting which were corroborated by the colonel's own notes and concerned themselves with the training of undercover operatives in South America, as it related to the War on Drugs. The marine officer had recently arrived at the Pentagon, returning from three years of operations in Colombia and Peru, and he was simply briefing the colonel on the multiple programs the US had started in these two countries and others. When Captain Hill of the State Police had asked why they had met off-site, the Marine had revealed they had done so at the colonel's request, because he had misplaced his Pentagon badge and had found it easier to relocate the meeting rather than going back home to find it. Of course, this had been an added twist into the fate of the colonel that day, since the badge had been taken by the cleaning lady when she had been cleaning the colonel's office earlier that day. Obviously, it had occurred to Eric that the colonel might have a secret file somewhere that was like a time bomb. He had therefore ordered a full analysis of the colonel private activities, going back five years, and none of the officers had been able to pinpoint any unusual event. They had noted the trips to Melroy, Pennsylvania, but since the colonel's parents lived there, and they happened at regular intervals during the weekends or at Thanksgiving time, the investigators had deducted the colonel was simply on a family visit. After receiving the results of the investigation, Eric felt secure that there was no time bomb. Nevertheless, he maintained his guard up, and Mrs Hightower's telephone was tapped, and a High Alert Notice (HAN) had been issued in conjunction with the name Hightower. Supported by the Echelon program, HAN was focusing on any traffic that included the name Hightower, whether on email, on Internet searches, or during phone conversations which were being monitored by the supercomputers operating deep in underground bunkers at Fort Meade.

While Eric was feeling more confident with every passing day that nothing would come from the Hightower case. That was until he got a transcript from a phone call. It stated that the voice had been altered—a picture came through his mind of Schwarzenegger speaking with an altered voice in *True Lies*, and he wondered if the voice of the caller had sounded like that.

'General Bernard?'

'Speaking.'

'I have documents about you and LICHI KLESH.'

'I have no idea what you are talking about.'

'Yes, you do!'

'Fuck you!'

And the general had apparently hung up on the call. Eric was fuming that the general had been so stupid as to use foul language and hanging up on the caller. These actions showed beyond the shadow of a doubt that the general admitted knowing about LICHI KLESH. 'What a bloody idiot!' Eric thought. Now the caller would be even more aggressive. Eric also knew in a flash that the caller had to be related to Hightower. That bastard had probably stashed a file somewhere and it only came to light now, over two months after his death. The HAN had failed to produce any result, so the contacts had to have never mentioned the name of Hightower, or if they did, they used face-to-face meetings and the US Mail, the only two truly secure means of communication in the cyber world. The effort would now have to be on identifying the caller. As in every series B thriller, he had used a public phone, and although it put him square on Madison Drive in Washington DC, the avenue in front of the museums was one of the busiest in the city and attempts to find a witness to the call would be futile. Nevertheless, Eric called up a task force to try to minimise the damage that the series of calls—as he was sure there would be more—could do to operations. There had to be a link between Hightower and the caller. Eric asked that all people who had ever had any connection, however tenuous, with Hightower be identified. It was a huge task. Jérome, a former Quebec resident and a long-time member of Eric's staff remarked: 'Unless the caller was picked entirely at random. If I had been in Hightower's shoes, knowing that you would do exactly that—going through every person I had ever even talked to – I would have picked a completely random individual.'

'Keep going, Eric encouraged him.'

First, I would have made sure that no information would be passed to anyone who had had anything to do with me. Second, I would have gone through the list of SF and Special Warfare officers, who, although not linked to me, had either a key interest in getting to the bottom of the Algeria fiasco, or, had a personal axe to grind with Bernard. Now, the information had to be stored someplace. This is the second part of the equation: where was it stored, with whom, and what protocol was followed to send the information.

'You are so right!' commented Eric. 'Forget about looking for a person linked to Hightower! But who would this officer be?'

'I think we don't need to look very far from the apple tree,' added Jerome. 'There is one officer who meets both criteria. . .' Jerome did not have the time to end the sentence, as Eric interjected: 'Of course! The guy in Morocco! By now, he knows he and his partner were betrayed and he wants to know why and by whom. If he received Hightower's info, then, he knows by whom. The question is "what do we do?"'

'In my opinion,' Jerome was already talking, so he continued, 'we should help him. Frankly, when you look at it, Bernard is an embarrassment. How he managed to get three stars is beyond me. The guy's mind is pickled. He gets wasted almost every night, he gets in bar fights at the drop of a hat, he sleeps with every call girl in DC and Northern Virginia, and I would not be surprised if he did drugs as well. If he weren't the cousin of the Speaker of the House, he would have been fired a long time ago. But, I transgress to personal matters here. On the professional side, we have had suspicions that some of the money he spends so liberally did not come from his monthly salary. Granted, a three-star makes about $10,000 a month, but when you spend $1,500 a night on a call girl, the math is not that difficult to figure out he is on the take from someone. So, we had his accounts examined. As you all know, his salary is $13,575 per month. Yet, over the past month, he has had eight visits with call girls, with a minimum tab of $1,500 each, which makes it $12,000. Then he had his Ferrari 456 GT services, and that bill was $4,229, which put him in the red by almost three grand. That was before the anniversary party for General Foley at the Palm, where he spent another $8,734, and the meals at various restaurants in town. Then, Mike and I went through his accounts. The credit cards show a level of expenditure similar to this every month. Yet, the payments do not come from his own accounts, because, believe it or not, he has not touched his checking account in over a year, and he has slightly over 160 grand in it. Savings account is the same: over seventy grand. Mike and I checked everything, and we are certain, he has no revenue from anywhere else. SO, who pays his expenses? The payment is on an automatic debit from an account at the Royal Bank of Canada in Port Lucaya. The RBC has refused to grant us access to the data on the account paying the bill. However, we traced the funds via Echelon, and we can say without the shadow of a doubt that the money is coming from Saudi Arabia. So, our conclusions are that the general is a major security risk who has been betraying the United States for at least two years. If our guy knows this, considering that he has already disposed of basically a dozen people and that his partner was killed, I would not bet on the general's longevity.'

'Excellent,' continued Eric. This is far more than I expected in such a short time. Bravo Jerome! So, we have a basic decision, yet again here. Since General Bernard is in such trouble, we have three options: one, use the information to blackmail him; two, let the guy do the dirty work for us—assuming this is what he intends to do; and three, help him. What do you gentlemen think?'

There were four people attending the meeting, and the conversation was rather animated between all four. Finally, a consensus was reached that the general had gone past the limits of acceptable risk and that he should be pushed out of his position. Eric asked for proposals, and once again, Jerome came to the rescue.

This is how an ambitious reporter working at the Washington Daily came to receive anonymous information regarding the military career and the associated medals General Bernard was displaying on his uniform. The lengthy explanation that had arrived in Gerry Billings' inbox was that the general was wearing enhancing devices, a 'V' for valour on his Army Commendation Medal and Army Achievement Medal ribbons when wearing his Class A uniform. Since he was sure that the reporter had no idea what the medals were and what a V for Valour was, the note went into detailed explanations of all. 'The Army Commendation Medal is a mid-level decoration, which is presented for sustained acts of heroism or meritorious service. For valorous actions in direct contact with an enemy force, but of a lesser degree than required for the award of other decorations such as the Bronze Star, the V device may be authorised as an attachment to the decoration,' the note read. 'As for the Army Achievement Medal,' the letter continued, 'it is a military decoration that is a means to recognise the contributions of junior officers and enlisted personnel who are not eligible to receive the higher Army Commendation Medal. No V device is associated with this medal.' At first, Gerry failed to grasp the significance of the information and wondered who would care about it. Yet, the note was explicit in stating that 'the general was wearing these V devices without proper authorisation and certainly without any associated documentation and that he was a fraud. Such information should be made public as we cannot allow a general who has daily and unrestrained access to the president to be what amounts to a liar.' Gerry half-heartedly briefed the editor about the article he was planning to write, and to his astonishment, the woman had exclaimed, 'This is dynamite! This asshole Bernard has it coming, one way or the other! This is brilliant stuff!' Surprised at the unusual expletive, Gerry produced a compelling piece. Three days later, on its Wednesday edition which was the one with the greatest distribution, the discredit campaign started. This was particularly easy, because the reporter had also found out that the unmarried Bernard had a massive alcohol problem and that he had employed the services of call girls even while the head of one of the most secretive organisations in the military establishment. It was reported that in addition to wearing illegal decorations, less than a month before, the general had been thrown out of the Willard Hotel bar a few yards from the White House, after he had started two fights. He had later been found sprawled out on the sidewalk on H Street with a head injury that had required seven stitches. Everything had been kept under wraps, yet this would have been cause enough for a junior officer to lose his security clearance. Particularly since the general had no independent recollection of being thrown out of the Willard—a few days later, he could not understand why he was denied access to the same bar—and he certainly had no idea how he had ended up on H Street or how he had gotten the head injury. While the call girls were after all a private matter, nothing that concerned the Chief of Special Warfare was private. Employing call girls was a security risk, especially when combined with the ethylic comas that the general experienced on a regular basis. The two were a deadly mixture for the operatives in the field. The same day as the article came out, the chief of staff of the army convoked General Bernard to his office to ensure he understood the seriousness of the accusations and that he had to take hold of himself. However, the chief of staff was far more concerned with the display of unauthorised decorations, and he started his own investigation in the matter. General Bernard naturally denied any wrongdoing and explained that just like everyone else, he liked to let off a little steam during the weekend. As for the call girls, he could not see the problem, since he was not married, had always been discreet and courteous to them.

A few days after the article publication, the general was seating in his office, daydreaming about what could have been, and how his position had become so vulnerable within the matter of two weeks. If the reporters were suddenly interested in what he was wearing on his ribbons, they were sure to dig much deeper, and find him out. There was no way he could cover his tracks. He was lucid enough to know that driven by his excesses with women and alcohol, he had been completely careless and had made no effort to even pretend he was not receiving contributions from abroad. However, he rationalised that in a sense he had done it for the United States. Through his efforts, there was a balance of power in Algeria, with the Front Islamique making no progress, the government of President Ben Buraddi being reinforced through a couple of successful military operations for which he, General Bernard, had provided the key, until this one operation had flopped. Only now they told him that that Major Power was the gold medal holder in competitive shooting! Who ever heard of sending such a man on a mission! Why not fucking Superman while they were at it? And the other imbeciles had sent a fucking Renault with stupid motherfuckers to take him out? Why not send a fucking grandmother? And when they had him cornered, when they had sent helicopters, a company of infantry, and a reconnaissance plane, he had been able to outsmart them and escape! Some people are beyond help. He came back to the reality, and now, he was the one who was beyond help. He was one move away to be checkmated. There really was no way out of it. The telephone rang. It was the same disguised voice.

'I know all about your accounts. I know where the money is coming from.'

But this time, the caller had hung up, not even interested in having further explanations, discussions, or expressing demands. His game was up. He considered the options. The easiest option was to resign from the army immediately and move overseas in an undisclosed location, and hope for the best. This one was viable until *he* found him again. And the general knew that this Major Power, or whoever he was, would never stop looking for him. He would also lose everything he owned. The next option was to do nothing, to let the course of the investigation that was sure to follow take place, and face the music whenever it started playing. But, when he was discovered, he would face years in jail at Leavenworth, and most likely, he would receive a life sentence. Not an option really. Of course, there was the final option. . . He could pretend that the news of his improperly wearing decorations had distraught him so much that he felt he could no longer face the soldiers of his army after such a lie. He was looking at his three options and could not find another one. He was jolted out of his reverie by the telephone. He would never leave him alone now. . .

'I hope you sleep well at night. In the meantime, meet me tomorrow at 4:00 p.m. at 38°43'27.60N 77°02'32.01'W. Be there.'

He barely had time to copy down the numbers, and the phone went dead. Like he was going to be. A fucking major ordering a three-star around like he was a domestique! His world had come to an end. He would have to opt for the last option. Two days on, the Washington Daily ran a front page article.

Commander, Special Warfare Found Dead!

WASHINGTON—One of the nation's most senior army generals, Lieutenant General George T. Bernard, died Friday from an apparent self-inflicted gunshot wound. The general had learned through the Washington Daily that questions were being raised about his integrity related to his improper wearing of decorations on his uniform and official photo. The Washington Daily has learned from the Special Warfare Command that Bernard wrote a suicide note.

Sources said that in the handwritten note address to the soldiers, Bernard stated that he had decided to commit suicide because of the questions raised about his wearing of 'V' for valour medals on his ribbons. Army officials decided that they would not release the letter although it is address to the soldiers. 'The army considers suicide to be a private matter, and therefore will not make any documents public following the suicide of any service member' declared a Pentagon spokesman.

A US Army official who had met with Bernard in the days prior to his death indicated that the general was deeply concerned about the impropriety that had surfaced in newspapers around the country, and that he felt it undermined his ability to lead soldiers.

General Bernard, a veteran of over 28 years of military service was the commander of a special warfare organisation. His lifeless body was discovered at a rest stop on the George Washington Memorial Highway, on the Potomac River, a few miles south from his office. He was transported to the Hybla Valley Trauma Center. An emergency room surgeon said Bernard was already dead when he arrived at the facility at 4:45 p.m. EDT. The only thing that the surgeon could do was confirm the general's death.

The Washington Daily had published a story that called into question two medals Bernard had received during his career. The paper had uncovered evidence that Bernard for the better part of his career had inappropriately displayed 'V' for valour on the medals in question.

According to a source who has seen Bernard's note to the soldiers, Bernard wrote that he wore the Vs because he thought he was entitled to them.

Brigadier General O'Hara, who had met Bernard two days prior to his death, said he had informed Bernard of a formal inquiry that had been directed by the chief of staff of the army on the medals incident.

'General Bernard was very depressed by the news,' said O'Hara.

The army would not confirm that Bernard's wound was self-inflicted. 'General Bernard occupied a very sensitive position, and we will not comment on the circumstances of his death,' said O'Gara. Army Secretary

John Mitchell said the Mount Vernon police was investigating Bernard's death. Earlier, a Pentagon official had stated it was definitely a suicide. According to sources familiar with the investigation, a 357 was used in the shooting. It apparently belonged to the general.

The president expressed his deep sadness about Bernard's untimely death, stated that he had served the country in an exemplary manner for the better part of thirty years.

The Virginia Police concluded that Bernard had shot himself in the heart. The autopsy report was obviously not released. The Pentagon issued a simple statement that the inquiry about General Bernard's alleged unauthorised wearing of decorations had been closed. In his office, Eric conducted a debrief of the operation, still not sure whether Bernard had actually shot himself or had been shot. Charlie had been at the scene, but the general had walked down to the river in a place where he could not be observed, and the shot had been fired after the person who had told him to show up had arrived. So he was pretty sure that the general had been assisted in his suicide, while Jerome thought that the 'shit he had discovered would have been enough for anyone to commit suicide'. Whatever the truth, and Eric was not going to investigate them any further, the problem was solved.

'Gentlemen, we can safely state that we have eliminated a security risk. People make choices and they have to live and die by them. We have verified all the information, and General Bernard had been receiving payments from Saudi Arabia for three years. I personally debriefed POTUS late last night, and he ordered an investigation of generals and admirals on the payroll. I thank you for your good work on this one, and wish you a good rest of the day. For now, the operation in Algeria was safe.'

CHAPTER 15

Max woke up suddenly. Night had already fallen. He had slept soundly after taking a hot shower and, even if for a few hours. He remembered why he was there. He had decided that the authorities knew of any room that had been reserved for him and that he could not spend a night there. He also had decided that any car provided by the embassy, however careful his colleagues were, was equipped with a tracking device. He went to the hotel shop and bought a map of Morocco. Then he proceeded to start his social engineering operation. He went to the front door of the hotel and observed the valets' comings and goings. He got close enough to see which car was keys were tagged with which registry number. He identified cars that were arriving with suitcases—there were not that many—and he decided on a Renault that arrived with a single man who looked like a salesman. He saw that he was given ticket 0976. He followed him discreetly to the reception and stayed far enough away to hear his name, and to hear which room he was being assigned. He registered everything, and went for a meal. It was in the same dining room that Colonel Andrews was having dinner with his Moroccan girlfriend. Max immediately noticed the North African beauty of the woman, and when he walked by the table, he also heard that the man had an American accent and that he was wearing a West Point ring. Max knew there would be no more than three army officers at the embassy, so there was a 33% chance the man was Colonel Andrews. Max walked passed swiftly, not wanting to make contact with him when a third party was present. Actually, he did not want to make contact with him at all, because anything he said would put him at risk. Instead, he made a long detour through the back of the restaurant, went back to his room, and ordered room service. It was better to think in any case. He had to get out of the freaking place, but he could not do it by plane or via Tangiers, it was simply too risky. He had to find a place to commandeer a boat and get to Spain. He decided that his best option would be to go through Ceuta. If he made it there, it was only sixteen miles to Gibraltar. He could take the ferry, although he knew he would not be in control as the ferry had to go back into Moroccan territorial waters, and he would be like a sitting duck in case the Moroccans decided to board it. He thought that he had a far better chance by going to the Ceuta marina and finding a fishing boat that would accept to take him straight to Gibraltar, or better to Spain.

The alarm clock rang early although Max did not have that far to go, only about 190 miles, but he wanted to ensure he did not meet anybody who might identify him. With the hat, the sunglasses, and his unshaven look, it was probably safer than he had been a few days earlier. For a moment, he forgot that the entire Moroccan police force was looking for him. Then he realised he had put himself into an inextricable situation. He felt discouragement take him over and he had to meditate before he found again the motivation to move. He was exhausted by the stress, still suffered from the ordeal in the desert, and he dreamt of a soft bed where he could sleep without worrying about his safety, where he would have regained the peace that had been with him before he had stepped into the C-130. But there was no going back, these days were gone forever. He hated the cliché, but it was his Pandora's Box. He felt drained. It was five in the morning and he was more tired than he had felt when he had gone to bed. He dragged himself to the shower, thinking that the hot water would wake him up, but if it did he did not notice. He needed to be sharp, to be on his guards, but this morning, nothing clicked. He thought it would get better later. He dressed and went to use the vanity phone in the hallway, where he dialled the reception, asking for his car to be brought up by the valet—he gave the number of his so-called ticket stub 0976 and went to sit down in one of the armchairs, to give plenty of time to the valet to fetch 'his' car. He waited fifteen minutes and took the elevator down. The Renault was waiting. And so was the valet for the ticket stub. Max figured there was no valet who would not accept the explanation that Max had forgotten the stub in his room, especially if the explanation was accompanied with the usual tip. But this valet must have gotten up from the wrong side of the bed, as he demanded to see the stub or he would not release the car. Max tried to reason with him, to no avail. Fortunately, it was early in the morning and no one was around. After two or three minutes, the valet still was no budging. He was as stubborn as a mule. Max walked to the driver's side of the car, so that the next scene could take place at least partly concealed from the hotel reception. The valet followed him. Max turned around suddenly and struck the diminutive valet with such force and power into the stomach that the valet folded in half on the ground trying to catch his breath. No sound was coming out of him except the noise of his lungs gasping for air. Max opened the trunk, shoved him in it, and drove off. The hotel will think that the valet had either stolen a car or had gone off the job. Max was amused that he would lose his job regardless. He cursed himself for not thinking of taking the small booze bottles from the room bar. He could have forced the valet to drink them, put him behind the wheel, and abandoned the car on the side of the road. He still could do it. . . He took the N6 but the valet started banging with all his might on the body of the car, while yelling at the top of his lungs that he was being kidnapped. Max had to stop the car. He turned around and told the terrified valet that he was a serial killer—this was true actually, thought Max—and that if did not shut the fuck

THE DATURA SOLUTION

up, he would be the next victim. With peace restored, Max took the A1 in the direction of Kénitra. It was still early and there was little traffic. Max had been re-energised by the incident with the valet, and he drove exactly within the speed limit. At Kénitra, he obliqued to the Northeast in the direction of Souk el Arba du Rharb. About halfway there, the warned the valet to be quiet 'if he knew what was good for him' and he stopped at a coffee vendor for a cup of the thick Moroccan coffee, he relieved himself and drove on. He took the N13 to Ouazzane, making sure he avoided the Autoroutes which were patrolled by the police. By eleven in the morning, he was in Tétouan, and he figured it was time to abandon the car. He was twenty-five miles from Ceuta. He finally found a convenience store that was open, bought a litre of vodka, and drove into the isolated Meruda Ruins. He opened the trunk, put a gun to the head of the valet and told him to drink the vodka. The valet hesitated, but when Max cocked the pistol, he drank as fast as was humanly possible. Then, he helped behind the wheel and told him not to move. It was not a difficult task since the vodka acted rather quickly on the small man. By the time Max was ready to go, the valet has passed out behind the wheel. Max threw the keys into the Tétouan River as he walked across the N2 bridge. Max walked to the bus station and he took the bus to Ceuta. While he was waiting for the bus, Max slid the hat over his face and pretended to be sleeping. At 1:45, he boarded the bus, took the last seat in the rear right corner, and again pretended to be sleeping. He had kept the weapons with him and wondered how he was going to get through the Spanish border at Ceuta. At the border, the bus stopped and the officials of customs inspected passports, checking almost every bag as they walked through the bus. While he had been pretending to sleep, Max had been very busy digging a cache for his weapons under the soft cushion of the bus seat. When the official asked for his passport and his bag, Max presented Monsieur Dupont's passport and a bag containing two changes of clothes. Satisfied, the official walked out of the bus. At the same time, the Moroccan police was issuing an alert for a stolen Renault and APB for the valet. The warrant for Monsieur Dupont's arrest had gone out a few minutes earlier.

When the custom official went back to his office, his captain showed him the picture they had received from Morocco and asked him if any of the people of the bus matched the photo. The official remembered the man with the hat, took his time to consider the photo, and after about thirty seconds, declared that the guy might have been on the bus. The thirty seconds of hesitation were enough for Max to pick up his weapons, put them in his bag, stagger to the front of the bus, pretend he was ready to vomit, and ask the driver to do an emergency stop. The driver obliged and the bus took off. As soon as the bus was out of site, Max started walking rapidly towards Prince Alfonso, while taking his hat off and changing into a different jacket. He was already a different person that the one who had been in the bus. He found a vagrant walking in the opposite direction, and he gave him the hat and the jacket he had just taken off. . . The decoy worked, and once again, Max's escape had been so well timed, he could hardly believe it. He saw the white and green cars of the Guardia Civil rush the poor man and take him into custody. Max was halfway up the hill already, intent on finding a place for the night before crossing over into Spain the following day. From there, he could get to a safe house he had set up in Southern France. He walked the two and a half miles to the Ulysses Hotel, Calle de Caloens, while enjoying the sight of the Portuguese fortress. As he walked he was leery of any police or suspicious activity. He would have liked to stroll down the road with Chantal, really enjoying the sights, but as he kept alert, he could not even think of her or her love. He was a hunted man, and he could ill afford to let his guard down to have emotions about the one he loved so dearly. She would understand. And the worst part was that he could not even call her without either revealing his position or putting her in danger. He was in a city where people were happy, had wives to go home to, had friends, and lived normal lives. He could not even think about his wife as he was scared that the

THE DATURA SOLUTION

mere thought of her embrace would distract him so much as to cost him his life or his freedom. He would be safe only once he was back in the United States.

At the embassy, the heat had subsided now that it was pretty clear the guy had managed to slip out of Morocco and into Spanish territory. Now, instead, it had passed on to Spain. The ambassador was not keen on having the guy in Spain and feared the moment he had to go explain to the prime minister. In any case, since there was nothing the embassy would do, could do, or was required to do, there was not much chance of this thing bubbling up to the surface. The ambassador to Spain also had some important business connections and interests to protect. Although he was not as bold as his colleague in Morocco, his wife the marvellous Elena Danielova had used her personal connections shamelessly to increase the volume of her personal fortune which was already enormous since her former husband Oleksandr Krasnaief had died in the hands of her current husband, a fact she still ignored. Elena had inherited the entire empire, but at first, she had made the decision to have a triumvirate of Oleksandr's former associates run it rather than jeopardising it to her ignorance of business matters. But, day by day, she had learned more about it, and now, almost four years after her former husband's death, she had an active part in running it. At this stage of her life, it was estimated that the empire had grown to a massive $31 billion, a third of it acquired after she had taken over the conglomerate. She was now 29 years old, and her business savvy was now as dangerous as her beauty was remarkable. In the two years they had been in Spain, she had bought and sold hotels, developments, housing, luxury villas, and she had become the leading real estate tycoon of Spain. She was now developing a luxury apartment and hotel complex in Sotogrande. She had financed the entire venture with 500 million euros from funds she had borrowed at advantageous rates from the Santander Bank, and it was rumoured that all of the apartments had been sold out for four times the initial investment. Outside of her marriage, Mrs Elena McMillan was a happy woman, who was being chauffeured to her business meetings in a charcoal armoured Rolls Royce Phantom.

    Max was starving by the time he finally managed to get his room. He would not go out unless he had to, so once again he ordered room service. He watched the news, but he had now slipped off the radar screen, and there was no mention of him either on the Moroccan TV or on the Spanish one. The Moroccans did not want to bring him up, or they would have to admit that one man had outsmarted their police after killing two men in Rabat, and the Spaniards certainly did not want to accept that they had let him enter the country undetected. In Rabat, Colonel Andrews admired the masterful way in which the guy had escaped the Moroccan police. In Langley, Eric was satisfied that the guy was out of Morocco, but he was not sure how to handle matters now. He had heard nothing more from General Kelly's office, so in one sense this was good. And he had no reason to take any further action. Let the guy blend back in, he had served his country well and Eric's purposes even better. He wishes he knew his identity, because he certainly could have used him again.

    Max did not sleep well. He was too weary of being discovered, so he spent the entire night coming in and out of sleep. It reminded him of the time when he had been on guard duty in Angola in his first operation as a lieutenant. There was no way to stay awake, and yet, there was no way to fall asleep, so the brain navigated in a sort of comatose no man's land that it could not really control. It was a loss of consciousness and yet the brain remained conscious enough to distinguish the abnormal cracking of a twig, or the slosh of water in a canteen hanging on the belt of a careless soldier, and in an instant, the brain was wide-awake commanding the index finger to push the button that triggered the silent alarm system that alerted them of the danger, while at the same time switching the right index turned on the night vision scope on the rifle, finding the target in bright green on the forest background. And then squeezing the well-oiled trigger, releasing a bullet muffled by the silencer, and watching the silhouette collapse and gradually lose the brightness of its green as life seeped out of him, and then go back to the comatose state again and keeping the team alive. The sun never came early enough, and that day in Ceuta, Max felt the same way—it had not come fast enough. He was tired. He ordered breakfast and turned the TV on. He found out that a reward had been set for the capture of his alter ego Monsieur Lefort. He checked his weapons, picked up his bag, and left the room. He walked to the Marina and found a fishing boat to be chartered. It was November, so the captain was glad to take on a customer. However, the captain became a lot less cooperative when Max told him he needed a passage to continental Spain. Only after Max had increased the fee to a thousand dollars did the captain agree to a passage. It was a thirty-mile ride, but it was a ride to a safe house. At about eight thirty, the forty-seven footer left the harbour, due north for the coast of Spain. Max kept an eye on the captain. He was certain that he was going to try something to get the $20,000 reward. When the captain went down into the boat, Max followed him silently after having pocketed the Glock. The captain was calling the Spanish Coast Guard (CG). Max told him, 'I know what the fuck you are doing. Hang up!' The Captain disregarded Max and kept trying to raise the CG. Max pulled the Glock and chambered a round. At the sound of the slide rebounding into place, the captain dropped the mike and lunged for Max. The man was far heavier than Max, and in the confines of the galley, he had the momentum, immobilising Max and trying to get the pistol. Max worked his left hand free and as the man focused on grabbing the Glock from him, Max reached for his testicles and pulled them out backward in a jerking movement. The captain immediately released his grip while shouting 'Shit'! Max took advantage of the momentous hesitation and hit the man in the face with the pistol, but pain was not to stop the main desire to get the reward money, neither did the threat of the pistol. Recovering quickly, the man charged like a bull at Max. Max did not hesitate and released a round into the

Captain's right leg. 'What the fuck' yelled the Captain, 'why the fuck did you shoot me? You son of a bitch!' Max simply answered, 'If you want to live just take me to fucking Spain and shut the fuck up! Get topside and do the fucking job I paid you to do! IF you don't get me to the Spanish Coast in thirty fucking minutes, you fucking die! You go it, dumb shit?' The captain obeyed and there were no more incidents despite the profuse bleeding that was coming out of the pants leg. Max knew he should do something about it, but he simply did not care. If the man was to die, it was his destiny, and Max was tired of interfering. He was completely indifferent to the fate of the fat man seating in the captain's chair. The man reeked of unhealthy sweat and Max was still infected by his repulsive body odour. The fucker might as well die, he stank too much, and now Max's clothes smelled like him. Fuck! A few moments later, as they approached the Spanish coast, the Captain leaned over to the right against the railing, and as the boat hit a bigger wave, the man was bumped out of the chair, slid down the side of the boat, and fell in the water. That's a new one on me, thought Max. He got up, went to the controls, turned the boat around, and doubled back to the body that was floating face down in the water. It was clear that the man was dead. Max made no effort to retrieve him, and piloted the boat as close to the coast he could. He did not want to beach it, nor did he want to have to swim, but the thought that if he came too close to the beach, the boat would end up on it anyhow. So he put on more gas and beached it on the deserted beach. He took his bag, jumped out, and made his way to the road. Luckily, he saw a sign for Sotogrande and he started walking towards the town which he knew nothing about. As he was already engaged on the bridge over the Rio Guadario, he was caught in an accident that had taken place at the other end. He accelerated his pace so that he could clear it before the cops arrived. He was halfway across when a charcoal Rolls Royce passed him. The car came to a halt because of the obstacle to the flow of traffic. A man came out from the accident scene and went to the driver's door. Since Max had been walking on the left side of the road facing traffic, he had a clear view of what was going on. Immediately, he thought something was suspicious. He reached into his bag and pulled the Glock out. Almost at the same time, the man standing outside the car put his hand inside the window of the car, which the driver had rolled down, and he pulled him halfway out. When the driver's head had cleared the car, the man pulled a gun and shot him. Max knelt down, took aim, and shot the assailant—he knew it was a carjacking or a kidnapping. He was not one to get involved in other people's business, but he could not remain indifferent to the scene. Another man came from behind the accident and tried to get into the Rolls. By that time, Max was so close, he did not even need to aim carefully. One bullet, and the man was down. Max cautiously approached the scene—he did not want to be shot while minding someone else's business. The day was not going well at all—it was barely noon, he had had to shoot three people, hit left shoulder plate was killing him because of the assault of the other cretin, and now the only thing he needed was to be shot. He made sure the pistols were out of reach of the two guys he had shot. He saw a third one drive away in a Mercedes S Class. He pulled the driver completely out of the door of the Rolls, opened it, and saw a beautiful woman cowering in the back seat. He lowered the glass partition.

'If you have to kill me, don't make me suffer, one bullet in the back of the head.' The words pronounced with a distinct Russian accent were flowing out of tow beautiful lips with the harmony of a Prokofiev melody.

'I am not here to kill you. I don't even know who you are! I am a commando from the US Army who just happened to be passing by. We need to get out of here quickly! Where were you going?'

'Never mind where I was going!' she answered. 'Take me back to Madrid, I am the wife of the US Ambassador.'

Max did a U-turn, and leaving all the casualties where they were lying on the road, he started back towards Malaga. But this was without taking account Elena's business acumen. Hesitantly she asked, 'Can you keep quiet about these dreadful people, darling?'

'Of course, I can. Don't worry about that!'

'Then, take me to my business meeting in Sotogrande. You'll wait for me, won't you?'

'Yes, I'll wait for you.'

And Elena called the ambassador's office so that he could make that little mess go away on the bridge to Sotogrande. Which of course he would, since his wife was under diplomatic immunity, and so was now Max!

After that, everything passed in from of Max's eyes as if in a dream. He fully grasped the meaning of Descartes's third maxim that we need to 'accustom ourselves to the persuasion that, except our own thoughts, there is nothing absolutely in our power.' Max lost complete control of the situation, and he seemed powerless to stop an act that could only make his situation worse. Of course, the events of the past few days had already changed him in a way he could not possibly yet understand. Later, he would never be able to figure out whether Lena had drugged him, bewitched him, or of he was just so exhausted mentally or physically that he could no longer say no, tell right from wrong, or simply decide what he wanted to do. Max realised he was facing the dangerous daughter of Helios—a woman who was now in charge of his life, and he did not feel like fighting at all. After her meeting, she sat next to Max in the front of the car and she casually asked him to drive her to her hotel. There, she invited him to go to the restaurant, and from the very beginning, max figured she intended him to spend the night with her. She first ordered a bottle of Dom Pérignon to celebrate the success of her business transactions. Then they had dinner—it had already been prepared according to her desires, and as he was to find out, every dinner with her included Malossol Caviar—talking about the day's event, and what they did in general. Max tried to keep it vague, but she very quickly understood he was in fact this Monsieur Lefort that everybody was looking for.

'Am I in mortal danger?' she joked.

But she shuddered as well at the thought that the man she was in the process of seducing had killed two people in front of her very eyes. Yet her thoughts were somewhere else as well. Was she falling in love with him, or was it simply the lust of the female for the alpha male? Because if she had ever met an alpha male, Max was it! Her first husband was simply a violent brute, not a leader, not an alpha male, and her current husband . . . he was as far from the alpha male as the earth is from the Andromeda galaxy—light years away. She had no respect for either of the two, and she had never loved them. Both had been marriages that had advanced her life: the first one had brought more money she could possibly spend in a lifetime, and the other one had brought her the US citizenship and the diplomatic immunity of an ambassador's wife. As the evening went on, with the assistance of two bottles of Marques de Vargas Rioja, they became more and more intimate, and closer and closer physically. Max could not control his erection, and she did not hesitate to feel it through his pants. After dinner, they had a couple of shots of vodka 'to guard against the headache the wine could give us', she told Max. They naturally had their hands on each other's thighs, and they kissed passionately as they waited for the elevator. In between kisses, she told him 'you are safe with me, I will never betray you!' And from the way she said it, looking straight into his eyes, Max could read the intensity of her thoughts and knew he could trust her. He also knew that at that moment she had fallen in love with him, and the words she had pronounced were more powerful and meaningful than the banality of a mere love declaration. By the time they got to her penthouse, she had already taken her panties off, and almost had experienced an orgasm as Max had simply caressed her between the legs. This touch, this gentle movement of his finger in the soft wetness of her intimacy, this burgeoning pleasure that was going to become so intense over the course of the evening and the night, this simple gesture that could have been a one off—had they been different people, had they not been Max and Lena—this incredible discovery between these two extraordinary human beings, this very instant that lasted a few tens of seconds changed their lives forever.

CHAPTER 16

Max reported as instructed at 0900 hours at the office of Colonel Perkins in the classified location that was the legal branch of the Special Programs that were run around the world at different times. The nondescript building in one of the new commercial developments in the Chantilly area seemed innocuous enough, but as soon as Max walked in to report, he instantly realised that the interview would be anything but routine. Colonel Perkins sat in a standard nondescript disinfected office, with the obligatory nature scene print on the wall, the heavy mahogany desk, quilted leather armchairs, and the overshiny coffee table on which were thrown copies of the *Washington Post* and the *New York Times*. The officer certainly did not maintain any military bearing: he had dishevelled long hair, wore an ill-fitting suit, and was clearly overweight. He contrasted to the point of clashing with Max who was incredibly fit, tanned, wore a new suit purchased and fitted at Joseph A. Banks, and had a very short airborne-style haircut. Max took an instant dislike for him, and his slovenly fat and sweaty hands disgusted him. Max hoped he would never have to touch him and wondered how any woman could ever get intimate with what he considered a repulsive man. There were no credentials on the walls, and the desk was bare except for a yellow legal pad and a K-Mart ballpoint pen. Max saluted and stated, 'Major Russ Kent, reporting as ordered!' Max used his LICHI KLESS assigned army ID alias to hide and protect his real identity.

The colonel's reaction was one of surprise and immediate disdain: 'Cut that soldier crap, major! I don't need to listen to this bullshit, keep it for your retarded friends in the Special Forces!'

Instantly, Max lost his temper: 'Then, fuck you, *Colonel*, and have a good day!' Max responded, and he turned around and grabbed the door knob.

'The charges against you are murder, it's up to you to leave. . .' the lawyer remarked.

This got Max's attention and also calmed the colonel down:

'Sit down. You are being investigated for the events that happened on or about 15 October in Algeria. The army would like to know how a US Army major and four members of the Gendarmerie were killed in an operation that had no rules of engagement against members of a foreign nation's military forces. Further, the widow of Major Steve Uvenshko (the colonel mispronounced his name), who we believe was your operation's partner, has stated that you and her had had a romantic liaison and that you took this opportunity to kill her husband because she had refused to divorce him. So, you see that this so-called black operation has made its way into the crime pages of the paper. . .'

'Let me tell you something, Colonel. First of all, at no time in my life have I ever been in Algeria. Second, I have no idea who Major Yuvensho (Max purposely mispronounced the name as if he had heard it for the first time) is, and third, I never met his wife or obviously had an affair with her. Furthermore, according to US law, even if your allegations were true, which they are not, you could not prosecute anyone for a crime committed in a location where US law has no jurisdiction. Finally, and I know where you are going with this, this does not fall under a war crimes event because the conditions are simply not present. You see, Colonel, you know nothing about me, and you think that you are going to have me shake in my Bostonians by barking at me like some junkyard bulldog, but I have studied law as well. Just as a reminder, a war crime implies that a violation was committed against the adherence of the laws of war, that there was a failure to adhere to the norms of procedure and to the rules of battle, such as attacking those displaying a peaceful flag of truce, or using that same flag as a ruse of war to mount an attack. You could also investigate my alleged mistreatment of prisoners of war or civilians, or maybe I committed mass murder and genocide . . . No, Colonel, I have absolutely no reason to be here in your office. This meeting is over. You can take your fucking investigation and shove it up your ass, with the compliments of the retards in the green berets!'

This time, Max got up and walked out of the office, and slammed the door. What really bothered him more than anything else was that Steve had breached the secrecy of the LICHI KLESH program by telling his wife that he was going on an operation, and by revealing to her Max's identity. And in this case, Jennifer did know Max's identity, so he was clearly compromised.

Max drove a few miles from the meeting place, found a pay phone, and dialled the number in Canada that would connect him with the program. He provided his classified password and informed them of the breach of security caused by his late teammate, and of his conversation with the colonel. He was told to go purchase a throwaway cell phone and to call back at 1600 hours. In the meantime, Max was at a loss about how to employ his time. He and Rebecca had not talked for over three months, and he was now talking to Lena every day, sometimes three or four times a day. The previous night they had spent over two hours on the phone and had ended up having an intensely satisfying phone sex session. Lena had been surprised by the pleasure she had experienced. She had told him in her at times awkward English: 'I am really a shy girl, but you wake up the craziest and the most insolent desires in me, you know every one of my fantasies. How do you do this? My whole thoughts and imagination belong to you. You are the object of my secret dreams and vulgar desires. I do not feel a shame, thinking about such things with you. I think it's natural with you. I think, it's cool, when partners can discuss everything with each other. It's cool, if they are able to discuss the intimate details. I am so glad, that I have an opportunity to chat with my beloved Max on this subject. It's cool, that you care about me and want to make a pleasure to me even such a way. You know, dear Max, every time we speak, me remains such strong desire to make love with you, that I become crazy, such hot dreams appear in my mind. I have never thought that I dare to discuss such things with a man. But I feel so easy and good, when I am discussing such things with you, that I become happy. It's so cool feeling.' On the other hand, he had not shared that type of intimacy with Rebecca, and the few times when he had tried to call her, he had only gotten her answering machine, even at night, when she should have been home. There was no sense in being obstinate. Max did not even feel any particular sadness. It was the result of a natural process. Either he had become indifferent, or the pain would come later. He thought the reason he was not affected was that he had found true love with Lena. A love such as he and Rebecca had never shared. He took his cell phone and deleted the contact. Rebecca no longer existed. He decided to call Lena, but she was not available. He went back to the hotel and since the weather was rather nice, he decided to go for a jog along the Potomac River. It would be his first run since October. While he was running, he thought about the next few days. He had been put on standby and was free to relocate anywhere he wanted. There was no training planned, and Lena, having asked him to live with her in Europe, he needed to give her an answer, because if he did that, he would have to resign his commission. He could not possibly stay in the army and live with Lena. He would miss her too much. While he felt almost no feelings towards Rebecca, he missed Lena every moment of the day. He was delighted that she had decided to fly in for the coming weekend. He was already staying at the Willard in the Jenny Lind Suite which Lena had reserved for them the moment she had learned of his going to

Washington. While the décor was a bit out of character for him, he knew that it would fit perfectly with Lena when she arrived later in the week. But many events would take place before the moment when he could hold her in his arms.

CHAPTER 17

It was a hot evening. Lena and Max had left the Rolls in the care of the valet at the Casino. They had walked down to the Miramar Restaurant, and every man would turn around to admire the beauty of the young woman, to see her long legs on high heels, her thighs hardly concealed by her black minidress, and to look at her perfectly trimmed long blond hair that harmoniously hung to the middle of her back. She was glowing with confidence, happiness, and the anticipation of sexual passion. They sat down to have dinner on the open air terrace overlooking the luxury yachts anchored in the harbour. One of those, the 120-foot-long Princess of Russia, was hers, and this is where she intended to take Max to spend the night for the first time. She wanted it to be a surprise. After a deliberate and fantastic meal, full of innuendos, sensuality, and repressed sexuality between them, they walked back slowly up the hill, still attracting the looks of the tourists who were wondering how this guy could be so lucky to be with her. She loved to make the anticipation for lovemaking last even longer, and they took the time to enjoy the fragrance of flowers in the Casino gardens. Max held her close to him, and they marvelled at the sight of the placid sea under the almost full moon, while cruise ships slid noiselessly to the horizon on the way to Italy. They watched as their distant lights faded into the darkness, and as they looked left,

THE DATURA SOLUTION

in the distance, they could see the mountains of Italy diving into the sea, their shores lit up and shimmering in the warm air. They kissed passionately for the first time of the evening as they absorbed these magnificent sights and these fantastic moments which they were both stealing from other people, and from the frenetic passage of time. They were not thinking about that as they were both aroused. They could not keep their hands from their bodies. He positioned himself behind her, as she was still leaning on the stone balustrade, discretely stroking her perfectly shaped breasts swollen with desire and she could feel his manhood against your buttocks. As they walked down towards the seashore, she stopped under a rubber tree that shrouded them in complete obscurity, and she kissed him with that unrestrained passion he knew so well and loved so much. At the same time, she took off her panties soaked with her wetness and playfully caressed his face with them. She was now completely naked under her dress, and her juices were dripping down her gorgeous legs, to which the moon gave a slivery glow. She was completely overwhelmed by desire, and at that stage, he had to be in complete control because she lost consciousness of where she was. She guided his hand between her thighs, and he started to caress her slowly at first, but he sensed the tension in your body which was a sign he knew well by then, and he continued faster until she reached an orgasm so intense she have to hold on to his shoulders, and bite into them to prevent herself from screaming. When she recovered, she simply took his hands and they walked on to the beach as if nothing had happened between them. They did not talk, she did not marvel at how good it had been for her, but the way she held his hand told him far more than words could have.

    He had been completely taken by surprise by her intense passion the first time they had made love when she had rocked her head from side to side as he brought her to orgasm time after time. The tsunamis of amorous passion had overwhelmed her in a way she did not even know they could, as she had lain exhausted, on the brink of passing out night after night, as he catered only to her pleasure. This is where both he and she had discovered the passionate woman she was, the orgasmic Venus that was hiding behind her cold and business-like appearance. She had given herself to him without restrictions, taboos, or conditions, and he had allowed her to discover herself a new woman. He was as pleased by her own satisfaction as by his. She was surprised by how long and profound his lovemaking was. She had told him that one of the things that had attracted her to him was his virility, and night after night, she understood that his lovemaking was virility at its purest. She discovered ways that the hands of a man could touch that she had never suspected. She loved his hands. And he showed her that his hands loved her entire body. He caressed her head, feathered over her face, tickled her spine in a way that made her shudder from pleasure, he rubbed her arms, pinched her nipples, teased her clitoris, massaged her feet, touched her thighs for long moments before finally allowing her to explode as he went back to her intimacy. He used his fingers in ways he had had never known they could be used. He glorified her in as many ways he possibly could and she pushed her athletic and strong body towards him, indicating how much she loved it, how much she enjoyed it. It was an unending series of pleasure waves, of orgasms that burst out of her in exhausting vibrations and with a violence that almost looked painful. She was receptive to all of his lovemaking. She was on a voyage of discovery, and he was leading her there with all of his love. From the very first day he had known how to read her body, how to measure the pressure he had to put on certain parts of hers, how to moderate the rhythm, how to increase the speed or the intensity of his touch, when to stop, when to start again. She had been amazed by the quality of the love. He had asked her if this was how she had imagined their lovemaking. She had been apprehensive, fearing that under the polished and virile varnish, the lovemaking would be as disappointing as with the other men she had known. But the first night, when they had kissed, hesitantly at first, and then with a passion that she had never experienced, when he had softly massage her head through her hair with his elegant and powerful hands, she had realised that his persona was indeed extraordinary. That very instant had been the point of no return. He had undressed her, ever so slowly in a deliberate manner that put her satisfaction ahead of everything else. He had known not to rush things, and that manner had already caused her to shake uncontrollably in expectation of the lovemaking. He had taken his time, spending so many moments caressing and rubbing her back that she was aching for him to turn to her shapely breasts. He had known she wanted that, but he made every effort not to touch them. When he finally barely effleuraged her nipples, she had almost collapsed. She was longing for his touch all over her, but he had refused to again be carried away by the immediate desire he had of her. He had undressed her, one piece of clothing at the time, dropping each on the floor, and ensuring he caressed her, kissed her, and coached her into following his rhythm. Only once she had been totally naked had he taken her by the hand and led her into the bedroom. He had asked for nothing in return. He had not been concerned by his own pleasure. He was there for her, and for her only and alone. Once in the bedroom, he had continued to focus on her, kissing her with such hunger for her love that she had pushed his head down in between her legs. Her first orgasm had been so violent, she had kicked him in the head with her knees. She was a passionate woman indeed. The lovemaking went on for hours until she could not stand it any longer, until her body was so satisfied there was no longer any way she could receive pleasure. She had never met a man who could outlast her. She realised after that first evening that no other man could ever satisfy her again. 'How can I survive after our paths part?' she had asked. He pretended there was an answer, but really there was none. When he would be gone from her life, she would be left with her hunger for him, for the passion he had created in her. He felt guilty for that. At a point in time in the uncertainty of the future, she would be left with the memory, and she would enjoy the memory of these precious moments. She would never again be satisfied. It was a great moment of revelation. He answered that he was like Socrates, he had allowed her to discover the inner truth about herself, and it was impossible to hide that truth any longer. She now knew. She would have to deal with it. She would have to do it alone once he was gone. And every night became more intense. Every wave of pleasure created more pleasure. Every action created more desire. Every satiation created more hunger. Every act became more sophisticated. Every penetration became more intense. Every abandon required more abandon. Acts that she thought were unachievable were achieved. Penetration she had imagined to be too painful, procured her pleasure so intense that she passed out.

When they got to the beach, it was completely deserted and bathed in almost total darkness but for the rays of the moon. They quickly undressed, and he admired the curves of her body in the moonlight as she ran to the water. They plunged into the comforting and refreshing sea and swam to the row of linear buoys that supported the net protecting the beach from the jellyfish, and they kissed again, their tongues penetrating fully and freely as the small waves lapped their faces. And holding on to the buoys, in the deep water they make love. They expressed their pleasure in ways that made her yet a different woman, a woman who had been longing for an experience like that but had never known she could have it. They swam back to the beach, their bodies still hungry for each other, but she told him to wait, she had something special in mind. They finally walked out, put their clothes back on our wet bodies, and heard the distant Saint Charles church tower ring faintly for two o'clock in the morning. Instead of walking to the Rolls, and driving back to the Vista Palace, she took him to the harbour on foot, and there, halfway down the pier, she took him to the Princess of Russia, where a party was going on at the rhythm of electro house music. They enjoyed a glass of champagne, danced a few times, and then she took him by the hand to the private apartments, locked the door behind them, and she undressed. He could not believe it. She must be mad! She pulled him to her, and whispered softly, 'This is your boat, my love, I just gave it to you this afternoon. . .' She did not give him the time to answer, she pulled his pants down and she asked him to continue with the lovemaking session as the boat swayed lazily in the movement of the sea below. The window was wide open and with the fresh breeze of the night adding to the sensuality of the moment, he took care of her better than she ever thought it was possible to be pleasured, in positions that brought them absolute intimacy as his imagination guided their eroticism. There was not a single part of her body that he did not explore. Her skin was so electrified that his mere touch brought her pleasure. He caressed her, licked her, kissed her, penetrated her, made love to her three caves, and she did not want the night to stop. Her body shaken and exhausted by a series of orgasms that lasted until early morning, they finally fell asleep, naked, she snuggling against him, a satisfied and fulfilled woman, dreaming of more nights like this, as the first rays of the sun appeared on the eastern sky.

By the time he woke up, it was already lunch time. He got up slowly, trying to find his bearings in the unfamiliar surroundings. He took great care not to wake her up. He found the shower, the hot water helping him recover from the incredible night. Then he recalled she had told him this was her . . . no, his yacht? It did not make any sense. He dressed in his rumpled pants and shirt, foregoing the underwear, and went on deck. There, the waiter was ready to serve lunch. It was a lunch he wished he could share with her—Caspian Sea caviar, vichyssoise, foie gras, lobster on a bed of salad, cheeses from France, fresh raspberries, tiramisu, and a choice of Beluga vodka or Chateau d'Yquem. Of course, the newspapers of the day (*Nice-Matin, The Herald Tribune, The Financial Times, Pravda*) were arranged on a nearby table. The waiter apologised and stated that the *New York Times* should arrive by two because of a slight technical problem. Behind him, in the salon, Max could follow CNN news on a huge plasma screen. And this was all his? She appeared at almost the same time the New York Times arrived. She was dressed in a turquoise kimono, and he could tell she wore nothing underneath. She kissed and remarked that he should dress better to greet her. As he said he would if he had any clothes to wear, she told him he should have looked in the closet. She took him by the hand to the apartments, and opened a walk-in closet that was full of clothes, from the most casual to the most formal, all in his size—42 long jackets, 34/34 pants, and 15 ½–36 shirts. 'Do you think you can find something to wear?' she joked. But before he could answer, she had entwined her body around his and was kissing him in a way that he now knew meant only one thing. 'Let's take these old things off you,' she said, and she pulled him into the bathroom to make love under the shower.

As they emerged from the cabin, it was mid-afternoon. She sat down on the deck to enjoy her lunch, while he had some tea.

'So how do you like your boat?' she asked with a gleam in her eyes.

'I don't know, I have seen only one room,' he replied jokingly. 'I adore it, Lena, but isn't it a bit much?'

'Not for my vice president,' she added with her entire body expression adopting the cold and calculating demeanour of the businesswoman she was.

It is true that during the past few weeks, he had been more and more engaged in her business, giving her his insight, helping her prepare files, pointing out to her elements she simply did not have because she had never lived permanently in Europe until her husband's posting to Spain. He had made her discover Monaco, and she was now heavily invested in the construction of a new high rise that was already providing over 150 per cent on her investment. She had figured that a yacht worth a mere $10 million was actually a less than fair reward on a deal that was bringing her over $420 million in pre-tax profits. That is why she had already pre-paid all of the ship's operating expenses, to include all personnel, for five years, and had authorised an unlimited amount of fuel to be purchased on the vessel's account. But the reality of the offer is that she could not live without max any longer. She had spent the last six weeks exclusively with him, and she could not bear the idea of being separated from him. Of course, there would business trips and obligations that she or he will have to attend alone, but she was looking at the long-term, and she did not want him to walk out of her life.

She had taken down all barriers, all taboos to satisfy him, just as he had. Their relationship was one of absolute love and commitment to each other which translated in unrestrained physical pleasure. While people would have judged them and belittled their relationship as lust, they saw it as pure truth. Shame or unease had disappeared from their lives, and they had given themselves to each other without any restriction. They felt comfortable expressing their most secret desires, their most obscure obsessions, the unfulfilled fantasies and pleasures they had been dreaming about for their entire adult life without finding anyone who would understand them. They did not even have to speak. A simple pressure, a small gesture is all they needed to commit to another act that allowed them to dive deeper and deeper into each other's secret minds. She was able to reach a serenity that she had never experienced before, and she absolutely knew she would never experience with any other partner. There was no love and no pleasure outside of their relationship. Everything else, every love, every sexual encounter before she had met him had simply been pure mediocrity. And what she had thought had been fantastic simply had turned out to be common place in comparison to the intensity of their passion. For the first time she had reached orgasm from all of her sexual parts at once, she had told him on a Monday night. It was an experience she had been hoping for and no one had cared to give her. She had no boundaries on what she was ready to do for him either. She had never had a partner as receptive as him. This was a reciprocal feeling and he had assured her she was unique in all the meanings of the word. It was as if his mind had been cloned and implanted in hers: they wanted the same thing, the same forbidden pleasures, the same stimulations that had been denied them for a lifetime. She had always wanted to be stimulated from different parts of her body and to reach such an intensity of stimulation that she would climax without her intimacy being even touched. There had been many unsuccessful attempts with many partners in achieving this. But he was different. She had never felt anything like this, she told him. She did not even know it was possible, she added once she had recovered. 'How did you know?' she inquired, 'How did you know to give me pleasure like this?' He had just felt it, he had captured her sensitivity, he had felt that she would love it. This is why they were extraordinary lovers. She had not had to ask, she had not had to talk, they had clearly measured the level of trust and complicity between them, and in turn, they only wanted one thing, satisfy each other in ways that they could only do when they were together. Their imagination ran uncontrolled, and their desire to discover was boundless. Stuck in her drudgery of lovemaking with her husband and he with his wife, their encounters had been like climbing the highest peak in the Alps. It was an adventurous track to the top, discovering new sensations, reaching the summit in an explosion of exhilaration, and then, having to come down to the reality of everyday life and the boredom of sea level existence. She had decided she could not stand it any longer, and unbeknownst to Max, Lena had already served the divorce papers on her husband. This would prove to have dangerous consequences.

CHAPTER 18

The man made his way between the strands of concertina wire under the watchful eye of the guard standing on the roof of the admissions building. He was walking slowly under the low cloud cover on this early April day. It was morning. He was moving like a person who really didn't want to leave. Yet, his stay had been terminated by the GUIN, the Central Prison Authority. He had lost track of time in there, and frankly he had found comfort in the fraternity of convicts, living each day without thinking of the one after, submitting to the routine tasks of the penitentiary colony, and yet becoming a leader in the closed environment community. He remembered his first day, when he had found himself in front of that same administrative building, dazed by the events of the previous days and by how swiftly he had been transferred from Krysti in Sankt-Petersburg to the middle of nowhere. The place had a name for sure, Uluntskaya, but he had no idea where he was geographically. Even twenty-four years later, he had no concept of where he was. Then, he had been afraid of going in. Today, he was afraid of leaving. The compound gate had been closed behind him, and in a few more steps, he would reach the outer barrier that separated his world from the outside. He still had his hands crossed behind his back, as was standard in the Russian penitentiary system: prisoner always walked with their hands crossed behind their back. On his right hand knuckles the word 'МОЙ БРАТЬ', my brother, had been spelled, but only the half of the letters had been tattooed 'М-Й Р-Т'. The missing letters were tattooed on the knuckles of his prison brother, so that once they would be reunited, their interlaced knuckles would then spell the complete words. It had been the hardest thing in the past fifteen years, to leave Vladimir behind. They had bunked together from the very first day of his arrival, and Vladimir had helped him survive the first few months. After that, they had become friends, and despite the penitentiary attempts to rotate prisoners around them, they had always managed to find enough money to bribe the guards into leaving them together. And once he had established himself as one of the leaders, the guards did not even mention bunk rotation again, so keen were they in having him keep peace among the prisoners. For their last night, they had shared a bottle of Standard vodka, delivered by one of the guards, but today, he was about to leave it all behind and face the harshness of the central Siberian monochromatic landscape opening up in front of him. He was cold. The prison had given him some cheap civilian clothes, shoes that were of man-made material and that would soon fall apart in the mud of the road leading away from the prison. He wished he had not had to go. He would have to do it all over again. There was no life waiting for him on the outside. He was sure he would not even make it as far as Moscow. Actually, he was pretty sure he would be back in jail within a few days. He had no future. One does not become a model citizen at the age of 44 after spending over half of that in prison for murder. He had the cathedral with the five onion domes tattooed on his back, and he also wore the ace of clubs on his shoulder, a testimony to the nature of his crime. The guard in camouflage fatigues pulled the last gate open. He hesitated. The guard shouted some obscenity at him, and he finally moved. There was not a house in sight; there certainly had to be a town somewhere near. Everything the prison used came in by truck. Instinctively, he turned left, towards the West and Moscow and eventually Saint Petersburg. The walk would be a long

THE DATURA SOLUTION

one. He had not cared about geography in school, but he estimated he had to walk about 4,000 kilometres to reach Moscow. At a rate of about 40 kilometres a day, it would take him about 100 days. The GUIN had given him the grand sum of 158,400 roubles for his labour during the past twenty-four years, which amounted to about 18 roubles a day, but before he could get out, the tax office had collected 18 per cent of the amount, which left just over $3,500. Three thousand five hundred dollars for twenty-four years of work. . . He figured he would have more than enough to reach Moscow, if he wasn't robbed before then. It was the most money he had ever had in his life. He heard the noise of a truck, but it was going the wrong way, and in any case the truck drivers were reluctant to pick up released prisoners since one of them had killed a driver to steal his truck a few years back. The road was a sloppy mess of mud, and within a few minutes of walking, the man-made material had soaked enough humidity that his feet were now wet. He was not used to walking long distances, and he wondered where he would spend the night. On his left and right the only thing he could see was fir trees. There seemed to be no end to their monotonous expansion. He would have to spend the night in the woods although he was leery of the Siberian spider that would bite and infect you with an incurable disease that left you dead in less than a week. At the age of 44, Ivan Petrovich Egorov was already exhausted by the type of life he had led. He had not always been that way, but things had changed when he was in my ninth year. Up to that time, he had been under the care of my grandmother who was a benevolent woman. She did not know what anger was, and with her soft voice, gentle manners and love, she could get anything she wanted out of him. There was never a cross word, and she would readily declare to whoever wanted to hear that he was a perfect child. She would use the cliché that I was 'adorable like an angel' a way of saying that he was a model of good behaviour. However, when his mother had decided to stay home to watch over my young brother—a thing she had not done for him as she had left him in the care of his grandmother—the responsibilities of watching over him were gradually transferred from his grandmother to his mother, and he started to feel the crutches of malevolence take over his life. The final blow was delivered to me when his grandparents had been awarded a larger apartment by the Communist Party, and they had moved from the apartment they occupied right above his family's, to a new home overlooking the Neva at 15 Malukhtinskiy Prospekt. Although this new apartment was no more than a thirty-minute walk from where he lived with his parents, the absence of a calming force above them had released a massive flow of evil he was to live with for the following eight years. He never understood how his mother could be so angry, abusive, violent, and plain mean all the time. His mother used terror management to get things out of him. There was no love, there was no gentleness, and there were no soft-spoken requests. There were only excessive demands to participate in housework or to excel in school that were immediately followed by threats of bodily harm in case these demands were not met. And if they were not met exactly to the letter, there were beatings and public humiliation. Personal initiative and independent thinking were severely repressed and punished. For example, if she sent him to the store to buy a cabbage from the vendor named Valery, and he was out of cabbage, and decided that he should get it from another vendor, he was sure to be yelled at when he returned home. He was convinced his mother had been trained by the KGB when she questioned: 'Did you buy the cabbage at Valery's?' He would tell the truth that he had not because he was out of them. She would then question where he had gotten them. If he said he had gotten it from old Radzensky, without warning, she would slap him across the face, telling me that he had not followed her instructions, that she had wanted the special cabbage from Valery, and that he would never amount to anything in life, that I would end up being a street sweeper, like the Tadjiks—as in his mother's caste system, the street sweeper was an 'untouchable'. She would go into an uncontrolled rage, demanding he return the cabbage and get a refund, and threatening him with more bodily harm if he

THE DATURA SOLUTION

failed to return with the exact change she expected. It was a house of terror. He would have to walk back to the market, explain to old Radzensky his situation, and the old man would comment 'With a mother like that. . .' he would not finish his sentence, shaking his head, and letting the other customers think of a proper ending. Old Radzensky would mumble about lunatics like her and refund the price of the cabbage, and he would return home. Once he finally made it home, he would be subjected to more yelling from his mother demanding to know what had taken him such a long time, taking the cat of seven tails, and flogging his bare legs to 'teach him how to move faster', and then she would send him back to the market to get a cabbage from another vendor, looking at her watch and giving him exactly thirty minutes to go down to the market and back. He started to live in a persistent state of fear, his stomach knotting up at the mere notion of getting home. He no longer had any love for the woman who demanded to be called his mother, and he started to hate her, many times wishing her dead over the course of the following years. He felt absolutely no guilt to wishing her all types of evil, and hoping for a quick liberation from her insanity. He decided his mother simply hated him, and it would be years before he could figure out why. In the meantime, he learned avoidance. Later he would learn lying, dissimulation, and retaliation.

He tried to get relief from the Catholic Church, but by that time he had already burnt all bridges with this organisation—which was at least as abusive as his mother. The priest he talked to preached respect for the authority of the parents, obedience, and bearing our pain just as the allegoric figure of Jesus Christ had done. His final statement that we were all sinners and that we had to endure punishment as a way to redeem our sins simply did not make sense. It was a cowardly way out of reporting his mother to child services, and to force him to come back into the fold of an organisation he had already decided was utterly worthless and not respectable. By then he had figured out that all people in a position to influence the behaviour of his mother were linked by a vast silence conspiracy. And he remembered that his grandmother had always told me to mind my own business, to let fighting dogs fight it out. He suddenly realised how flawed such reasoning and attitude was, as nobody would bring him relief. He was in a permanent struggle against his mother who at times simply was clinically mad. He had to find a way to beat her, to have her break down before he did. She could torment him physically, but he soon learned that he could torment her psychologically and emotionally. It really happened by mistake. He already knew she cared far more about his newborn brother than she did about him. One day, as he had been told to watch his brother in his pram—again under strict orders not to mess up—his brother began to get agitated and to have a fit of gesticulating and yelling. He was old enough to sit up in the pram, and he started rocking it back and forth until he managed to tip it over in a huge crash that dislodged its collapsible roof. Upon hearing the commotion, his mother came running into the room to pick up his brother, ensuring that the fucking little angel was okay. She yelled at the top of her lungs that he was an incompetent imbecile who would never get anywhere in life since he was not even able to watch a small child. But she was so concerned by the health of his brother that she forgot to beat him. He also understood the anguish the mere possibility that his brother was hurt had caused her. From that point on, he had my first weapon. He caused all types of small accidents for his brother, accidents that he knew he could not be blamed for, like leaving the broom in his path as he was trying to learn how to walk—the broom could have fallen out of its place by itself—so that he would fall flat on the tile floor of the kitchen, cutting his lips, and causing blood to stain his clothes. His mother would go out of her mind every time he was hurt, and since he could not possibly be blamed for 'acts of God' he would go scot-free. The anguish he caused his mother became his most effective weapon. So he observed her closely, trying to find her hot buttons. Every time he found one, he would add it to his list of weapons. He slowly drifted out of the house simply to be free of her.

After spending his later teenage years as a street corner drug trafficker, he had taken over an entire city block by the time he was 18, in a universe of valance where there was absolutely no value to the life of a single man. He had attracted the attention of one the then-KGB senior officers because of the excesses of his violent acts, using his trademark execution technique, beheading with a chainsaw. The officer had actually been amused at the technique and had wondered why the KGB had not thought of it before. He offered a deal to him: his protection for a cut of the profits, and accept doing some dirty work for the KGB in the interest of Mother Russia's national security—work that would be highly remunerated. Of course, he could not have predicted that within less than two years, Mother Russia would have collapsed, the KGB officer would have become a drug lord, and that he would end up being arrested and sentenced to a long prison stay. It had happened very quickly. The KGB officer had commandeered the assassination of a drug dealer that threatened his own position, and he had not realised that by doing that, he would become a dangerous rival to that same KGB officer. The hit had taken place flawlessly. He had gone to the Chornaya Koshka club to celebrate, had enjoyed a sizable quantity of vodka, had picked two girls from the club unending supply of young prostitutes, had driven his Beemer to his apartment on what still Leninskyi Prospekt (there had been no time to change street names yet), and after some light amusement with the girls, he had fallen asleep. At five in the morning, the door to his apartment was torn off its hinges by the powerful ram of the Quick Intervention Squad of the new VSB (successor to the KGB), the officers had rushed in full combat fatigues and armed as if they were attacking the Kremlin, they had thrown the sheet of the bed, brutalised the two girls into a corner of the room, put a gun to his head, had handcuffed him, and taken him down to the police car waiting for him entirely naked. They had refused to let him get dressed as part of the humiliation treatment he would be subjected until his trial. The squad leader had first helped himself to one of the two girls, and then he had 'searched' the apartment, making an easy $72,000 that he had stashed in various parts of the flat. The official report stated a weapon, which would later be identified as the murder weapon, had been discovered together with a significant amount of drugs—actually the report should have said staggering, but the squad members had helped themselves to a large portion of theme for later resale—but that no cash had been stored in the apartment. Later on, at the trial, Lieutenant Ivachenko testified under oath that this had been the case. Nobody asked why such a low-ranking officer could arrive at the trial venue in a brand new Mercedes S500, which had been delivered from Bremen Spezial Personelkraftwagen AG, Bremen SP in short, and why such an officer needed an armoured car. Only Ivan knew. What he did not know, but was to figure out over the course of the years what that his former KGB officer friend had actually turned him in into the VSB after he had convinced the VSB to put a $20,000 reward on Ivan's head. Thus, the murder of a drug kingpin had cost the former KGB officer not a cent—he actually had made money—and he had gotten rid of two potential rivals in a single operation. It was a brilliant operation that had gotten the attention of a former colleague of his who had launched a political career in the now rebaptised Sankt Petersburg Oblast. Politicians needed money to finance campaigns and the former KGB officer, a certain Oleksandr Ivanovich Krasnaief, had plenty of it. In turn, favours to politicians turned into more opportunities to make insane amounts of money by capturing industrial facilities, a feat that could only be accomplished thanks to the professional killers and personal guard the drug lords maintained on their payroll. Soon Oleksandr controlled the entire Sankt Petersburg political class, and a myriad industries going all the way to Moscow, Kazan, and Ekaterinburg. Oleksandr, a veteran of Afghanistan—he had loved that war that had allowed him and a few colleagues to establish their own opium trade route, thus eliminating the Chechen middlemen—did not have any problem getting involved in fire fights. Thus, he conquered the Yakutsk diamond mines as well

THE DATURA SOLUTION

as part of the gold mines, leading an army of his acolytes equipped with the best weapons he could purchase from the West. There were always foreign interests represented by retired diplomats or rogue weapon dealers that were ready to deliver the best hardware the West had to offer, and that far surpassed the already aging Soviet arsenal. One he had figured out that Oleksandr had betrayed him—it came through bits of information brought in by other convicts, Ivan had lived night and day with a single purpose: getting revenge. He had made every effort to gain the trust of the GUIN so that he could get released early. He had followed Oleksandr's career. The man he had vowed to kill, was now a multi-billionaire, a friend of the Russian prime minister, who could visit the Kremlin whenever he wished, and who was essential to the funding of the National Party. The president was a member of the board of his industrial empire, and the prime minister was the vice president of his Russian Field Mining Company. Ivan realised that having access to him would be an impossibility, that his dream of revenge would never take place, and then he became concerned that Oleksandr may well decide to do away with him instead. Oleksandr had to have thought of the eventuality that Ivan wanted to kill him. And then, one rainy autumn evening, he had learned that Oleksandr had died of a so-called heart attack at the headquarters of his company in Yakutsk. Ivan felt cheated. He had wanted to kill him. At the same time, he was able to relax again, knowing that the man who probably had wanted him dead had died first. But from that day forward, Ivan's life had lost its meaning. He had lived for revenge. He had nothing at all to walk out for: no family, no friends—all his friends were the convicts inside the penitentiary, no girl, no job, no illegal business, and no contacts. He was a tired man who no longer had a purpose. He continued living by habit, also knowing that he had now lost touch with the drug networks, and that he also was no longer in that good a shape to get contracts—younger guys with more experience were a dime a dozen. In the last two years of his incarceration, he had found solace in political extremism and nazism. He had become a founder of a new prison gang that called itself the White Brotherhood, and now as he was walking out the door, he was also losing the authority the position he had created had given him. The Brotherhood had been so popular that even some of the guards had joined it. But, now as darkness crept over the barren landscape Ivan was alone, and had found no place to spend the night. He realised that the GUIN released prisoners like him in the hope that they would simply die on the way to civilisation. He did not have the skills or the knowledge that would allow him to survive in that expanse. He also knew that there were wolves around—he had them howling many times from the safety of the penitential barracks, wolves that were supposed to never attack people. Yet a few years before, a member of the working party who had been forgotten behind was fatally mauled by wolves. He had been attacked by at least three wolves as the sun was setting and the wolves were probably starving due to the effects of a long winter. Ivan tried to hurry his pace, but the mud had already rendered his shoes useless and the going was harder and harder. Outside of two trucks, he had seen no traffic all day. Then he thought about it and figured it was Sunday. He would just have to survive that day and he would be safe—he would find a ride in the morning. When he was about to give up, he heard the roar of an engine revving up to keep the momentum to the wheels and maintain a high speed on the treacherous quagmire. Ivan got out of the way, certain he would be hit if he stayed in the path of what had to be a four-wheel drive. The lights were on, so Ivan could not identify it. The vehicle pulled up to him and stopped. The window went down, and he was ordered more than invited in. 'Take of your fucking mud floppers first, I don't want that shit all over the range,' the man added. Ivan did as he was told, and climbed in. The heat felt good. None of the two men in the Range Rover talked, and Ivan, used to the prison, kept his mouth shut—he could go days without speaking a word. They rode for a good three hours before they reached one of these typical uninviting Siberian villages made up of a few wooden houses, an onion roof church, and a main street that is simply a dirt track. The men stopped in front of a house that was barely distinguishable in the dark. The passenger gave Ivan a pair of galoshes, and they went in. They were served a dinner of cabbage beef and potatoes and were given a bed each in the freezing house. Ivan went outside to pee, rejoined his bed, and fell asleep immediately. The following morning, the first thing Max did was to verify that he had not been robbed. They did not wash, brush their teeth, or shave. They were given breakfast and they were on the road again. Neither man had exchanged a word with Ivan, and it suited him fine. He felt no need to ask any questions. After twenty-four years in the brink, he was used to his questions having no answers, so he had simply stopped asking questions. They drove for another four days, and every night the scenario was the same, and every morning it was the same again. On the fifth day, they reached the small Kolpashevo Airport near the city of Tomsk. The Range Rover pulled on to the landing strip and they waited. Over two hours later, a Citation landed and refuelled. When the refuelling operations were completed, the passenger told Ivan to get the fuck out and get on the fucking plane. Ivan followed his instructions without a word. In five days, he had not uttered a single syllable. His remarkable ability to keep his pie hole shut was reported to Sankt Petersburg. The Citation flew directly to Sankt Petersburg. Ivan was given the best meal he had eaten in almost twenty-five years and a glass of champagne. He fell asleep and did not wake up until wheels down at Pulkovo Airport in Sankt Petersburg. There, a Mercedes GL was waiting for him. An hour later, he was stepping into the Astoria Hotel. He was given a suite, and an envelope. The instructions were simple: using the money inside the envelope, he had the whole day to make himself presentable for a meeting with important people. The note recommended he spend the bulk of the $20,000 at the Emporio Armani on Bolshoi Prospekt. He was also instructed to get a haircut from the hotel barber. Ivan put the envelope in his pocket and rode the elevator to his room. He was not sleepy despite the fact that it was close to one in the morning. For the first time in his life, he watched CNN. The next day, Ivan did as he was told, got a modern haircut, grabbed a cab to the Emporio, and bought underwear, five shirts, ties, five suits, three pairs of shoes all under the supervision of the experienced fashion manager. And he still had over five grand left. When he got out of the shop, no one would have recognised the man who had walked out of a penitentiary less than a week before. Had it not been for the stupid tattoo on his knuckles, Ivan would have been taken for a high-powered businessman as he was to meet in the morrow. There was no way to hide the tattoos, and at least nobody could see the ones on his chest, shoulder, or back. Although when the people at the Emporio had seen them, they had known exactly where Ivan was arriving from. But they did not care—they had made a $15,000 sale. Ivan took a few steps outside the shop and then decided that he should have spent the entire amount. He went back and did just that.

The following day, according to very specific instructions that had been relayed to him through the front desk, Ivan was ready to be picked up at eleven o'clock. He had transformed himself entirely, but the oafishness he had acquired at the penal colony was visible under the polish of the Armani suit and the patent leather shoes, and no amount of grooming or fashion would take this away anytime soon. He still caught himself walking with his hands behind his back, giving away for everyone to see where he had just come from. And there was the question of the criminal tattoos on his fingers. Everybody knew immediately. At eleven, another Mercedes came to collect Ivan. No words were exchanged. They just drove him about town to the meeting place—he assumed. He had no idea who he was going to meet, where, or for what purpose. He just hoped he would not be executed. The drive did not take long to Ladozhskyi Vakzal. Pulling up to one of the round buildings on the right side of the railway station, Ivan was welcome by a hostess who took him to an office on the top floor. There, the entire environment changed from post-Soviet pseudo-Western offices to a luxury in office decoration that Ivan had never imagined and was straight from the plushest offices in New York City. Ivan felt ill at ease and completely foreign to the office that he was ushered in. A man in his sixties stood up to welcome him as if Ivan had been an important head of state, and as if Ivan knew him. Coffee and tea with an assortment of Fortnum and Mason delicacies were waiting on a coffee table.

'Welcome, Ivan Petrovich! I hope the travel and accommodations have not been too demanding on you . . . blah blah blah.'

Ivan could not focus, he could not hear anything that was being said, and he could not understand what was going on. His mind could not work that fast yet, or would it ever? He could only get bribes of what was being said: plenty of time, lunch, coffee, old friend, task . . . he simply could not get it. He answered with monosyllabic agreements, nor sure what he was agreeing to. He had not even gotten the name of his host. His host was in the middle of saying 'of course, Mister Egorov, this is all new to you, and we are going a bit fast' . . . A bit fast, Ivan thought, how about way too fast? He realised how decrepit his intellect had become while in the GUIN's custody, how atrophied his neurons had become, and this man he did not know was apparently thinking that he could be of service to him? He could barely figure out where he was. Then he remembered 'Ladozhskyi Vakzal'. Ladozhskyi Vakzal, Ivan repeated mentally as if to have something concrete to hold on to. During that time, this man did not stop talking, making key points, projecting ideas, ensuring that Ivan could understand everything. And Ivan froze when he asked, 'So, what do you think?' Ivan could not even utter a word. He thought nothing! His head was full of emptiness; it was a massive vacuum, compared to which space was overpopulated. He was utterly incapable of aligning two words together, even less a coherent thought. Time passed, the question had been asked minutes ago, it seemed. Ivan could still not say anything. The host thought he was pondering the right answer, but there would be no answer, because Ivan was losing his mind. He could not understand anything any longer outside of wood cutting duty, cigarette rations, the White Brotherhood, and the cycle of meals in the prison refectory. He was nothing more than a walking zombie. He finally mustered enough brain power to state:

'I think we should talk more about it.'

'Of course, continue his host, we should. I tell you what, let's go to lunch and we can discuss it further!'

Ivan caught the word lunch. But he wanted to be away from there. He wanted to be relieved of the pain of not understanding another human being talking, not even knowing what he was supposed to think about. In the back of the room, he caught one of the bodyguards rolling in eyes up. Yes, he was lamentable. He was a piece of human refuse on the shoulder of life highway. He was a nothing that had been made to dress up and look good, but he still had no idea why. And now, while he thought he was being taken to a restaurant for lunch, they simply moved to a room two doors down from the office, in what was labelled as the Executive Dining Room, and he was invited to sit at a table covered with the finest grain linen. The food arrived, and he was even more uncomfortable. He was served French dishes he had never seen, escargots he did not know how to eat, quails he did not know how to cut, cheeses he had no concept about, and finally, a flaming Baked Alaska he had never seen. It was as if the host was trying everything to embarrass him. And the variety of wines that were served! He had no idea how to drink them. It reminded him of a Russian folktale, the wolf and the stork, when the wolf invites the stork for dinner, but the stork cannot eat out of the fancy China the wolf is using. After lunch, and with no more understanding of what was expected, the host took him back to the office.

'So we are all set, then Ivan Petrovich?' asked the host.

Incapable to acknowledge that he had become what medical science calls a Cretin while in Siberia, Ivan was content to emit an unconvincing yes.

'I know what I am asking you to do is difficult, and we appreciate your accepting it. Here is a little something to tie you over while we prepare the instructions. In the meantime, of course you will be my guest at the Astoria, unless you prefer another hotel? Enjoy our beautiful city, Ivan Petrovich!'

'Yes, thank you!' Ivan was finally able to say. He had only captured the meaning of enjoy the city, Astoria, and instructions. He nevertheless accepted the envelope that was ended to him.

Once he was back in the car, he tried to make sense of everything he had been told, and especially why he was given another envelope full of money. He also realised he needed to go a doctor in a hurry because his mind was completely gone. As he returned to his room, his head still spinning from the events of the morning and lunch, he opened the envelope, and it contained three stacks of $100 bills. Thirty-thousand dollars! But for what?

Ivan lay down on the bed. He tried to think. Slowly he reconstituted some of the conversation. It had to do with that pig Oleksandr Ivanovich. But he could not figure out why. Wasn't he dead? Yes, it came back to him now; it had to do with his wife. It would be a good way to get revenge to. . . What? He jumped up in his bed! That's what it was! He had agreed to kill Oleksandr Ivanovich's wife as a means to get revenge on the man who had sent him to the penitentiary. 'What the fuck?' thought Ivan. He didn't want to kill anybody, a woman even less than anyone else. But now he was committed, and he knew the law of the Mafia. Once you accept a job, it is too late to go back. There is only one way out of it, death. Well, that put things in perspective.

There had been a time when he had been able to think, a time when the chancy and equivocal nature of life had challenged his understanding of the human condition. Long ago, in a place that was only a foggy landscape of broken down and rotting buildings, he had lost track of the ideologies. The unending boredom of religious rites had put me to sleep on the train taking him out of the vast expenses of conformism. He had listened to their fairy tales. He had been told about unrealities. He had known that there was a tribe in America, the Lakota, that believed each star was the soul of a dead comrade. He wondered if they had a word for star, and what relation it had with the reality of fusion reaction. He had asked what would happen if another tribe someplace in Africa or in Australia thought the same thing. How would the stars be divided, and whose ancestors would actually be stars? How could this mess be sorted out? What gave the right to the Lakota to say that the North Star was the father of their nation? What if he wanted that star to be his own great-grandfather? The beliefs of the Lakota were summarily swept away and his questions supposedly answered by the statement that the stars were nothing but celestial bodies, and that what the Lakota believed was a senseless legend, that was indeed amusing, but had no validity. Dismissing the religious beliefs of the Lakotas was fine with him. During his entire childhood he had been given information that was simply to be discarded a few months or a few years later. The revelation that there was no such thing as fairies, or Santa Claus, or witches, was another step in the process to confirm that there was no one to turn to, no fourth dimension. Now, as he was losing his mind, he wished he had a fourth dimension to go back to, but it was too late, as it was too late to come back on the contract. He was a man of barely 45 who felt like he was 90 and about to die.

CHAPTER 19

Lena did not realise for a long time, and not even after she had been his wife for several months what trap she had fallen into and what error she had made when she had married George. She had been blissfully unaware of his multiple affairs before and after he had met her and her naïveté could only be explained by her lack of sophistication. She had been born in what had been the Leningrad, and her parents, lower working-class Soviet citizens, had raised her in the ignorance of the world that is typical to that class of people around the world. They idolised the Soviet dictators and believe that they were the paragon of virtue described in official propaganda. She owed her own success to the fortune of her remarkable beauty, which had led many of the apartment block building where she lived to wonder who her real parents actually were. Some rumours insisted that the Fermyer parents could have created such fine-looking girls. There were some of the most homely and ignorant occupants of the block, lacking even the most modest modicum of politeness that was the standard of Soviet neighbours. People had concluded that genetics worked in extraordinarily incomprehensible ways. In any case, Lena's genetics simply did not add up. She had known abuse ever since she had been a little girl. The only way her father knew to teach her anything was to beat her. Many times, she had gone to school with bruises on her body or face, and the teachers had simply ignored the entire matter. As soon as she had been able to she had escaped the drudgery and filth of the small flat she had known all of her life, and she had moved in with another teenager, eager to conquer the new world that the collapse of the Soviet Union had allowed her to discover. She had visited a model agency and had been instantly accepted. Within a short time, she was in demand from Russian magazines in Moscow, and she had been able to move into a nice apartment, which would have seen rather common to most people, but represented a life achievement for her. Of course, her local fame had attracted suitors, and she had shown the same lack of sophistication in selecting her lovers that she had in choosing a flat. They had mainly been truck drivers or factory workers, and they had brought nothing to her life. Rather the opposite, as one of them had stolen her life savings from her. When she had been approached by another agency to become a hostess at events for rich businessmen, the timing had been perfect as she had not reached the fame that she was to know through her contract with the Krassiva fashion house, and she had run out of money. It is during one of her engagements at the Sankt Petersburg Convention Center that Oleksandr Krasnaief had first laid eyes on her. Her marriage to the oligarch had been as happy as two people equally ignorant of the ways of the world could be. Certainly, he had money and could travel with her around the globe to his exclusive properties, but outside of this, he had brought her very little. The son of a miner in the Yakutsk diamond mines, he had the physical appearance of an ox, and the disposition of a bear. Used to abusing vodka, devoid of any education whatsoever, and yet a ruthless businessman, he had used her as a trophy wife, and as an outlet for his rare sexual needs.

While she had suffered abuse from some of her lovers, and the occasional slap or punch from Oleksandr when he was drunk—she had been so scared to lose everything, she had forgiven him without ever confronting him—nothing had prepared her for the sexual and physical violence of the respectable man who was now her husband

and the ambassador of the United States to Spain. The night he had slapped after she had made what she had thought to be a helpful comment on his lack of erection, was a turning point in their sexual relationship. A few evenings later, as soon as he had entered the rococo bedroom of the Ambassador's Residence, George had partially untied his tie while removing it. Without a word, he had approached Lena, still holding the tie in his hands, had grabbed her wrists and had tied them together with a brutality that had told her immediately it was not a game. Never before had he shown such a penchant for violence during sex. She was stunned and shocked at once. He had then pulled so violently and suddenly that she had stumbled and had almost fallen. He had thrown the tie over the crossbar that supported the bed canopy, between the two bedposts, and had attached her there, with her arms way above her head. He had torn her clothes off revealing her nakedness, her perfect white buttocks, and her shapely breasts. He then had taken off his patent leather belt, and folding it in half had started beating her with a vicious pleasure. After a few strikes, he had managed to work himself out of his pants, and switching the belt to the left hand he had masturbated with the right hand. Lena had been screaming in fear and pain, knowing full well that nobody would come to her rescue, while her husband delighted in seeing her back and buttocks turning red from the hits he was inflicting. She had begged him to stop—expecting him to rape her—but she had also noticed that as she begged, his erection grew bigger and the stronger than she had ever seen on him. And all the time he was beating her, he was cursing her, calling her the foulest names a man can call a woman. For Lena, it lasted an eternity, but for her husband it was very quick. He reached his climax within a couple of minutes, making sure he came on her violet-red ass, and he cursed her, 'You see what you had me do, you fucking bitch! It's all wasted! Now I cannot fuck you! Oh, you are laughing, eh! I'll teach you to laugh at me, you whore! I'll leave you fucking tied like this all night. That will teach you, you fucking piece of Russian shit!' And with that he had walked out of the bedroom, slammed the door, and left her hanging there all night. He had gone to his private bedroom, changed and had driven to visit Xin. The exercise with Lena had simply aroused him further.

It was the maid who found her in the morning and detached her. Lena had collapsed in her arms, and the maid had helped her sore body to the shower. She had had to cancel all of her appointments that day and had recovered in bed. She had had the locks changed and sworn to herself that *he* would never have access to her again. That evening, as George came to get her an official dinner at the Embassy of Morocco, he behaved as if the incident had never taken place. He had made no mention of her treatment, and since she did not answer him when he spoke, they never approached the issue. The only difference was that she had refused to join him. Having predicted that, George had called Xin and had instructed her to get ready as planned and to serve as his substitute wife for the evening. In the hands of Xin, George had become more and more reliant on sadism to reach full sexual gratification. Pleasure now meant that he had to abuse humiliate, hurt, degrade, and dominate a woman. Xin had been smart enough to channel all of George's deviance onto other women, whether occasional partners or the ever more demanding Martine Fournier-Lenotre who enjoyed masochism at least as much as George enjoyed sadism.

Lena stood firm to her decision to never again let George touch her. She refused to submit herself to another beating, and be the object of abuse which George explored with Michelle. But if he could not hurt her physically, George systematically tried to destroy her self-esteem. He became intrusive about her whereabouts, constantly needing to know where she was, what she was thinking, feeling, and becoming clinically jealous. She had other things to worry about, and he did not care than she was at the head of global conglomerate. He called her names, referring to her as 'nothing but a Russian mouzhik' or a 'Russian whore'. He tried to lock her up in the residence to keep her from her appointments or scheduled travels. He went as far as calling her private pilot and telling him that Lena needed him to fly to Paris to pick her up, while in fact she was on her way to the airport for her flight to Paris. And to explain her absence at formal events which she should have attended, he said that she had fallen ill and was being treated at a mental institution. Of course, the next day, the news was all over town, and investors started to question whether they should continue their venture with her. For all others, George McMillan remained the gentleman, the successful upstart who was the US Ambassador to Spain, the charming handsome man who was married to the most wonderful of all women, Lena, and the concerned husband of a mentally sick wife. The fact that he came to functions accompanied by the lovely Xin had shocked many. But after he had explained his wife's ailment, people simply looked at it as an almost normal thing. Especially since George had introduced Xin as his executive secretary, implying that he had been a successful investment banker before becoming ambassador, and that Xin had been his right-hand woman. At the residence, he became more controlling, demanding he knows in advance of all her activities, companions, whereabouts, and male encounters. One afternoon, he saw her talk to the marines captain in charge of the embassy detail and had him reassigned on the spot. This is when George, ever more frustrated by his impotence to control Lena and the ineffectiveness of his passive aggression, became even more brazen in his abuse. On the Fourth of July, when she had accepted to attend the garden party at the US Embassy, he persisted to look at her threateningly during the entire event, even using hostile gestures, and when the guests had left, he had smashed things around the residence, especially those that she had chosen or brought from Russia. After that day, the intensity of verbal abuse, degradation, cursing, name calling, and verbal threats escalated once more. This is when Lena decided to get her own villa, and she never appeared in public with the ambassador again. She had completely separated from him, and she consulted with her lawyers to ensure that in case of her death not a penny could possibly go to

George. She purchased her own Rolls, hired her own driver, her own body guards, and extended her real estate investments outside of Spain, into Southern France, Italy, and especially London, which had been designated as the Olympic city. She contacted the best divorce lawyer in Virginia and initiated divorce proceedings. Of course, George realised he had gone too far when all access to her financial wealth was cut off. She had been making so much money that she had never bothered to refuse George's request for a couple of million dollars here and there, especially that he claimed they were to enhance the image of the United States during official functions. Now this generosity had stopped. Since he had no longer any physical access to her, he sent her emails begging her to forgive him that he had changed, that he would not behave in such a naughty way—he had even put a smiley face next to the word, and his promises were accompanied by a contractual engagement. But when she answered him that no amount of begging or supplication could make her change her mind, he responded with emails full of anger ad bile, calling her a Russian whore, and writing her that he would tell the whole world how she had treated him and that her citizenship would be taken back. After that email from him, she simply added him to her junk email list.

Her marriage was ruined, but her life was not. And she was quite happy about it. On the positive side, she was now a US citizen, she was an ambassador's wife—at least on paper—she benefited from having a diplomatic passport, she had whichever connection she wanted, she was on first name basis with the president of the United States, and with the prime minister of Russia, her personal fortune was immense, and she no longer had a sexually deviant husband to put up with. She laughed at the thought of her husband calling her a Russian muzhik. Of course, she made sure that everyone in Madrid knew the ambassador was impotent, and she hired a private investigation agency to warn all of the call girl agencies that the ambassador was a violent man that got his kicks out of severely beating women. Soon Lena had her own followers and the real estate opportunities she was developing,

THE DATURA SOLUTION

together with her ventures around the world, were the reason why her luxurious villa on Calle de la Infanta Silva soon became known as US Embassy B. Within two months of moving in, Lena had purchased the entire building and had started a complete refurbishing of the property. A year later, the villa apartments that had been renting for 10,000 euros a night were being rented for three times that much. When rock stars came to Madrid, they stayed there as Lena had added a twenty-four-hours-a-day catering service. The amortisation of the building upgrade was so rapid that it took half of the anticipated time. People in the construction community around noticed her business savvy and started wanting to close deals with her. She was like King Cresses: everything she touched turned into gold. Within two years of her arriving in Madrid, Lena was at the head of a real estate investment and construction empire that was unequalled in Spain, was also the biggest to span the three Latin countries, and had invested heavily on the London market. Everywhere, jetsetters were likely to stay, she owned prime location property to include Portofino, Notting Hill, Monte Carlo, or Saint Tropez. Rumour had it that only the prince of Monaco owned more real estate in Monaco than Lena. In addition, she ran a company that rented super yachts to the super wealthy, and whether in Porto Cervo, or Nassau's Paradise Island, if one sailed in with a leased super yacht, more likely than not it was part of Lena's expanding fleet. She had just ordered the refurbishment of the Princess of Russia from a Turkish shipyard for over $50 million. The boat would boast floors made of antique wood, bathrooms decorated with lapis lazuli, white marble and gold, and furniture that had belonged to tsar Peter the Great. As Lena became more and more successful, she lapsed back into what Freud called the latency stage and repressed all of her sexual desires and her sexual drive. The woman who had been so passionate and so sexual—or at least she had thought—showed absolutely no interest in sex, so focused was she on stamping out the pain of her failed marriage, and on collecting more wealth. This is the woman Max had met in Spain on the way to saving himself. Later when she had told him that, Max had been amazed by her courage. He had also immediately despised and hated the ambassador. And yet, he failed to remember the words of the fortune teller: 'I see chaos, destruction, and disruption on a primal level.'

CHAPTER 20

When she travelled, she would call him at least once a daily, and she texted him several times a day. It was particularly important because while she was away in Sankt Petersburg, he was managing her business from Monaco. She was supposed to come back on 22 December, and they were preparing the traditional Christmas party at the Louis XV, the restaurant in the Hotel de Paris, kitty corner from the casino. They had had an unpleasant discussion about a business matter the previous day, and when she did not text him or call him on 11 December, he figured she was mad. She had told him before, 'If you hurt me, I'll hurt you,' but he had never taken these words seriously, and she certainly had never applied them to their relationship. Actually, Max decided that her silence was completely out of character. He had texted her several times that day and got no answer, and every time he had called her he only got the message in Russian telling him that the number for that cell phone was currently unavailable. Throughout the day as the business matters required his attention, he found it disconcerting and he was angry that she would not answer, but he did not have the time to think about it much. As he sat down in The Princess of Russia luxurious dining room where they had so many times made love, he suddenly realised that her behaviour was abnormal. Never before had she ignored him for an entire day. He called her at least three dozen times and got no answer. Finally, he searched and found her mother's phone number, but by the time he reached her, it was past ten o'clock at night and she had not seen or heard from her daughter. She was pretty upset about it because Lena had invited her for lunch at the Grand Hotel Restaurant, she had dressed up in her best clothes, and Lena had never come to get her 'not even a phone call', she complained. By the time he hung up, Max was convinced that Lena had had a problem—something was wrong, he was sure of it. He did not know what to do. He could not call the Sankt Petersburg Police, he could not call a Special Warfare Unit, and then he thought about it. . . Why not simply call her hotel? He was so concerned by the time he dialled the number '7 for Russia, 8-813, no 812' that his hands were shaking and that it took him four times to get through to the reception. And when they connected him to the Imperial Suite, there was no answer. He called back asking if anyone knew of Lena McMillan's whereabouts. The answer was even more worrying because nobody had seen her since the evening before and she had not picked up her mail. Max was now certain that foul play was involved. He then asked the reception to connect him to the room where the pilots of her private jet stayed, and the receptionist stated that they were not in their room, because he had seen both of them go to the bar. Max insisted he get one of them. Once the pilot finally got on the phone, he reported he had not seen Lena since they had landed four days before. When Max shared his concerns, the pilot asked what he was to do. Max knew immediately what should be done now that the adrenaline had started pumping. 'Fly back to Nice as soon as you can, and take me to Sankt Petersburg! When can you be here?' The pilot thought about it, made a brief calculation, and said that if they left early in the morning he could have the Learjet in Nice by 8:30 and with refuelling and turnaround time, they would be back in Sankt Petersburg by mid-afternoon. Max then called Heli Air, the Monaco Helicopter service, and booked himself and two other passengers on the 8:00 a.m. flight. Before packing his clothes,

Max called John, his head of security, and together, they assembled the necessary weapons to prepare themselves for the trip, because it was now clear that they would be entering a dangerous zone. John suggested they bring along Dmitry, a former VDV major and Russian emigrant who was part of the yacht's security detail. They went to the ship's armoury and selected Glock Model 31 pistols which use .357 calibre ammunition, have extremely high muzzle velocity and superior precision even at medium range, a couple of AR-15 which had been modified to have the automatic capability of the M-16, and at John's recommendation three 40-mm MGLs (Multiple Grenade Launchers) which he had acquired from the black market in South Africa. They also packed armoured executive travel vests, and John then called the twenty-four-hour One-Limo armoured limousine service in Sankt Petersburg and reserved a car for the following days. Max served a couple of Glenfiddich whiskys, and he called his chief of operations so that he could conduct business for the following few days as he was embarking on a mission, which he did not tell him was a matter of life and death for Lena.

Max was restless—he drifted in and out of sleep several times, as he worried for Lena's life. He knew her safety had long been compromised. He tried to see how he could approach it. The first thing was to find out where she had been the day before and at what time of the day she had disappeared. He also thought he would need local assistance, and he looked for private detective agencies that could help him. He went to the computer and noted the coordinates of the Private Detectives Lagoda, which boasted three former KGB officers on its staff. This would be their first stop. Deep inside, Max knew it was too late. He had experienced it before during his days of weapons trading in Russia. If you were in the way, you died. He remembered how Ed Cameron, an associate of his who had gone solo had been gunned down in the Kievskaya subway station in broad daylight as he was walking from the Radisson hotel to the underground shops to apparently get a souvenir for his wife. He also remembered Olaf

Gustafsen, the Norwegian businessman who had told him during a dinner—that was to be last—at the Metropol how the Russian mafia was trying to buy him out at ten cents to the dollar, and how he had turned them down. The next morning, the waste disposal workers had found his body on the stretch of grass between the parking lot and the hotel. When the police had arrived, they had found the window of his seventeenth floor room wide open. The chief investigator had ruled the death a suicide. The Russian Mafia had become so powerful as to operate without any boundaries, and without being subjected to the rule of law. One could not fight it, and anyone whose business interests were above the $100 million mark was certainly a target of the mafia's attention.

Once they landed in Sankt Petersburg, Max and John went directly to Gangutskaya Ulitsa where PD Lagoda was located. It was already night time although it was barely three in the afternoon, and it gave the entire city an appearance of gloom and despair, the same despair that filled Max's soul. The meeting with Boris Potunov did not improve his state of mind either. Potunov was an overweight man with no manners, a ruffian who had pushed people around and probably actively participated in torture when he was a KGB officer, a major general in fact, a man who projected a constant spray of spittle as he spoke, who wore a shirt too small for his bovine neck, and whose stomach was so fat he could barely reach the keyboard while seating behind his desk. But his truly repulsive physique was compensated by a knowledge of Sankt Petersburg that he had collected from over forty years of service in the city. He knew all about Elena Alexandrovna, about the so-called heart attack her husband had suffered, which Potunov confirmed had most likely been a massive injection of KCI (potassium chloride) laced with sodium thiopental. Potunov mentioned that most of the empire previously owned by Oleksandr Krasnaief, was now under the control of Petr Danielovich Popov, a now untouchable ruthless thug 'even more ruthless then me', joked Potunov, as he poured another round of Impierskiy vodka, homemade at the restaurant of the same name. Although the fat slob annoyed Max, he did recognise that Juba knew his stuff.

'What do you mean most of the empire?' asked Max.

'Yes, Gaspadin Max,' continued Potunov, 'most of it. Apparently you are not aware of this. When Oleksandr died, Lena was able to dispose of almost all of the assets—at a fraction of their real price, of course, but it made no difference to her since there was so much money. But Oleksandr had made her the sole owner of two very desirable assets for tax purposes. I do not think she even knew that. The first one is the Maksinovna diamond mine, which has revenue in the higher range of hundreds of millions of dollars, and the second one is the highly strategic cobalt mine of Zolotiy Liess, which produces the cobalt which is used even in the production of your famous F-15 jets. The mere ownership of these two mines, which are a subject of great envy, is enough to put her life in danger in our beautiful federation of all Russia. The oligarchs are continuing their fratricide wars to control all natural resources in Russia, and since Elena Alexandrovna owned these two, getting rid of her after having her sign the properties over is a practical means of conducting a very effective business transaction. And if they do not get her to sign the titles over, and they kill her, my dear Gaspadin Max, you are next on the list. . . Gaspadin Max, I will give you one piece of advice: either Elena Alexandrovna is already dead, and there is nothing that your presence here will accomplish, except getting you killed; or she is not dead but will be soon—and you will not find her before she is dead—and you are still going to get killed as well. My advice is for you to not even stay the night in our lovely dark city. Simply turn around, go back, and start mourning. You will never find her alive. Of this I am certain. She represents over $1.5 billion of annual revenue that these people want. People who are so close to the prime minister that they fuck the same whores, people who are financing "his" Olympic Games, people who are so protected they can kill Oleksandr Valerovich, who was a friend of the president, and get away with it. You, two goons with peashooters, and a hard dick cannot possibly do anything. Even if you get to kill the head of the brotherhood, they will all come after you. You remember what happened to the village of Lidice after the Czechs killed Heydrich? Exactly the same thing will happen to you, and that pretty yacht of yours, the . . . oh yes, the Princess of Russia, will become the most unsafe place in the harbour of Monaco. . . Boom!'

'Surely, you don't expect me to just fucking walk away, do you?' Max was losing his temper. He knew the situation was as desperate as Potunov described, but he was not going to admit defeat so easily. 'Is there a way to negotiate with these fucks?' he asked.

'Gaspadin Max, I have a simple question for you: did the Jews have a way to negotiate with the Nazis? This is exactly the same way! These motherfuckers have entire armies at their disposal. They are entrenched in the entire country! There is nothing you can do, unless, of course, you want to declare war on their organisation. It will not save Lena. Her, you can forget about her entirely. She is like you say in American "collateral damage". But you can ally yourself with a rival group and bring down the fuckers who killed them, and recover your assets, and . . . make me a rich man, Gaspadin Max. You have this choice . . . If you are considering it, they, by all means stay in our lovely city, and you will be under protection. However, you must realise that by doing so you are declaring war to the Frunze Group— this is how they call themselves since they are Russians who came back from Kyrgyzstan, you know Bishkek, the old city of Frunze, capital of the gloriously shitty republic of Kyrgyzstan?'

'You are telling me that 1) I will not recover Lena alive, and 2) that if I stay here tonight, I am effectively launching myself into the oligarchs' war?' summarised Max. 'And I would have to drag your fat ass around as my partner? You must be fucking insane! How the fuck can you expect me to accept to these terms? I don't give a shit about the motherfucking assets! The only thing I care about is Lena. If I cannot get her back, your entire fucking country of motherfucking shit can go to fucking hell!' Max was shouting by then, but it only amused

Potunov who was contemplating the riches he could get from such a man who was now effectively an oligarch himself and a man of action not afraid of a few bullets flying around his head. Potunov decided that this was a man he could admire.

'Yes, Gaspadin Max, you will have to partner with the big sack of shit seating on this chair. You are right, I am a big sack of shit—and one that failed to get rich at the right moment . . . But this fat ass, as you say, has still control of about half of the FSB forces which are commanded by officers I trained. Once we have the funding you can provide, you will have your own mafia here, except, it will be a legal one,' Potunov laughed, amused by the irony, 'and one that is entrenched all over Russia as well—just like your enemies. I tell you what, Gaspadin Max, why don't you stay here tonight, we'll put out the rumour that your pilots had reached their flying hours limit and that they could not fly back, think about it, and in the morning you can tell me what you decide . . . I assume you will be staying in Lena's suite. If so, I will be sending a security details to the hotel, some of the best FSB men—there will be about ten of them watching over you. Let's meet back here in the morning, about ten?' Potunov stood up with difficulty, shaking Max's hand and taking him to the door.

On the way to the hotel, Max was in no mood to talk. John, a former officer veteran of 2 Para, recipient of the Victoria Cross, who had seen action in Iraq and Afghanistan, was not a talkative man to start with. He was all military efficiency without the need for bombastic behaviour. He had killed more men in combat than Max, and contrarily to Max, he had been rewarded for it. They settled in their respective rooms at the Grand Hotel, and Max immediately noticed that, as he had expected from Russians, the security detail was there, well-armed, and especially highly visible. They escorted Max and John to the private dining room they had reserved, where Dmitry joined them. As the junior member of the trio, Dmitry was there as an adviser, since both Max and John spoke Russian, their intent was to use Dmitry as a technical resource. Over the appetizer of 'Karat Caviar', ossetra sturgeon caviar from Israel since the Russians had managed to fish out all of the sturgeons in the Caspian Sea, Max and John discussed the situation. Did they have an appetite to get involved in a war in Russia to control $1.5 billion of revenue? There was no logical reason to do so. POR Enterprises, for Princess of Russia Enterprises, had assets of over $16 billion, and they currently generated about $3 billion from investments in the stock markets around the world, and construction and real estate in Europe and exotic tourist destinations. Since Lena had made Max the co-owner of the corporation, all of the assets would revert to him in the case of her death, so there was no financial motivation to enter into a destructive conflict.

'Yes,' interjected Dmitry, 'but do you think that you will be safe after they get what they want form Lena? Do you think you are going to be sheltered from their greed to come and repossess the assets that were financed from money they now realised they should never have paid Lena? And if they decide that this is what they want to do, you, actually all of us, will be under great danger. The mere association with Lena's name will be sufficient to have us sentenced to death, you know that, Max.'

'He's got a point, added John with his 2 Para accent. The moment they went after Lena, they actually went after you. They know perfectly well you'll never forgive them. And they know who you were then . . . they know you will try to go after them. They have no choice but to take you out, mate. Old Potunov knows that, that's why he has this detail protecting you. You are his best asset. It is early Christmas for him. He has already figured out that you have no choice but bring the fight to the bloody bastards. Anything else, you might as well blow your brains out right now. You may not like what he looks like, but that Potunov has a brain and he uses it!'

'So you are both telling me I am fucked regardless?' asked Max.

'Well yes, yes and no,' replied John. 'The way I see it, you have four choices: one, you get out of here and run, and you are going to have to run for the rest of your life; two, you go on the offense and you put them on the run, then you become one of the oligarchs clique and you become a friend of the prime minister; three, you turn over all of your assets to the Frunze Group, this is the from riches to rags scenario; and four, you end it all tonight and you blow your brains out in spectacular fashion in this beautifully decorated dining hall. You have no other choices. Well, you could also include disappearing and becoming a hermit in those mountains of Arizona you like so much, are they the Santa Ritas?'

'You know I will not run, I will not give all the assets away and bring the mafia into perfectly legal business, I will not commit suicide, and as for the mountains, you always get it wrong . . . It is the *Dragoon Mountains*, and they can wait for me . . . I am not he hermit type, thank you very much,' responded Max.

'Then it leaves only one option,' concluded John.

They continued with dinner which included sterlet fish, one of Lena's favourites. Max had not had the time to really think about her disappearance, but once he got back to the Imperial Suite, he could not help feel the powerlessness to rescue the woman he loved above all. He went to bed but he was not been able to find any sleep. He relived every night he had spent with her in this very room, in this very bed. The desire to touch her skin excited his virility beyond limits, to the point where he could stand it no longer. The pain in his loin was physical as well. He could have chosen to relieve it, but in a sense it would have been like being unfaithful to her. He thought of her in a mafia holding cell, lying in the dark in despair, tortured and knowing her death was near and unavoidable. If she was alive she was thinking of him, and he had to think of her so that she could feel his thoughts reaching out to her. She, too, would find no relief to her torture. He tossed and turned all night, hearing the distant palace clock tower count the hours as they went and he found no rest. He dozed off for a while only to be awakened by a nightmare. He was at the office, working at his corner office, overlooking the street. He was absorbed in a document, and he did not hear her arrive. He felt a tap on his right shoulder. She had returned in the glory of her beauty, with her radiating blond hair reflecting light like a halo around her head. Surprised, he got up, turned around, took her in his arms, and kissed her with the pent-up passion of the separation. Then as he felt the sensation of her tongue touching his as if it was real, he watched her disintegrate in a dust of particles, and he woke up in a sweat. But now, the sensation of the kiss had simply made the matters worse. He got up to go to the bathroom. He thought of her even more, and he saw the reflection of her face into the mirror, as if she was combing her hair after making love. He broke down and sobbed. He went back to bed, knowing the futility of his attempt to find sleep. He waited with anticipation for the morning to come, for the meeting with Old Potunov, as John called him. He got up again, messed around with the laptop, scanning the Russian news to see if there was any information about her. He drank another whisky. That helped him find sleep. He dozed off for a couple of hours. At six in the morning, he woke up to the noise of traffic in the street below. He wanted the night to be over, and at the same time, he felt such emptiness at not having her with him at that moment, cosy in the cocoon of the heavy quilt, and able to enjoy the warmth of her body. Time passed. He did not want to get up. For what purpose would he do that? He had lost interest in everything that had counted for him. His own life would no longer matter if he could not share it with her. Yet, he knew he had a heavy fight in front of him, and despite the sadness, the despair, the tears, and the sobbing, in the morning, he would have to be equal to the old Max, the one that had survived North Africa and Spain. He mustered the souvenir of her face, he fixed in his memory every last detail of her eyes, of her smile, of her nose. He knew he would never see them again, and he sobbed quietly into the pillow. When the wake up service called him with breakfast ready in the dining room, he was a wreck.

THE DATURA SOLUTION

At nine forty-five, all three of them got into the armoured Mercedes for the short drive to Gangutskaya Ulitsa, and they were escorted in front and in the back by two official SUVs of the FSB. When they entered Potunov's office, there were several other people around the conference table. Potunov himself had dressed up. He was wearing a white Egyptian cotton shirt, a Hugo Boss suit (Max recognised it immediately), and he had made himself rather presentable. He joked about it: 'You see, Gaspadin Max, this is what a sack of shit looks like when it dresses up!' Potunov introduced the people around the table by their first names only, telling Max they were all in the FSB, either in Sankt Petersburg or in Moscow (one colonel general had flown in from Moscow), or in other back organisations. 'You must realise, Gaspadin Max, commented the colonel general, that although Igor Petrovich fucks the same whores as our prime minister, this does not mean that the prime minister either likes it, or likes him.' Max concluded that Igor Petrovich was the head of the Frunze group. 'As a matter of fact, continued the general, our prime minister does not like it all. Of course, Igor Petrovich is protected, the prime minister needs him and his money—and you know why—but if somebody was going to get rid of Igor Petrovich, the prime minister would rant and rave in public, but privately he would be very grateful. You see, one thing that is really not good about Igor Petrovich is that he is not from Sankt Petersburg. He cannot be trusted. Our friend Potunov, on the other hand, as I, is from our Venice of the North. So our enterprise would be well received from the Kremlin.'

'Gentlemen, it seems you are assuming I have taken the decision to get into a mafia war,' commented Max while smiling.

'Mister Max, you would disappoint us greatly if you were naïve enough to think that we had not listened to every one word of your conversations,' responded the general.

'General, you know that I would never disappoint you!' retorted Max, but the point now consists of figuring out where Igor Petrovich is and hitting him. I believe that we should go on the offense before they do themselves. I know exactly how vulnerable we all are. The sooner we attack, the stronger our position becomes. But before we talk about that, what do you gentlemen know about Lena's whereabouts?'

A more junior officer at the far corner of the conference table scratched his neck and started talking hesitantly.

'The Frunze Group is known throughout Russia for its excessive brutality. If, and this is a big if, if Lena is in their hands, I must warn you that in the past seven or eight years, since they acquired the notoriety they have today, they have never released a single hostage alive. One of our undercover agents has described a process that consists in imprisoning the person in a completely dark and soundproofed cell, thus depriving it of all sensory stimuli, while starving it and providing just enough water for survival. This can last two to five days, after which they open the cell, make the person do whatever they need it to do—in your case sign papers—and the person is executed on the spot. Usually a bullet in the neck. If she is in their hands, she is most likely already dead.'

'Okay, Colonel,' Max guessed he was a colonel, 'you can cut the shit. You know exactly where she is and whether she is dead or alive, so tell me and get it over with!'

'Well, continued the colonel, we knew where she was yesterday when you arrived. Potunov called us and we activated Plan Red and actually found out that she is in Frunze's hands and that she was being held in the Gatchina area, but she was moved during the night, and, the reason we know she was moved is that. . .' The colonel hesitated, not knowing if he should continue. Max came to his help:

'The reason you know they moved her is because you found her body,' Max stated.

This did not hide the embarrassment of the colonel:

'Yes, we found her body. I am sorry.'

Nobody moved or said anything, waiting for Max's reaction. He hid his face in his hands, elbows on the table. The wind had been knocked out of him. He needed to meditate, he needed a moment to recover. They all waited. After about two or three minutes, Potunov asked him if he needed privacy. Max shook his head no. In the meantime, he saw the future disappear in front of him, he saw the happiness he had grown accustomed to simply vanish. He was a desperate man. He was like a wounded tiger, whose fight for survival stops at nothing as he gets cornered. 'No more Mister Nice Guy,' he would have joked in happier days. He would destroy all of Russia, if he had to, to get the motherfuckers! Finally, he looked up at the assembly of people around the room. They were surprised that no tears were visible, but Max had never had the habit of public crying. What scared even Potunov was the hatred and savage determination in Max's eyes. Even John, who had known Max for three years, had never seen such look in his eyes.

'Gentlemen, on 8 September 1941, the Nazis came to then Leningrad and proceeded with the total destruction of the city. I want you all to get inspired by the brutality and pitilessness in the history of your city, and to put the same determination in destroying the Frunze Group as the Nazis put in destroying your city. The first order of business is to develop an operations plan, and I want it done by tomorrow night. Period. The second order of business is to plan the assassination of Igor Petrovich. You tell me where he is, and I'll take care of the fucker. Third, I believe Potunov, the general, and I have to agree on some parameters. Fourth, I am running this operation, and things will be done my way or not at all. And finally, I want the Frunze Group destroyed by Christmas. We have eleven days. Any objections?'

Nobody said anything. Nobody dared disagree—they had worked all their lives for dictators, and they knew better than disagreeing with men who had power. A second general gave orders to the colonels in the room, and they went into an adjacent office to start planning with John and Dmitry. The colonel general, Potunov, and Max went into Potunov's private office to discuss the financial terms.

CHAPTER 21

Max did not leave Potunov's office until late in the evening. He, Potunov, and the colonel general, who finally had revealed his name as Andrei Andreiovich Andropov (his nickname was Triple A), had agreed to a very lucrative arrangement for all three men. Under the terms they reached, Max would retain control of 51 per cent of the mines in Yakutsk, and Potunov and Andrei would split the remaining 49 per cent. As for the assets they would seize from the Frunze Group, it was agreed that Max would take 40 per cent, and his associates would split the remainder as they saw fit between themselves and whoever was still standing and needed to be compensated. A lawyer was called in after lunch to draw the legal documents, and the entire package was signed by the time they went home. In the other office, planning for operations aimed at taking down the Frunze Group were advancing rapidly. In Max's absence, John had taken over the leadership of the team. It was decided that it would be a multi-prong attack destined at absolutely destroying the organisation. John, very much the Para officer again, briefed Max, Potunov, and Andrei:

'We will strike simultaneously at six targets on 25 December. This will allow us to meet your deadline, to have a reasonable planning time, and to have an absolute surprise advantage. We will strike at zero hour ten Moscow time, a time when everybody is in the middle of

THE DATURA SOLUTION

celebrating Christmas, either drinking, opening presents, or fucking their wives or girlfriends, or both. We are therefore putting in place seven teams. Team One will be led by yourself and will hit Igor Petrovich in his villa on the Island of Capri where our intelligence tells us he is planning to spend the night of Christmas with some close associates—this will allow us to eliminate about half of the more senior leaders of the Group, to include all of the Frunze associates. Team Two will hit the headquarters of the Group at Ladozhskyi Vakzal. The reason we are doing this is that the rest of the leadership will be there celebrating Christmas in the penthouse of the building. While the strike at Capri will be a shoot and kill approach, the one at Ladozhskyi Vakzal will be brutal. Colonel Onegin has already procured a thousand kilos of explosives that are going to be installed in the heating system of the floor below the penthouse. At 0010 on 25 December, Merry Christmas, the whole top floor will be pulverised including Frunze members, wives, prostitutes, cooks, and servers. We will make sure that the bodies of a couple of Chechens are recovered within the wreckage, of course. Again, this is in line with the orders you gave to approach this like the siege of Leningrad. The other targets will be less spectacular but nevertheless of a nature to destroy the group: one of the key FSB officers is a member of the Group. General Kozlov is the FSB second-in-command, and he will be executed by a team of elite Spetsnaz Unit Alfa will gun down the general wherever he is at H Hour. In his safe, papers will be found incriminating him in the illegal trafficking of nuclear material with Iran, and Unit Alfa will use weapons consistent with those in the Iranian Revolutionary Army, thus giving credence to a deal gone wrong theory. The fourth target will be the director of the aluminium works in Krasnovarsk, the reason being that this gentleman is the brother of Igor Petrovich and is seen as his successor. We will send a special assassination team from the KGB. The fifth target is another one of Igor's close associates who is serving a ten year jail sentence at Vladimirskyi Central. One of the other prisoners will take care of him. Finally, the sixth target will be the head of the Sankt Petersburg Police which is both a favour to our friend Potunov and will allow us to promote a gentleman much favourable to our cause. At the same time we eliminate these people, a few Christmas presents will go to a list of seventy-two people who will become instantly favourable to our cause. We have identified Christmas gifts that go from $1 million at minister level to $50,000 to federal judges. The total bill comes out to about 11 million, and I did not think you would object.

'John, this is perfect! Fantastic work to you and the team!' commented Max.

'Well thank you, John answered. Of course the planning of each operation has already been assigned to key individuals, and for security purposes we will not meet as a group. There will be no reporting on the planning to avoid moles figuring out what is going on before it happens. Orders have been given on this plan and they will be followed to bring success to the entire operation. Now and I need to sort out the Capri operation. Our code word for it is simply Operation One.'

They left at nine o'clock and returned to the hotel. Max had eaten nothing all day. The news of Lena's death had not hit him yet, and he was bracing himself when he would be alone in the suite with her toiletries spread out on the shelf in the bathroom, her clothes in the closet, her shoes, and everything that had been such cherished objects simply because they were hers. The three men want to dinner, careful not to talk about anything remotely related to the day's activities. The mood was one of restraint even if John made the occasional joke. For the most part, they dined in silence, respecting Max's mourning of the woman who had made him happy beyond his wildest dreams. This woman was now gone forever, and he could not understand it. He knew from experience that the pain and the horrible feeling of despair would hit him sooner or later, and he was not looking forward to it. It would always be there. They had shared so much complicity and so many adventures together that there could never be another Lena. He gazed into the distance unable to move and to detach his eyes from the wall where he was visualising her. He also knew that little by little her features would erode inside his head, that he would lose her pixel by pixel, until there would be a day when he would barely be able to see her. And the only things he would have to remember her by would be a few hundreds of still pictures and a few hours of videos.

He waited until the very last moment to go back to the empty suite, holding on to the impossible hope that she would somehow be there when he walked in. But the suite had remained stubbornly empty. A few days before, he had watched her slender figure reluctantly walk towards the awaiting Rolls, her black leather coat tightly wrapped around her, her red scarf peeking out from under her blond hair. He had wished her to turn around, to look at him one more time, so that he could engrave in his mind her beauty, even as the streaks of tears run down her pretty face. She had not turned around, even as he followed her silhouette disappearing inside the car. He followed her as she drove away along the pier. He knew that she could not have left him if she had looked back. He knew the intensity of the sadness she was experiencing, a sadness whose strength could only match the intensity of her passion for him. He watched finally as the Rolls vanished into the traffic, and she had now vanished into the nothingness of permanent absence. He was sitting on the bed, her clothes, the only reminder of her presence in his life. The chair she liked so much was desperately cold. He thought about how he had caressed her small hand, how he had barely touched her, and how she had shuddered at the reminiscence of the touching that had revealed her passion to him a few days before. She had taken his hand and had pushed it between her legs, where he had felt her dampness. He had not wanted her to go. He had wanted time to stop, he had told her it was dangerous for her to go to Russia, that the mafia notwithstanding, she was too well known, and this alone was a danger. If he had only been more forceful! How he wanted to have these precious moments back. And now the sadness became unbearable. He was overwhelmed by an uncontrollable desire to cry, to let her know how vulnerable without her, him the soldier who had faced danger with stoicism. He could not face her leaving for ever. When she had stood up to go to the bathroom to prepare for the night, he felt his entire life summarised in a Mikhail Krug song Тебе Моя Последняя Любовь. He made every effort possible to control the pain, a pain he had never known could be so devastating. He stumbled and collapsed on the floor sobbing uncontrollably and shouting his pain like a wounded animal. She would not want to see him like this, but there was nothing he could do. He wanted to be strong for her, but he had to let the pain do its work, he had to let the pain destroy him so that he could be rebuilt. He had to have these attacks of pain and sorrow in private to make sure that nobody's resolve would weaken. Now that the only person worth living was gone, he did not give a fuck about anything else. He no longer had the strength to care. He was angry with himself for not having accompanied her. If he had, she might still be alive, or they would have died together, which was better than surviving with the unbearable pain. He did not know how he fell asleep, but sometime around two in the morning he woke up freezing, in the foetal position, on the floor exactly where he had been taken down by the pain. He got up like an old man—he was a complete wreck, the shadow of the real Max. He fell back on his knees, crawled to the bathroom, and vomited his entire dinner into the commode. He set on the floor, knocked out like a boxer who has just received an uppercut to the temple and tries to figure out where he is, why some guy is counting, trying to sort out if it would be a good thing to get up, or whether he should just stay down. Max's mind was completely enveloped in a thick grey fog from which he could not shake it. He sat there, unable to decide what he should do. He was in worse shape than when he had been recovered in Morocco. Then the pain was physical. Now it was mental. There was no IV drip that could fix this type of pain. Yes there was, he suddenly thought—whisky. He could drink himself into oblivion. He tried to stand to get to the liquor cabinet faster, but his legs could not carry him. With the acrid bitter taste of vomit in his mouth, he did not have the wherewithal to brush his teeth or to rinse his mouth. He crawled back to the bedroom. Everything around him was spinning. His head was captured into a whirlwind of nothingness and blackness. He closed his eyes, but the spinning and the disorientation did not stop. He barely made it up to the bed, mustering the strength to climb on it. He lay on it, pulled the cover, and closed his eyes. Suddenly, he shook in panic as his brain shut down and went into a place it had never been to. Max had passed out.

This is where the groom found him when he delivered breakfast at eight as Max had requested. Max could hardly move. The man called the reception and asked for a 'врач' to be sent up. Max did not have the courage to object, telling the man he was okay, it would pass, there was nothing a doctor could do. The groom sat him up in bed, served him coffee, gave him orange juice, while the hotel manager himself came to the room to see what was the matter with a valued customer who was paying over $2,600 a night—one has to take care of such economic assets. Half an hour later the doctor arrived. He declared the patient on the verge of exhaustion, recommended three days of rest and gave him a shot of vitamin B12, and prescribed a cure of the same vitamin. Max refused any mind-altering drug, and the doctor was satisfied that the patient would soon be better. When John arrived as scheduled at none, Max was still in bed, dishevelled and finishing the last of the coffee.

'Rough night, eh,' remarked John.

'You have no idea,' replied Max.

'We can go ahead without you today, Max. We are mainly gathering intelligence.'

'Thanks, John. But you know it's not my style. Give me an hour and I will be there. Don't worry, I just need time to get hold of myself.'

'Okay, no problem. I'll be off. I'll send the car back with Dmitry. See you there.'

'Bye, John. Thanks. I appreciate it,' Max assured him.

Outside the hotel, the armoured Mercedes was waiting together with the special security detail. The rear right passenger door of the car was open. Each of the trucks of the FSB had a door open and a guard with a Kalashnikov at the ready was surveying the scene. The assassin lunged out from behind the valet's desk. He pulled out a silencer-equipped revolver and five three rounds almost point blank at John as he was ready to step into the car. He immediately collapsed on the ground, his face barely missing the edge of the car chassis, he slid under the car where his head wedged itself under the body of the car. He did not lose consciousness and he heard all hell break lose above his head, he distinctly distinguished the rain of expanded brass cartridges from the Kalashnikovs rebound next to him, he heard the terror screams of the bystanders, and he heard bodies fall or hit the floor to get out of the line of fire. He heard the heavy handgun that had been used against him hit the pavement, which he thought meant his assassin had been hit, he heard the other guards come out of the SUVs, run around them, and also start shooting. 'Fuck,' John thought, 'there was only one bloody guy. How many people are they shooting?' And then as fast as it had started, it all stopped. He heard the last cartridge fall and bounce around on the hard surface, and there was silence. And there was the smell of gunpowder all around him. That smell revitalised him. It brought back the soldier in him. He tried to push himself from under the car, but the pain in his back was too sharp. At the same time, he felt two strong hands pull on each of his legs, and he was unwedged. They help him stand up. 'It's over. We got the fuck!' the captain, head of the detail, told him. John surveyed the carnage, and thought, 'With all the people you hit, I am sure glad you didn't miss him!' There was blood everywhere, expended cartridges were littering the floor by the dozen, and there were at least four dead, or soon to be dead, people.

'Which one was it?' asked John.

'The blotnoy is the one with the fancy suit.' The captain pointed at the man's hand that bore the blue tattoos М-Й-Р-Т. 'A fucking convict,' added the captain as he spat in the dead man's general direction, more out of principle than in an attempt to actually spit on him.

'And the others?' inquired John.

The man looked at him like he was stupid and simply shrugged his shoulders. Then he inquired: 'Are you okay?'

'Never felt better!' replied John. But the humour was lost on the Russian whose body was full of adrenaline. The detail had called for a cleanup crew and the only thing that mattered to the captain was that John was still alive.

'What do you want to do?' asked the captain.

'I am going to go back to my room as soon as I can breathe again and change my bullet proof vest.'

'No need for that. We have some in the trucks. Ivan, get a flak jacket over here—large!' ordered the major.

They gave the jacket to John, they pushed him into the Mercedes and they left minus one of the two SUVs. The protection detail had just been extended to inside the hotel and the men of the FSB were soon guarding Max's door. While driving to the office, John who probably had broken ribs thought how lucky he had been that the assassin had been incompetent. He should have aimed for the head. If he had, John would be dead by now. He called Max and told him what had happened.

The news shook max out of his torpor, out of his feeling sorry for himself. And he found a new energy, as if he too had smelled the familiar scent of gunpowder. That smell that soldiers find nauseating at first, but that they gradually develop a liking for, a smell that is comfortable when the shit hits the fan and the weapons are firing in defence of the position, the smell that they all miss after they leave the army. The smell is *the* army smell. He showered and his torments for the night were gone. He dressed and opted for two flak jackets: the civilian one John was wearing, and the military grade that the Russians had brought up. He then went to the safe and packed two Glocks with four magazines. The second one was for John. At nine thirty, he left the room in famous shape, and escorted by the FSB detail, he made his way to the lobby that had been cleared by hotel security. Outside, the cleanup was still going on. John had been right: '*they* had not fucked around!' They obviously did not care about collateral damage. When he got to Potunov's' office, he was waiting for him.

'So, Gaspadin Max, what do you think of our troop's efficiency? I think we had a lucky call, but the little fuck is dead. By the way, you will be interested to know that the weapon is of the same calibre that killed your wife. And that piece of shit probably mistook John for you. We are certain you were intended to be the target.'

John realised that he needed to see Lena's body, that he needed to make arrangements for the funeral, that he needed to cancel the Christmas party. Or should he? And then, turning to Potunov:

'If you knew I was the intended target, why didn't you call us and warn us?'

'You see, Gaspadin Max, our intelligence is not yet flowing efficiently. We learned about it a few minutes too late. Believe me, after the document we signed yesterday, I want to keep you alive more than anybody in the world. Actually, I want to stay alive myself! I lost four kilos since your first visit. Of course, I carry so much shit around that you could not notice. . .'

The first order was to tighten up the security around the team. They decided that the planning should be done independently in the six groups that were planning action, so as to minimise the necessity to travel and make their movements obvious. Potunov dispatched an anti-explosive detail to the hotel, and the top floor where Max and John were staying, as well as the floor below, was evacuated, all issues except the elevator locked and a guard detail was put in place by each door.

THE DATURA SOLUTION

The ROE were simple: shoot on sight and without warning anyone outside of six persons: Max, John, Dmitry, the hotel manager and two stewards who were specially assigned to their service and wore a special uniform. The ROE was even more extreme for the floor below, as the orders were to kill on sight anyone who ventured there.

By mid-afternoon, the coroner called and stated that Lena's body was ready for Max's viewing. The Mercedes and the two escort cars made their way through traffic quickly, the sirens of the escort blasting their way through the lines of traffic in typical Russian manner, with little regards to the rights of the citizens. Within twenty minutes, they had reached the salmon-coloured building that was the Sankt Petersburg City Morgue. The coroner, Professor Valentin Grishko, met them at the top of the few steps leading into the building. He shook Max's hand without a word, knowing from experience that words were useless in such moments of mourning and tragedy. Thankfully, his service had prepared the body for viewing in a private room, and Max was spared the sight of the steel drawers. They entered the second door on the right into a brightly lit room. The state-of-the art power stretcher, which contrasted with the rundown appearance of the entire building, was there in the middle of the room with a white sheet over the body. Max braced himself for the sight of Lena. The Professor slowly pulled the sheet of the body. The woman was naked under it, so out of respect he only uncovered the face.

'Sons of bitches!' exclaimed Max, startling the Professor who had remained stone faced up to that time. 'How the fuck can they do that to me? Motherfuckers!'

He said no more. Looking for the captain, he asked him to dial Potunov, right away:

'What the fuck?' yelled Max, 'what is the meaning of this shit? You went through all of this simply to get an agreement with me?'

'I don't understand' ventured Potunov, sensing the volatility of the situation and Max's rage over the airwaves, 'what are you so worked up about Gaspadin Max?'

'Oh, cut the Gaspadin shit, won't you? You know it's not her! Why the fuck do you go through all of this to have me sign over the assets to you?' demanded Max.

'Careful, this is not a secure line. What the fuck, it's not her? Well, if it is not, you should be happy! And you should come back here right away so that we can figure out where the fuck they are holding her. I call a meeting. Come back. But I assure you, I know nothing of what you are talking about. It makes no sense,' responded Potunov.

'Okay.' Max closed the phone and told the captain to take him back, while he was telling the flabbergasted Professor Grishko that the woman was not Lena.

But something in the Professor's demeanour told him he had known about it the whole time.

Back in the office with Potunov, the first thing Max asked was that the professor be arrested and made to talk. He knew what was going on. Within the hour, the professor was in the basement of the FSB Headquarters in Sankt Petersburg, and his ordeal started. The second order of business was to have a special task forced charged with finding Lena. One key element is that the would-be killer had been identified as Ivan Petrovich who had been released from the penitentiary in April after serving twenty-four years for murder. Of specific interest was the dirt that was recovered from his shoe soles that came from only one place in Sankt Petersburg and was immediately recognisable as that of the semi-abandoned Palace of G. . . This meant that either Ivan Petrovich liked to visit crumbling palaces of the tsar, or that he had a good reason to go there. And surveillance had already been put into place to verify the second possibility. Max decided to rely on the FSB to find Lena—he personally had no access to intelligence, but they agreed that any information should be shared with him and that any decision point should be reviewed and agreed with him. And he made clear that regardless of the new situation, the arrangements reached the day before were valid and that all attacks should proceed as planned.

CHAPTER 22

The courier arrived at the US Embassy in Madrid on Calle Serano. He presented his credentials and was admitted into the underground garage. He parked the car, a Chrysler 300 C, in one of the reserved slots and made his way to the top floor, punching in the ambassador's personal code to have direct access to his office suite. The courier, a retired CIA operative, who was now working for George McMillan's Green Ventures Corporation, or GV Corp, had been at the service of the ambassador for five years, while George was still a Wall Street banker. Ricardo Gonzales was of Cuban descent and had spent almost his entire career in South America. He was now particularly useful to the ambassador because Spanish was his mother tongue (the ambassador of course did not know ten words of Spanish), and because he could 'take care of problems'. In George's world, there were always problems that needed to be 'taken care of'. And Ricardo, in mafia terms, was both a house painter and a carpenter. In other words, he could terminate a problem and make it disappear. In the ambassador's world, no one used the world 'kill'. It was always innuendos, references to a kitchen that need to be repainted, to an obstacle that needed to be taken out, or to a courtesy that needed to be extended. The ambassador, in all of his maturity, business acumen, and knowledge of human nature, had proven to be rather shallow and naïve in the way he had recruited Ricardo. Ricardo had been recommended to him by a business partner also from Cuban origins, the famous Juan-Javier Peres who had made headlines in the Seventies because of his daring escape from Cuba aboard a homemade plane he had fabricated from garbage cans and an old 440 Dodge engine. Coming from an advisor in Cuban affairs to the president, the recommendation was solid, and George had not bothered to further check either Ricardo's background or Juan-Javier's motivation. If he had bothered to inquire, he would have found that Ricardo had been a double agent at the service of both the United States and the Chilean military junta, and that Juan-Javier wanted to have one of his men deep inside George's organisation, thus giving him a powerful advantage during negotiations with the ambassador or any of his corporations. In this manner, Ricardo continued his vocation of being a double agent. In a world of Armani suits, elegant evening dresses, charity events at the Lincoln Center, and weekends in the Hamptons, the world of George and Juan-Javier was just as ruthless, if not more, than that in which the Frunze Group operated. It was simply far more discreet and subtle. What the ambassador should have been careful about as well is how he treated Ricardo. For example, upon delivery of the package to the ambassador, George had taken the package and had dismissed Ricardo with a shooing of the hand as if he were a dog, or some sort of lower form of life. Ricardo did not like that and greatly resented this affront. What the ambassador should have been more careful of as well was that Ricardo had hoped that rubbing shoulders with a man as rich as George and working with him for over eleven years, some of that money would have trickled down to him. But Ricardo received a salary of just over $120,000 year without the benefit of bonuses or profit sharing on the deals that he had helped 'negotiate'. Ricardo knew a lot about the ambassador. He knew how a ruthless sleazy 'bastardo' he was, and he knew that if he tried to quit, the ambassador would not hesitate to have him taken care of. One could not do that much dirty work and simply walk away. So Ricardo had come to the logical conclusion that either the ambassador had to die or Ricardo did. The two of them had come to the point of the relationship where neither was safe as long as the other one lived. This is why Ricardo had bugged every place where the ambassador conducted business, to include the armoured suburban that he used for his so-called driving meetings, arrogantly thinking that no bugs could be set in a car. 'He has seen too many movies,' thought Ricardo. And this is also why Ricardo had not hesitated to open the package he was carrying back. From whatever he could make out from the documents (Ricardo did not read Russian), he saw they dealt with mining companies, since the names were in Latin letters. He already knew from the bugs that the ambassador was so angry at his ex-wife that he had resolved to steal her Russian business from her. Ricardo knew that this information was very valuable to Max (he knew of Max—who didn't?) and that the more valuable information, the more perishable it was. Later that day, he informed the ambassador that he needed to take an early Christmas vacation to go 'spend Christmas with a Russian woman he had met'. Indeed, he caught a cab to the Madrid airport, and on the way there he called the Princess of Russia to arrange a meeting with Max. When he found out that Max was not there, he tried to get his cell phone number, but was denied access to it. However, he was given the number of the head of security, John—no last name.

It was already past six thirty at night when John's cell rang. It had been another gruelling day of planning and the injuries he had sustained in the shooting were not getting any better. A visit to the American Clinic of Sankt Petersburg on Moika Embankment revealed what he had known already that he had broken ribs, four to be exact, and he had refused to take the pain killer the doctor wanted to give him. The pain would shoot out intensely at times, depending on a movement, and he would instantly be soaked in sweat. He did not recognise the number of the caller, but he recognised the country prefix '34' was Spain.

'This is John,' he answered.

'John, this is Fonso, I am calling you about Lena,' started Ricardo. 'I think you are wondering where she is, and I have information that may help you stop wondering.' Then he stopped talking.

'Hold on, Fonso. Are you saying you are calling from Spain and you know about Lena? So, let me tell you what I think: 1) your name is not Fonso, fair enough; 2) you are either in Russia or were in Russia not long ago; and 3) you are associated with that piece of shit McMillan. So, you have to put your cards on the table right now, or I fucking hang up,' responded John.

'A bit hot under the collar, aren't you? Is it because of the pain? Well, here is my answer: 1) you know I am not going to tell you my name, 2) yes obviously, 3) sometimes the people who are associated with someone no longer want to be so, 4) I need money to be able to enjoy life, and 5) if you hang up, you will hang up on the only person who knows where Lena is and is willing to sell you the info.'

'Hold on, I am putting you on hold,' and John turned to Max, and said, 'You need to listen to this: either the guy is a fraud or we have a lead.'

John put the loudspeaker on and reconnected the call:

'Fonso, I am back and Max is with me. Talk to us.'

'Hello, Max,' started Ricardo, 'well I was in Russia two days ago, where I had to pick up some interesting papers for the ambassador. These papers had to do with your interests Max, and in doing so, I had to go pick them up where they had been signed. And where they were signed, this is where the person who signed them is. And the person who signed them is Lena. You agree to the transaction, I give you the following information: 1) what the papers were, 2) what is McMillan's part in this, and 3) the address where Lena is, plus any other information you want. In return, you give me $10 million now and $10 million when you find Lena. Do we have a deal?'

John was signalling to say no by shaking his head from side to side. Instead in his cool and deep masculine voice, Max said:

'How are you doing Ricardo? Long time no see! I always knew that one day you would come through for me! Give me your account and routing number. I am sending you $10 million. But, how do I know you will call me back once you receive the money? How do I know you will not be run over by the freakin' bus, eh? So, here is what I want you to do. I want you to give me all of the information now. I will send you $25 million, but I want the info now. Either you trust me, or you let Lena die. And if you do, Ricardo, I swear that there is not a place on earth where you can hide and I cannot find you. So, here is my proposal, and it is non-negotiable: you give me the info you have, I send you $25 million now, and we arrange a meeting where I can debrief you of all the other information, or you tell me nothing, I send you nothing, and if Lena dies, so do you. You have thirty seconds to think about it. Starting . . . Now!'

The seconds passed. There was silence at the other end. John whispered to Max, 'You know you are insane, right?' Then Ricardo's voice:

'Okay. I'll give you the information, but if you double cross me, I will come for you, Max.'

'Fair enough,' responded Max, 'but you won't have to.'

'First things first. My account data: First Caribbean International Bank, Nassau, the Bahamas, routing number 1229548-9, account number 494885. You got it?'

'Yes, Ricardo, we got it.'

And Ricardo spilled the beans:

'For months, the ambassador has been talking about setting things right, and how he wanted to make sure that was supposed to be his would be his again. Well, he planned this whole thing with some guys working from the Russian embassy, here in Madrid, to have Lena forced into signing over the papers of her mining companies to him. He tried with threats, and that did not work, so finally he decided to have her kidnapped and coerced into signing the papers. I know all of this because I bugged his office, his residence, and his car. I was out of the office for a couple of days, and suddenly I did not hear about Plan B as he called it. Then, four days ago, he tells me to drive—not fly—to drive to Russia and go pick up a package in Leningrad—he still cannot figure out the city changed names. Needless to say, I didn't freaking drive. I drove to the airport and flew. Anyhow, when I got there I went to the Radisson Hotel and I called this number that George had given me. Within one hour, a car came to pick me up. The windows were tinted, but I still figured out where we were going while pretending I was not. So we drove east of the city for about thirty minutes, to an abandoned village in the middle of no place and we go to Souiradna Barrack. It's a bunch of small wooden buildings, and you can see people coming for a long way. There was a guard outside the third building and the car stopped in front of it. I was frisked, my ID was checked, and I went in to the house. The place was a wreck. Again I pretended to see nothing, and they gave me the package of documents for that sleaze bag. I got back in the car, and they drove me back to the hotel. The next morning I was gone. There were six guys with heavy artillery watching that place—you don't need that many goons to watch a fucking letter. So, I figured that this is where Lena is. But one thing is clear that shithead McMillan organised the kidnapping.'

'Okay, Ricardo, your story holds the road,' commented Max. The transfer should be effective in about thirty minutes. But if this shit does not hold the road, start fucking running, buddy. Anything else?'

'In any case, I would go at night, NVGs, handguns with silencers, leave the cars about two miles out, and do it all in cotton. I would not go with leg infantry. Just two or three people tops. Good luck!'

The connection went dead. In Madrid, Ricardo considered how he could negotiate the information he had just received with the ambassador. He set down at one of the cafes in the airport, and thought about it. After the second beer, he had come to the conclusion that being of service to the ambassador, other than what was required under his current employment, would actually further threaten his life.

THE DATURA SOLUTION

The ambassador was worse than he was himself. So, in the end, it was not his sense of chivalry or gratitude that prevented Ricardo from selling Max out, but simply the cold logic of conducting business with scoundrels.

In Sankt Petersburg, Max was faced with the necessity of making a quick decision. He went to his laptop, opened Google Earth, and keyed in Souiradna Barrack, and he soon was able to see pictures of the area and of the village. It was now after 7:00 p.m., and there was no need to alert the entire FSB organisation. He would do it alone. He knew John was not up to it, not with four broken ribs. So, he called Dmitry and explained what was expected. Dmitry insisted that this was completely insane, but that as long as he had time to write his will, he would go along. Then Max called the FSB captain. He was about an hour in getting there, since he had been at a meeting regarding the Ladozhskyi Vakzal. When he got there, Max explained to him what he expected from him. He had two hours to get them NVGs, camos, high-powered rifles with scope and silencers, and if he wanted he could join them in the attack. The captain, a veteran of Chechnya and the Spetsnaz who wore a тельник under his uniform, agreed on the spot. He would be back in less than two hours. So the team included Max, Dmitry, and the captain. John had to reluctantly agree that his condition would prevent him to even walk the two miles to the target. When the captain arrived less than two hours later, as he had promised, he offered the services of a driver, who could come and pick them up on site after the operation, and a vehicle. Before getting all of the gear ready, they drew the plan of attack. They would conduct a three-pronged attack: Dmitry would arc to the left, so that he would be facing the door, the captain would arc to the right. When they were in position, Max, who would have stayed about 200 metres from the entrance to Souiradna Barrack, would use a rifle to shoot the guard. They would wait for his relief to arrive and Max, who would have advanced to the house in the meantime, would shoot him with one of the Glocks, point blank. Max and Dmitry would enter first and kill any one of male gender they encountered. The captain would follow.

'By the way, what is your name?' asked Max.

'Simnatsat,' answered the captain.

'Simnatsat, like seventeen?'

'Yes, like seventeen.'

Anyway, Simnatsat would immediately find the way to the cellar and investigate it with Dmitry. Any male found there should be shot without questions.

'Okay,' said Simnatsat, 'what about power? Are you planning to cut power? Because if these fucks have the advantage of having lights, we are toast with our NVGs. I can take care of it. Have power go out at 0225 hours.'

'Why at that time?' inquired Max.

'Because all of these guys who work for Frunze were part of the Morskaya Pekhota, and in the Morskaya Pekhota, they change guards, not on the hour, but on the half hour. So if we are in position at 0225 hours, the electric goes out—they probably won't even know—Max shoots the guard at 0226 hours. I creep up to the side of the building, and I shoot the guard coming out to replace him, then Max will have covered the 200 metres, and he is the first one in, with Dmitry as cover.'

'Agreed. Dmitry, any objections?'

'No, I'm good,' he answered.

The plan also received John's approval and the men inspected and prepared the weapons. They had ample time before the departure time which was set at 0030 hours. John managed to convince them they should take two cars, so that he could tag along. He would ride in the Merc with Dmitry, while Max and Simnatsat rode in the FSB car. Simnatsat called to ensure the power would be shut down in the entire district at 0225, and he threatened the electric company worker with death if this was not done according to his request. He commented that there were only two ways to motivate people in Russia: bribes or the threat of death. Then Max ordered room service, and while they were waiting for it, Max zeroed the sniper rifle, using the bed cover designs as zero targets. The steward did not even flinch at the display of military hardware strewn all around the room, nor at the fact that live 7.62-mm bullets were being fired in the room. After they ate, they spent the following two hours rehearsing the operation in the room, and rehearsing Plan B in case there was no guard outside. Then they wrapped all of their weapons in black garbage bags so that no spent cartridges would be left behind.

Using the GPS device, they parked the cars two miles from Souiradna Barrack. They got out of the cars, and bundled up in the camo winter gear, they made their way towards the target area. There was some snow but not enough to make the going particularly tough. During the first moments, they checked that their individual radios were off and that none of their gear made any noise while walking. They advanced in complete silence. There was nothing more to be said. They knew what they had to do, and all three were professional soldiers even if two of them were no longer active duty. At one point Max checked their advance and determined they were progressing too fast. The key to success was to arrive just in time. They had decided to arrive no sooner than 0220 hours, and when they saw the Barrack in front of them, they checked the distance by laser and they were only 500 metres away, and over fifteen minutes early. The three men separated and lay on the frozen ground waiting for Max's signal. At 0215 hours, Max motioned for them to move forward. He waited five minutes, and crouching down to keep his profile as low to the ground as possible, he moved to within 150 metres from the house because he had identified a small bump behind which he could find cover. He adopted a fully prone shooting position and partially unwrapped the 'Police' model of the SVD sniper rifle. He did not need to chamber a round because this had already been done at the hotel to minimise any noise on site. He uncovered the PSO-1 optical sight, acquired the guard in his crosshair, which he placed squarely on the man's head. He checked his watch and at precisely 0225, he squeezed the super sensitive trigger. He felt the familiar recoil of the weapon against his shoulder as the firing pin hit the cartridge and released a 7.62-mm down range through the silencer. Before he could register the slight pang of the bullet exiting the muzzle, and before he could enjoy the pungent smell of the gunpowder, he saw the head of the guard being pushed back, being jerked to the left, and exploding towards the wall of the house. The man fell heavily on the ground, dead already, and making a raucous that could probably be heard from the cars. Almost immediately the door opened, and a voice he could clearly hear asked 'What the fuck is going on?' As the man was stepping out, Max released a second round aiming for his head. He was spot on, and the second guard joined the first one in a heap on the ground. Simnatsat and Dmitry then rushed into the house, in an improvised change of plan as Max abandoned the rifle and pulled out the Glock, mentally preparing to rush down to the cellar. By the time he reached the house, Dmitry had already found the stairs going down and had disappeared below. Simnatsat was following him, and Max stayed upstairs to secure the area. The entire operation had lasted less than three minutes. From downstairs, Max heard the soft report of the muffled handguns and the distinctive thud of at least two bodies falling. He heard Dmitry called the cars on the personal radio, and he heard the driver acknowledging the instructions. Then Dmitry came up, and told Max, 'You should go downstairs,' as he proceeded to search the ground floor and continue secure the house.

What Max saw downstairs was a scene of devastation. Three men were slowly finishing bleeding to death, while a fourth one was on his knees with his hands on his head, in jaw hanging in a sure sign that it had been broken, and he too was bleeding abundantly from the mouth. Simnatsat had the pistol to the back of his neck. 'Look behind me,' he told Max, 'then tell me what you want me to do with this fucking piece of shit.' As he looked behind the captain, what Max saw tore at his heart. Chained to the wall, naked and shivering from cold and fright, dehydrated, bleeding from the beatings, blood caked over her face, covered in her own faeces, and barely conscious, Max had to collect all of his memories to recognise Lena. She, on the other hand, was too damaged to be able to recognise him. He took his jacket and covered her nakedness. Then he tried to find a way to detach her, but her hands had been padlocked into heavy metal rings.

'Ask him where the keys are!'

'They are in his pocket, gurgled the wounded man, pointing at one of his dead or dying accomplices.'

Max went over, found the keys, and as he was passing the last survivor, he kicked him as hard as he could in the ribs with the heavy combat boot. He heard the ribs crack, and he proceeded to unchain Lena. She dropped off the wall unconscious. Max told Simnatsat, 'Just shoot that fucker, and help me bring her up. 'Without any hesitation, the captain followed Max's instructions. Outside, the cars were waiting. None of the men bothered counting how many dead bodies there were. Simnatsat got the extra camo uniform and gave it to Max so he could dress Lena who was barely breathing. He got her into the Merc with the captain. John simply asked, 'American Hospital, right?' Max agreed. Dmitry took the driving duty, with John in the passenger seat. As they were turning around, he saw Simnatsat throw a thermal grenade into the house, and the FSB car followed them. Before they turned onto the road out, Max recovered the SVD, and as he returned to the car, the house was already engulfed in flames.

The ride to the American Hospital proved very taxing on Lena's feeble body. The motion of the car apparently made her sick, and she vomited bile, as she had not eaten anything in days. On the way there, John called the hospital, telling them about the emergency, so that when they arrived, Doctor Beregovna was already waiting. She happened to live not far from the hospital and had readily accepted to come to meet with the poor woman. Upon seeing the patient for the first time, as she was rolled into the hospital on a gurney, her hopes to actually save her vanished. Her first priority was to rehydrate and feed her. After the IV was hooked up, she asked Max to leave, so that she could go about the business of saving her without interference and drama. Max walked to the waiting room where the other three men were assessing the result of the evening. Simnatsat was amazed at the success and stated that the three of them had 'terminated nine enemy targets' without losing a single element of the team, and while rescuing the hostage. 'Too bad you were not around at Beslan!' he said, referring to the tragic end to the hostage situation at the Beslan school when the FSB had failed at rescuing over 300 hostages, mainly children, who had died in the operation. Max was indeed satisfied but knew that Lena's life held by a thread. He also knew that if they had not intervened that night, Lena would have died, no matter what. The next order of business was to protect her now that she was in hospital. Simnatsat had already made the proper calls to get an elite detail at the hospital, and Max would stand guard himself. A while later, he sent John and Dmitry back to the hotel, and he fell asleep in the waiting room as the FSB detail was put into place. At about seven in the morning, Doctor Beregovna woke him up, gave him a cup of coffee, and told him to follow her to her office. Once they were seating down, she briefed him on the situation:

'Gaspadin Max, you know as well as I do that your wife is in critical condition and that she is much closer to death than to life. Your rescue operation last night—or rather this morning—could not have been better timed, because she would not have survived another day. First, she is severely dehydrated, and as far as we can tell she has not had anything to eat in at least five days, so our first priority continues to be to hydrate her and to feed her. Unfortunately, she is unable to eat because she has a broken jaw. We did a complete scan of her body, and the brutality to which she was submitted is extreme. The list of her injuries is alarming: outside of the broken jaw, she is suffering from two fractures to the skull, one on the left temporal bone, the other one to the occipital bone—the trauma of the beatings caused some swelling of the brain, and we can only hope that her brain was not damaged—both of her zygomatic bones have been crushed, and they will require plastic surgery to reconstruct them, she has a detached retina in her left eye, and we have already scheduled surgery for this morning. This is an injury that cannot wait. Of course, we have already immobilised her jaw—we have wired it shut. In addition, you may have noticed that she had lost several teeth, to include all of the front teeth. Now we go to more serious injuries. Every one of her ribs had been broken—I have never seen that, Gaspadin Max—and two of them have punctured her left lung which collapsed. Obviously, we rectified this situation and she is now under respirator, and the lung should recover. She has a lacerated liver, a broken solar plexus and she has some damage to her kidneys, the extent of which we cannot determine yet. She has several broken bones in her hands, her feet, she has a broken left arm, and also a broken tibia in her left leg. Finally, you are without doubt I am sure that she has been raped. Additionally to being raped by sexual organs, she was raped with multiple object including broom handles and broken glass bottles—we extracted glass shards from her anus and vagina. And she was rendered sterile by the forced penetration into her uterus. From a medical point of view, even taken one at the time some of these injuries are life-threatening. But, when you add them all together in a body that has suffered from malnutrition and dehydration, they become a deadly cocktail. And Gaspadin Max, at this point, we cannot assess the extent of her brain damage. For now, we put her in a medical coma so that she can recover without feeling the pain the injuries are causing her. In two to three days, we will slowly bring her out of it, and we will monitor her progress. We are doing everything we can, but we are not optimistic. We will be talking to our neurologist this morning to determine if she will need surgery to fix the temporal fracture. We cannot know for sure at this point if bone fragments have embedded themselves into her brain. I know what you are going to ask me, and I will be very frank with you. My colleagues and I are estimating her chances of survival at about 10%. The next two weeks will be critical. I would like to fly her to a private clinic in Western Europe where more can be done at once, but Gaspadin Max, we are stuck here in Sankt Petersburg, and you have the best care available in this city. Do you have any questions?'

'Yes. First I want to thank you for your efforts to save her. Second, as you well imagine Lena has her own private physician, Professeur Calmet of the Salpetriere in Paris. Would it be beneficial to fly him here to further assess her condition?'

'Gaspadin Max, we welcome such an eminent colleague, but as long as she is in a coma his presence would not benefit us. I would recommend that once she is out of the coma, yes he should visit and give us his opinion of the patient. And I hope that whoever did that you catch them!'

'Doctor, when can I see her?'

'We'll take you to her now.'

Doctor Beregovna got up and led Max to where Lena was resting. On the way there, Max told the doctor that he would put a security detail to protect her, because anyone who was in contact with Lena was in danger.

CHAPTER 23

Lena passed away peacefully, without further pain, her tormented body quietly shutting down, while Max was holding her hand. The American Hospital staff had attempted to keep her alive all day long, and they had transported her from one surgical unit to another, to the point where Doctor Beregovna herself, who had been so dedicated to keeping Lena alive, had had to give up. There was nothing more to do. Her body simply was shutting down. One by one, her organs had stopped functioning and even the intravenous feeding was not sufficient to keep her from losing further weight. Her once beautiful legs that had made the envy of every man in Monaco were tortured skin and bones, and her hand already had that look of the hands of the dead. Her pretty face was now a mangled mess with her cheekbones gone and further scars purposely made with a razor to increase the damage. She would need months of plastic surgery to rebuild her face. As the hours passed, Max felt that he had done the right thing by rescuing her, but that at the same time, the misery she would have to suffer to try to recover from this ordeal had twisted the value of his chivalrous act. He questioned himself. Had he been right to rescue her? Of course, he would answer, she will pull through, and he will get the best surgeons in the world to reconstruct her face. He would get the surgeons from 90210. And if she did not make it, he had given her the decency of passing away with him at her side, not in some filthy basement where rats would have eaten her face. At the same time, a rage he had never known was taking over his entire mind, his entire body. Whoever had done that, and he knew exactly who it was, would never get away with it. George McMillan would die, and he would die a horrible death. The executioners were already all dead, the head honcho would die soon enough, yet McMillan probably did not think he had it coming. But he did!

Max had conferred with all the doctors, and they had finally agreed that there was no sense in tormenting Lena any longer. There was no sense in attempting a new surgery that would only further weaken her body and they had all given everything they could for the past forty-eight hours. The injuries were so deep there was no way to artificially maintain her alive. Max had walked back to her room, his head low, and he had simply held her hand. A few hours later, it was exactly twenty-three past midnight, he had felt her hand relax, and the heart monitor had gone blank with the stupid alarm going off on that single unending note. He had not had to close her eyes since she had never re-opened them, and the greatest sadness in his life had rolled over him. He had started crying like he did not remember ever crying in life, and for an entire hour, he had wept, incapable of stopping, unable to control his emotions. Doctor Beregovna had allowed him the time he needed with Lena, and during that time he said goodbye to her. He thought of all the good times, since their encounter just a year before in Spain, where he had saved her life, until now, where he had tried to save her again but had arrived too late. He thanked her for everything she had given her: happiness, trust, loyalty, her gorgeous body, and immense wealth. He told how he had changed so much with her, and how he loved her, how he would never find another woman like her, and how he would miss her for the rest of his life. He swore to avenge her, and then he felt pain like never before. He felt destroyed, as if hit by lightning, as if hyenas were gnawing at his entrails and pulling his guts out of his belly. Now, Max came

THE DATURA SOLUTION

to the realisation that this was where it all ended. Sankt Petersburg. As the moment for the final separation approached, Max still sat on the hospital chair, while people passed in the hallway indifferent to the drama that was playing out on this tiny piece of real estate. He would have liked to hold her body tight against his, but it was of no use, and yet he was unable to separate, and tears flowed down his cheeks. His eyes hurt from the tears and from that insurmountable pain that had taken over his entire body. His entire body, his back, his stomach, his head were pure pain. There was not even any sense in sitting here; there was no sense in prolonging the moment into the unavoidable separation. He was still bewildered by the speed of her passing, and nothing anybody could say or do at this moment would make him feel any better. He felt like a starving plant in the desert, slowly succumbing to the realisation that nothing would ever be the same in his life, that he would never again make love to this perfect woman, that he would never again experience the incredible emotional and physical pleasure she brought him, that he would never again be whole and feel like a man, and that he would never again love a woman like he had loved her. At these thoughts a new tsunami of sadness and despair overcame him, and he knew he had to dig deep inside him to physically survive the separation. Even the revenge he had sworn would not allow him to survive. He could not understand the level of pain Lena's death was inflicting on him. He could not imagine living without her, without the touch of her thin and elegant hands on his body, without the gentle kiss of her full lips on his sex, without the passion that they had experienced when they had been together. The thought of all the riches she had bestowed on him was not enough to jolt him out of the dazed stupor into which he had fallen. Finally, like a death row inmate he let go of her hand, he pushed the chair back and it made a little scrapping sound on the floor, his feet slowly and reluctantly started carrying him out of the room, into the unknown of the rest of his life. There would always be two dates in his life, November 1, when they had made love the first time, and

December 19. But his life would never be the same after December 19. There would be before December 19, and after December 19. After December 19, hope would be gone from his life, and there would never again be the passionate love between them. He opened the door to the room, a defeated man, into the hallway, stopping on the threshold, hoping that she would suddenly start talking. Instead, the woman he had loved more than anything in the world, the woman he knew he could not live without, the woman for whom he was now openly crying in public, the woman he would regret for the rest of her life, this woman whom he had cherished was slowly starting to decay. He looked back one last time, and saw her waxen face, almost unrecognisable from the pretty young woman she had been, and he stepped into the hallway, letting the door slowly close behind him with a muffled thump. Yet, in the morning, he would have to keep going, he would have to plan the killing of more people, inflict on others the same pain he was suffering now. His life had crumbled from under him, his happiness was gone forever, and he could barely breathe, his chest oppressed by a pain he knew would end up killing him if he did not react right here, right now. He slowly made his way down to Doctor Beregovna's office, his vision blurred by the flow of tears still flowing freely down his cheeks. He turned around a last time, looked at the door, almost rushed back inside, and at the last moment decided to keep going to the doctor's office. He had become the zombie of his own sorrow. He was an empty shell. There was nothing left of the euphoria of the night when they had rescued her not even two days before. That night as he found his way back to his hotel, he imagined her walking next to him, as they had so often done. Overwhelmed with sadness, oblivious to his surroundings, he became irremediably lost and wandered around the city in the bitter cold until early morning, when he finally met a woman and asked her for the way back to Mikhailovskaya Ulitsa. He had gone straight to the breakfast room and had drunk a couple of stakani of vodka before asking for a cup of coffee. He started to think that the Russian way to handle pain by ingesting massive amounts of inebriating liquids had some merit. He spent the day boozing, trying to make sense of the events of the night, and organising those of the following few days. Since it was Monday, he decided the best he could do was to abide by Lena's wishes that she be cremated. He had his people contact the best private crematorium in Sankt Petersburg and plans were made for her to be processed the following day. According to her wishes she would then be placed into an urn and into the wall of the salon of the Princess of Russia until such time as it was sold or sank. If it were to be sold, she wanted her ashes to be spread about the Casino Gardens where she had experienced so much pleasure and where so many memories linked her to Max.

Lena's rescue had been admired by Potunov who had now taken the lead of the events of Christmas night, for it had become clear that Max was in no shape to invest himself in that planning. Since Lena had been transported to the hospital, Max had spent every minute there. Potunov had progressed very well on all fronts, but the Island of Capri was giving him some trouble. He did not have the understanding of the geography, or of Italy, and he certainly thought that dropping a bunch of Russians down there would not go unnoticed. As could have been expected the villa which Igor Petrovich occupied was an exclusive compound set on the eastern end of the island at the end of a cul-de-sac, via Italo Pergolesi. The villa was a set of three buildings, surrounded by a forest of pine trees, from where one could see Mount Vesuvius. The main residence was a sprawling arrangement of constructions going back to Roman times that covered over 20,000 square feet. The garage for five cars was directly across the driveway, while the guards and domestiques slept in an eleven-room house set back from the main house and to its east. Igor Petrovich was hated by the natives after he had rebaptised the villa which had been the Villa Pliny for as long as people could remember to the unimaginative Villa Nouvelle, which simply meant New Villa. The Italians scoffed at the name and were now calling it Villa Nuvoloni—Villa Cloud of Locusts. They despised the new occupants even if they did good business with them. Like Giancarlo, the grocer who delivered food there and who would say 'Solo perchè vendi un pomodoro a qualcuno non ti fa amico con lui, Madonna!' when people vented their anger at for the money he was making 'con questi Russi di merda, che sono tutti maladetti!' Max was well aware that the Russians were the object of universal hostility since they had purchased the property and the surrounding area for the unnameable sum of $22 million. He knew that because as soon as it had been the plan to attack the villa on 25 December, he had contacted Luigi di Filippis, a former Italian-born Green Beret 'fearless men' as the Ballade says, who often worked for the corporation. Luigi had been collecting information, and thanks to the latent hostility towards 'i Russi', he had had no difficulty obtaining the diagram of the security system, learning how many guards were there (surprisingly it was only eleven), what their processes were, and any other information he had wanted to glean. He had also discovered per chance—while listening to street kids bragging about breaking into 'la Villa'—that there was an ancient Roman sewage tunnel leading from the villa to an area overlooking the sea a few hundred metres to the North East. Luigi had followed one of these kids and had pretended to be a Russian demanding to know where the conduit was, and that if he told anybody else he and his chumps were sure to be, and he had slid his right thumb over his throat. The kid had received the message loud and clear and had shown Luigi the entrance. The next day, Luigi had returned with a torch and had been surprised to see that the conduit was about one metre in diameter, relatively free of debris, and that it came out in the middle of a bunch of bushes without any type of device preventing access to the compound. While the Russians had spent almost $1 million in motion sensors, CTV, and an operation centre to ensure the security of the head of the Frunze Group, they had yet to figure out this massive lapse in their security system. Within three days, Luigi had given a full report to Max. By mid-afternoon, Max had showered, dressed, and in general regained enough composure that he could go to Potunov's office to continue planning. His head was surprisingly clear and his thinking so focused that he knew exactly how the operation should be conducted.

Potunov was amazed to see him and to realise that he was as sharp as usual. Max told him, 'There is one thing soldiers know how to do, and this is getting wasted and looking like they never had a drink.' Of course condolences were presented, vodka was consumed, and Potunov gave him an update, which could be summarised as 'everything is getting in place and will go as scheduled' except for Capri. Like Max had anticipated, Potunov was ill-prepared for operations in Italy. Simnatsat was there with them and introduced Captain Muzhov, another black operations officer from the Special Branch of the FSB, who would take over some of Simnatsat duties now that he had been promoted to major—a promotion that was retroactive to 1 November. Max included both of them in the planning. On a butcher paper block, Max drew the compound from memory, and placed the important features: the three buildings and the entrance to the conduit:

'This is what I have in mind: our operation will launch at 0010 (Max said at zero-zero-one-zero) hours, so the first thing we need to do is put out their CTV, remote sensors and laser surveillance system. This can be done remotely by hacking into their system, which is located in the basement of the guard house (he pointed at the butcher paper). We have the entire schematics of the system right here, and he took the thick envelope from his suitcase, to include the sys admin login passwords and ID, which the system maintenance people in Italy have been very happy to share with us for a modest amount of greenbacks. I would like you to assign the two best hackers in Russia to already hack into it and put in Trojan horses deep into the OS that will trigger at zero hours on 25 December with the aim of disabling the entire system. Potunov, Simnatsat? What do you say?'

'You can leave this to me,' said Potunov, 'I know exactly who to put on this.' Looking at Simnatsat, he added, 'You know Georg Mikailovich, right? You know the guy who hacked into the servers of the NSA, and he did it with Alex Romanovich. I think these two will be happy to concoct just the right Trojan for us. I'll get them here tomorrow, and we can go over what we want and what they can do.'

'Yes,' continued Max, because the key is to disable the system entirely but ensure it continues to provide output as if it were working. In other words all sensors, captors, and cameras will be off, but the central control room will think that everything is working just fine. Next, is the issue of the invading force. Three considerations: one, how many men we need; two, how we get them there without raising suspicion; and three, how do we attack? The number of members in the intervention force, code name Saint Nickolas Choir, depends on two factors: the number of guards and the number of guests, since this is going to be a cleanup operation. The guest list was recovered from an Italian hacker who accessed Igor Petrovich's laptop—he does this routinely, and in this memory stick, we have the entire database of this scumbag, again, acquired for a modest amount of greenbacks—and the guest list includes thirty-two people total: Igor's closest associates, lawyers, and various prostitutes. I have no interest in having a massacre of the women there. So I will eliminate them from the operation, although collateral damage cannot be excluded, we will not consider women as targets—especially since none of them are Igor's close associates. This means that the number of male guests is fourteen because there are eighteen women on the list. So, we have a potential of twenty-five total enemy combatants. Two of them will be at or near the gate, two people will be in the guard house, and of course, the help is not part of the enemy combatants. So we will need two people to take care of the gate guards, four to investigate the operations centre, the plan for which are right here, and I estimate twenty to take care of the remaining twenty-one. Gentlemen, what do you think?'

THE DATURA SOLUTION

Both men agreed that it made perfect sense and that a contingent of twenty-six should be adequate. To which of course needed to be added Captain Muzhov, who would be the commander on the ground, Simnatsat who wanted to make sure everything went smoothly and he earned his half million dollars, and of course, Max who wanted to see Igor Petrovich dead.

'So now that we agree on the numbers, how do we get the men there and the weapons? The men should use the various ferries available to get to the island from both Sorrento and Naples. It would be too conspicuous to hire a boat and land with almost thirty men speaking Russian. We will start infiltrating forces on to the island on 24 December in the morning, and host them in various hotels and inns around the island. We will rendezvous on foot at the entrance of the conduit where we will dress into our black combat fatigues at 2300 hours. All weapons will be also waiting there, courtesy of the Russian diplomatic suitcase, which you, Potunov are arranging. At 0010 hours, we will get out of the tunnel and start the attack, which Captain—actually I should say Major—Simnatsat will plan and brief us about. However, one challenge we have is to ensure the helicopter which Igor uses is disabled. So we'll need someone to take it out—as for the pilots, we can only assume they will be within the confines of the compound.'

The rest of the afternoon was occupied planning the details of the attack, selecting the teams and notifying them to report at the FSB facility in Kolpino so that they could start getting their orders and rehearsing their roles.

The following day, accompanied by Lena's mother, Max went to the crematorium, and at 2:00 p.m., Lena's body, which had been set in an oak casket, was processed into the infinity of the cosmos. Per Lena's wishes, there was no service, only Max and her mother whose sadness needed no witnesses. Max offered support to the woman, but there was nobody there to support him. John who had only known Lena as her employer had offered to go, but Max had asked him to keep the moment private between him and Lena. What no one knew, not even her mother, is that since Max's birthday just over two months before, Lena had been Max's wife. They had gotten married in a civil ceremony in the vanilla-coloured Mairie de Monaco, grabbing two witnesses from among the customers at the Restaurant du Rocher where they had had lunch before Lena had told him she had arranged everything as a surprise. They had kept this their secret, and Max would never tell anyone now. The only person to know of course was Lena's and Max's lawyers since they had subsequently changed their wills. Lena's mother did not know, and because she had not enjoyed the best of relationships with her mother, Lena had not wanted to tell her. Now, telling her would have served no purpose. As the casket containing Lena's body was pushed into the retort, temperatures reached over 1,000 degrees Celsius and Lena's soft tissues and organs vaporised and oxidised becoming again stardust escaping through the exhaust system. Vodka was served as the process went on for the next two hours. Once the cremation was completed, the attendant used the cremulator to process the remains into a consistent powder. To contain the ashes, Max had carefully chosen a yellow, gold, and white Meissen China urn with a double snake handle, a gadrooned flared foot, and it bore the crossed swords mark in blue underglaze. He had obtained it at an antique dealer at the corner of Nevskiy Prospekt and Ulitsa Konosheynaya. Max handed the urn to the attendant and watched as the last of the ashes were transferred to the elegant container, which Lena would have loved. The cover was sealed, more vodka was consumed, and a little after four thirty, Max climbed back into the armoured Merc, while Lena's mother refusing a ride, walked home alone despite the frigid cold.

> Full with sorrow
> Inevitably let go
> Of what has been
> And will not be tomorrow

recited Max mentally, as he cradled the urn in his arm. He went to the hotel and he set the urn on the dining room table. He returned to Potunov's and attacked another phase of planning that involved getting Ricardo's help—after what he had paid him, Ricardo owned at least one favour, Max thought.

By the time he arrived at the office, Potunov was able to announce that his hackers, Georg and Alex, had been able to penetrate Villa Nouvelle's computer system. Georg was actually in the office and looked like a tormented intellectual from a Dostoyevsky novel. He explained that he had gotten into the system by the backdoor, avoided the honeypot—whatever that is, thought Max—had left markers all the way and had already taken control of the system twice with a standard Trojan Horse that he had developed. No anti-virus could possibly detect the Trojan because it was a private one that had not been used against Microsoft, nor was it intended to be used that way. In any case, they had also protected it with a custom-made virus that would destroy the system if it was tempered with. The Trojan was encrypted and reproduced itself every time the password to the computer system was entered. Max was interested in only one thing 'Did you test it?' Yes, of course they had, had continued the hacking genius. Like he had said, they had taken over the system twice already, once manually, once by activating the Trojan at 14:14, and they had disabled the cameras and sensors from the office. At that point, they had verified that the console indicated to the operator that all systems were operating normally. 'Frankly, concluded the hacker, it was not very challenging.' Max thought that not challenging equalled good. Potunov also informed Max that the assault teams had been formed and that the training had started. Simnatsat arrived a bit later and stated that Captain Muzhov had everything under control. He also discussed the issue of disposing of the bodies. Simnatsat was of the opinion that everything should be left as clean as possible. Sure, there would be bullet holes here and there, but 'we cannot leave twenty dead behind, can we?' In order to remedy the situation, he suggested that body bags should be available for at least thirty bodies and that a catering truck bearing the advert of the famous Sorrento catering company Uzzano should be used to evacuate the casualties. This would involve getting a boat there—we can steal one from the harbour in Capri—and we can easily dump the bodies out in international waters. 'During that time, the assault team will turn into a cleanup crew, and since we will have regained control of the sensors and cameras, from the outside everything will look normal. Now, the bigger question of course is what do we do with the survivors who are all witnesses? Frankly Max, I would apply the motto, Leave no witnesses behind.'

'You want to kill them all?' asked Max.

'Well, if you find a better way, you tell me! But I haven't found one yet. If we let them live, can you imagine what they are going to tell the fucking papers? What I suggest we do is simply take the place over. Kill everybody, and pretend nothing ever happened there. If someone comes looking for anything, like the cops might after people who were at the party disappeared, everything will be clean, and the walls will have been repaired. There will be nothing to find, I guarantee you. Since there is not a single Italian there, the cops are never going to come looking for anything anyway, will they? We were ready to kill up to sixteen people, now it is like thirty-two . . . What the fuck? Mother Russia will recover!'

The problem, Max had to recon, was that the major was right. Either they did it thoroughly or they didn't do it. They really had no choice. But this was some crazy freakin' plan—if they pulled it off, it would be a miracle.

'Okay. Let's say we agree to your plan. Now we need two trucks to carry the bodies. We need to transfer them onto the boat, then we have to dodge the Guarda Costiera—not a big issue on Christmas morning—but how do you get the bodies to sink? You have them in body bags that are full of air, their lungs are full of air, as they decompose they produce gases that also add to their buoyancy, a

THE DATURA SOLUTION

week later you have thirty plus bodies floating around . . . Also, this would be an extraordinary massacre, even for the mafia. You may not remember that during the most famous mafia massacre, the Ciaculli massacre, only seven people died.'

'Tak, Max, we are going to have to do what the navy does: bury them at sea! We ask the Russian Navy to get us ocean burial shrouds and some weights, and we are good! We can put a few rounds through their chests for good measure, but this should be able to do the trick! Only problem of course is that we need 75 kilos of weight per body. If we have thirty, that's about two and a half tons! We'll think about it. The best thing is that if they ever resurface, which is truly unlikely, they will be in naval shrouds. Further, the depths in the Tyrrhenian Sea are around 1,200 metres which is twice the recommended depth for sea burial, so none of the bodies are ever likely to surface again. And as far as the Ciaculli massacre, we may set a new record but nobody will ever know about it.'

'You have thought of everything, haven't you?' commented Max.

'Tak, I have thought of everything, but I have not solved everything. But first things, first. Do you agree we need to dispose of all of them?'

CHAPTER 24

It was a normal day at the embassy in Madrid. Ambassador McMillan had just concluded his weekly 9:00 a.m. staff meeting, which he routinely held on Tuesdays, his calendar was clear until after lunch. . . Maybe he could sneak out to see one of the call girls he met with regularly. He was seriously considering this possibility when the phone rang. It was his secretary who told him somebody from Russia wanted to talk to him. He picked up the phone and sat down in one of the lavish leather armchairs facing the bay window with a view of the city. It was a cold day, even for Madrid, and he could feel the chill of the weather through the window. Nothing like it must be in Russia, though, he thought to himself. At first he had a hard time sorting out the heavy Russian accent, the hesitant English, the weird sentence construction, and the skipping of articles and other words:

'Gaspadin Georg, this Oleks Anatolievich. You Gaspadin Georg McMillan?'

'Yes, I am Ambassador McMillan. Why are you calling me?'

'Oh, yes, I very sorry, of course, Ambassador McMillan. Well, I head of Mining Registration Office. This office of Ministry of Finance that requires registration of all new ownerships of mines and natural resources. I work directly for Minister Volkov, who great friend of your country. He brought to attention of me that to you now belong two

THE DATURA SOLUTION

very important mining facilities in territory of Russian Federation, and that these, like all such industrial complexes had to from you re-registered by new owner within fifteen of superb transaction. You aware of rules Ambassador McMillan?'

'No, I cannot say that I was,' replied the ambassador, 'what do I have to do?'

'Like everything else in Russia, it not easy matter I afraid of. Registration has to have in person. We know it very difficult for important man like you. So, Minister Volkov invites to you. He send personal plane to take you to Moscow and you his guest. You bring title papers and registration fee for dollars of one million for one mine, and millionov three for other mine. Minister see you and we celebrate in Moscow at very nice dacha of minister with very nice Russian girls. When of you possible come?'

George did not really like this shit, but on the other hand, what could he do. The fifteen days were up during the Christmas break which he planned to spend in Snow Valley with two call girls he had already hired from Madame Nicole in California, and he had been assured they were better than porn stars. He did not want to spoil that, so he agreed that the sooner would be the better, and said:

'How about tomorrow? Can the plane pick me up tomorrow, let's say at nine in Madrid?'

'Of course, Ambassador, of course. Please give me your email address, and I will send you all necessary information. Registration to pay in form cash—no paper trail, Ambassador McMillan, no paper trail. For me do you questions have?'

'No, no question. I'll wait for your instructions. Can I have your number in case I need to reach you?'

'Of course. 7 for Russia, 984 495 795. Now, email address?'

The ambassador gave Oleks his email address, and the call was concluded. Next, George called the US Embassy in Russia to verify that Oleks Anatolievich was in fact a staff member of the Russian Ministry of Finance working for Minister Volkov and that his number checked out. In fact the Bureau of Commerce at the Embassy knew Oleks quite well and qualified him as a true friend of the US Embassy, a civil servant who was pretty much okay. Satisfied by the answer, the ambassador called the vice president at Santander Bank that managed his personal accounts and instructed him to prepare two boxes of money, one for $1 million, and the other for $3 million for a cash transaction, the nature of which was legal and none of the business of the VP. He asked that both packages be delivered at the residence, to avoid having to go get them himself since that 'fucking Ricardo is not around when you need him'. He thought it was about time to get rid of him. He had noticed an attitude lately with him, and with the services he had rendered, he knew way too much for the ambassador to be safe as he considered the future. He had to go. He would take care of that when he returned from Snow Valley. The ambassador looked at his Outlook calendar, found out he could easily cancel his 2:00 p.m. appointment, and called the escort service for an afternoon of sex. He had decided that the Russian transaction needed to be celebrated as it would clearly and legally establish his ownership of the mines, he had illegally obtained.

When he got back to his residence, it was ten o'clock at night. He had had an evening of debauchery, with two of the best hookers Spain—via Hungary—could provide, and they had dined in bed, using the body of the beautiful Anna as a table while at the same time committing the lewdest possible sexual acts, which included sodomising the 'table' with a piece of salmon, which the other girl ate it from the other side. He had paid them handsomely of their services and for the cocaine and meth they had brought. So despite the exhaustion of the evening, he felt in top shape after using meth to get back in action. He checked his email, and everything was set for the morning. He sent a quick note to Oleks confirming he would be there and looking forward to meeting him. The meth had given him a new life, so he called Serena, his live-in housekeeper and occasional sexual partner, on the house phone and asked her to come down to his bedroom if she wanted to make an 'extra five Bens'. Of course, she did. And he told her to come down naked. When she arrived, he tied her to one of the bed posts, took his favourite Gucci belt, and got an incredible erection from beating her back, ass, and legs. Then, without preparation, he raped her anus, and reached a violent climax in her rectum. He detached her, and shoved ten $100 bills in her vagina. The woman had never seen such violence from 'His Excellency' as she called him during the day and decided to leave his service as soon as she could find a new position. Satisfied by his performance, George had a glass of Bourbon and went to bed. At five in the morning, he was up already. He made coffee, watched some porn on the Internet, and masturbated for almost an hour before deciding he just couldn't get it up that morning. He took a shower, got ready, and at eight o'clock, the embassy driver loaded the money that had been packed into two GAG aluminium suitcases, the ambassador's Louis Vuitton travel bag, and they were on their way to the General Aviation terminal. The Falcon with the tail number indicated in the email was already waiting. The crew loaded the luggage and gave George an envelope. Inside, on the high-quality vellum with the arms of Russian embossed on the top left corner was a note from the minister of finance:

Your Excellency,

Please enjoy your trip to Moscow with my compliments. The two stewardesses on this flight will provide you with whatever service Your Excellency wishes. My trusted Oleks will be at the airport to welcome you.

Best Regards,
Antoni Volkov

The flight was delightful, and George would have loved to take advantage of the services of the two long-legged, perfectly shaped

Russian stewardesses, had he not been haunted by the fear of not being able to have an erection. He went to the toilets and tried to get one going by remembering the whipping he had given Serena the night before, but he could not produce an erection. So he ate the excellent caviar, drank some vodka, and in general did not pay much attention to what was going on. If he had, he would have seen that the plane had taken an unusual route to get to Moscow from Madrid. Of course, he could not know either that about one third of the way there, the plane had rendezvoused with another Falcon flying in from England, that the transponder had been turned off, and that by shadowing the other Falcon, the plane carrying George McMillan to Russia had disappeared from the air, from the radars, and that George McMillan was already a dead man. About thirty minutes before landing, George was given another vodka—he was already tipsy from the quantity he had consumed—but this vodka somehow was different. It was a lemon vodka with a spicy taste which he had never had before, and he found it quite interesting. Within a few minutes, he felt some pressure on each side of head, by the temples. Oh no, he thought, I am not going to be drunk as I have to meet Oleks! He asked the stewardess for a cup of coffee. As she went to the galley, George experienced a violent headache, and he was suddenly scared of passing out. He thought his was not a good day. First he could not get it up, and now, this headache. He fought not to pass out, and he started sweating from fear and from pain. The migraine headache was taking over his entire brain, and he had lost his focus. Suddenly, he could not put together any thoughts, except that of fighting to stay conscious. He vaguely saw the stewardess bring him a cup of coffee. He feebly tried to take it, moving a hesitant hand forward, but it fell back on his lap, and he passed out. He did not feel or see the plane land at a non-descript airfield near the small city of Razan, about 100 miles south east of Moscow. If he had he would have realised that this could not be good.

The black Suburban was waiting at the airport. The one Falcon landed, while the other went on to Moscow to refuel. As soon as the door opened, Max and Dmitry got the ambassador out. By now, he was in semi-consciousness and was only partially ambulatory. They handcuffed his hands behind his back and pushed him unceremoniously into the Suburban. Then they placed ankle chains on his ankles. In his delirium, he said with a slurred speech, like a drunk:

'Don't forget the money, and don't forget the titles, they are in my Vuitton bag.'

Of course all of the suitcases had already been loaded. The driver took a southern direction, and they soon reached an abandoned compound that had once been the barracks for KGB unit Eighty-Six. Simnatsat jumped out and unlocked the rusty gate, the vehicle made its way through the deep snow, and stopped in front of Building 939. Max opened the door, grabbed the ambassador by his tie, and violently pulled him out of the Suburban with a rage that filled George with fear, even in his semi-comatose shape. He fell heavily head first into the layers of snow that cushioned his fall. Max took an Opinel out of his pocket and cut the clothes off the ambassador, so that he was now naked in the minus twenty degrees Celsius weather. Without shoes or clothes, they marched him into the building. It was damp and just as cold as outside. As they got to the top of the stairs leading to the basement, Max kicked him hard in the buttocks, and he fell tumbling down the stairs, in shouts of pain as his already frozen body hit the steps and finally the floor. Dmitry returned to the Suburban, picked up the discarded clothing, and threw it inside the building. Then he went back to the Suburban, sat down in the comfort of the heated vehicle, and found a radio station playing Russian house music—a mix by Voluminial was playing. The events taking place in Building 939 were of no concern to him.

Downstairs, helped by Simnatsat who was becoming a true accomplice, Max hung the ambassador by the handcuffs to an overhead pipe. His feet barely touched the ground. Max told him:

'So did you enjoy having Lena tortured? Well, we are going to serve you the same recipe, except worse, because I don't even need your signature! You know why? Because your title papers are fake! You went through all of this shit for not a thing! Funny, right? Your fucking friends fucked you over, you piece of shit!'

The ambassador who was already shaking from head to toe from the devastating effects of the cold was about to answer, but he did not have the time, because Max had grabbed a piece of steel pipe, and using it like a baseball bat, he had swung with full force into his prisoner's rib cage. The three men clearly heard the ribs crack and break. The ambassador let out a scream of pain that echoed in the empty basement.

'Please, don't hurt me! I'll give you whatever you want! Do you want money? I have money!'

Max asked him if he enjoyed crying and pleading like a girl, because since he had twenty-four ribs, he was going to enjoy this twenty-four times. And he hit him again, on the other side. Then he said, 'Well you should like that, you like to beat women, so you should like being beaten! Didn't you beat Serena last night? Oh, and you like to rape her asshole! I forgot!' Max swung him around and simply shoved the steel pipe into George's anus. He screamed even louder in pain! 'Oh, if you scream so much, it must be because you like it! It's like sex, the more they scream, the more they like it, right?' Max took the pipe out, pulling some guts out with it, while blood and faeces dripped on the floor. He shoved it again into what had been George's anus, but was now an ugly wound of faeces, guts, and blood dripping out of his ass between his legs. He pulled the pipe out again and shoved it a third time. He commented, 'We are leaving it there for later, I have plenty more!' Then Simnatsat, anxious to participate, took his commando knife, swung the already dying man around, and said, 'Look, he does not even have a hard on! I guess if it doesn't fucking work any longer, you don't need it!' and joining his action to his words, he grabbed George's dick and balls, and sliced them off with the razor-sharp heavy blade, and threw the package on the dirty floor. The wound produced a heavy flow of blood, and Simnatsat declared,

THE DATURA SOLUTION

'Don't worry asshole, you won't bleed to death.' He took a dirty rag, poured vodka over it, and shoved between George's legs, then taped it there with duct tape. George had long passed out form the pain that no human could possibly have handled. And yet, that pain woke him up and caused him to scream at the top of his lungs before fainting. Max took the vodka bottle and broke it on George's head, the cold liquid bringing him out of his fainting again, so that he could feel the pain, and the life slowly dripping out of his body. Simnatsat turned to Max, and said, 'Why don't we go eat?' Max answered that it was a good idea, and to make sure 'fucking asshole', as they called him now, did not die from exposure, they turned on the oil furnace next to him, and left its door open. Immediately, the area was less cold, and by the time they came back, it would actually be almost bearable. As they were leaving, Max did not even turn around to look at George, and they disappeared upstairs.

Of course, there was no way they would leave the fucking asshole unattended for long, and they simply went to the Suburban to have a packed lunch of caviar, pork escalopes, roasted eggplant, bread, onion, and of course vodka. Then, they settled in the heat of the truck and enjoyed the warmth. Max told Simnatsat that he would get half of the bounty brought by the fucking asshole, and for the first time since he had met him, Max saw him smile. Max was taking no sadistic pleasure in torturing the former ambassador. It was a duty he had in towards Lena. It was something her had to do. He had promised her he would avenge her, and this is what he was doing. He was applying revenge in the most Sicilian of ways. His fate had already been sealed and he wanted to kill him and see terror in his eyes. He wanted his soul to be so tormented that it could never find its way to the underworld. He wanted to see the same terror in his eyes that he had seen in Lena's eyes the night of her rescue. And the skill consisted at inflicting maximum pain and grievous injuries while keeping the victim alive for as long as possible. But he knew he would never have the patience to torture him until midnight as he had planned. Max would not waste eight hours of his life to deal with McMillan. He did not even feel anything, just an irresistible impatience to be done with it, and to get out of there. With the death of Lena, the hope for happiness had been destroyed, and he knew that the fantastic days of the previous summer on the Princess of Russia would never be again. With her death, Max had changed. The ruthlessness that he had shown in the past had turned into an unstoppable brutality that was matched only by Simnatsat's. He was not afraid of whom he had become, as he knew he would regain his balance once the task at hand was completed, but until then, there would be no pity, no safe haven for any of the people who had been guilty of any trespassing against Lena. The remnant of a man downstairs was a mere peon on the chessboard, and he had no value. Simnatsat and Max got out of the Suburban and went back downstairs. Their victim was either passed, or was sleeping or dead, and neither man could tell which one it was. Max picked up a steel pipe and swung onto the ambassador's chest. It extracted a yelp of pain from him. Then George murmured: 'Listen we can make a deal, you and me. I can turn over my assets to you, let me live!' Max laughed.

'I thought you would say that . . . Unfortunately for you, here, in my hand, is your will. That's the will you wrote in favour of Lena. You then wrote another will after the divorce. And here, is yet another one dated 15 December. In this will, you are turning over all of your businesses and assets to Lena. Yes, I know you never wrote it, and you never signed it. But what difference does it make? You signature is on it—a pretty authentic signature, since it is yours. . . You should have been more careful with the papers Ricardo gave you to sign. . . When you sign a blank piece of paper, anybody can write anything they want above the signature. As far as your law firm is concerned, Fisher, Farris, and Gauthier, I can assure you that like all other lawyers, they are for sale. And in exchange for a petty $20 million, he authenticated your signature, transferring to Lena your entire $4-billion fortune. . . And since Lena left everything she owned to me. . .You have in front of you, the new owner of all your assets! Pretty cool, no? It thought you would agree with me! Well, we are not here to talk about business, are we?'

Max pulled the steel pipe out of George anus and he pushed it back in with such violence, the entire three feet went inside him. He knew he had basically killed him. There was no sense in continuing. He asked Simnatsat to help him detach him, and the body of the former ambassador to Spain fell to the ground, inanimate. Max grabbed a wood board that he and Simnatsat used as a stretcher, they lay George on top, and slowly, they started feeding the board and George into the blazing furnace, alive. Simnatsat asked, 'Where the fuck did you learn this shit?' 'Ever read the methods of the Einsatzgruppen?' replied Max. The pain of being burnt alive revived George who tried a futile attempt to escape. Max knew that as long as the legs were burning. 'His Excellency' would suffer abominable pain. But no pain was bad enough to expurgate having killed Lena. Max commented that by now the news had been released that for unknown reasons, the private jet taking Ambassador McMillan to a diplomatic meeting had been lost in the Atlantic off the coast of France. The plane had suddenly disappeared from the radar screens and any attempt to find it or the wreckage had failed. He had no idea if the ambassador heard, but if he did, the last thing that he would have learned upon dying was that his murder would go unpunished. That morning after the ambassador had left, Ricardo had gone to both the residence and the ambassador's office, and using a powerful electromagnet, he had wiped both all computer hard drives clean.

Max threw in the clothes and the shoes in the furnace. It took over two hours for the powerful oil burner in Building 939 to turn the last of George's body into industrial ash. Simnatsat and Max spoke about the future. Max needed him to remain in the FSB for the moment, although he would have liked him to work directly for him when John was unavailable as was the case today. Regardless, Max, would pay him an annual stipend of a $500,000 base, and additional fees as required. The money would be deposited in an account in Macao. This suited

Simnatsat just fine, and he asked Max to deposit the $2 million in that account as well, rather than giving him the cash that was in the car. Max agreed. They were about to turn off the furnace, when Max reminded Simnatsat to 'not forget his balls'. They had almost forgotten to dispose of the small insignificant shrivelled package. Simnatsat threw it in the furnace. They washed their hands with vodka, waited ten minutes, and walked out. They drove out of the compound's gate. Simnatsat locked the gate. They drove about 500 metres when Simnatsat rolled down the window, stuck out his arm, and pushed a button on a remote control. Building 939 imploded and collapsed in a cloud of dust and rubble. Simnatsat rolled the window back up, and turning to Max added 'Just in case,' And for the second time that day, he smiled, proud of a job well done. Three hours later, the three of them were pulling up in front of the Sheraton Palace in Moscow on Tverskaya. It had been a long day and the three men simply retired to their own rooms. That night, with the sense of finally having rendered justice, Max, for the first time since Lena's disappearance, was able to sleep well.

CHAPTER 25

Captain Muzhov's soldiers had been training and rehearsing the operation for almost ten days when they had to prepare to infiltrate the Island of Capri. During the planning of the operation, a consensus had been reached that weapon use should be kept to a minimum to accomplish two goals. First, minimise the amount of blood that would have to be cleaned up, and second, to avoid damage to the villa which would have to be fixed. After multiple tests, the FSB detachment, operating under complete lock out and secrecy, had opted to promote the use of lethal quantities of suphentanyl that would be dispensed through several modified LPO-50 flamethrowers, a Russian weapon that could deliver one gallon of liquid spray in a less than four seconds, and with volatile density sufficient to incapacitate or kill anyone within twenty metres of the nozzle. Part of the rehearsals had been focusing on managing this deadly drug by testing it on pigs. Tests were done in a closed environment, simulating the operation centre and the rooms of the villa, in the open, simulating the guard gate, and of course in the semi-open area of the villa terrace. Rehearsals had taken place in the icy cold weather, and inside a vast hangar where temperatures could be raised to anticipate the ten to fourteen degrees Centigrade expected in Capri. Care was taken to test the gas with open flames in case the villa used a barbecue or open-flame heaters on the terrace. All tests had been highly successful and showed that the concentration of gas selected would kill 65 per cent of the animals, and incapacitate another 30 per cent. This left 5 per cent of the animals to be dealt with by other means, and in the case of Capri, this would represent at most three people. And this assumed that people had the same reaction to the gas as pigs. To ensure planning was correct, Captain Muzhov had also tested the gas on two prisoners that had been sentenced to death, but had been allowed to 'escape'. Since the escape had been rigged, they were recaptured by the FSB, thus disappearing from the GUIN books, and they had been available for this critical testing. These live tests confirmed the effectiveness of the doses that the unit was planning to use. Captain Muzhov believed that it was better to overplan and deploy more resources than needed, he had modified seven units, although in reality only four would be needed: one in the operations centre, one at the gate, and two at the villa. Of course, the assault force would be wearing the standard GP-5 gas mask, the so-called Aardvark gas mask, which also had been tested on the two 'escaped convicts' to ensure it offered the required protection against suphentanyl. Max had approved the use of the gas as it allowed to ensure the excesses of bloodletting were prevented. It also provided the possibility that noncritical personnel could actually be allowed to survive. It would be difficult for them to piece together any of the events after falling into the semicomatose state caused by the gas. Simnatsat scoffed the idea of limiting the elimination to the 'critical personnel' reminding Max of his siege of Leningrad comments. Finally, Max had told him, 'Listen, you and Muzhov are in charge, you go ahead and you have carte blanche. The only thing I want to personally make sure of is that I see that motherfucker Igor Petrovich dead and buried.' Simnatsat had smiled, having finally achieved the level of understanding that he had been seeking. From that point on, the operation was freed of any constraints and could proceed with the unrestrained ruthlessness typical of Russian military operations. Except that in this case, Simnatsat and Muzhov made it clear that there would be no pillaging, no raping, no destruction of property, and that in exchange every soldier would get a $10,000 bonus, but only if these rules of engagement were respected. On that grey Monday afternoon when the major had introduced the idea of the bonus, all twenty-five men of the assault contingent took a pledge to respect the ROE imposed by the operation.

The question of how to enter Italy had never been an issue. There was no way the Special Unit would apply for visas, or use real identities, so they were simply issued forged diplomatic passports from various European Community countries, and the men did not need any further ID. On 21 December, they simply started boarding various flights from Petersburg to Rome, Milan, Nice, and Naples according to a well-established plan, so that no flight carried more than a single man. Once in Italy, they converged on their own towards Capri, one at the time either via the Naples ferry or the Sorrento one. On key element was that they should not be seen together and that there could be no connection between any of them. The specialised equipment, which had been disguised as diving gear arrived via Max's Falcon at the Naples Airport, coming from Nice. In Nice, thanks to a set of fake US diplomatic passports, John and Max were not even given a cursory look when the custom officers had approached the plane. From the airplane, the gear was loaded on to a 'borrowed' van thanks to Luigi, and then transferred into a rented fourteen-metre Endeavour 42 power cruiser. Thus, the crucial Phase One of the operation was completed by the evening of December 23, and the men as well as the equipment were on the island. The plan was for Phase Two to start at 1900 hours so that the convergence to the conduit could be done in a gradual manner. The men started arriving at ten-minute intervals, and because night had already fallen, no one could possibly notice them. However, the first three men who had arrived had donned black combat fatigues, put on NVGs, and established a security perimeter just in case. In Petersburg, Georg and Alex had already reported they were in control of the operations centre, according to a change in plans. The system had been so easy to break into and to fool, they had decided to forgo the Trojan and take over manually. Even better, they had been able to repurpose the cameras within the Ops Centre and they were transmitting the feed directly into a monitor inside the conduit, so that the men assigned to attack it had a visual of it before going in. Exactly as planned, 23 men plus Captain Muzhov, Simnatsat and Max were ready to go at 2330 hours. At 2345 hours, the LPO-50s were strapped to the seven men who would carry out the gas attack. As they approached the head of the conduit, they could hear the party going on above. The first four men to get out would carry conventional weapons (of course every weapon had a silencer) and establish a security perimeter. As the other men got out, they would advance in complete silence, and they had trained for days on how to move without making noise, 'something that was new to Russian military operations,' Captain Muzhov had joked. It also had been agreed that the entire operation would be conducted wearing the Aardvark until the all clear was given by the NBC specialist, Starshiy Serzhant Bedev. This was agreed for three reasons: the obvious one to protect the assault team from the effect of the gas, the second one to keep the faces masked and thus not recognisable, and finally to add an element of terror since the gas mask had this effect on most people. The men heard the cheering and celebration of Christmas with the boat hooting their horns in the harbour below. They had not realised the excellent opportunity this created, and Captain Muzhov quickly improvised to exploit this tactical advantage. He immediately ordered the men to don their masks, and at 0001 hour, nine minutes ahead of schedule, the first man exited the conduit into the cool night air. There had been no time to turn off the lights, and Simnatsat messaged Petersburg to forgo this part of the plan, as the assault would be done by then. The operation started like clockwork. The perimeter was established, and the three men assigned the Ops Centre rushed forward. All of the doors combinations had been disabled by the hackers in Petersburg, and they rushed in, down the stairs, exactly as they had rehearsed, opened the door to the Ops Centre, sprayed the gas, and as the jet was being propelled out of the tank, one of the operators reached for his weapon, which he had negligently left into the shoulder harness that he had put on the chair's back. As he reached for it, the gas took effect and he simply slumped forward and fell out of his chair. The other guard had been so close to the jet that he had been hit immediately and had already collapsed. This went so fast that they were reporting 'Ops Centre secure' before the second team had even reached the gate. There the two guards that were too far apart to hit them both with gas at once. As the FSB soldier released the jet towards the first one, the second one continued to watch scattered fireworks and the hissing sound of the gas, camouflaged by the boats still blowing their horns in celebration did not catch his attention. He was dispatched within a few second also, as the assault team got to the terrace. Most guests were as well watching scattered fireworks and had their backs to the assault team. Some of the men heard a man—probably Igor—state 'Motherfucker! We could have had fireworks! Anatoly, where is Anatoly? Where is my fucking Anatoly?' and as he turned around to look for Anatoly, he caught sight of the FSB assault team, and let out 'What the fuck?' as the gas was released and the entire group of men and women fell pell-mell over each other or trying to run away from the source of the spray which was clearly visible in the lights. At the gate, the two catering trucks carrying the Navy burial bags were already backing up into the compound, driven by the remaining two FSB soldiers who had been under Luigi's personal care for the previous couple of days. The vans were equipped each with a container similar to those used by the airlines and that can be rolled on and rolled off the planes. On the terrace, things were going perfectly, and now the team proceeded with a thorough search of the villa. Arriving in the third bedroom, they found the man who was probably Anatoly in bed with two women, and before he had the time to even utter a protest, the gas had been released and the three of them were already drifting into semi-consciousness. The problem arose in the fourth bedroom because whoever was in it had been alerted by the unusual sounds. Actually, there were two men in the room, who had been enjoying gay sex less than a minute before as the state of their penis indicated. But, even though they were naked, they were now ready for combat. As Sergeant Korovin entered the room, he was hit in the chest with a 9mm bullet fired from a Beretta. He stumbled backward but was saved by his ceramic flak jacket. Having lost his breath and his balance, he nevertheless recovered fast enough to let go two rounds of his Glock 357, one of which killed one of the men instantly while the other one realising the futility of the situation put his gun down and was sprayed by the deadly gas. It took another fifteen minutes to declare the villa secure. Starshiy Serzhant Bedev declared the all clear at 0024 hours, and the men continued to fill the burial bags with the bodies—they did not care whether they were dead or alive. Max and Simnatsat looked for Igor Petrovich, which they found and positively identified. However, he was still alive. Simnatsat took a syringe out of a medical kit, filled about four cubic centimetres of cyanide, and gave the fatal injection to Igor himself. Within seconds, Igor's heart had stopped beating. He was put in a burial bag, and like the others, he was stored in one of the containers. Simultaneously, the cleaning of the fourth bedroom was taking place, to ensure no blood traces could be found. Using an ammonia-based solution that was brought in the catering trucks, the team cleaned up the entire area. They used a black light to ensure they had removed all blood traces, and proceeded to find the second bullet. Since they had used silencers, the bullet had not penetrated the wall very far, and it was easy to remove it. They used a small Black and Decker vacuum cleaner to clean up the floor from any plaster, and they then made the bed. The other soldiers were busy carrying the burial bags to the vans, and a total of forty-two bodies were thus recovered and stored in the containers. In the meantime, the Ops Centre had been sanitised, and two of the FSB soldiers were now replacing the guards. Together with a contingent of eight soldiers and Captain Muzhov, they would stay behind to maintain the pretence that nothing had changed within the villa. At Max's demand no news of the other activities had been forwarded to the team so as to not distract them. At 0100 hours, he got a simple one letter text message 'E' which had been decided would be the indication that all five of the other missions had succeeded. He shared the news with Simnatsat, while the catering vans were leaving the premises. They drove three fourths of a mile down the hairpins of via Don Giobbe Ruoco to the intersection with Piazzetta Angelo Ferraro, where they made the sharp right to rejoin the awaiting super yacht *Alabaster* which was waiting for a catering delivery. At the yacht, the vans backed up in turn to metallic rollers that had been installed for the purpose of rolling the containers onto the deck. From there they were lifted on pallet stackers and further moved into the living room. The rollers were removed, stowed in the living room, the doors closed and locked, and the FSB squad provided security from this point on. The two vans drove away to a prearranged garage, where they were sanitised, quickly stripped of their catering company stickers, made to look like a moving company van, and readied to take the ferry back to Naples. Once in Naples, they would be abandoned with the keys in the ignition. Within a few days, they would probably have been sold to a customer in Eastern Europe, and nobody would ever see them again.

 The captain as well as the crew of the *Alabaster* had been removed for the purpose of this operation, and members of the Naval Spetsnaz had replaced them. These naval personnel, just like the FSB soldiers, were participating in a top secret operation, and like them they were subject to the nondisclosure of classified information. This made the men on board highly reliable because they would never talk about the events of the night. Every soldier and sailor on the mission had signed a binding nondisclosure agreement under the Russian Federation Classified Mission Program. Furthermore each man had had to sign a specific binding agreement for this mission. Any disclosure of defence-related events carried a minimum mandatory sentence of ten years of hard labour. This had allowed Max to actually bring the Navy crew on board the *Alabaster* for two weeks of training on the ship systems. Since the crew was already certified on various Russian naval vessels, they were now, if not certified, at last very proficient in the handling of the *Alabaster*. By the time the containers were transferred on board, it was close to two in the morning and it had been decided to not steam out immediately after their loading, but rather at around four in the morning. Max had opted to stay on board and to receive the feed from CNN regarding any event in Russia. Captain Muzhov had now secured the villa, the security systems were back on line, there had been very little disruption to the property. Everything had gone as smoothly as possible. The security weakness of the compound—the conduit—having been identified, an explosive charge had been emplaced a few metres short of the entrance, and it would be detonated during New Year's Day celebrations when a massive firework was planned. In the meantime, additional sensors had been installed, and concertina rolls had been deployed through the entire length of the conduit. A guard detail was also patrolling its exit into the compound. Life in the villa was exactly as it should be on the early morning of a Christmas day. Even the most scrutinising observer could not have said that ownership had changed during the night.

As soon as he flicked the TV on, Max could tell the attack on Ladozhskyi Vakzal had been highly successful. Under the 'Breaking News' ribbon at the bottom of the screen, it was announced that Chechen rebels had attacked a peaceful Christmas party in Petersburg and that the explosion had killed at least eighty-four people. Max knew that the party had included 120 guests, so the annihilation of the Frunze Group was in the process of taking place. Again, for security reasons, it had been decided that no communication would take place from Petersburg to Capri. The only call Max had made had been to John who was recovering in Monaco about the Princess with his new Ukrainian girlfriend, a tall, elegant brunette with the body of a supermodel, who had also brought with her 'her best friend, if you don't mind' as she had told John. Her best friend was her carbon copy as a blonde. He had called John to wish him a merry Christmas, after the success in Capri had been certain. Of course, John had not answered his cell phone. As CNN made a mess of the reporting, Max decided it was time to go to bed. He poured himself a glass of eighteen-year Glenfiddich and hit the sack as he felt the *Alabaster* get on its way. He lay down and was so exhausted by the day's events that he was asleep before having time to finish his whisky. When Max woke up, it was already broad daylight and the *Alabaster* was a third of the way to Sardinia. Max did not even think of the day as Christmas day. If he had, a massive wave of sadness would have taken hold of him, and he would have been incapable of functioning. He would have thought of Lena, and how they had spent the previous Christmas in Zermatt, skiing, enjoying each other, having raclette, and making love in front of the raging fire in their living room. He would have thought of the many small gifts they had given each other during the day and how they had promised to spend every Christmas day of their life in the same way, focusing on their happiness. He brushed the mere thought of Christmas out of his mind, took a shower, and went to the state room where he got brunch. He called the captain of his ship and Simnatsat so that they could join him. The report of the night was that there was nothing to report 'a big NTR' stated Simnatsat. Max inquired if there were any ships around, but there was little to no traffic on the Tyrrhenian, so things looked good. The three men discussed the possibility of getting rid of the containers then rather than later. There was no ship within twenty nautical miles, and they were now above the Vavilov Plain where the depth of the water was over 2,000 metres, which made this a perfect dumping ground. Simnatsat had confirmed that the explosive charges were set and ready to go on both containers, so it was up to Max to give the go ahead. Max was of the opinion that a night time dump would have been better, but in fact, they could be surprised by another vessel just as well at night time. So he gave the go ahead. During the morning explosive had been attached to the sides, the bottom and the top of the two containers. The principle was that instead of dumping the bodies one by one, which would have taken a long time, the opening of each bag, the manipulation of each body, the loading in each bag of 175 pounds, and the closing of each bag, the containers themselves would be dumped. Since they had buoyancy and would not have sunk on their own, shape charges were being used to punch sixteen one-foot-wide holes in their sides, bottom and top. This would allow them to fill with water, to sink to the bottom of the sea and solve once and for all the problem of anybody coming back up to the surface. The charges would be detonated after the containers had been dumped into the sea. The sailors reinstalled the rails as fast as they had taken them down the night before. Within thirty minutes, they were fastened well enough to allow the containers to splash into the sea. The ship's captain verified his radar and again provided an all clear. The pallet stacker was brought forward and the ship itself came to a stop. The ship Zodiac was lowered in the water so that the result of the operation could be verified and it moved away from the *Alabaster*. The soldiers lined up the first container onto the steel rollers, they pushed the heavy load and slowly it gathered speed until gravity pulled it overboard. It splashed lazily into the water in a spray of white foam, submerging just below the surface. The explosive specialist waited until it had drifted about 100 metres from the *Alabaster*, he keyed the remote, and the sixteen charges detonated in one single report. The container slowly tilted on its side, releasing air bubbles and a few pieces of human flesh and bones. The Zodiac crew went to its location and confirmed that it had disappeared from sight. The same procedure was followed for the second container, but from the beginning, it refused to cooperate. First, it got misaligned and it took the entire contingent of soldiers and sailors to lift it, right it back onto the tracks, and get it going again. Then, for some reason, instead of falling right side up into the water, it tilted on its side, and now the effect of the charges was not going to be as predictable. Indeed when the explosive specialist detonated the charges, they merely shook the container and nothing happened further. Instead of sinking directly, the angle of the bodies inside it and the way the holes were now misaligned compared to their intended position caused it to neither sink fully, nor surface. Simnatsat gave a couple of orders. The Zodiac came back to the ship, and two RPG-7 anti-tank rockets were handled to the Zodiac crew. It was only after they had fired the second rocket into the recalcitrant container that it finally started sinking for good. In the meantime, small fragments of body, clothing, and body bags were floating on the water. Simnatsat was clearly not amused. He had another soldier bring a handful of hand grenades that were thrown in the area where fragments were floating, and they too were finally disposed of in the spray of explosions caused by the grenades. In the meantime, the sailors had been disassembling the steel rollers and on the count of three they threw them overboard as well. They finally grabbed the pallet stacker, and it too followed the containers and the steel rollers into the abyss. The Zodiac was brought back on board, and the *Alabaster* resumed its course to Porto Cervo. The voyage continued uninterrupted. At Porto Cervo, the Russian crew members and the FSB soldiers disembarked and the ship was released to the care of its normal crew, which had to prepare it for a New Year cruise starting two days later from Malta. The Russians transferred to another boat that was waiting for them to take them back to Sevastopol and to their military occupations. However, Simnatsat remained on board as Max and he had additional business to discuss, and the helicopter pilots who were to take them back to Monaco had not arrived yet because of airline delays.

That evening, Max decided that it was normal for him to call Potunov, and according to a protocol they had designed, they did not talk about the events in Russia, although in fact, this is the only thing they talked about.

'Allo, Potunov, so how are you doing, my friend?'

'I am doing like five peas in a pod. Fantastic! How about you?'

'I have been enjoying my vacation, reading Pliny, and this is an interesting book to read when you are in Capri! You know that the

Romans used eels to entertain themselves, by throwing slaves into a pond and seeing them being eaten alive. One day, they had this Roman aristocrat throw thirty-two slaves into the eels basin, and all of them were eaten! Can you believe it? And the next day, he had another contingent of slaves take over the running of the household, as if nothing had happened. The neighbours did not even know what happened! Now tell me about you what have you been up to?'

'I am doing okay, but you know my aunt, Larissa Viktorievna, right, the one who lived in Karpino, at 122 on Bolshaya Ulitsa, well, she died. There was an autopsy, and they said that she had been poisoned by food from the Caucasus. And the police closed the file, because the doctors found the poison we thought in her veins. In any case, may she rest in peace. It is a good thing that she never learned that her cousin Konstantin never came back from his mission in Iran!'

'Wow, you are full of good news, aren't you? Well, I am truly sorry to hear about the bad news. I hope you have some better news about you friend that was looking for a job. Did he find one?'

'Oh, that was a stroke of luck, let me tell you! You know he wanted to be a plant manager, right? Over the past two days he was contacted and one job became available when the guy who had it suddenly decided to resign. So he got it! And this is not all the good news. Remember Vliadimir? You remember how he had that bad back all the time, right? Well, he found this great chiropractor in Moscow: he uses the metal technique, you know with the magnetic properties, bingo he felt better after the first visit. And what about you? When are you coming back?'

'I am waiting for the air force to show up, then I'll be back at my normal place. I give you a call once I am there, okay? Oh, tell me one thing? Your friend Stefan Pavlovich, how is he doing? He is not pissed off that I didn't go to his Christmas party, is he?'

'Oh, him, no! He likes gifts so much, that since he received yours, he is your best friend. He told me your gift was the best he ever received! I don't know what the fuck you gave him, but you sure impressed him. Actually, he has invited you to stop by at his Moscow home. You need to do that. He is having a party on 19 January. I already made arrangements for you to stay at a nice place. You need to bring Sasha as well, and if your English friend can come, he is also invited. He wants to have a big dinner, and everything. So, that's about all the news.'

Max turned to Simnatsat, and commented:

'We have full success on the entire front! And it is becoming very dangerous: you and I were invited to visit with your prime minister! Well, this should be the occasion to open a bottle of champagne and celebrate!'

Max called the butler for a bottle of Laurent Perrier and some caviar. Over the course of the month, they had worked together, Max had come to appreciate Simnatsat's qualities, and even felt a certain kinship for him. After all, he had accompanied him in every challenge he had faced in these past few days, and he had proven to be a powerful ally. In addition, it was clear that Simnatsat was a highly educated man, who had class when he needed to, and was not simply a ruffian. This is why max had wanted to have some time with him to discuss his future. While they were sipping champagne and delighting in the quality of the caviar, Max approached the question of who was Simnatsat. Max had to be tactful because he knew of the major's reluctance to talk about himself. Yet, a special bond had been created between the two men. It was the bond of the brotherhood of arms, братсво, as they said in the VDV forces. So when max asked him about himself, Simnatsat finding more courage in Champagne slowly revealed his background.

'Of course, my name is not Simnatsat. Before the revolution, my family was part of the group that includes the Princes of the Blood, and my ancestor was ranked seventeenth in the order of succession to the throne. This is why I took the name Simnatsat as my operational name. Our name then was Vorgunin, and Prince Vorgunin was also one of the generals of the Imperial Army. During the bloodletting of the revolution, the entire Vorgunin family fared no better than the Romanovs and they were all massacred with the exception of the surviving prince, the general's son who was a prisoner of war of the Kaiser. Because he was also related to the Kaiser, of course being a prisoner of war meant that he lived in a large villa in Berlin that was his property to start with. Nevertheless, he alone survived. When the Bolsheviks had decided that enough killings had taken place, Vorgunin stupidly came back and was sent to the gulags. How he managed to perpetuate the family line is a mystery to me, but eventually the Bolsheviks lost interest and the Vorgunins came back to Petersburg and started doing what they were good at, being soldiers. During the entire time of the communist rule, people would still refer to us a Prince Vorgunin, and even today, people who know me call me Prince Vorgunin. Over the past twenty years, we have also been able to recover some of the properties that were ours, mainly farmland and a few buildings here and there. But we—actually I should say I—I had to sell them because I did not have the money to fix them. I simply kept a small pavilion where I live, and now, thanks to the funds you so graciously provided to me, I will be able to restore it to its pre-revolutionary splendour. So, this is it. My family spent seventy years hiding, running, and trying to survive. I am the only survivor of the blood line, and I need to start thinking about a family. But with the job I have, it is not so easy. It is rather difficult going from feeding a live man into a furnace to a loving wife and family. In any case, I was lucky enough to be able to attend the University of Moscow, to get an economics degree, and to later attend King's College and get an MBA. So I should be all set for when I quit the FSB.'

Simnatsat had just confirmed what Max had asked Potunov to find out about the major. It was a habit of Max to never ask questions for which he did not have the answer already. . .

'Well, this is what I wanted to talk to you about. These operations that we have been conducting have come to an end, at least I hope so,' said Max. 'We have established ourselves, consolidated our assets, and now we need to hold our position, and simply repel eventual assaults. Plus we have Potunov and . . . to assist. What I came to realise during the past two months is how close to death we all are. And the man I usually rely the most upon, John, not only almost died, but he also became totally unavailable at a critical moment. If it had not been for you, who stepped in and exercised remarkable leadership, we would not have succeeded. So, here is my proposal. I would like you to come on board to work as a 'consigliere'. I use a term that has been hijacked by the Italian mafia term, but I am actually referring to the way the Principality of Venice was run during the Middle Ages, that was led by a doge and a consigliere ducale. I think this term describes the functions best. I want you to be my adviser or counsellor. I would like you to eventually represent me at important business meetings that I cannot attend. This will require that you become familiar with the corporation business of course. And finally, the consigliere is to be my close, trusted friend and confidant. What will you receive in exchange? I am proposing a package that my lawyers have drafter for you, of a base pay of two mil a year (US dollars) and a participation in the company net profit of 1 per cent. So that you know, 1 per cent of last year's net profit was over four mil. Naturally, you have to move to Monaco, because I need you next to me at all times.'

'Since you have drafted the contract in my real name, you already knew everything about me didn't you? I like that,' commented Prince Vorgunin with a smile as he switched to English. 'You are a smart man, one I can learn a lot from. Actually, I thought a lot about what I want to do with the rest of my life. At one time I had for a goal to rebuild the fortune of the Vorgunins, but at the end of the day, who cares? I am not even married. I already own hundreds of thousands of acres, and I am not interested at all in the bloody country life, so . . . I thought killing people would never get old, but to speak frankly, after this last month with you . . . well, I think I am a bit tired of it. The problem I had until this very moment was that I had no alternative. So despite the fact that a reasonable man should think about such offers, and ponder, and reflect, I am a paratrooper after all, so I'll act like one. It is not at the moment to jump out that you have to decide whether you want to jump or not, it is throughout the weeks of training that you make your decision. Here it is the same thing. I had anticipated this conversation, and I am ready to accept.'

Reaching for the contract lying on the coffee table, he started reading it.

'So, what should I call you now, Simnatsat, Prince Vorgunin, Arkady, Arkady Kirillovich?' joked Max.

'Just call me AK. And in business, I can be AK Vorgunin. Although I am still a Prince of the Blood, since we do not have tsar, it does not make much sense to parade the title around...'

AK finished reading the contract which was actually very short, and he signed it. Next, he called Potunov to have him arrange his resignation from the FSB. Max also told him he could stay on the Princess until he found a suitable apartment in Monaco.

CHAPTER 26

It had been a month since the events in Petersburg. Max had lived with such intensity since then, it already felt like Lena had died months ago. Yet, the pain was so intense of her absence that he would suddenly realise it was such a short time, he should be hurting much more, and he felt guilty for not feeling more miserable. The Meissen China urn was sitting on the shelf in the ship's state room, and every day since he had placed it there on New Year's Eve, Max came in the evening, sat on an armchair facing it, and spent time with Lena while he listened to Wagner's Siegfried Funeral March from the Götterdämmerung. Every day he reminisced about the past, about the short time they had had together, and about the future he now had to face alone. He thought about certain clothes that she had worn, like that November day when she wore a purple Nina Ricci suit that made her hair even more radiant blond. He distinctly remembered the power of her femininity and of her sexuality that evening, and the look of happiness in her eyes. He had surprised her by taking her to a special dinner at his 'second office' as he had come to call the Café de Paris. She had enjoyed seeing how he knew everybody there, how he had a nice word with all of the waiters, how he had gone out of his way to ask Pierre about his sick little boy, and how he had so discreetly and delicately given him an envelope to help him pay for the costs of hospitalisation.

She knew that there had been as much money in the envelope as Pierre earned in a year of waiting on tables. They had eaten leisurely, from courses not on the menu, but courses Max had pre-ordered and that the chef had prepared specially for them. He had told her how he was going to make love to her later and she had begged to stop his graphic descriptions unless she would have an orgasm right in the middle of the restaurant. 'That's the purpose of my telling you all of this,' he had told her. And he had not stopped until he had seen her tense up and admit she had had an orgasm. After dinner, instead of going back to the harbour and the Princess of Russia, he took her arm and led her into the casino. She had thought the idea strange given Max's complete lack of interest in gambling. But instead of turning left into the game rooms, he had turned right and to her delight had taken her to the Salle Garnier for the ballet Gisele. She had realised how much she appreciated Max's gift to organise events so well, to always surprise her and make it look like it was a spur of the moment thing although it had required a good deal of planning. She had wrapped her arm around his chest and had kissed him tenderly.

During the ballet, Max had nonchalantly caressed her knee, and her neighbour had not been able to keep his eyes on the scene. At intermission, they had had a glass of champagne, and in the corner of a window, he had whispered in her ear all of the vulgar sexy things he wanted to do to her later. She had begged him to stop because her sex was opening and releasing a flood of juices that were running down her alabaster thighs. He had paid no attention to it and had continued. She had been squirming as if needing to go to the bathroom. Finally, she had been saved by the bell ringing and indicating for them to return to their seats and she had had to borrow his handkerchief to wipe her thighs . . . During the rest of the ballet, he had simply touched her thighs and had squeezed them slightly. After the ballet, instead of walking down the avenue des Spélugues to the harbour, he had taken her across the street to the Hotel de Paris for a drink, as they had many times. She had told him, 'I'm not hungry or thirsty, let's go home! There are only two things I want to do right now, and neither can be done in the middle of the bar!' But he had not been in a hurry. They had sat at a table, and her smile had revealed all of her sexual desire, her anticipation, and her passion for him. He had excused himself so that he could go to the bathroom and had disappeared for a long time. After a while the waiter had come to her table and had given her an envelope with a note and a key card. It had simply stated 'Room 425'. She had not believed he had planned the whole hotel thing as well. She ran to the room where she found him in his sexy pyjama bottom, serving her a glass of Krug, her favourite champagne. She did not even touch the glass and jumped on him with a passion he had never experienced before. Every night as he played the Funeral March, he resuscitated a short episode of their lives together, and when the music ended, it was as if she had been still alive for the five minutes and thirty-five seconds of the recording. The music would then switch to Siegfried's Idyll, and seven minutes and forty-four seconds later, Max would come out of his deep communion with Lena and wonder how he could manage to keep going. He had killed a lot of people to avenge her, becoming one of the Russian prime minister's favourite oligarchs in the process, and he often reflected that no amount of killing or bloodletting would ever bring her back, that no amount of slaughtering change anything to the fact that he had to move on, and eventually to find the woman who would replace Lena. And he felt such guilt about replacing her, that he could not even envision this possibility.

The next day he had to get things in order to go meet with his associates joining him in Moscow prior to the audience with the prime minister. Max's new executive assistant, Chantal, a very competent 35-year-old from Paris, whose subtle beauty was matched by incredible intelligence, had reserved the rooms at the Ritz-Carlton on Tverskaya. The hotel was only a few hundred metres away from the Kremlin offices of the prime minister, but a motorcade had been arranged because it would have been unthinkable for people of Max's importance to simply go to the Kremlin on foot. It was impressive to be invited there, and it was fundamental that the movement there also be impressive. At the Ritz, in the Washington Meeting Room that had been set up for dinner, Max, AK, John, Potunov, and Triple A mapped out the meeting with Prime Minister Pavel Burushin. This was the first meeting between the five men since Lena's death. Max had asked AK to tell them not to talk about her, as he wasn't sure he could control his emotions if they simply mentioned her name. As Max entered the meeting room, Chantal called him on his personal cell phone, which number was known only by six people. Chantal had been selected by Lena in a rigorous interview process to replace another executive assistant who had decided to launch a real estate venture of her own after witnessing Lena's success in that business. Max thought about the connection between the two women and thought about the trust Lena had placed in Chantal as he answered his iPhone. There was a change to the meeting with the prime minister because he had to go to Sochi the following day instead of meeting with Max and his team. So they had an extra day of planning. In addition, the construction season was in full swing again and several documents needed Max's signature, and she was sending them by fax. The activities related to Max's businesses meant that he now had to spend a lot of time with Chantal, either on the phone or in person. Outside of AK, she was the person he talked to the most. And as she was telling him about the construction in Spain, the property acquisition in Morocco, and the building in London, he could not help visualise her long-volumed blond hair, and her green eyes. The meeting started with the announcement of the delay, and a round of Beluga vodka. Outside of enjoying the gourmet cuisine of the Ritz-Carlton, the agenda included a complete review of the attacks and their aftermath, the conciliatory position to adopt with Burushin, and the amount of funds they were ready to pump into his sporting events, starting with the winter Olympics, and looking at the soccer world cup, and finally the Formula 1 grand prix.

THE DATURA SOLUTION

The attack on Capri had been completely understated. Thanks to the calculated manner in which it had been conducted, the lack of spectacular explosions or reports, and the continuation of the routine activities at the villa, no one had even reported anything to the police. Luigi himself was astounded. Now, the vial had been shut down and secured, and the caretakers had moved back in. They would never know how close they had come to dying. Had they not decided to go visit with their oldest son in Civitavecchia for Christmas, they too would be resting under 2,000 metres of water. The name of the villa had been rectified to Villa Pliny, and there was no fall out whatsoever from the Italian side. On the Russian side, here and there a couple of inquiries had been made about the whereabouts of a relative or another, but since the people who had disappeared either were criminals, worked for criminals, or were involved in illegal activities, no one was really interested in having the police stick their noses into what clearly was not their business to know. So, there again, nobody really missed individuals like Igor Petrovich, the members of the Frunze Group, or the goons that accompanied them. They had simply vanished, and no one cared. When Burushin had been told by Triple A that Igor Petrovich had disappeared and was presumed dead, his answer had been typical of the regard he had for such people, and he had asked to make sure he was not the only one that disappeared. The Capri operation was an absolute success. The titles of all the Frunze Group properties had been transferred to a new joint venture that had been baptised the ARC, for Anglo-Russian Corporation, that now regrouped all of the assets that had at one time belonged to Oleksandr Krasnaief, to Lena, and to Igor Petrovich. The shares of the corporation had been issued according to the agreement between Potunov, Triple A, and Max, and had been revised to readjust to the economic reality of such a vast empire. Not only had the shares been realigned so as to make no distinction between Frunze and non-Frunze assets, but Max had retained the control of the entirety of the assets through the ownership of 50 per cent plus one share of the voting papers for ARC. Potunov, who was continuing his diet and looked better every day, as well as Triple A, had completely changed from a Soviet-styled slob to an elegant man of a certain age, doing his best to maintain himself physically. Both men were now wearing elegant attire from famous fashion houses such as Boss, Armani, or Salvatore Ferragamo.

Pravda has run a front page article on the attack of Sankt Petersburg:

> One hundred twenty-seven people were killed in the explosion at Ladozhskyi Vakzal in Sankt Petersburg. The explosion took place on Christmas night at ten past midnight while the staff of the company headquartered in Tower 1 was celebrating Christian Christmas and exchanging gifts. This attack was so violent that the entire top floor of the building was blown off, and not a single survivor was found in the debris. Ambulances dispatched at the scene could only take victims to funeral homes where many of them were still being identified. This has caused people in Petersburg to hunt down Chechens and beat them in retaliation for the attack. Hundreds of cars were set on fire, which necessitated the intervention of anti-riot police using tear gas to re-establish order. Among the dead were three prominent businessmen well known in the Petersburg community: Alexey Bornakovich, president of the Baltic Hockey Club, Sergey Ellisov, the chairman of the Leningrad Metals Stock Exchange, and Alexandr Popovich, president of the Tunganaskaya Mining Corporation.
>
> Prime Minister Burushin who flew from Moscow to Petersburg asked the population to remain calm while condemning an 'unqualified criminal act aimed at the very fabric of our motherland'. On a TV interview from the scene of the explosion, he called it an 'act of blind and

heinous terrorism which will not go unpunished', which according to him was 'clearly a Chechen operation'. Later on Christmas day, troops were put on high alert to initiate military operations against specific targets in Chechnya. When asked about his certainty to the Chechen link, the prime minister confirmed that perchance Chechen terrorists were intercepted and shot at the crime scene.

In Europe, France, the United Kingdom, and Italy immediately condemned this terrorist act and the French president called it a 'cowardly and senseless act that will hurt the cause of the Chechens'. The US president, Barrack Obama, also 'categorically condemned this abject and barbarian act' and stated that his country was ready to assist Russia as needed to track down the culprits and to provide necessary help in the war against terror.

In the Middle East, Arab leaders joined in the vigorous denunciation of this odious act. Saudi Arabia spoke of a 'criminal act which is condemned by our religion, our ethics, and international standards'. Iraq's deputy prime minister, Abdullah Asfar, expressed concern about the response of Russia and pleaded for Russia to 'moderate its response in Chechnya'. Iran also condemned this act and presented its condolences to the Russian Federation.

Four persons of Chechen origin are confirmed dead at the scene. Two were found under the rubble, apparently caught in the building before they had time to escape, and two shot by Municipal Police agents who intercepted them perchance as they were fleeing the scene. One of those shot had a cell phone that was apparently used to detonate the explosives set in the building. All four of these individuals had railroad tickets for the Sankt Petersburg to Moscow Express train in their pockets. In addition, another seven suspects were being held within the framework of the investigation, according to an FSB source. Ten other potential suspects have been released, and interrogations are being held around the clock. The authorities who have clearly determined that the terrorist act was perpetrated by Chechens with the assistance of 'foreign elements' have already submitted a preliminary to Prime Minister Burushin. Finally, a videotape was received by NTV that shows one of the men shot by the Petersburg Municipal Police promising to 'severely punish the Russian people for the atrocities against the Chechen people'. Prime Minister Burushin promised that retaliation would be forthcoming and of a scale 'commensurate to the destruction brought upon the peaceful city of Petersburg'. The prime minister also declared five days of mourning for the dead of Ladozhskyi Vakzal.

For Max and the Consortium, the Ladozhskyi Vakzal explosion had also been an unqualified success. All of the explosives used through the Machiavellian plot designed by Colonel Onegin could be traced back to explosives 'stolen' from the Russian army in Chechnya. The colonel had made sure that the DNA of the explosive was readily recognisable. Further, the placing of two Chechen rebels within the building before it exploded was an undeniable proof that they had been there. Finally, the shooting by FSB forces of two men escaping the building as it blew up was the cherry on the cake, since both men were known Chechen terrorists who had been fooled into making videotapes threatening that very building. The two men had been captured by the FSB which never revealed that they were the FSB. Instead they had convinced them they had been recruited by a top secret unit of Chechen terrorists. They had made the tapes proclaiming they would strike a deadly blow to Criminal Mother Russia. A few moments before the building had blown up, they had been released by the 'secret unit' with railroad tickets for the 03:55 a.m. train to Moscow. They had been told that at the Moscow station, someone would be in touch with them to give them further instructions. Of course, the two man, the driver, and the guy riding shotgun, and all gotten out of the car, embraced, and as the Chechen were walking away towards the station, they had shot them in the back with silencers, in a manner consistent with the way two terrorists would have been shot. The aftermath of the explosion had been massive and a great opportunity for President Burushin to demonstrate his leadership. He had flown to Petersburg on Christmas day, which really wasn't Christmas day for him since he was orthodox, and he had toured the remnants of the building, personally going to the rescue area and giving a hand to the rescuers as they had pulled yet another victim form under the rubble. He had spoken to and consoled the families of the victims, declared the area a disaster area so that it would be funded by federal money for cleanup and reconstruction, and he had also awarded every family a stipend to tie them over during the coming days. Of course, he had declared five days of mourning, and he was going to stay in Petersburg for the funeral mass, where he had directed the Red Army Choir would sing. His decisive action, his grabbing of the initiative, his exposure to cameras, and his promise for retaliation had boosted his popularity among all Russians, and given a demonstration to the leaders of other countries how to truly exploit a disaster. The man behind this strategic achievement had been none of other than Andrei Andropov, who had prepared in advance all of the speeches, transportation and logistics to make Burushin really look good. A few days later, Triple A had been promoted to the place left vacant by the unfortunate accident of General Kozlov whose helicopter had crashed while he was flying home to Nizhny Novgorod from a meeting in Kazan. Triple A was now the second most feared man in Russia. But the Ladozhskyi Vakzal event was further exploited to renew the offensive in Chechnya, and as the five men were having a sumptuous dinner in the dark mahogany half-panel room with cream damask on the wall, while they were sitting in the comfortable royal blue armchairs and drinking expensive champagne, artillery fire could be heard all over the high mountains of Chechnya where Russian infantry was ruthlessly dealing with the nest of terrorists that had committed such atrocities in Petersburg. The success of the operation was guaranteed through the disinformation campaign that was being conducted by the FSB. Friendly losses would be understated, and enemy casualties inflated. President Burushin would look like a great military leader as well, and the First Channel News, the famous ORT, would show rows and rows of dead rebels, which in reality were civilians fallen victim to collateral damage and hastily dressed to look like Chechen rebels. In Petersburg, nobody would care: they only wanted to see Chechens die for what they had done on Christmas night.

As stated, the Alpha Unit had done a perfect job in disguising General Kozlov's assassination as a helicopter accident. It had been particularly easy as the team specialised in this type of accidents. Even if it caused the death of three people instead of one, limiting damages was not a prerequisite of the mission. Since papers were later found in Kozlov's safe implicating him in a scheme to sell nuclear technology to Iran, the untimely death of the general also provided Burushin with a means to chastise Iran for meddling in Russian affairs, and to appease the United States by declaring that many of the Russo-Iranian transactions that had been conducted over the past three years were the subject of top-down review that was sure to lead to a better support of the United States in the difficult matter of their relationship with the ayatollahs. The funny part was that after living so long with propaganda, lies, and half-truths, Burushin could not tell any longer where the truth actually was. In any case, as long as it served his political career, it really did not matter to him, and after Kozlov's revelation, he was now getting good press from the United States. But since Burushin was far from stupid, he also knew that all of these events on the night of the twenty-fourth of December had been masterfully planned, and that someone, he had no way of knowing at that time, was striking a heavy blow in the war to control industries and officials. He knew on Christmas morning that the undercurrents of power had shifted, and that even he had to be careful, because any faction that had that much power could certainly jeopardise his own career. Then he thought about it on the way to Petersburg: that faction was on his side. They were putting in place all of the tools to make him look good and to enhance his position. The help that Andrei Andropov had provided clearly indicated that he was a member of that faction. This I why he had made the decision that he should replace Kozlov. When Andrei Andreiovich met him in Petersburg, he had taken him to the side to thank him and ask him to get that meeting organised that had just been delayed by one day. At that time, Burushin had said nothing about a promotion. As the day unfolded and Triple A demonstrated time and again his dedication to the task of making Burushin look good, Andrei slowly fed Burushin bits of information to reveal the motivation and the nature of the man behind this campaign of re-establishing the popularity of the prime minister. When Burushin pretended to be shocked by the number of dead upon which he had to rebuild his popularity, Andrei had simply told him that not one of us can be blamed or held accountable for the atrocities these despicable Chechens had committed. The prime minister had looked at him sideways with a look that was asking as clearly as if he had spoken 'You don't really expect me to believe this bullshit, do you?' Two days later, Andrei had been promoted, and the prime minister had acknowledged the generous contribution made by Andrei's friends to his Sochi project.

Of all the Christmas night events, the less spectacular had been the disappearance of Igor Petrovich's brother who had been spending time with his wife and four children in Igor's dacha outside Moscow, on the small Kratovo Lake, near the village of Zhukovskyi. Yet it proved the more troublesome. The team had strict instructions not to harm either the wife or the children, and since it had snowed heavily, and intervention would have left footprints. So they had waited until after the planned time of attack. When their victim had finally come out by himself on December 27, they had followed him, and ran him off the road as he was turning left onto Muromskaya to go to the village. At first he had thought it was a simple traffic accident, but realising it had to do with his brother, he had started yelling 'Help! Help! They want to kill me! Help!' and the sounds had carried far away in the icy December air. At the same time, he had attempted to run away, yelling even louder, 'You are mistaken, I am not Igor Petrovich, I am his brother! I am Sergei!' But one of the men had judged necessary to reassure him, 'Don't worry Sergei, we know who you are! Your brother's already fucking dead anyhow!' Sergei had run even faster, but it was no use. He struggled in the deep snow while his assailants, strong, young army Spetsnaz had no problems. They finally dragged him back to their car. One of them hit him hard on the head so that he lost consciousness and they shoved him into the trunk. They subsequently worked for almost half an hour getting Sergei's car back on the road. They started off in the opposite direction to the town and drove to an isolated cross-country path in Bolotsyei. There, they took him out of the trunk, sat him down in his car. One of the two men grabbed Sergei's left hand, put a pistol with silencer in it, brought it to Sergei's temple as he was regaining consciousness and pulled the trigger. He then removed the silencer and shut the door as Sergei's lifeless body slumped to the right and on the passenger seat. They backed off and left back towards Moscow. 'I thought we would never have that motherfucker!' commented one of the two men. 'Yeah, it was fucked up, wasn't it?' When the body was found two days later, it had snowed again, so the footprints were not visible. Although the inquest concluded it was most likely a suicide, the prosecutor was convinced it was actually a pure and simple murder. He knew of the relationship of the victim with the mob, he also knew he was Ivan Petrovich's brother, so there was no need to waste too much time on this one, and bring oneself to the attention of the mob. They would take care of it themselves. So, the affair was filed as a suicide, to the loud protests of Sergei's wife who had by then figured out her brother-in-law had also vanished. 'I bring that to the attention of the president himself,' she threatened. The next day, she received the visit of a high-ranking member of the FSB that took all of her information, listened to her grievances, and asked her in the name of Prime Minister Burushin if she needed anything, and if she had enough money to raise the children. When she answered affirmatively that money was not a problem, the official left. But he was the same official that attended her husband's funeral, and she understood immediately from this second appearance that there was a consistent threatening message attached to that presence. This was confirmed when the official approached her to present his condolences and told her that the prime minister had set up a pension fund for her children to attend the best universities possible. Once she got home that night, she thought the matter over: her husband was gone, he had been a key mob figure, she knew this day would happen one day, nothing that she could do would bring him back—actually, she thought, would she want him back—and the future of the children required her survival. The following day, she went to the prosecutor's office and signed all the witness statement supporting the theory of suicide in her husband's death.

By the time Max got to Moscow, the Ladozhskyi Vakzal events had been largely forgotten by the general public and by the press. This had been helped by the fact that Russia had suffered yet another mining disaster in Siberia at the Saharskaya Mine where fifty plus miners had been killed right off, and another forty were trapped almost a mile underground. The ongoing saga of failed rescue attempts, the primetime pictures of women sobbing in the frozen landscape, and the lambasting of mine owners by the politicians had all of the elements of the dramas the Russians are so fond off. The longer the trapped miners survived the more people were interested and the more it sent the Petersburg dead to oblivion, since after all their death had happened in a few seconds, and no footage existed of the explosion. The dead had been buried, the debris almost cleaned up, and a construction company had already been contracted by the owner to rebuild the building exactly like it was before the next New Year. It should have been no surprise that the construction company belonged to the consortium which Max now headed. The men in the Washington Room at the Ritz-Carlton agreed that the prime minister had been pacified and that he understood how the consortium had helped him already. The senior Russian members went further in stating that they actually owned the prime minister, by now, and that rather than being conciliatory to him, it was the opposite. He had to be conciliatory to them. There were two reasons for this and they were simple. First, they could bring him down as fast as they had brought him up. It was a matter of staging the right event, and his leadership could be compromised as easily as it had been built up. Second, he had to know that a group that could dispose of the number two officer in the FSB could dispose of anybody in Russia, prime minister included. The consequence of this was that the prime minister had to know that the army that counted, the one that contained the true professional soldiers, this army was no loyal to any politician. This army was loyal to its leaders, to its officers, and to those who could bring them money. None of the politicians had ever been able to either pay the pensions the Russian Federation had promised them, or even to allow them to earn enough money so that they did not need to be waiters in Moscow restaurants to have enough money for their families to live on. Yet, there were organisations like the Consortium—the three men decided to adopt this name after using it all evening to describe their holdings—who came along and actually paid for their services and allowed them to live with dignity. This is who these men were now loyal to. And the Consortium did not ask them to do this the Russian Federation had not asked them to do before: the assassination of political figures, the mass killing of hundreds of Chechens, and the complete destruction of Grozny were of such scale as to make the events of 25 December look truly benign. As Andrei Andreiovich had remarked, 'We did away with about 120 people at Ladozhskyi Vakzal, that's not even a tenth of the people we blew up in a single building during the third campaign of Grozny.' All men agreed that in order to 'play the game' and to not have to face the taxation office raids, they had to pretend to be subservient to the prime minister. If they did not want to play that game, there was only one solution, and that was to eliminate him. During the meeting, this had to be made very clear. So, now they had to submit to his endless begging for money for 'his' projects. They had to decide how much money they accepted to part with instead of killing the prime minister. Basically, they were ready to assign his life a monetary value. Up to that amount, keeping the Burushin alive was a viable economic proposition; above that amount, it no longer was, and he would have to be disposed of, especially if the Consortium ever had to face the tax office. Andrei Andreiovich stated firmly that the entire tax office would be blown up by Chechens if they even suggested coming after the Consortium. He had already passed the message along, and furthermore, since their entire offices were bugged, he knew exactly which civil servant said what, and it was easy enough to rough up a couple of people as a pre-emptive measure. If a couple had to be disembowelled and left to rot in a dark alley of a Moscow suburb, it could also be arranged, had Andrei Andreiovich concluded. So, they started working on the figures. Rustelecom had invested over $120 million in the Winter Olympics. The Rus-Yak Bank had committed to about $100 million. But the other oligarchs had only provided funds well below the $20-million mark. Andrei Andreiovich produced the up-to-date list of the twenty-one oligarchs and the amount they had contributed and none of them had spent that much, and the average was just over twelve mil. As a newcomer to the group, Max should not try to impress, nor should he be too cheap. But most of all, he should never underestimate the position of power that he was in. Burushin owed him his future. Max argued that politicians have no memory and no conscience, and that the Consortium should remember that at all times. The boost the Consortium had given Burushin was in the past, and therefore, it no longer existed. Max was of the opinion that the Consortium should be fair but also absolutely ruthless with Burushin. Max was not about to treat him with kid's gloves. In Max's view, Burushin was like a prostitute: you paid her to get a set of services, you got the services you paid for, and at the same time, you always had to be on your guards and ensure she did not rob you or murder you while supplying the services. All men laughed and agreed, and they started joking and calling Burushin 'Burusuka', from his last name and 'suka' the word for bitch in Russian. In the end, it was decided that the Consortium would offer $12 million as a contribution for the Winter Olympics, and in return, they would get the contract for the entire security of the games, which amounted to somewhere around a billion dollars. If this went through, the Consortium would double the investment to $24 million. The proposal would be made while emphasising that the Consortium would ensure the 'absolute security of the prime minister', a clear way to express the threat to his life without stating it.

CHAPTER 27

It had been a slow process. At first, he had found Chantal to be attractive with her lively deep-blue eyes, her charming French accent when she spoke English, her smile that caused four dimples to form on her cheeks, her blond hair, and her intelligence. But he had not been able to say that he had been attracted to her in a physical sense. She wore conservative clothes that succeeded in hiding her body quite effectively. The only thing he could make out of her body was that she had beautiful legs. But he had not been carried away by passion like he had been with Lena. Lena had been stunningly beautiful, but Chantal did not emit this immediate need to love her passionately. Her effect on Max was to be far deeper in the sense that she became his best friend over the weeks and months that followed Lena's death. Without really realising it, she became far more of an adviser than Vorgunin would ever be. She arranged all of the meetings, she knew where Max was at all times, she was the only person to have full access to him, and she and he talked at least two to three hours a day about business issues. Over the months, he even forgot that she was married, and started talking to her as if she weren't, as if she was completely available to him. The fact that he thought about her from the moment he woke up until the moment he went to bed did not really trigger in him the idea that he was falling in love with her, and she with him.

There were business imperatives that required them to talk every day, and that required them to meet frequently whether on the Princess of Russia or at the Café de Paris. During these meetings at the Café de Paris, it was obvious to the waiting staff that Chantal was not simply an executive assistant, and many of them speculated whether Chantal was one day going to replace Lena, who was still in everybody's mind. While Max was oblivious to these thoughts and while he would have laughed at the speculations regarding him and Chantal, this was not the case for Chantal. The day she had come to the interview with Lena, she had met Max, and during the briefing, he had given her on the operations he controlled within Lena's business, Chantal had been impressed by his intelligence, comprehension of the world, and experience in a way that no other man had ever impressed her before. In addition, she had found him incredibly attractive. When she had seen him depart the offices of the Princess of Russia to go to another appointment in France, she had followed him with her eyes, hoping that he would turn around, so she could see him one more time, and wishing she was part of his world. But he had not turned around and she had then desired with all her soul that she would get the job with Lena, so that she could be close to Max. And even in the interview she had had with Max, Chantal thought she had detected indicators that Max was not insensitive to her. But she had dismissed all of this as nonsense. She was a married woman with two children, a woman who had never had the slightest thought of being unfaithful to her husband, and a woman who would never do that, even if life with her husband was far from meeting her needs and from fulfilling her. On that very first day, when she knew Max had a relationship with Lena, when she knew she had a duty as a wife to be faithful to her husband, and when she knew Max could not possibly have any interest in her, she rejected the very notion that she could have fallen in love with him, and yet, as she would discover later, on that very first day, she *had* fallen in love with him.

THE DATURA SOLUTION

Almost a year after Lena's death, Max and Chantal had travelled together to New York. Because of a shortage of hotels, they had had to stay he on the East Side, she on the West Side. They had spent every moment of the day together, and he had invited her to dinner every night. Despite this, he had kept his distance from her, not wanting to disturb her marital life, which of course he did not know was nonexistent. It was September 11, and they had met an important client downtown, a client that was about to commit to purchasing over 50 per cent of a building they were in the process of building in London with Atlas Enterprises. The meeting had gone very well, and Max and Chantal had walked out of the building happy with the outcome, ready to return to their respective hotels to catch planes she to Argentina, he back to Monaco. He had rushed to the cab, thinking she was running behind him in the driving rain. But when he had turned around, she had been nowhere to be seen. He had called her but her cell phone had remained silent. He had had no choice but to drive off, and he had understood immediately. The idea of being separated from him for the coming two weeks had been too much, and she would not have been able to control her emotions. She had taken refuge in a diner and had waited for him to leave before jumping in a taxi and going to her own terminal at JFK. That day, Max came to regard as the day he had become conscious that he had fallen in love with her. Her absence weighed on him, and his heart was hurting, knowing how much she was missing him. He was cursing himself for having changed plans at the last minute, deciding to return to Monaco rather than going to Buenos Aires with her. During that trip, she had called him every day, supposedly for business matters, but in fact neither he nor she was fooling each other, and they both knew with certainty that next time they met, they would become lovers. He had come to the conclusion that this love that they had been repressing for almost a year, this intimacy which they had built, this almost daily contact, this complicity they shared were simply stronger than any resolution he had made to stay faithful to Lena or to respect the fact that Chantal was married. He could not fight this any longer. Max could not believe how the feelings he had for Chantal were so intense and so deep, that even the memory of Lena could not prevent him from wishing with all his heart and soul that Chantal become his mistress. He could not recall such intensity from the love he had experienced with Lena. With her it had been quick, almost immediate, and it had been a passionate entry into a freedom of loving he had known with only one other woman before, but there had not been this building of an entire relationship for a year before he would even exchange a kiss with her.

CHAPTER 28

29 January

The flight back from Sochi should have been a routine one. The weather was perfect, visibility was excellent, and Prime Minister Burushin had been assured by Captain Ivanov that he would be back in Moscow by dinner time as planned. The prime minister had already arranged his appointment with the gorgeous and highly talented Galina Churchiskaya, a tall call girl who had been the November centrefold of *On*, the sexually explicit Russian magazine that was now outselling American erotic publications in Russia. The fact that the prime minister's nephew owned the magazine had not escaped her, and she felt rather proud of the way she was able to manage the business relationship she had with Burush, as she called him. She had skills in the bedroom that far exceeded those of her competitors, but the prime minister was not particularly happy to have to share her abilities with pop stars, Mafia bosses and even leading ecclesiastic elders. Her rates had become truly unmanageable over the previous few weeks. To go all the way, or as he liked to call 'from the attic to the cellar' now cost $15,000 per night, and Burushin was considering simply buying her services for life for a set amount rather than having to go through the drudgery of having to make appointments with her so-called agent, and often finding out she was already engaged with another member of his social circle. He then had to resort to hiring the services of much less performing women who although they were professionals lacked Galina's skills. She was a true artist. He was thinking of his last session with her, when he had experienced every sort of sexual position possible between a man and a woman. She had finished the session by a fabulous rimming while masturbating him, and she had penetrated his rectum with her middle finger as he came on her face. It had been one of the most intense experiences of his sexual life. He was daydreaming about this performance and was already feeling an erection when he was taken out of his reverie as the Tupolev started to shake violently. His erection and the thoughts of Galina immediately gave way to a cold sweat as the plane started plunging towards the ground as if it were a dive bomber. The shaking got worse as the speed increased. The stewardess—whom he had thought of seducing a few moments before—was projected forward into the bulkhead, and Burushin who was not wearing his seatbelt joined her there after his attempts to remain in his seat failed. He braced himself for the impact and crashed violently into the woman, cracking her ribs, and splitting her lip as he hit her with his head. She swore at him and let out a cry of pain. The forces of gravity were stronger than either, and he was crushing her despite his efforts not to do so. Despite the dire situation, there was no warning from the cockpit. The pilots did not communicate, and Burushin immediately knew that the plane was suffering a terminal problem. He cursed himself for wanting to fly a Russian-made plane, a Tupolev 154 'to show the example' instead of a Boeing or an Airbus like everyone around him had so strongly recommended. He knew that statistically, the Tupolev 154 had one of the poorest safety records in the world. Yet, he also knew that the crashes had all been caused by human error rather than a flaw in the design of the aircraft. And now, he wondered what his crew had bungled up in the cabin to cause the aircraft to so violently shake and plunge into an uncontrolled nose dive. When he heard one of the engines explode, Burushin knew he would never again see Galina. He tried to have a last erotic thought, but the few seconds he had left to live and the urgency to think it through were not conducive to sexual activity, especially since the stewardess has gone into a panic and was repeating that they were going to die. Burushin expressed the thought that he wished 'the bitch would shut the fuck up'. He did not have the time to transform the thought into words. The impact was colossal and the prime minister of Russia was vaporised in an infernal fireball as the plane scattered itself into a million small and unrecognisable pieces.

The news reached the Internet at 3:16 p.m. GMT, when Russian officials announced to the world the embarrassing news that the plane of the prime minister, VVS-2 (they had copied the name on the US vice president's plane name but had to abbreviate the excessively long Voyenno-Vozdushnye Sily to VVS) had crashed for unknown reasons as it flew between Sochi and Moscow, in the vicinity of the city of Lipetsk. Immediately, the Ministry of Defense had issued a statement implying that the plane crash was the result of terrorist activities conducted by agents of the Georgian Government. However, Russian media simply reported that the plane had suddenly lost altitude and that the calls from the Voronezh air controllers had remained unanswered. Russian media also reported that the President of Russia, Sergei Komissarov, had tears in his eyes when he had come on TV to announce the death of the prime minister to the people of Russia. He had also announced that the Deputy Prime Minister Alexey Shadrin would be running the day-to-day business of the government and that a week of national mourning had been declared, starting with two minutes of silence the following day at twelve noon, Moscow time. Sergei Komissarov had added, 'The Russian Federation must function and will function.' He had also warned potential enemies that the Russian Federation would not let its guard down and that any foreign power trying to take advantage of the situation would be 'severely punished by Russian Armed Forces'. And to make sure the message was clear, he had put all forces on alert for the next forty-eight hours. In Moscow, people had immediately taken to the street and gathered on Red Square. Mourners had started to lay flowers and light candles in front of the Lenin Mausoleum, as a crowd carrying innumerable white, red, and blue flags occupied the area between the GUM store and the Kremlin walls. 'I am shattered, I don't know what to say, I don't know what to do. He was our father to us all,' Antonia Romanova had declared on Russian TV as she was laying a bunch of flowers on Red Square. All over the country, in the main city of the federation, similar scenes were being orchestrated, while mourners gathered, many of them sharing genuine tears for their former prime minister. At the same time, Galina cursed the gods that had deprived him of her best-paying customer, and furthermore, one she had liked to perform for. She took the decision that she had to replace him, and she started forging her plans on the spot.

While the Russian Emergencies Ministry told the world the plane had crashed at 1348 hours Moscow time, the Voronezh Regional Governor confirmed on Russian TV that no one had survived. And while thousands of Muscovites marched outside the Kremlin, they were offered a last look at the office of the prime minister, identifiable by its lit window, as it had been every night when he worked there. Little did the people know that the light had always remained on when Burushin had been entertaining Galina. And lately, it had been almost every night. Max and his team tried to make sense of the event. There was no use in waiting in Moscow. Suddenly, the entire political map had been torn apart as if by a powerful earthquake, and the power the Consortium had built around the prime minister had been reduced to nil. Thinking about it, they came to the conclusion that the plane crash had been a direct attack on the Consortium. There could be little doubt about it. It was decided that Max would leave right away as the situation had acquired a volatility that certainly carried a definite part of danger for any foreigner who had achieved as much notoriety as he had. And the more the crowds manifested a spontaneous outpouring of grief and expressed anger at foreign influences, the more it became risky for Max to stay in town. Stunned people, visibly moved to tears, and who until then had violently disagreed with Burushin's policies and lifestyle, had now become his staunchest defenders, united by a hatred of these foreign influences which President Komissarov had denounced. With hundreds of Russian flags being unfurled on Red Square, the extremists of the far-right movement 'Rodinna' mingled into the crowd and started to organise a demonstration asking that Georgia be punished for assassinating the prime minister. At the Ritz-Carlton, Max packed his bags and called the concierge to get the Mercedes ready. He had decided to leave immediately as nothing positive could possibly take place now. As the car pulled out onto Tverskaya Avenue, traffic was at a standstill and throngs of people were converging onto Red Square. It took over three and a half hours to get to Domodedovo Airport, and everywhere it was the same litany of women wiping tears from their eyes, and men unable to believe that their beloved prime minister, whom they had loathed the day before, was now dead. Finally, after going through the lethargic procedures of civil aviation, Max boarded the Falcon and was on the way to Nice.

On TV and on the radio, the usual platitudes were being served to the multitude. There were of course numerous eyewitness interviews. There was the man who had heard an explosion, and when he had looked up, he had seen a plane nose-diving towards the ground, and then he had heard the huge noise of the explosion and he knew no one could have survived. And no, he did not know it was the prime minister's plane. There were of course all sorts of preliminary reports, which simply stated the obvious and clearly put the blame on a terrorist act: the plane was in perfect condition, the pilots were faultless, veterans of thousands of hours flying the Tupolev 154, the crash was simply no accident. Captain Ivanov's biography was broadcast ad nauseum, showing him in the uniform of a MIG-29 fighter pilot, a veteran of tens of missions over Afghanistan. He was a man who had been personally chosen by the prime minister. The preliminary reports summarised that the plane had 'suffered an explosion in flight, had fallen to the ground and broken up into pieces,' the expert said. 'There were no survivors in that crash.' Naturally, Georgian media who had been keen to put the blame on anybody but Georgia carried claims that the plane's crew were at fault for the crash. They had already planted the idea in international circles that the flight controllers had noticed some irregularities in flight patterns leading to the suggestion that the plane landed in Voronezh. But as far as they knew, the crew had not even answered the radio calls.

Simultaneously, conspiracy theorists had stated that this was an assassination conducted by the black operations of the VSB which wanted to take over Russia and re-establish the rule of the Communist Party. Russian Deputy Prime Minister Alexey Shadrin had already visited the crash site, after saying he would personally oversee the investigation into the crash. 'Everything must be done to establish the reasons for this tragedy in the shortest possible time,' he had said.

Since he was a former KGB officer, this fuelled the rumours that his investigation was a sham destined to hide the truth about the real assassins. In the late evening as Max had already taken off, Russian officials announced that all the bodies had been recovered from the scene and were being taken to Moscow for identification. Actually, this was an absurd overstatement, as the only remains that had been found had been a couple of shoes—yet to be attributed to anyone—and the frozen solid heart of what would have been either the pilot or the co-pilot. The Emergency Minister also proudly commented that both of the plane's flight information recorders had been found, recovered, and that they had been flown to Moscow where they were being examined. At the FSB offices, General Andropov was already at work activating the plan that would allow him to regain advantage of the situation now that the prime minister was dead. The Consortium had succeeded in making him totally subservient to the Consortium interests. Now, he had set the wheels in motion that would allow him, and not the Consortium to ensure that Alexey Shadrin, who would undoubtedly become the new prime minister, would become his servant into a new Consortium-inspired structure. The deputy prime minister was well known by the FSB. They had gigabyte upon gigabyte of information on him, and in this massive amount of data, General Andropov had already implanted the fabricated lies that were to make the new prime minister his peon. This was also the dream opportunity to eliminate rivals and threats while the power was in limbo, but he had to strike fast. This would serve his purpose while nobody with authority could contest his actions or hold him accountable for anything. Of course, he had to be weary of the other FSB generals who were sure to attempt the same manoeuvre. Nevertheless, he continued to use the Consortium as a conduit for his actions. The Consortium had agreed to handle this situation in exactly the same way they had handled the Petersburg explosion. Every member of the Consortium knew perfectly well that their plan would have one result, and one result only, war against Georgia. To this end, Potunov had already heavily invested in the armaments industry, and any conflict that Russia launched into would greatly improve his financial situation as well as the Consortium's. The Consortium was now an uncontrollable machine that ate everything in front of it. To survive and to grow, it now needed the blood of thousands of men who would die avenging the life of a prime minister that had been despised and ridiculed during his lifetime and whose integrity had been so low, he was not worth the life of a single man.

In the ensuing days, General Andropov's services, which he had established as a separate entity under Captain Muzhov who had been promoted to major and subsequently speed-tracked to Lieutenant Colonel for services rendered to Mother Russia. It went without saying that Colonel Muzhov was now an indirect employee of the Consortium and that his Monaco bank account under the false identity of Andrei Grovalchuk was growing at a rate related to the complexity and sophistication of the work he was doing for the Consortium. These J-Services, as they were now code-named, had been able to 'capture' a Georgian operative who under interrogation—but especially thanks to the bribe of $50,000—had signed a confession and had confirmed that he had been witness to a conversation a few weeks hence in which the blowing up of the prime minister's plane had been debated. This operative, whose name was to remain anonymous at the moment for his protection, had even given specific details of the place, time, and date of the meeting and he had provided the names of three people who had attended the meeting. Nobody would ever know that the names had been provided to him by J-Services before his so-called confession. The three names were those of agents of the Republic of Georgia that had been caught spying on Russian Federation territory during the brief conflict of 2008. Having considered that he may one day have need of such people, General Andropov had had them delivered to a top secret detention centre, where they had been imprisoned for several years in total isolation. So, it was an easy task to give their names to their star witness and provide the new prime minister a complete report on the involvement of Georgia in the crash. This served three purposes. First, it established the same strong link between the prime minister and a key member of the Consortium, as had existed before. Second, it showed the speed with which the prime minister was able to provide reliable information to the public, and in this moment of crisis, the delivery of such quick news was key to re-establish trust in the office of the prime minister. And third, it allowed Russia to have a legitimacy to demand apologies from Georgia and escalate the crisis anyway it chose without receiving blatant criticism from other countries. Naturally, this entire scheme was completed by the planting of false information on Georgian Internet servers, information that showed coded email traffic between an office of the security services in Georgia and their operatives in Russia—the three men in detention. It was given to the brilliant mind of the gifted Alex Romanovich to flawlessly fabricate and embed these emails on various servers around the world. Photographs had also been photoshopped showing any of the three men in the company of the Georgian president, minister of defence, or other well-known figures. All photographs went back to at least 2007 and demonstrated the close link between the plotters and the members of the regime. These pictures were rather effective when a week after the tragedy, Prime Minister Shadrin was able to hold a press conference identifying the three plotters, showing their pictures, then showing them shaking hand with the Georgian president, and revealing the content of coded emails between the Georgians and their operative—content that had of course been transliterated into Russian. These emails were particularly damaging since they gave the time and date of flight of the Russian prime minister and contained the code phrase 'Our grandmother is waiting for her khartcho tonight'. Khartcho referred to the Georgian beef broth with rice, herbs, and walnuts, and tonight, as the prime minister pointed out, was the day of Prime Minister Burushin's death on 29 January. The prime minister in interim—who was now certain to become the permanent occupant of the Kremlin—had made a very convincing demonstration, a demonstration for which he had been coached by General Andropov. The prime minister was now mulling far greater responsibilities for the man who had become his greatest supporter during the past week. Following a visit to his 'gadalka', whom he consulted on a regular basis, the soothsayer—who had received the rather unpleasant visit of FSB men in the meantime—had affirmed that she saw someone with a last name starting with *A* that would play a major role in his life. The idea had come into his mind that General Andropov would make an excellent minister of defence.

While the prime minister was getting the glory of the progress of the investigation, Triple A had been working on producing the three men. From the moment the prime minister's plane had crashed, General Andropov had had two major concerns. First he had to produce a fake Russia's Interstate Aviation Committee (IAC) investigation report. And this had to be convincing enough to pass scrutiny with Aviakor—the company that maintained the president and the prime minister planes—with Jane's—the international aviation magazine would undoubtedly launch its own investigation—but most of all with the FAA. Second, he wanted to make sure that the three Georgian operatives reappeared, and of course, it was out of the question that they would reappear alive. After the very public speech of the new prime minister stating that he would conduct the investigation himself, there had been a parade of high-ranking officers and civilians offering their assistance to help him conduct the investigation. But only one of them had come through with a partially completed report which he had summarised to the prime minister in a manner that allowed him, Alexei Shadrin, to once and for all take care of the Georgian problem, or not. When he had pushed General Andropov for more answers with questions that clearly demonstrated his knowledge and understanding of Andropov's subterfuge, the prime minister had been delighted by the coherence of the general's thought and by his unwavering confidence in defending the most outrageous lies. So it came to the point where the prime minister wanted a meeting a day with General Andropov and that he asked him for advice on maintaining his immediate supervisor at the head of the FSB. When Andropov had produced several reports of examinations by eminent professors of the Moscow Serbsky Institute, the most famous psychiatric hospital in Russia, including a report signed by its eminent director, Tatiana Dmitrieva, showing beyond the shadow of a doubt that the director of the FSB had the early symptoms of the onset of Alzheimer's, the new prime minister issued an order on the spot removing the director and promoting General Andropov to this role. The gadalka's prophecy was self-fulfilling. The prime minister and the general now had a complete understanding of each other, and the general would deliver because with every step forward in the development of his career and in the power it allowed him to have, he made millions of dollars through intimidation, theft,

THE DATURA SOLUTION

extortion, and industrial and business deals, which only *he* could make because unbeknownst to all, he was really already in charge of Russia. Within a few days, he had become the force to be reckoned with, and Potunov was making Max well aware of this exceptional rise in power that meant only one thing: General Andropov had become a very dangerous ally and soon would become a very dangerous enemy. Max relied on daily calls with Potunov, but Andropov was now completely out of reach. Max knew perfectly well that the situation needed to be brought under control. He could not let Andropov progress to the point where he did not need Max any longer, or thought he did not need Max. And Max was not about to lose his dearly won assets in Russia, Lena's legacy.

In the meantime, in their prison, the three Georgians who were still segregated had been given a better diet for several days and were now hopeful they would be released. In Moscow, the newspapers had managed to get the name of the Georgian informer. But this was no accident. General Andropov knew perfectly well that any man who is paid $50,000 to sign false statements can also be bought by the next person for double that price to say that the statements were indeed false. By arranging for his name to be released to the media, the general had signed the man's death warrant. He would be the first of thousands of people to die, and it bothered the general not at all. The man, a certain Abkhaz Guermoulian, would be found stabbed in his cell. How another prisoner could get into the isolation cell which Abkhaz occupied was never satisfactorily explained, because it could not be explained. The fact was that an FSB agent had been given a set of all the keys to the isolation wing as well as the key to Abkhaz's cell, and that he had slit his throat as instructed. He had then gotten into his Volkswagen Passat and when he had almost reached his home in one of the massive apartment buildings that ring the city of Moscow, near the Chaussée Entuziastov, where his wife Svetlana was waiting, the fifty pounds of explosives that had been installed on the bottom of his car were remotely detonated via a cell phone and the life of the assassin had been terminated. Neither the man who had installed the explosives nor the man who had dialled the number to detonate them had any idea they had just killed an FSB colleague. And this is the way General Andropov wanted to keep it. Knowledge had to be compartmented, and again, according to the motto he had adopted from Max, he was sure to 'leave no witness behind'. Of course, the press could possibly have linked the two events, but every reporter in Moscow knew that long-term survival meant staying away from the business of the FSB and its most powerful leaders. Everything was done to the benefit of Mother Russia, claimed the Rodinna slogan, and there was no greater defender of Mother Russia than General Andropov. So it came that two cousins Mustapha Guermoulian and Abkhaz Guermoulian, who had not even known each other, had fallen victim one to the United States because of his own actions, and the other to Russia, simply because he had been at the wrong place at the right time.

Three days after these events, General Andropov confided to the prime minister that the Georgian terrorists who had blown up the previous prime minister's plane had been located within the confines of the Russian Federation and that J-Services were hunting them down. The prime minister had no comments except to state 'tell me when it is over'. From this short sentence, General Andropov concluded that the prime minister's wish was that the men never have the opportunity to see the inside of a courtroom and that their miserable lives should be terminated as soon as feasible. That night was Valentine's Day and since the period of mourning was over, the prime minister attended the ballet Cinderella at the Bolchoi to mark the event. It was a Siberian night, with temperatures well below thirty degrees. Yet, as he entered the Bolchoi, he had taken a few moments to give an impromptu interview during which he had declared that he was very close to finding 'the saboteurs who think they can come to Russia, commit their horrific murders, and then run home and not be punished!' From that point on, the prime minister pushed Andropov hard to get a 'final resolution, if you know what I mean'. General Andropov decided to proceed like the Nazis had done in Prague when hunting down the assassins of Heydrich. He gave his instructions to Colonel Muzhov, who picked the abandoned village of Uzhginskaya in the Perm Oblast. The village was completely deserted save for one old woman who still lived in one of the houses with her two dogs. The colonel had three of his men set up a semi-permanent residence in the church, making sure they left plenty of Georgian gear and products as evidence. But as soon as they had approached the village, the old lady's dogs that were unaccustomed to human presence except for that of their master had started barking. The three men were going to let them be, but as the woman came out, she started yelling at them, and they knew they could not let such a vocal witness survive. If she talked, she might well see and state that the three dead Georgians were not the ones that had occupied the village. Without hesitation, and according to their rules of engagement, one of the men stepped forward and shot the old woman in the chest. Then, he shot the dogs. Without even a cursory look at the house they went on. It is only after they had gone about 200 metres that they thought it would be good to pillage the house, 'like Georgian sons of bitches would have done.' They ransacked the house, taking food, whatever few rubbles they found, and all of the vodka. Then, they dragged the woman in the house and raped her with a flashlight, 'just like the Georgian sons of bitches would have done'. One of the men burst out laughing, and it became their logo. They joked about it, and with everything they did, they added 'like the Georgian sons of bitches would have done!' During the night of 21 February, a squad of FSB elite troops 'assaulted' the church using weapons with silencers. They did not hesitate to use a massive amount of ammunition from multiple rifles. Then, three of them went into the church and fired different rifles from inside the church, as if they were the three Georgians defending themselves. If there had been any witnesses, they would have had the clear illusion that a gun battle had taken place between a platoon of J-services and three Georgian terrorists. The three men, who had been brought up from their prison facilities, had been given the clothes of partisan fighters, and had been given an opportunity to test fire the newest Russian weapons, so that their uniforms would bear the powder signature of people involved in combat. They had been absolutely flabbergasted and had never understood why they had been dragged from jail and given the opportunity to test fire the weapons. They understood even less why they were then transported by helicopter to Uzhginskaya and were then taken to the church blindfolded. Their emotions went from elation to pure terror and turned into the conviction they would die moments before they were tied to specific locations in the church with ropes: one at the door of the church, one at the large side window, and another in the steps going up to the church tower. Then a new fake assault took place, this time with no silencers, while 'defenders' were shooting from the church. The noise of FSB armoured vehicles was heard. The gun battle lasted about ten minutes. Finally, the three Georgians were shot several times where they had been roped. The ropes were quickly removed. The bodies were placed to imitate the way combatants may have died in a fire fight, and pictures of the scene were taken to show how the Georgian rebels had died fighting FSB troops.

The next day, Prime Minister Shadrin called a press conference at lunch time, just like he had seen President Obama do so effectively on CNN. At the announced time, the prime minister appeared on all major TV stations in Russia, speaking from his office in the Kremlin:

'Fellow Russian Citizens. Last night during a raid of a rare violence, the security forces of the Russian Federation assaulted a church in the small village of Uzhginskaya in the Perm Oblast and defeated a unit of Georgian terrorists that had taken refuge there following their assassination of our former prime minister. The raid was conducted starting at 02:30 a.m. by a platoon of our elite forces. The exchange of gun fire lasted for about twenty-six minutes during which more than 1,500 rounds of ammunition were expended on each side. From what we can piece together, the criminals had taken refuge in a small house on what used to be the main street of the village, which is now abandoned. In that house, they murdered an old pensioner and her three dogs, and repeatedly raped her. Upon detecting the approach of the security forces, they realised they were surrounded and transferred to the village church that provided better defensive positions, and which they had prepared ahead of time. The three Georgian terrorists were killed during the gun battle. Several documents, their passports, articles, and a laptop were recovered and show without the shadow of a doubt that they were of Georgian origin, and that they were operating under the instructions of the government of the Republic of Georgia. These operatives had been introduced into Russia prior to our victorious war in Ossetia, and their operation against Prime Minister Burushin had been planned since that time, as revealed by the content of their laptop hard drive. As for the victim of the three men, Maria Alexandrovna Lershinskaya, she was the sole inhabitant of the village. We know nothing of her, except that she had family somewhere in Russia. We found a postcard with this content dated from five years ago for May Day: "Dear Granny. Congratulations for the 1st of May. Be healthy, best regards and many smiles to you. But what we want most of all is that you come and visit and make the acquaintance of your granddaughter. Sincerely, your family". We don't know if she ever met her granddaughter. But I can tell you that reprisals are inevitable. At this point I want to thank our security forces for their effectiveness and courage in bringing to an end this tragic episode in the history of our country. We have the pictures and names of the three individuals and they will be made public by my office later this afternoon. I personally do not want to dirty my mouth by pronouncing the names of vile criminals who are no better than rabid dogs and who were seeking the destruction of Russia. I believe that this summarises the situation and I will answer two questions.'

The first question did not concern the Uzhginskaya raid at all and was asked by the *Pravda* correspondent, Mikhail Adamov:

'Mr Prime Minister, the Prime Minister Burushin was flying in a Tupolev 154, a Soviet-designed plane that was more than twenty years old. Are there any plans in the future to upgrade our political leaders' planes?'

'I take exception to your question as it seems to imply that the crash of the plane was due to a mechanical failure rather than to explosives that had been placed on board, traces of which have been recovered from the crash site. This being stated, our aviation maintenance company, Aviakor, had just finished a total overhaul of the plane on December 27, and the plane had received its new Airworthiness Certificate on 4 January. As for the age of the plane, we are well aware that our planes are old and that no plane has been produced at the Tupolev factory in more than twenty years. Prior to the event, and I want to emphasise these words, "prior to the event", the Russian Federation had already contracted with the Airbus Company to purchase two brand new A-320 Prestige airliners to transport the president as well as the prime minister. These airplanes are due to be delivered in the spring of this year.'

The second question was from the correspondent of the *International Herald Tribune*, John Smiley, who asked a question about security forces.

'Mr Prime Minister, ever since we heard about this raid, my colleagues and I have been surprised by the restraint used by the security forces to fight the three terrorists. In past incidents, your security forces have been characterised by a rather muscular approach, and a use of force often disproportionate to the threat. Could you please explain to us why only one platoon was committed to this operation?'

'Thank you, John, for your question! We have learned a lot from watching CNN! As you know, in the beginning of February, we had a change in the leadership of our security forces. At that time, I instructed General Andropov to modernise our approach to security problems, to bring Russia on par with Western countries. I believe that

THE DATURA SOLUTION

the resolution of the Uzhginskaya situation is an example of how we are dealing with such events under my watch. I commend General Andropov for the restraint our forces have shown. Yet, I am glad you are calling the expenditure of over 1,500 rounds of ammunition "restraint". I thank you all for attending.'

And the prime minister, copying his style on President Obama, quickly left the room, albeit without smiling, as this would have been totally inappropriate to his Russian audience.

That same afternoon, Prime Minister Shadrin was officialised by the Duma as the new prime minister. At five he started consultations to revamp the cabinet, naming a close associate from Petersburg as his deputy, and holding private talks with General Andropov. That evening, the Kremlin announced that General Andropov had been nominated to the post of defence minister. 'In this time of crisis, it is the choice of the president and of the prime minister to recognise one of the best soldiers of Russia and nominate him as the next minister of defence. We both feel that having a career soldier with over thirty years of experience is in the best interest of our country as we must ensure our military is ready for any potential military action against the wolves who are howling at our doorstep,' read the communiqué from the prime minister's office. The prime minister had been adamant that the general would cumulate the jobs of defence minister and FSB director, but that he could nominate an interim director to assist him. The next call General Andropov made was to Potunov, who far from the sack of shit he had been, had now lost the best part of eighty pounds and was regaining his edge, that of a very dangerous man and a man who was as fierce as a bear and as cunning as a silver fox. Andropov had decided that it would be good to have him close. So it was that the civilian job of defence minister was now occupied by a general, and the military job of FSB director was entrusted to a civilian. And since Potunov was from Petersburg, the prime minister was very laudatory of the choice.

CHAPTER 29

Max had been following the Russia events and trying to make sense of them, wondering how he could influence them. In the days between the death of the former prime minister and the nomination of General Andropov to defence minister, Max had realised he was losing control of the entire situation. He felt like Mary Shelley's hero: having created Frankenstein he was unable to keep him under control. With his friends in such high places of power, Max fully understood that on first examination, they no longer needed him. He now had to find a way to maintain his assets, and to ensure he did not die during a plane trip. Upon his return from Moscow, Max had held daily crisis meetings with Arkady, during which they had been planning ways to regain the momentum they had been enjoying only a few days before. On the third day, they came to the conclusion they needed an ally within the fortress, their Trojan horse. Arkady suggested they should enlist the services of the only person who could access any of the information in the vaults of the FSB, and any of the data in its Tempest protected computers. It was time to get in touch with Georg Mikhailovich. But there was no way to contact him directly without immediately compromising his situation, as every telephone number they used was sure to being monitored. They had clear evidence that their phones were under surveillance, that anyone they called would be put under surveillance as a matter of routine. Therefore, they had to make physical contact in Petersburg, an F2F meeting, as they said for face to face. Max considered the challenge under every possible angle. He knew very well that any associate he had was now at risk. The entire Consortium was at risk, and he himself was eminently hesitant to return to Russia, knowing that his main partners had become more powerful than he. He had already started realising that his association with Arkady now represented a great danger to both of them, and he had put him under surveillance. The surveillance included a daily report of all his activities and phone calls, as well as monitoring of all the money transfers in and out of the corporate accounts, but also of his personal accounts. And it did not take long for the Agence Rogier to give its first report of a direct conversation between Arkady and Triple A. It was an innocent conversation between two comrades and partners, and yet, Max immediately felt the ominous threat that filtered through the words, a threat that was straight out of the old methods of the Soviet Union. From that one conversation, Max knew that Arkady would be under tremendous pressure from the Russian state to get back to the fold, become a double agent, and betray him. In subsequent conversations, Max analysed how the minister of defence made more inroads in recruiting Arkady, promising him that by helping dismember the Consortium and returning to Russia the assets of the Consortium, Minister Andropov would be able to return to Arkady all of the real estate and titles of the Vorgunin family. He went as far as allowing Arkady to again be entitled to be officially called Prince Vorgunin in a decree that he had ensured the new prime minister could sign and even get through by the parliament. So that the decision would have the force of a law it could be published in the Official Edicts of the Russian Federation. Max saw how all of the challenges he and Arkady had survived, all of the financial advantages he had granted him, and all of the power he had given him stood for very little compared to the satisfaction of travelling through time and once again establishing the Vorgunin family as one the most prominent families in Russia. Max knew there was nothing he could tell Arkady, and nothing he could do that would prevent him from choosing being Prince Vorgunin over living on the Princess of Russia. Once again, Max was facing the loss of all the Russia assets, unless he decided to fight for them, a fight that would cost many lives. While Max was incapable to figure out what to do, with every passing day, he was losing Arkady more and more to the song of the sirens. He came to call him Ulysses, forgetting that Ulysses had been able to resist the song of the sirens. Completely out of his character, Max was hesitating, getting up late, sitting in the large sofa, looking at the velociraptor skeleton, and daydreaming for hours at the time. He ate and sat, stopped going to the gym, and within a few days, he did not fit any longer in his Massimo Dutti jeans. He switched to sweat pants and stopped shaving. From the depth of his depressed state and torpor, he became angry at himself. If he continued like this he would betray Lena. She had died in the belief that she could master Russians, and now the Russians were about to strike back at the heart of Max's assets. He did not feel ready to fight for them any longer, and he felt deeply shocked and despondent by the fact that Arkady was conducting what could be termed negotiations with the people who were his partners and had obviously already betrayed him. The idea to collect information about the new Russian leaders was still a valid one, and the idea of fabricating fake information about them was certainly still valid. This was a method the Soviets would never hesitate to use. The issue now was to get to the people who could fabricate it and penetrate the Russian computer systems to ensure that it would act as a Trojan horse, slowly infecting the system, at appropriate moments. And the bigger issue for Max was to get motivated to do it. Instead he sank further into despair, drinking alone in the state room until he became so angry with himself that he turned to violence. In one of his bouts of rage, he threw his laptop at the velociraptor and actually broke the fragile bones of the lower jaw. In his darkest moments, he would blast Wagner's music into the boat stereo system. On one such occasion, the Monaco Police had even boarded his boat to make him turn it down after his neighbours had complained. He knew that many people would have to die before the situation could be sorted out, and he wondered if Lena would have agreed with the hecatomb he would have to unleash to regain the upper hand. She had died defending her assets, there could be no mercy. In a moment of lucidity, Max made a list of all of his associates and placed them into two columns: reliable and unreliable.

This is the same thing General Andropov was doing in Moscow in the top secret facility of the Ministry of Defence. While Triple A was clearly on Max's list, Max featured prominently on the general's own list. But the two lists had a clearly different purpose and presented various levels of threat to the people who were unfortunate enough to be identified on the dreadful pieces of paper bearing their names. Max's list was a tool to be used for decision making on fighting to keep the Russian assets of his corporation, while Andropov had already issued much more sinister instructions. He had called a meeting of his most trusted advisers, including Potunov who although part of the Interior Ministry was now under the complete control of the minister of defence. Andropov had reminded them of a little known historic fact that had been the inspiration for the vilest Soviet methods. General Andropov, who detested the Soviet regime and all things communist, had therefore preferred to inspire himself from the equally vile precedents of the Nazis. Hidden behind a wall located in one of its multiple offices with restricted access, there was a passage, known of only eleven people. This passage led to a top secret meeting room known as the 'Malyutinskaya' after Malyutin, the inventor of matryoshka dolls. Inside this room was a Faraday caged room, and inside it was a bubble, with a conference table for six people. When Potunov first entered, the Malyutinskaya, it immediately reminded him of the meeting room of Wewelsburg Castle, and unfortunately, the comparison was far from stopping there. Andropov seated his guests, which included Potunov, the chief of staff of the Armed Forces, the Commander of the Army, the Commander of FSB Forces, and the Commander of Penitentiaries, and he held the following discourse:

'If you recall your history, you will remember that on 7 December 1941, on the same day, the Japanese attacked Pearl Harbor, Himmler issued his famous Nacht und Nebel order, or Night and Fog, the goal of which was to arrest regime opponents and simply make them disappear under the so-called cover of night and fog. Nobody would ever know what happened to them, and the families could never find any information about them. We are faced today with an extraordinary threat to our country, a threat that is insidious, pernicious, and knows no boundaries. In these extraordinary times, we need unusual measures, measures that will squelch our enemies, bring terror into their hearts, and save our country from further collapsing into anarchy. When a terrorist group can come into Russia undetected and assassinate our prime minister, you must agree with me that we cannot just conduct business as usual, and that it is up to us to preserve the fabric of our Russian homeland. It is up to us to preserve its unity, and to send a powerful message to our enemies, both domestic and foreign that we will stop at no measure to keep our homeland safe. So, gentlemen, we are hereby launching our own program, code name "Noch y Tuman", abbreviated NYT according to Directive 09-04-26:

> Preamble—Within the territory of the Federation of all Russias, independent groups and other elements hostile to the Russian Homeland have increased their efforts against the integrity of the Russian Federation since Christmas 2010. The amount and danger of these activities force the Russian State to take severe measures as a deterrent. The following directives are therefore applied.
>
> Directive 1—Within the territory of Chechnya, the adequate punishment for offenses committed against the Russian Federation or the forces of the Russian Federation which

endanger their security or state of readiness is on principle the death penalty, or imprisonment for life at one of the absolute security facilities within the Russian Federation.

Directive 2—The offenses listed at Directive 1 when they take place outside of the territory of Chechnya are to be dealt in the same manner if it is probable that a death sentence would result from a trial.

Directive 3—All personnel arrested under Directives 1 and 2 are subject to military procedures. In case Russian, territorial, or foreign authorities inquire about such prisoners, they are to be told that they have been arrested but that national security does not allow any further information.

Directive 4—The Army and FSB Commanders in Chechnya and in the Russian Federation are personally responsible for the observance of this decree.

Directive 5—The chief of staff of the Armed Forces together with the director of the FSB determines how this decree will be applied. They are authorised to explain and issue executive orders and supplements.

Gentlemen, this decree is not open for discussion, and if any of you dissent with my decision, I will accept your resignation within the next six hours. If you dissent and do not resign, and later on decide you do not want to apply this decree, I will consider you to be part of elements hostile to the Russian Federation, and will treat you as such. That's all.'

General Andropov stood up and walked out of the Malyutinskaya. Potunov who had by now trimmed himself back to a slender version of his previous self and was taking his new job as seriously and honestly as he could, suddenly realised that his position had become untenable. He remembered his history very well and knew that Field Marshal Keitel had been sentenced to death at the Nuremberg trial for supporting and applying the 7 December 1941 Decree. The application of General Andropov's decree would make him a war criminal under the Geneva Convention and international institutions. He knew that resigning would mean his end and he would be lucky to escape the so-called 'absolute security facilities'. The present showed that his past decision to involved Triple A in the Consortium had been the wrong one and he now had to figure out how to survive his future. On the way back to Lubyanka Square in the armoured Mercedes which he had inherited upon taking office, Potunov, who was stuck in one of Moscow's now legendary traffic jams, was deep in thought. He had never been squeamish about executing a few people who had plotted against what was then the Soviet Union. He had not hesitated to demonstrate his dedication to the good of the state when he had led special units to the assault of Chechen positions, which had turned up to become mere blood baths of whoever was on the other side. And he certainly had not tergiversated about plotting a bombing and an assault against rival mafia gangs to become the immensely wealthy man he was now. But, in each case, he had done so as a personal choice. He had been a young lieutenant when the Soviet Union had asked him to run down anti-communist elements in Frunze, and a captain full of hopes for glory when serving in Chechnya. He had bloodied his hands to become rich, but in fact, he had had nothing to do with the killings. He had simply agreed with the plan and let others do the dirty work. And in modern Russia, he did not know any of the oligarchs who had not done the same. He ought to know, since he now had access to all of their records. The new twist that Andropov had added to his life was not of his liking. He could not see applying Nazi-inspired decrees to the Russian population. Because this was what Andropov was turning Russia into: a Nazi regime. He had already vastly increased the power of the FSB to arrest, detain, and interrogate people, and Potunov knew that Andropov's only ambitions were to increase his wealth and control more and more of Russia's natural resources and production facilities to do so. Andropov was using the NYT Decree to further his wealth, and the first victims of the decree would be those who had made him rich and powerful

THE DATURA SOLUTION

to start with: Potunov, Max, and Simnatsat. All three had to be on Andropov's warrants list, even as Andropov talked to Simnatsat about restoring his former titles and assets. Potunov had put Andropov's phone under surveillance from the moment he had been nominated as the new defence minister. It was clear in Potunov's mind that as long as he was useful to Andropov, that is to say as long as he carried out his policies and allowed him to feed his greed for money and power, he would be relatively safe, but from the moment he stepped out of line, he would end up in the absolute security cells. As much as he could think about it, he could only come up with four choices. The first one, which was repulsive to him, was to go along with the NYT Decree and serve Andropov without hesitation in spite of his dislike or what he was about to do. The second one was to resign as Andropov had offered, and he knew that the signing of his resignation would be the same thing as signing his own death warrant. The third was to simply run away from Russia—he had already stashed millions of dollars in bank accounts around the world—and imitate Trotsky in the hope that the FSB assassins would never catch up with him. The fourth was to stay in his position, pretend to go along with Andropov's madness and use all of his time to bring Andropov's downfall. In spite of Andropov's power and state machinery, he had made plenty of powerful enemies, all well documented within the FSB files, and it would be relatively easy to mobilise these forces to organise the events that would cause Andropov's downfall. Unfortunately, Potunov also knew that Andropov had secured loans to the other men who had attended the meeting in the Malyutinskaya, another trick Andropov had no doubt learned from the Nazis. For example, the chief of staff of the Armed Forces was now seating on a $5-million loan that he had used to buy an extravagant villa in Portofino and a yacht that he could never have been able to otherwise afford. As long as he supported Andropov's positions and goals, the loan would never be called. To ensure long-term support, the loan papers also contained a pardon clause that was to be executed ten years after Andropov left office. In other Andropov's ten years in his job or higher, these loans would be pardoned. In addition, to make sure he was safe, in the case of Andropov's untimely death, the loans would immediately be called. So, however much the other attendees disagreed with Andropov, none of them was about to resign, and the suggestion they could resign had been aimed at Potunov alone, since Andropov had no means to control his Consortium partner, as Max had made both men of equal wealth. Of course, if Potunov died, then Andropov would be sure to double his fortune instantly.

In Monaco, Max dove into the depths of his self-induced depression. He locked all doors to his suite and let his associates run the business. He was no longer available for any decision, and the only people having access to him were the delivery boys of the Ferrati Liquor Store, who allowed him to mix cocktails that wiped his mind blank of the doubts he was experiencing. Max could not even remember where he was. One night, he opened the door to the deck, he stumbled onto the wooden floor, lost his balance, and fell overboard. He was already unconscious by the time he hit the water, and the cool water of the harbour slightly smelling of diesel did not wake him up. It was only the quick thinking and rapid actions of his neighbours who saved him from drowning. In the hospital, he submitted to the treatment, and within a week, and taking a regular dose of Prozac, Max was on the way to recovery. It was as if he had just come out of a dream. Everything he had lived in the past five weeks was a blur, like these dreams we experience in the middle of the night and can only remember vaguely. When he went back to the boat, he could not understand how he had even been able to hurt the velociraptor. His first concern was to have an expert come and restore it. His next concern was to find out what had happened to his circle of employees, and in particular, Arkady.

CHAPTER 30

He immediately knew where he was. There was no other place like this in Russia, and possibly on earth. He knew he was not in a grave, although in fact the place would become it eventually. There was no light and no sound, and all tactile stimuli had been reduced to their most minimal expression. There was not a single item that provided any potentiality of human comfort. He could feel the clamminess permeate his body, and the acrid and pervading smell of the curing concrete invade his lungs. It would be the only smell he would know until his days were up. In the solitude of his confinement he was naked, and the ambient temperature was barely high enough to keep him from shivering. There was only a wool blanket on the bed—a simple shelf of concrete that was ever colder than the ambient air, and it stank of naphthalene. The material itched against his cold and damp skin, and it reminded of the sweaters his mother forced him wear in the days of the Soviet Union. So many times he had promised himself that he would never touch the rough wool that tortured his body mercilessly. Yet, he had completed the circle. Some things never changed. Nevertheless, he used it as his only defence against the humidity and the frigid air. Thankfully after a few weeks, it would have the stench of his own filth, and the wool might have been worn down to an acceptable level of discomfort. The good side of it was there were no bugs, or at least if there were, he could not see them, since his cell was forever plunged in total darkness. Food, or what the penitentiary administration served as food after the bureaucrats had helped themselves to the money allocated to food, was not enough to keep him alive in the long run. The last meal—if he could call it a meal—had been a watery soup of oats mixed with a few leaves of cabbage. He had not had any protein since his arrival and has received only one fruit. He wondered how long it would take for him to get scurvy. There was no means whatsoever of maintaining any hygiene. There was a small sink with a tap which dispensed only freezing water. The toilet was a simple hole in the right corner of the cell and did not flush so that the smell persisted long after he had gone. No toilet paper was provided. There was no way to wash, as no soap was ever issued, and there certainly was no way to dry oneself, except with the blanket. There was no way to shave either, or to cut one's hair, or to trim one's nails. There was no hope of ever getting a knife or to make a knife since the food was served without silverware of any sort. And the bowls in which the food was served were made of soft rubber, like Tupperware. They had removed every possibility of improving one's life. It was life as man must have known it before the age of stone. But the most challenging aspect of the situation was the boredom. There was nothing to do except to sit around or walk back and forth in the total darkness. There was nothing to occupy one's mind, and the prisoners were meant to die without ever hearing a human voice again. He tried to estimate how long it would take him to go completely insane. He could not even measure the time he spent there because there was no day or night, and because all the meals were the same. He could not tell breakfast from lunch or from dinner. As soon as he had arrived he had lost the notion of time. Food was delivered through a small door at the bottom of the cell door, and even then, the delivery made hardly a sound, and the obscurity remained. There was no variance to the process. They had even made this a boring event. Once he had eaten, he had to push the bowl out through the trap door: he had learned that failure to do that resulted in no food being delivered until the bowls from the previous meal had been recovered. Yet, although his situation was now more desperate than ever, in a sense it was a relief from the physical pain he had been subjected to over the previous six months, when he had suffered through a variety of torture methods, such as the swallow, depravation of water, the respirator, extreme cold, the box, and most of all, sleep deprivation. His body vividly remembered the pain and his mind the terror of being forced naked into the box that was no wider than the width of a regular red brick. The first time, he had almost suffocated before he had had time to figure out the frightening way of getting air into his lungs, by inclining his head upward and literally sucking whatever fetid air was above him. And that was before he had realised that there was nothing he could do about the incessant biting of bedbugs that were breeding in the narrow space in the millions. When he had been taken out of the box after what had seemed an eternity but had in fact been just over two days, he had collapsed on the floor of the prison hallway while one of the guards had urinated on him before kicking him in the chest and breaking at least one of his ribs. Then, other guards wearing gas masks had arrived and had sprayed him with a powerful insecticide that burned every each of his skin as if he had been rolled in stinging nettles, and that had penetrated deep into his lungs, causing a helplessness he had not experienced since he had had his first asthma attack as a small child. The guards had taken a perverted pleasure in sodomising him with the sprayer nozzle and filling his rectum with the foul liquid that had caused him even more suffering and internal bleeding. At that very point he had ceased being a man and had been reduced to the level of a toy that would soon be broken by the infantile mind of the people in charge of running the penitentiary administration. In all the years he had spent serving the Russian Federation, he had never imagined the possibility that he could become a victim of the system. Not once. As his interrogation period had come to an end, he had had to face the worst of the terror this administration had to offer: the water-filled cell. It had been originally designed to prevent a prisoner from sleeping but had been modified to actually kill him. After days of mistreatments and torture that clearly had their genesis in the Middle Ages and had been put in place by the Stalinist regime, he was dragged half-dead to a cell that opened up on a hole full with water. Naked, he had been thrown into the ice-cold water that was just over seven feet deep, preventing him from sleeping and filling him with the primal fear of drowning. If he tried to stand on his tiptoes he would soon lose his balance as he sank into sleep standing up and gulped in a mouthful of the foulest sewage that he had ever smelled and tasted. Within a few moments he understood that he would never survive that ordeal as the cold started to numb his mind while rats, seemingly impervious to the frigid water, had started to nibble on the lobes of his ears. The poison of the water had started filling his lungs, his stomach, and was slowly infiltrating his body through the pores of his skin. Even though he had had no substantial food in days, he started wrenching, but the only thing that came was bile. He knew he would die one of three ways: drowned, poisoned, or from pneumonia. And the rats would eat whatever part of his body they could reach. He had to get out of there, as he realised that no secret justified a torment such as this. He had also rationalised that he had been arrested over six months before and that anyone connected to him would have had plenty of time to modify their operations accordingly. In the meantime, the foulness of the water was attacking every mucous membrane of his body, and he also recognised with both terror and great inner peace that it was a matter of minutes before he would be so weakened and incapacitated that he would be unable to bang on the door—the signal that he was ready to sign the confession the authorities had wanted to extract from him. After all the weeks of suffering and agonising pain, he had been broken down. He would not die that way, drowned in that fetid liquid filled with vermin. He thought of Mikhail Krug's verse 'Хотя я банковал, жизнь разменяна' (No matter what I bet, life is decided) and in the last moment of consciousness he could muster, he feebly hit the door as he again swallowed a mouthful of the venom his body had been soaking in, hoping that the guards had heard his inadequate signal. He was going under, and as he lost consciousness he did not feel four powerful arms pulling him out of the fetid grave.

Now, the terror was different. It was a terror that removed all hope, and would soon fill him with an insanity from which he would never recover, a terror from which he would not survive, a terror that would first destroy him by depressing him beyond comprehension to the point where within a few months he would no longer care about what people on the outside called life. The facility had been built into the lava bed of Eastern Siberia, the same lava that had caused the Permian Extinction. The prison that had been baptised Perminskii Tsentral with a sense of humour that most likely escaped every one of its prisoners. It was the ultimate destination to eliminate elements of society that did not fit the arbitrary mould that had been set by the successive administrations, and now by the all-powerful administration of General Andropov. The construction had started ten years prior to his imprisonment under a secrecy that had caused the United States to rework the orbit of one of their military spy satellites and to commit several human intelligence resources to this uninhabited region of Siberia. The entire construction had proceeded under the cover of huge tents that had been stretched over an area extending the size of four football fields. A massive hole ten stories deep had been excavated before the construction of the extensive maze of concrete corridors and cells had been built. Once the prison had reached a level about one floor below the original terrain surface, the roof had been installed, and the former landscape and ground including the Siberian tundra had been recreated, leaving no trace at all of the construction below. Access was through a tunnel the entrance of which was located two miles away and linked to a dirt road that was often left impassable in winter. This meant that prisoners were transferred in and out only during the milder months of the year. Food supplies were stored for months before being served to prisoners, and vitamin C was added to their diet in the form of carbonated drinks. The cells were six feet square allowing for a three-foot-wide bed, a toilet, and a sink. What made the facility particular was that the prisoners lived in absolute isolation. From the moment they arrived there until they died—all of them had been sentenced to life in prison without parole—they would never see another human being, as all the support functions were fulfilled by robots. They never saw light either, as the cells as well as the hallways were not lit—there was not a single light bulb or any electricity in the entire building except for the recharging stations for the robots, which were located in the common area near the elevator shafts. Finally, the cells had regular air pumped from the surface air intake shafts located inside the access tunnels. These air intakes were booby trapped in case an intruder tried to use them to penetrate the facility. The hallways and common areas were filled with deadly argon gas that prevented any prisoner from escaping should he be able to open the steel doors that were locked with computer-controlled locking mechanisms. Extensive quantities of insulation had been used to ensure that the prisoners could not ever communicate between each other. Any banging on the doors or walls was to be left unanswered. Silence pervaded the entire prison and soon became insufferable to the prisoners. Since they were kept naked, had no use of sheets, the occupants of Perminskii Tsentral had no way to commit suicide except for apocarteresis, dehydration, or biting their own tongue off. The facility had been opened for seven years, and the twenty-eight guards assigned to it—more to process the annual summer arrivals than to prevent any escape—has never had to intervene to foil an escape plan. Now that he was in the facility, he had helped design and build, Prince Vorgunin started thinking about a way to escape. He knew he should act fast before the facility got to him, before the lack of vitamin D and other key minerals caused him to fall into the hell of depressive thinking and irreversible weakness accompanied by osteoporosis.

He sat down on the hard concrete shelf that would serve as his bed for the rest of his life if the penitentiary administration had its way. He was in complete darkness. Within a few days he would not be able to stand the light of even the greyest of days. He had no idea which cell he was in or which floor he had been assigned since prisoners were drugged before they were delivered to Perminskii Tsentral. He had been deposited into the cell without even being conscious of it. Now, as he made efforts to not think how far he had fallen, about his former life in Monaco, about the fortune he had left behind, or about the beautiful Nadya who had joined him from Odessa and who had been his only motivation to survive up to then. He had dreamt about her all day long during his ordeal, even when his jailers humiliated him, and when he was beaten, interrogated, and tortured. Nadya was his life jacket. In the delirious pain of the Kresky in Petersburg, he had been able to summon enough strength to remember the evening on the beach on the Black Sea. He remembered the day when Nadya and he were taking a slow walk along the Koktebel moonlit shore hand in hand, walking and talking to each other. They had stopped in a remote cove and spread their blanket on the beach. They had sat down, facing the Black Sea and had listened to the rhythmic sound of the soft waves caressing the sand. Max had kissed the back of her neck as he had wrapped his arms around her. He had slid his hand down across her breasts. Her nipples had already been hard and erect under the swimsuit as he had taken them between his fingers and pinched them softly. She had moaned as he had kissed the back of her ear. She had giggled in anticipation at what she had known what was coming next. He had turned around to face her as she had leaned down and pressed her lips softly to his. He remembered the soft touch of her flesh, the soft perfume of her breath. She had moaned softly as his tongue had slowly licked her lips. They had kissed long and passionately while his hands had squeezed her engorged breasts. They had parted lips and had looked deep into each other's eyes. They had recognised the passion they had for each other, him the rich Prince

Vorgunin, and she the simple but irresistibly pretty girl from Odessa. They had both smiled with understanding and sexual desire. He had taken her into his arms and had again kissed her tenderly. She had whispered into his ear, 'I want you honey.' These days were so far in the past. They had been both his motivation to survive and his greatest sorrow. Surely Nadya had no idea where he was. And he had not been able to communicate with her in over half a year. He had no idea what the Russian government was doing, and he had ceased to care. He was simply focused on one more effort to recover from the deadly situation he was in. He also had to adjust to the temperature of his cell which was supposed to be maintained at seventy-four degrees Fahrenheit. But often the temperature dropped below the set standard by a few degrees and men who were naked were extremely vulnerable to these fluctuations. Often, Arkady would start shivering and he sat in a ball in the corner of the cell, trying to prevent heat from escaping his body. Because of the lack of light, he, as the other prisoners, had no idea how many hours had passed, or days, and he had no concept of night and day. As meals were served at random intervals, there were no help to keep track of time—and there was no way to remember how many meals had been served. Arkady did not manage any better than the others on keeping mental records of this illusive dimension in their lives. Arkady thought daily of the story of Edmond Dantès and wished he had an Abbé Faria that would give him a means to escape.

Failing this, he tried to focus on a way not to lose his mind entirely. But it wondered aimlessly from thinking about how Max could rescue him, to the deepest of despairs when he convinced himself he could never be rescued, to the boat in Monaco, to the thought of women, all of the women he had known, to cursing himself for coming back to Russia, to asking himself how he could possibly get his mind busy for the rest of his life. He decided that after a while, he would just stop drinking and eating. It would be tough, but he would simply die from thirst after his kidneys failed. In the meantime, he decided to revise his Latin and to start speaking to himself only in

Latin. This would keep him occupied for at least one or two years. He would first revise all of the declensions. Immediately, he set to work with the first declension: rosa, rosa, rosam, rosae, rosae, rosa, rosae. But his mind could not stick to the grammar, as he saw himself in Latin class, seating next to the pretty Victoria, at Public School 483. She had hair the colour of a wheat field in the summer, and the red scarf of the school uniform made her even prettier. His mind went on to their first kiss during the Saint Petersburg White Nights, at the top of the Ferris wheel. He wondered where she was now. She was married for sure, she must have had children. Why had he not thought of looking her up before? Then he reminded himself of Nadya. She was so far back into time, it was as if she had never existed—the past no longer had any reality and his present was immobilised into the absence of a future. He started crying at the memory of those happy days that were lost forever and at his situation. It was so hopeless; there was no way out of it. And within a few minutes of starting Latin, he had abandoned the idea altogether as serving no purpose. The emptiness of time kept on going punctuated by the unsystematically systematic delivery of insipid food, the stinking up of his cell after he defecated, the endless hours of semi-sleepiness, and the laziness that robbed his body and his mind of the strength to exercise or to keep sinking into the hell of hopelessness. He confused Dantès with Dante and went from Monte Cristo to the Divine Comedy, and he wish he had known the poem to help him through the rest of his life. He also remembered that no prisoner had ever been released from Perminskii Tsentral and that the prison did not even exist on the penitentiary records. He laid down on what was now his bed, closed his eyes, and went to sleep. He never had any idea of how long he had slept, and when he was awakened by the delivery of yet a new bowl of soup, he could not tell if he had slept eight hours or five minutes. He just knew that it was another day, as he fooled himself into the illusion that he was able to count the number of meals in groups of three now, and although he had missed a few at the beginning, he had now started to tally the meals, and knew that he had lived through ninety-two cycles of three meals, which meant he had been there just over three months. He gave himself another ninety days, and he would apply Plan A, as he called it, which was the termination of his own life. Now that he thought about it, he should have indeed gulped the fetid water and drowned in the cell with the rats. The torture continued unabated. It soon became physical as his back was unable to cope with the discomfort of the concrete bed, and his muscle mass started disappearing. His beard has grown, as well as his hair, and they were soon infested with vermin that barely reacted to the weekly spray of insecticide that was mixed with the air for five minutes. He could not see, but became convinced that insects were crawling out of the hole in the floor that was used for a toilet. The revolting smell coming from the orifice had gagged him at first, but now, he had become used to it and he did not even pay attention to it any longer. Yet, he recoiled from it and it became a recurring hallucination that insects were invading his cell and crawling all over it in the obscurity. He remembered a Soviet bakery that he had worked in as a student, and how the thousands of cockroaches scrambled as soon as they turned on the light at night as they came to work. And yet none were to be seen during the day or when the place was lit. He thought he could feel the cockroaches running over him as he slept, and at regular intervals he would randomly slap the closest wall with his hand, convinced as he was that he would squash a great number of the insects. Yet, every time he did it, he did not feel the cracking of the shells under his palm, and he would deduct from it that he had missed them as he knew they could see in the dark, and he could not. In the obscurity, he swore he could feel the long antennae tickle his skin, and when an itch caught him behind his ear or on his nose, he was certain it was a cockroach testing his skin with his antennae. But he could not catch a single one as evidence of their role in making his life a living hell. By then the lack of vitamins and minerals in the Perminskii diet had made him incapable of logical reasoning and he could not comprehend that there was no truth or reality to the misery that he was needlessly adding to his life. On the other hand, it kept his mind occupied. He repurposed Jean-Paul Sartre's sentence 'L'enfer c'est les autres' to 'L'enfer c'est les cafards'.

He laughed at himself, the tough guy who was now afraid of cockroaches. He also thought of all the men he had personally condemned to the same fate he was experiencing, the forgotten prisoners, whose name would forever remain anonymous. And even if one saw their name later, one would have no idea who they were. They were like the people of Chernobyl: even when one read their name on a piece of paper in the files of the abandoned factories, they had no longer any meaning. He did not regret any of his past actions: he had acted for the good of Russia. Later, rather than Russia, he had served Max loyally while making a bundle of money. There was no regret to have. He remembered how they had killed that shit McMillan, and he thought they had been way too nice to him: Lena had suffered for over two weeks, and they had disposed of him in less than a day. They should have kept him alive and sent him to this place. Rotting in here for the rest of one's life—this was a good punishment. He had no qualm about doing exactly the same thing to others if he ever got out.

In a futile attempt at leaving a mark of his passage in a place where nobody could ever read it, he tried to engrave the sentence on the raw concrete of his walls. He only had his nails to do it, and it proved a long and painful task. He devised a method to measure exactly where he was in the cell so that he could resume writing when he had to stop. His fingers soon started bleeding from the attempt and he was satisfied that he could write the quotation in blood. Then he signed it, 'Arkady, Prince Vorgunin, aka Simnatsat'. This is when he started to talk to the wall, as if it were a person, a friend. He reminded himself of John Wayne's character in 'Blood Alley', Captain Tom Wilder, who spoke to an imaginary 'Baby'. At times he would yell at it, angry that he would not agree with him. He yelled in Russian, in French, in English. And the only answer he got was absolute silence. He wondered if he were the only prisoner there. For sure, if there had been others, they would have heard him and responded. Since there was no response, he became certain he was the only one in the entire facility, and he sank into the blackest of despairs. He could handle it if there had been others, but being the only one to suffer this much . . . he simply could not bear it. At the same time, he also lost count of the days he had been in there. When he realised this, he became angry, yelled at the wall for not reminding of counting the meals, beating it with his weakened fists and asking it to help him remember, for he could not even remember the last number of days that he had reached. He could not even be sure he had been there more than ninety days. His confusion was total. His mind was settling into a fog that would slowly numb his senses, his pain, his hopelessness, as he soon even forgot Nadya's name. He realised that and could not do anything about it. He went through hours of mental anguish before he finally got it back. Then he took the wall as his witness that she was Nadya, and yelled at him not to 'fucking forget her name, you useless fuck!' There were no longer any logical thoughts left in him. He remembered the song 'in Kolyma which is a white hell' and he suddenly realised he had not eaten the bowl of putrid food, which he now delighted to savour. He had become a hybridised creature, a mixture of Edmond Dantès and Chuck Noland.

CHAPTER 31

After Arkady had failed to return to Monaco within a couple of months, and Max had stopped receiving regular communications from him through the Secure Email Network they had been using, he knew that Arkady's attempt to successfully defeat General Andropov had gone drastically wrong. He could not, however, get any news from Russia without jeopardising the security of other people. He waited until he could provide Georg Mikhailovich with access to the Secure Email Network before he developed a plan of action, albeit remotely. In the meantime, the Consortium had been dissolved and as he had anticipated the faucet had been turned off on all revenues coming from Russia. After all of the fighting, all of the murders, the terrorist attacks and their retaliation, nothing remained of Lena's legacy except the meagre gain of a villa in Capri overlooking the Mediterranean, a villa she had never seen. Now, his best friend was lost somewhere in Russia. He knew that rescuing him would be paramount to declaring war on Andropov and his clique, as Andropov would know exactly where the initiative had initiated. Yet, Max could not sit by idly as Arkady rotted inside a Russian jail. Max was reluctant to launch a full-out war against Andropov, a war he knew he could not win. In his office aboard the Princess of Russia, Max could not reach a decision as to the course of action. He sought the advice of his trusted advisor

Chantal with whom he now maintained a passionate liaison. It seemed to her that the first priority was to find out where Arkady was being detained. Knowing Andropov as they both did, there could only be one place where Arkady was, the secret Perminskii Tsentral that he had talked about one time. Ironically, this was the facility Max had helped build when he was part of the FSB. Chantal suggested going through Arkady's laptop to see if any information could be gained from the device. Neither she nor Max were able to break through the defences and passwords of the computer, and yet, they were convinced that the solution was right there in the machine. Well aware that he could not rely on any of his former Russian friends, they also decided that the best way to deal with this would be to have Georg Mikhailovich do the work. Of course Georg had gone into hiding the moment Andropov had turned on his former allies, and finding him would be the greatest challenge. Max calculated that Arkady had been gone for over six months, and he knew that the time for action was running out. In a few more months given the conditions Arkady had described as prevailing at Perminskii Tsentral, his mind would be gone. He had to find Georg, bring him back to the West, have him hack into the prison system, have Arkady released, and hopefully returned to Monaco so that he could be treated. In the meantime, he would have to find a way to get to Andropov and bring him down. Slowly an idea took shape in Max's mind. He knew of Andropov's taste for wild salads—he had a predilection for wild spinach which he often had flow from Ukraine. Max also knew how easy it is to confuse datura plants with wild spinach. If there was a way to intercept the shipment of wild spinach and lace it with datura, or even better replace the wild spinach with datura, he may cause the death of Andropov in a way that would bring little suspicion to the event and would be blamed on the confusion between the two plants. Max decided that the best plant to use would be the *Datura metel*, which could be found in the hills above Monaco and had a particularly dangerous level of tropane alkaloids. The plant would be fatal if ingested in even a tiny quantity—a single leaf would be sufficient—and by the time the symptoms were linked to the salad and the datura, it would be too late to save anyone who had eaten of it. Max would be able to use his Ukrainian network to accomplish the deed, but the cost would be high. With this in mind, he asked his pilots to clear a flight path to Kerch-Voykovo while he contacted his trusted friend Alexei Tavtuch in his retirement villa in Koktebel, on the Black Sea. Alexei and Max went back at least twelve years when the two of them had conducted training after the Cold War. Later, they had entered in private business selling Ukrainian military hardware in Africa and the Middle East. The money they had made had allowed Alexei to purchase a lovely estate overlooking the famous nudist beach. It was time for Max to cash in his chits. From Kerch, Max flew a Kamov helicopter to his friend's backyard. With him he had brought several transplanted datura plants that were to provide the means to get rid of Andropov. Within a couple of hours, the situation had been evaluated, a plan of action set in place, and the proper suppliers in Ukraine had been contacted. For a massive amount of money, Petr Shashkilin, the director of Zilionaya Produktsya—the firm that normally shipped wild salads to the Andropov kitchen—agreed to lace his shipments with metel. He knew that this would be the end of his company, but the sum of money Max had been ready to provide made it a compelling proposition. With the $12 million that were to exchange hands, the director would leave Ukraine, resettle in the United States where his two children already lived and fulfil his life-long dream of living in Florida without ever having to work again. But first, he would have to be given a new name and passport, for anyone attacking the powerful defence minister was sure to be hunted down wherever he found refuge in the world. The contacts at the US Consulate were available to provide such a service, but any trace of the transaction could be found through a paper trail, and the director refused to agree to any arrangement that involved a person who could be interrogated and coerced into revealing his new name. Acquiring a US passport without leaving a paper trail within the territory of the Former Soviet Union was impossible. So, it was decided that Luigi would travel to Sao Paulo and purchase the documents there through the normal illegal means. This would delay the action, but also would allow Luigi to get the required documents and come back without leaving an obvious link to Ukraine. Three days later, Luigi was transacting the deal in a small damp and mouldy office two floors below the ground floor of the Sao Paulo Football Club Estádio do Morumbi. There, in the oppressive humidity of a room lit by a bare light bulb hanging hesitantly from a wire in the ceiling, the bodyguard of the club president had arranged for an ID cards reseller to provide a US passport, a social security card, a Florida State driver's license, and of course, a couple of credit cards, that would grant Petr Shashkilin his new identity and freedom, while the same action signed the death warrant of Andropov. Luigi gave the reseller the ID photos, and he went to work finalising the documents in the name of Peter Southfield, so that Petr's initials would remain the same. The transaction was cash only and the names were unknown—there would be no links that anyone involved would remember and the FSB would be hard-pressed to find it. It took the man a little more than an hour to doctor the documents and integrate the photos. There was no handshake, a simple sliding of the documents over the small desk. Yet, one could never be too careful, and as the cash was being pushed across the desk to the reseller, a signal that had been pre-arranged with Luigi, the bodyguard pulled a 9mm Beretta with a silencer and killed the ID cards reseller with a single shot to the temple. He pocketed the extra cash and took Luigi back to the Sao Paulo Airport, leaving the task of disposing of the body to a later time in the day. He deposited Luigi well off the departures terminal. The two men shook hands, and Luigi was on his way to Kiev to finalise the mission, which they had code named Operation Anthropoid, a bad omen reference to the assassination of Reinhardt Heydrich in 1942.

Once Petr had seen all of the documents that were to give him a new identity and his freedom, he agreed to launch the operation.

THE DATURA SOLUTION

On the given day, which was selected in accordance to the purchase orders from the defence minister's office, the package of wild salads was express-shipped to Arbatskaya Square. It happened to be October 24. The salad packages consisted of loose leaf salads of wild spinach, dandelions, marguerites, aspergettes, and borage. Substituted to the wild spinach among the packages were the deadly datura leaves. Now, it was up to chance to take over. In case the first batch did not work, it was agreed that Petr would stay on and manage the shipping of a second batch.

The cook at the ministry was used to Andropov's preference for wild salads. The packages had been x-rayed and checked for any harmful substances, but neither the FSB guards nor the cooks could possibly have recognised the datura metel leaves which resembled perfectly the wild spinach they were used to processing. Minister Andropov was having dinner with two of his closest advisers whom he had kept late for a working session. They all shared the meal's main course, a salt-crusted baked sea bass. The defence minister discussed matters of national importance and did not pay any attention to the salad he was eating which was essential to good digestion as he put it. His two guests were also invited to share the delicacy but preferred to pass, rather hesitant to eat marguerite flowers and dandelions. The evening work progressed well, and at about midnight, Andropov accompanied his guest to the door of his suite and wished them a good night. Without even brushing his teeth, he collapsed in bed, exhausted by the long day, the heavy dinner, and the quantities of vodka he had consumed. At about one in the morning, Andropov started experiencing difficulties breathing. At the same time, he suffered an anxiety attack which he thought was a heart attack. Not willing to show any weakness, he decided to treat this with vodka. As he stumbled more than walked to the vodka cabinet, he started sweating profusely, another sign of heart attack, he thought. He hesitated about calling his physician, but thought that if he did that, his political opponents would immediately take advantage of the situation to jockey for his succession. It was not to going to happen. He forced himself to reach the bottle of vodka. With a hesitating hand that shook like he had never shaken before, he poured himself a large glass of vodka. He drank it in one gulp, bottoms up, and put the glass down on the cabinet. No sooner had he done that he was overcome but an urge to vomit which he could not control. His already weakened body did not allow his legs to carry him to the bathroom, and he watched in horror as he started expelling vomit that fell in large splashes on the Tabriz rug which he had purchased for over $25,000, knowing that the acidity of the bile-filled liquid would ruin the carpet forever. As he made a valiant attempt to find his way to the bathroom, he slipped in his regurgitations and crashed heavily on the floor. Dazzled by the fall and stunned by the worsening of his conditions, he re-oriented his efforts to finding a phone—any phone—so that he could finally call his physician. As he crawled on the floor, his brain slowed down, and within a few minutes stopped actively functioning. He lost his sense of direction and became unable to find the right path to the phone. He realised that this was no ordinary stomach sickness, that something was drastically wrong, and that he was in a bad way. For the first time in his life, he wondered if he would be alive the next day, and while his mind had become incapacitated, another part of his brain was making it very clear to him that his life was about to end. He collapsed into unconsciousness, returned to voluntary cognitive processes for a few moments only to experience convulsions that sent his legs kicking into the little end table next to the couch. His entire body was being destroyed in a systematic manner, torn between the welcome complete darkness and the bright light that shone over the vodka cabinet but was linked to the horrible convulsions and pain. Then, everything went black as he gave up any fight and lay there in a pool of vomit in a deep coma. It was not yet two in the morning. The next day was a Sunday, and no one looked for him until he failed to show up for a one o'clock lunch with the president of Lukoil. At about two in the afternoon, the inanimate defence minister was being treated by the physicians at the Burdenko General Military Clinical Hospital, where Professor Fedorov, an expert cardiologist, was examining his famous and feared patient for heart attack signs. Everything pointed to some type of cardiac ailment, possibly generated by a stroke. He ordered a Pet-Scan to be conducted and surprisingly, it revealed no lesion either to the brain or the heart. While this examination was taking place, Professor Fedorov was being scrutinised by FSB agents dispatched to observe every word and act of the renowned doctor. He had no reason to order a stomach pump, since all the vomit indicated the patient had either expelled any food, or had digested it a long time before his being admitted to the hospital. Nor could the professor suspect that the condition of his patient was due to the ingestion of datura. Thus precious time was lost when the patient could still have been saved by drugs such as physostigmine or benzodiazepines. Professor Fedorov, sensing that things could go drastically wrong for him if the patient died in his care, resolved that he should include others into the diagnosis while the patient was still alive. Soon a college of seven of the best physicians in Moscow was at the patient's bedside. Andropov was now hooked up to machines that breathed for him and moved his blood for him, as his comatose condition had yet again worsened and he was clinically dead. Doctor Mikhail Bizotkov suggested that the patient may have fallen victim to carbon monoxide intoxication. Professor Fedorov remarked that the patient had been in their care for over six hours by then, and that since the half-life of carbon monoxide is only five hours and twenty minutes, the symptoms should be disappearing, not worsening. However, no one had a better suggestion, and they agreed to administer hyperbaric oxygen rather than normal air. After two hours of this futile effort, while the patient had not died, he certainly was not any better. Not a single person in the room thought about poisoning, and in any case, it was now far too late to be able to counter the effects of the massive ingestion of datura metel. The doctors agreed that there was nothing they could do. They reported the condition to the prime minister of Russia, and they watched as their patient was being kept alive by the machines. The defence minister had no family, so it was left to the doctors to decide his fate. They agreed to leave him on life support for seventy-two hours and see what his condition would be then. During that time, at Arbatskaya Square, the remnants of the defence minister's meal had been disposed of in the garbage processor and had been flushed down the sink into the Moscow sewage system. The plates with the defence minister's seal had been washed, dried, and put away. The packaging of the salad had been bagged into black garbage bags that had been disposed of in the dumpster, and as usual at nine in the morning, the waste disposal company emptied the dumpster into a garbage truck, as they did every morning, except on Christmas and New Year. In Kiev, Petr was anxiously waiting for news of Andropov's death to be able to resign his job for personal reasons and leave Ukraine forever. The FSB had of course started an investigation, and the best detectives had combed the defence minister's apartment looking for any suspicious signs, while the forensic scientists had collected the vomit off the carpet to conduct the standard analyses.

In Kiev, Petr had stayed in his home with his wife of thirty years, cloistered ready to leave at any time that Max would say. But Max had given different instructions to Luigi. However, cunning Petr had been in business, he was truly a naïve man who thought he could be involved in the assassination of the defence minister of Russia and survive. As the defence minister's condition came close to death, Luigi drove up to the Shashkilins' flat in a semi-rundown apartment block on the western side of the city in one of these nondescript streets that were the trademark of the Soviet Union. The driver who was no other than John helped the sexuagerians with their luggage and waited for them patiently as they and Luigi went back up to their apartment one last time and with tears in their eyes said a silent goodbye to the place where they had lived for a third of a century, where they had raised their daughters, and where they had hoped for a better life to come. Luigi felt as sad as they did, and for the first time in his life, he decided he was not ready to follow an order. The execution of these two people who were so full of hope, expectations, and sadness was simply beyond his strength. They locked their door for the last time, and Petr led his wife who was openly crying down the stairs.

'I cannot go,' she said. I cannot leave Ukraine. You go without me. I must stay here. I cannot go to your United States. I never wanted to leave Kiev, my friends, my family. This is where my parents are buried. This is where I want to spend the rest of my life.' And she stopped dead in the middle of the first flight of stairs.

'Shashenka, you cannot do that. It is all arranged. We will be happy. We are rich, Shashenka, we will buy a beautiful house by the ocean, we will see our daughters, our grandchildren. We will be in a beautiful country. I will never have to work again!'

'I don't give five kopecks for your beautiful country. My country is here! I have made up my mind! I will NOT go.'

She turned around, pulled the key out of her pocket book, and opened the door to the flat. Petr ran after her as Luigi's radio came alive with John becoming impatient in the car below and asking 'what the fuck is going on?' When Luigi explained, he directed him to forget about it and give them time to sort each other out. Luigi conveyed the message to Petr, who by then was in a full-fledged fight with his wife. John understood the danger of the situation and knew that information Petr had about Operation Anthropoid could inadvertently be disclosed in the exchange. It was now six o'clock in the morning since the Shashkilins were to catch the nine o'clock flight to Frankfurt before transferring to the transatlantic flight—or so they thought. John ordered Luigi down, gave him the wheel, and once they were about 300 metres away, he had Luigi stop, and he exited the vehicle. Under the cover of the still predominantly dark sky, he rushed back to the apartment building and quickly climbed the four flights of stairs. Once he reached the apartment, he could hear the Shashkilins arguing through the closed door. He knocked and the yelling stopped. Petr welcomed him into the small flat. Before he could close the door, John had shot him in the back of the head with a silenced Fort 14 handgun using Parabellum ammunition. John supported the body and slowly laid him down on the floor. He walked further into the apartment and found Shashenka in the kitchen preparing tea. She turned around, anger flashing out of her eyes and she started yelling again, this time at John for putting them in such a situation. He waited for her to pour the hot water into the teapot. Then she would have her head turned away from him. She would never know her husband was already dead. In fact she would never know she had been shot as the hollow point bullet penetrated the soft tissue in the back of her head just below the cranium and her entire cerebellum, spreading fragments into her medulla oblongata, and continuing its twisted path into her thalamus and further into her frontal lobe. Her heart beat a few more times. John held her up, putting her head into the sink, and lifting her body onto the kitchen counter to prevent the blood inundating the floor. Her heavy blood started pouring out of her wound and he saw her life slowly wasting away into the drain of the aging porcelain sink. The saucepan full of boiling water fell with a metallic sound and the hot water poured on John's left hand glove, going through the thin layer of leather almost instantly. He took no notice of the pain, focusing instead on the task at hand. He holstered his pistol, rummaged for dish towels and a garbage bag and rushed to the entrance where Petr's blood was continuing to empty. He lifted his head and put it in the garbage bag, wrapping it tightly around his throat. He then absorbed the blood already on the floor with the dish towels so that is would not sip thought to the floor below. He threw the towels in the sink where Petr's blood mixed with his wife's into the pipes leading to the Kiev sewers, and eventually to the immensity of the sea. Once John had made sure his shoes had no blood on them, he exited the apartment and silently but quickly walked back to the spot where Luigi had parked the car. The entire operation had lasted less than three minutes. Luigi started on his way without a word, knowing perfectly what had happened and not needing any explanation. Later they would take care of the bodies and ensure the flat was sanitised. They reported back to Max who was waiting for them at the Hyatt Regency.

On 29 October, the surgeons and the Medical College of Russian met to decide what to do with the defence minister. He had been on life support and in a deep coma from which he would never recover for four days. The meeting was to decide if any course of treatment could be recommended. No cause for his condition had been identified, and the official word was that the defence minister had worked so hard for the people of Russia that he had suffered a heart attack from which the heroic doctors of the Burdenko Hospital were attempting to save him. But they had all come to the same conclusion: whatever the disease was, it had progressed beyond the possibility of a remission. The defence minister would die regardless what happened. It was simply a matter of when. During that time, the FSB had been working hard to determine if this was a health incident, a suicide, or a murder. They had interrogated every person in the defence minister's staff, and the two people who had eaten his last meal with him had become persons of interest. In the purest Soviet style, these two unfortunates were imprisoned, tortured, and left to rot in the basement cells of the Lubyanka, which had again become the forbidding institution it had been under Stalin. Eventually they would be released, scarred, dishonoured, unable to ever work for the ministry, pensionless, and reduced to begging in the common area of some railroad station. The FSB wanted to look efficient and wanted to be able to close the case as fast as possible. After four days of lab work they had not identified any unusual content to the liquids and samples they had collected at the minister's apartment on Arbatskaya Square, and they had to admit that the sudden sickness of the minister was indeed a cardiac ailment. So, in the absence of any evidence to the contrary, the entire country, as well as its leadership, was content with the accepted theory of what ailed the minister. For the people, it was of far less interest than the upcoming soccer game between Dynamo Moskva and St Petersburg Zenith which was to take place on the Sunday afternoon, and the condition of the defence minister soon became an irrelevant piece of new. 'Let him die, and stop pestering us with what happens to the fucker' was the main opinion heard in the streets of Moscow. As for the Russian republics, nobody really cared who was defence minister anyhow. For Max, with Andropov out of the way, he now had access again to his oldest ally, Petrunov. And it was time to call upon him to try to get Arkady out of the hell of the Russian penitentiary system.

Lightning Source UK Ltd.
Milton Keynes UK
UKOW02n2139090616

275977UK00002B/23/P